BEAUTIFUL DILEMMA

BEAUTIFUL DILEMMA

ROSHUMA FLORENCE

Roshuma Florence

To God and my mother for giving me life.

CONTENTS

Dedication   iv

One
Jevon   1

Two
Akilah   10

Three
Jevon   18

Four
Akilah   26

Five
Jevon   38

Six
Akilah   44

Seven
Jevon   53

Eight
Akilah   62

Nine
Jevon   66

Ten
Akilah   78

Eleven
Jevon   85

Twelve
Akilah   94

Thirteen
Jevon   103

Fourteen
Akilah   110

Fifteen
Jevon   115

Sixteen
Akilah   121

Seventeen
Jevon   132

Eighteen
Akilah   139

Nineteen
Jevon   146

Twenty
Akilah   154

Twenty-One
Jevon   162

Twenty-Two
Akilah   166

Twenty-Three
Jevon   171

Twenty-Four
Akilah   175

Twenty-Five
Jevon   182

Twenty-Six
Akilah   193

Twenty-Seven
Jevon   200

Twenty-Eight
Akilah   207

Twenty-Nine
Jevon   217

Thirty
Akilah   225

Thirty-One
Jevon   231

Thirty-Two
Akilah   241

Thirty-Three
Jevon   255

Thirty-Four
Akilah   266

Thirty-Five
Jevon   269

Thirty-Six
Akilah   273

Thirty-Seven
Jevon   284

Thirty-Eight
Akilah   292

Thirty-Nine
Jevon   298

Forty
Akilah   307

Forty-One
Jevon   314

Forty-Two
Akilah   326

Forty-Three
Jevon   340

Forty-Four
Akilah   355

CHAPTER ONE

Jevon

Pops had been on my ass lately about my future plans. He thought I was better off going to college to become a doctor or something, but I just didn't have it in me. I knew what I wanted to do. I was meant to be a champion, and I'd be damned if anyone stopped me.

Today though, I decided not to push him any further and apply to a few colleges. Senior year had barely even begun, yet there I was, in the library of all places. I could think of at least a dozen better ways to spend my time.

College would only be a waste of money in the end. In what world would any championship competition wait for me to get a degree? By the time I finished wasting my time at a university, my competition would already be miles ahead of me.

I sighed heavily as I leaned back in the creaky old chair, catching a few dirty looks from the librarian upfront. It had been about three hours since I first arrived, and I only had one completed application to show for it.

Admittedly, when I first agreed to apply to schools, I didn't imagine it would take so long to turn one in. Almost every college wanted a resume, a list of references, and a statement of purpose.

You'd think I was applying for a job, with all the requirements on every page.

Up until now, my life had been consumed by Silat, a deadly martial arts form. I had nothing else to offer these schools. There were no other extracurriculars I was ever interested in, and my grades were average at best. What school wanted a fighter? It was useless trying to check boxes on a page that weren't made for me, a concept I couldn't seem to get through to my father.

I viewed school as a waiting area on the way to my next step. It was just another thing I had to go through before I could truly pursue my dreams. I didn't want to go to college. There was no need for it when I would only choose fighting in the end.

Fighting had always provided me a release. I often viewed it as my lifeline because without it I'd be lost, or dead, or both. Before learning martial arts, I was just a small, quiet kid with a bad temper. I didn't bother anybody, and I certainly didn't expect anybody to bother me, but life never actually went the way anyone planned.

After getting picked on one too many times, it didn't take long for the neighborhood kids to understand not to mess with me. I was small, but I was scrappy and I quickly learned my way around a few fights.

My parents soon realized that my temper would get me in serious trouble at some point, so they decided to put me in karate to learn some discipline along the way. After my first class, I knew it would be something I enjoyed. Not only was I good at it—I was great. I advanced to higher-division classes in no time.

Eventually, I began to learn different styles of fighting. Even now, I still felt that there was more out there for me. There was so much more out there that I couldn't and wouldn't find in college. I heaved another frustrated sigh as I balked over the next question on the application. It wanted to know what major I was interested in pursuing. There wasn't an option that appealed to me, but I half-heartedly hoped I would find a school with something even remotely close to my interests. Without even really looking, I checked an available box and moved on to the next question.

Movement on my right caused me to look up as the librarian approached me. She slit her eyes in my direction and placed a frail, old finger against her lips as she passed me. She all but sliced me open with disapproval. Unfazed, I smiled and scooted loudly away from my desk.

"Don't worry," I said in a normal voice. "I was just leaving."

Her eyes grew big, questioning my audacity, but I gathered my things and did just that. It was time for me to go anyway. One application was good enough to keep my pops off my back for the next week or two. With school starting back up soon, I'd have more than enough on my plate.

I headed out to my car and as soon as I turned my key in the ignition, my phone vibrated in my pocket. I didn't have to look to know that it was Jalissa, my ex-girlfriend, calling me. We'd broken up a month before school ended junior year. There was no word from her all summer long—she was too busy having fun with some dude in Florida. Still, having her call me now came as no surprise to me. Our on-and-off relationship was like clockwork, and Jalissa was right on time. I silently cursed myself as I pressed the button to answer the phone.

"What, Jalissa?" I asked, already exasperated.

Her voice was sickeningly sweet as she giggled on the other end. To her, nothing had changed between us. At least, that was the way she acted.

"Don't act like you haven't missed me."

Jalissa Anthony was nothing but a mind game, one I didn't feel like playing right now. It was my last year of high school, and I needed to be focused if I was ever going to prove to my dad that I could make it without a college degree.

"What do you want?"

"I was just thinking about you and decided to call. I missed you."

"Aren't you with somebody?" I countered.

"Jealous?"

"No."

"Sure," she said, and then all the humor left her voice. "But seriously though, how are you, Jevon?"

Before Jalissa and I had ever dated, we were friends. Out of our group of friends, she was the only one who truly understood my dread about going to college, only because she didn't want to go to college either. Jalissa had dreams of becoming a supermodel.

Pops was pretty hard on me. He never settled for anything less than perfection. It took me forever to convince him that fighting was more than just a hobby for me. As a young black kid, I understood why my father wanted more for me than just fighting. I knew all too well how dangerous it could've been for me had I not gained the discipline I needed to tame my temper.

"Well?" she asked when I went silent.

"I'm fine."

"I read about what happened in London a few months ago and I tried to call, but you never answered."

"I had nothing to say."

Jalissa sighed. "I know it probably feels like the world is against you right now, but you still have me in your corner."

She made hating her almost impossible when she said things like that. Honestly, it was good to know that she still cared to some degree.

"What happened over there?" she urged.

Images of the fight that I was trying to forget, the fight that had changed everything for me, suddenly flooded my brain. I remembered Jao Shang, my rival since the very beginning, with the most clarity.

At every national competition, he made it his sole mission to beat me. And not just beat me, but make me a target to the other fighters as well. He was a conniving little prick, and this summer's international competition was my chance to get my redemption.

Early in the fight, Shang had me nearly licking the floor mat from the beating he was giving me. It wasn't until close to the very end that I gained the upper hand. I would've won too, but my temper got the best of me.

At last, I'd thought, *I finally one-upped him.*

I wasn't going to give in. That determination was what caused me to blackout mid-fight. I got so lost in trying to beat Shang that I didn't take into account the damage I was doing until it was too late.

If not for the referee and security intervening, I'm almost positive I would've made a very serious mistake. Shang ended up winning by default, which earned me some huge demarcations in my national scores. It pushed me that much further away from my goal of becoming an Olympian.

"Keep reading the blogs," I said, "you'll find out everything you need to know."

"Jevon, don't be like that."

"I'm done talking about it. It happened. It's over. I gotta go."

Without giving her the chance to respond, I hung up and chucked my phone into the passenger seat. I shifted my car into drive and in no time, I was pulling into my driveway. The ride home from the library was a short one, but as I came to a stop in front of the garage door, I almost wished it had been longer.

One of the reasons I respected my father so much was because he knew how to be powerful without his fists. Michael Williams commanded respect just by walking into a room. I could spend my life learning all the fighting styles in the world, and I'd still try to gain his approval. So when I saw Pops standing on the stone steps at the front door with his arms crossed tightly against his chest, I got a little nervous. Slowly, I cut the engine and hopped out of the car.

"Hey, Pops," I said warily as I went to stand across from him. "What's up?"

"Did you apply to those business schools like I told you to?"

"Yeah, I did. I only finished one application for now, but I started on another one."

My father was instantly annoyed. I knew he would react that way, but I didn't understand why he couldn't wait until I got inside.

"We'll talk about that later, but for now, you got this in the mail."

It was a large, white envelope addressed to me. Inside was a letter, a flyer, and a few pamphlets. I went to read the letter, but Pops stopped me.

"It's about that competition where you lost your damn mind and almost ruined everything."

He never failed to remind me just how badly I'd screwed up. It wasn't like my father didn't completely believe in my dreams of becoming a fighter. Once he saw how good I was at it, he couldn't just ignore my talent. He was proud of being able to travel with me to all those competitions. After all, Michael Williams didn't believe in doing things halfway. It was in my blood to be the best. Pops just didn't want me to give up on my education in the process.

After the incident, I had received a lot of blowout from it all. People were calling me a monster, a cheater. Some even wanted me out of the competition circuit altogether, but with the help of a skilled PR team assembled by my dad, I was finally getting back into the good graces of some of the judges and viewers.

"What's the problem now?" I asked. "I thought everything was good."

"The problem is that not everybody believes you've changed, son. Some only see you as that violent person attacking Jao Shang on TV. You still have to convince these people that you're good."

"Pops, you know some of these 'people' you're talking about won't see me as anything but violent. I made a mistake, but so have lots of other fighters! Now, all of a sudden, I have to be the right kind of fighter? It's not fair."

My father knew just as well as I did that mixed martial arts was a biased sport.

"Well, son, that's the game you're playing. This was a risk we all took when you decided you wanted this career. You have to get in where you fit in, and if you can't do that, then we create our own space, but there's always a better way to go about it. The real question is: do you want it bad enough?"

"You know I do."

Pops grinned a little, satisfied with my answer.

"So, what do we do now?" I asked. "Has Dave said anything about it?"

I hadn't heard from my lawyer in weeks.

"Yeah, he did, and he thought it'd be a great idea for you to place yourself in an environment that will inspire these people to see you in a different light. Show them you have layers, that you're not just a kid who knows how to fight."

"Okay," I shrugged. "I'm down. Anything."

My father quirked a brow. I was pretty much down for anything that would get me where I needed to be.

"We're going to enroll you into Cambridge School of Arts."

. . . except that.

"An art school? Really, Pops?"

"Yes, Jevon, what's so wrong with that? You could learn some culture. It'd look good to the schools you're applying to."

"No, I'm not doing that. I'm not even artistic. What would I do at some art school?"

The thought alone seemed impossible, yet my father stared un-waveringly back at me.

"Find something other than fighting to put on your applications."

I scoffed. "I meant what do we do about my career? Nobody's gonna care that I go to some prissy art school. You're prepping me a future I don't even want."

"I'm preparing you for every obstacle, Jevon! You act like fighting is the only way, but what do you think will happen when you don't get the outcome you want? When the judges decide you're unfit to compete? When you're forced to sit on the sideline because you can't seem to control your anger?"

Pops's voice began to rise as he explained his point. It always came back to college. He had a way of slipping it into every conversation, like it was ultimately the end-all-be-all for me.

"If," I corrected him.

"Excuse me?"

"*If* I don't get the outcome I want. *If* the judges decide I'm unfit to compete. *If* I'm forced to sit on the sideline, then I'll find another way."

Pops held my gaze for a moment. He took me in with narrowed eyes. In that moment, I wasn't sure if he'd respond to me like my father, or my manager.

"Let's just hope it doesn't come to that," he said instead.

"There's got to be something else I can do, Dad," I tried again. "Anything else."

"No, it's already done. You start next week."

"What? How?"

"I called in a couple favors with the dean of admissions. We got him a deal on a house way above his tax bracket last year, and let's just say, I helped him tie up a few loose ends. He owed me."

"But I'm a senior this year. How do you know all of my grades will transfer over?"

"Since when did you care about your grades?"

"Since they're getting transferred over to another school."

"Look, what's done is done," he said with finality in his voice. "You decided you wanted this career. Be glad this is the only thing I'm asking of you. They could've taken you out of the league altogether."

He was right yet again, but yet again, it didn't make it better. I didn't want to move to a new school, not while I was comfortable finishing at Laney High. I understood then why Pops had approached me outside. With this news, there was only one reaction he would get from me.

My hands begin to twitch and clench themselves into tightly bound fists at my sides. My mouth clamped shut as I felt a dryness spread over my tongue. When my teeth began to grind together, I knew I needed to leave. I needed a release.

"I'm going to the dojo," I called over my shoulder as I made my way back to my car.

First college, and now this? I wasn't going to some prissy-ass art school. I'd make sure of it. Why did I have to change everything about me to prove I was a worthy enough fighter? It made no sense to me at all. My father didn't push me. He knew just as I did that my temper was flaring, and I had to leave. I didn't even look back as I peeled out of the driveway, and sped off into the distance.

CHAPTER TWO

Akilah

Senior year could never be *just* senior year at Cambridge School of Arts. It was all about what you were going to do afterward. I knew exactly what I wanted to do, and there wasn't a doubt in my mind about how I was getting there.

I was meant to be a muralist, painting my mark on the world as I saw fit. It was easy to be inspired by the world around me. Atlanta had such a colorful aesthetic. Most of the buildings were already decorated with artworks that highlighted our city's culture and influence. One day, my work would join them too.

Artistry ran in my family. My mom was a successful classical dancer in her day, and my dad was a renowned master chef at Le Bleu, a fancy restaurant downtown. Oddly enough though, my parents never saw me as a visual artist. They expected me to pursue a dancing career like my mother, or something a bit more practical, like my father.

While I was pretty good at dancing, I paled in comparison to my mother's talent. Paint, drawings, clay sculptures . . . art was my love and passion. With art, I could create my own world and happily live in it. What I loved most about it was the freedom that came along with it. There was no rhyme, rule, or rhythm to art. It just was.

"KIKI!" Momma yelled from downstairs. "Come eat breakfast!"

I was in the process of perfecting my makeup, adding a golden highlight to my brown skin and fresh set of lashes to accent my colorful eyeshadow. I tried to hurry and finish before she had to yell again. I had about a good thirty minutes before I was forced to rush out of the house. With one final glance in the mirror, I brushed my straightened hair down the length of my back, and added a thick coat of gloss to my lips. I looked good in my yellow halter dress.

"I just don't understand why you feel the need to cover yourself in all that makeup. You're beautiful just the way you are," Momma said when I finally made it to the kitchen.

Grabbing a plate of food, I resisted the urge to roll my eyes. She'd been saying that for years, but it never stopped me from wearing it. I viewed makeup as an art form, simply because I could create any look I wanted. She thought that I was covering myself, but to me, it was an expression of my artistry. I loved it.

"Momma, did you forget that you wore makeup as a dancer for all those years?"

"I was a classical dancer, sweetheart. We used makeup as an enhancement, not warrior paint."

I ignored the slight diss and dug into my food. It wasn't worth it to try and explain how times had changed, or that our sense of style was completely different. I finished quickly and dropped my plate into the sink.

Grabbing my bag of supplies from the counter in one hand and my book bag in the other, I headed out to my car. With any luck, I'd be just late enough to make an entrance, but not too late that I'd end up in detention on the first day.

It was nice out today. Though the sun scorched through my windshield like a heated lamp, it gave me the oomph I needed to hurry to school.

"Nice of you to join us, Miss Johnson," Mr. Patrick said as I finally made my way into homeroom. I had just missed the first bell, but I breezed through the door in time for the second bell to ring out.

"Good morning, Mr. Patrick." I smiled as I passed by his long desk to take a seat by the window.

"How did I know you would find a way to make an entrance?" my best friend Kayla teased from a desk in the row next to mine.

She looked even better than I did in her sequined jumpsuit. Her loose curls were swooped up into a high ponytail, and her dangly earrings brushed against her shoulders. Kayla's niche was fashion. She created a lot of the things that I wore on a daily basis, and I repaid her in art.

"How else am I supposed to arrive?" I asked, flipping my hair as I did so.

We both laughed at the uppity gesture and relaxed to discuss the new year. I couldn't wait to get to the studio. I was itching to finish the sculpture I'd started working on last semester.

"Settle down, class." Mr. Patrick was more irritated than usual, but class had barely begun. What could sour his mood already?

"We have a new student." He sighed.

The whole class, including me, all shared looks of confusion. Almost nobody could just transfer to CSA at the last minute. Only rarely were exceptions made early on in the year for really advanced students. This new kid had to be either really talented or really rich to be accepted at the last minute. Whatever the cause, it made him an easy target for whoever shared his niche. Any new student was automatically seen as competition, a threat.

Mr. Patrick directed our attention to the boy standing beside him, if you could even call him that. A boy, I mean. Standing at maybe six-foot-four, the tall dark-skinned boy at the front of the room made Mr. Patrick look extremely small in comparison. It was not only his height that set him apart. He was incredibly ripped.

"Class, this is Jevon Williams. Welcome to CSA, Jevon."

Jevon seemed unimpressed and uninterested. He looked around the room, hardly noticing the way we gawked at him, but I figured you'd have to be used to people staring when you looked the way he did.

"Now that's how you make an entrance," Kayla mumbled to me. "He's fine as hell!"

I couldn't disagree. In fact, I found myself staring at all of him from top to bottom. He was like a classical statue—all tall, strong, and regal in his stance. There wasn't a flaw on him anywhere in sight. He would definitely be interesting to draw.

I analyzed his features and committed them to memory for later. It was only when Jevon's eyes connected with mine that I took the hint to turn away. Everything about him screamed un-fuck-with-able. Clearly, he didn't appreciate being stared at; the look he gave me said it all.

"So, Jevon," Mr. Patrick said, "what's your niche?"

Jevon appeared confused.

"Uhh, your talent. What's your artistic talent?"

"Oh, I don't have one." Jevon said simply.

A wave of shock passed through the room. How did he end up in the best school of the arts in the entire city if he *didn't* have a talent? Why was he even here?

"Well that's impossible, otherwise you wouldn't be here," Mr. Patrick said.

Jevon shrugged. "It looks pretty possible on my end."

At that, Mr. Patrick dropped it and let Jevon take his seat. The only available seat was behind me, and Kayla all but pounced on him with her eyes as he walked by. Jevon looked good, there was no doubt about that. He was also very, very standoffish and reserved. When he got to his seat, he took to staring begrudgingly out the window for the most part.

I wondered what brought him here, and what could possibly make him to look so mean, so ungrateful for the incredible position he was in. Every now and then, I'd turn my head to get a peek at him out of my peripheral vision, and each time, he seemed more uncomfortable and out of place.

Eventually the bell rang and my examination was cut short. I grabbed both my bags and carried them over to my locker where they would stay until my class with Ms. Hazel in advanced visual arts.

After homeroom, we were required to endure core classes like math, science, and history, but later in the day, I got to go to the studio. It was my favorite part of everyday.

"Hey, Ms. Hazel." I waved to her as I took my place at my station.

My unfinished clay sculpture was there, exactly the way I left it. It was starting to dry and crack from sitting out for so long. There was even a small sheen of dust collecting around its edges.

"Hey, AJ."

Kayla and I learned a long time ago that it wasn't hard for people to mix us up with our similar sounding names, so I'd decided to go by my initials.

Ms. Hazel didn't waste time with introductions or any of that first day of school nonsense. We were seniors, so most of us were already acquainted with each other in some way. Without another word, I popped my earphones in and got to work.

I poured a liquid solution onto my sculpture to soften the clay before digging in. It had been so long since I last attempted this piece that I almost forgot what I was even trying to create. There was something about it that made the whole thing feel like child's play.

Taking one of the tools from my pouch, I carved into the surface of the clay and used my fingers to scrape out a pattern that would help define it more. I repeated this step until my nail beds were coated in the reddish-brown concoction.

Ms. Hazel approached my station after a while, placing a hand on my shoulder to get my attention. I popped one of the earphones out, careful to not get the clay in my hair.

"Will this be ready by the opening of the senior art show?" she asked.

Every year, CSA hosted an art show for senior visual arts students. Art critics and deans to some of the top schools in the country attended and offered opportunities to those who really stood out. The only opportunity I wanted was a spot at Ivory Middleton next year, my dream school.

"Yes, it will," I said confidently, even though I wasn't exactly sure where I was going with it yet.

Ms. Hazel cocked her head to the side with narrowed eyes. She stared at my shapeless mold like she was holding back a bundle of unspoken criticism. "Hmm."

"Hmm?" I mimicked. "What does that mean?"

"It means that sculpting isn't your strong suit. I think you should consider entering a painting for review. You have so much potential with a paint brush."

"Everybody's going to submit a painting," I argued. "I want to stand out! I want to create something so . . . brilliant that they have to notice me."

She chuckled softly. "It's not always about the wow factor, AJ. It's about how you make people feel when they view your work. Look at this." She pointed to side of my mold, where I had done the most damage with my digging. It had started to slowly tip over from the lack of support at the base. "How does that make you feel? Do you really think this best represents your talents?"

"Not yet, but it's not finished. I still have time."

"Don't spend too much time trying to be impressive. Work from the heart, and let your talent speak for itself."

Turning back to my leaning tower of nothing, I tried again to feel anything other than a growing disappointment. It shouldn't have been this hard to come up with something new. I wanted people to *feel* and *see* me through my work, but more than anything, I wanted them to be amazed. There was no way anybody could be amazed with what I had now.

"Just think about it, okay?" she said before leaving to check on another station.

I nodded as I thought about just balling up the clay and chucking it in the bin by the door. It was all a jumbled mess anyway.

"What's this?" Ms. Hazel asked.

At first, I thought she was talking to me, but as I looked up, I found her attention to be diverted to the door. The new boy was standing in the doorway, his head nearly reaching the top of the frame. He came into the room and handed her a slip. Ms. Hazel snatched it from his fingers and looked over it quickly, sharing that same irritated expression on Mr. Patrick's face from this morning.

"Have a seat." She directed him to the empty station in front of me.

He's an artist? Interesting.

I watched as he placed his things on the table and pulled out a long piece of graphing paper before settling down to begin his work. Jevon worked quietly at his station, never once getting up for new supplies or materials. Ms. Hazel came over to briefly give him instructions, and when she was done, he shifted to stare out the window like before.

My eyes grazed over him absentmindedly. I tended to stare off into space when I was searching for creativity. Typically, a good view or even a good song did the trick in helping me focus, but Jevon was blocking my view of the window. It forced me to stare at his back the whole time.

I started adding pieces of clay back to my mold as I kneaded it into submission. Unconsciously, my hands started pinching and folding lines into the mold. I let my fingers do all the work and I figured something would come to me.

Only when I looked down at my sculpture with fresh eyes did I realize the figure I'd created—a neck that curved into a broad set of shoulders and muscles that bulged out on the sides.

I did a wild double take. The resemblance was uncanny. Had I really been creating art inspired by Jevon?

I went to mash the whole thing up and start all over again, but then I noticed that *something* that was missing before. It wasn't in the minor details I'd added to the mold—it was in the sudden feeling of hope I got when I looked at it. The changes made a monumental difference to the overall effect and I knew then that I had to keep going.

For the rest of the class period, I watched Jevon openly. I studied the muscles and the contours of his back, following the lines almost perfectly in my clay. My sculpture came to life like magic in my hands.

By the time class was over, I had an incomplete bust of the boy sitting in front of me. I had a long way to go if I wanted to have something presentable for the exhibit, but the hope I felt was thrilling. I didn't know how, but somehow, I'd find a way to make him my muse.

CHAPTER THREE

Jevon

I tried in vain to get my mother to side with me against going to the art school. She hated the thought of me fighting. Ma had always been hyper-sensitive to the idea of me getting hurt or injured. I was convinced she hoped I'd take an interest in something else, something less violent.

It was a lost cause in the end. I'd spent the entire week before school in the dojo where I trained, staying until closing time every single day. The plan was to get all the frustration out of my system before heading into this new school. I hated that I was being forced to go to an art school. I wasn't artistic. It was like being thrown into a completely different playing field with no guide or instructions.

All day at school, I focused on keeping my head down and just getting through the day. So far, it had gone pretty smoothly, although the constant staring was hard to get used to. I was perfectly fine with being left alone to do my sentence in peace.

Then, during my lunch period, things got a little weird.

"Hey, you're the new kid, right?"

I looked up from my lunch to find a hand extended toward me.

My eyes followed that hand up to a face. It was a guy I recognized from a few of my core classes. He had his own unique sense of style that was a little odd for my tastes, but it kind of worked for him. He dressed like a DJ from the 80s, complete with the track suit, Adidas, a couple of gold chains, and a beanie.

I stared at his outstretched hand like the disturbance it was. With any luck, he'd catch the hint and go away. Nervously, he scratched at the back of his head and dropped his hand at his side.

"I'm Tommy," he tried again, "but you can just call me T."

Tommy sat down across from me and instantly made himself comfortable. He cast his tray of food to the side as he fiddled through his duffle bag on the floor.

"Jevon," I said finally. "What are you doing?"

Tommy pulled out a bunch of equipment that seemed to be used for producing music.

"Formally introducing myself."

He pulled two speakers out of his duffle bag and placed them on both ends of the table. When he was done, he flexed his fingers and popped the kinks in his neck like he was preparing for something big.

"Check it out," he said, and soon the cafeteria was filled with loud music.

The table in front of me vibrated with the beat, and I instantly looked around, expecting someone to come and tell us to shut up or keep it down. Most people ignored us altogether, probably used to some kid blasting his music out in the cafeteria.

I listened for a while, bobbing my head to his song. Tommy's music was admittedly pretty good. I wondered if I'd ever get used to this. All day, I found myself comparing Cambridge to Laney High. An act like this would've definitely landed us in detention at my old school.

The music came to a stop after a while, and so did all the wandering eyes. I waited for Tommy to pack his equipment back into his bag.

"That was dope, man," I admitted.

He nodded. "That was just a warm up. What's your niche?"

There was that question again.

"I don't have one."

Just like all the others before him, Tommy's face twisted up in that same look of confusion. Everyone here was so concerned with my talents. A part of me wanted to show them what I could really do, but the rational side of me warned against it. My fighting was to be used only in competition or in self-defense. With Tommy looking at me like he was waiting for the butt end of a joke, I could only shrug in return.

"You can't be serious, Jay."

Only my friends called me Jay, but I didn't object to it. I was learning quickly that Tommy made himself comfortable quite easily.

"I really don't have an artistic talent, or a niche, or whatever you want to call it."

"Then, why would you . . ." Tommy started to ask, but the more he stared at me, the more suspicious he became. "Wait, hold up. Don't I know you from somewhere?"

I shrugged and played it cool. If no one had looked me up yet, they would all discover who I was eventually. Tommy wasn't convinced. He brought a hand under his chin while he contemplated.

"What'd you say your name was again?"

"Jevon—"

"Williams!" Tommy interrupted me with a snap of his fingers. "That's why you look so familiar. You're Jevon Williams, the pro fighter, right?"

I nodded, not wanting to draw too much attention to myself.

"Huh." He leaned back in his seat. "That's weird. People usually get famous after they leave CSA, not the other way around."

"I'm not really famous."

"Famous enough. You don't need CSA."

My thoughts exactly. "Yeah, I know."

"Wait, so why are you really here?"

I considered the best way to explain my sudden acceptance to this school and drew a blank. None of my father's logic would make any sense to him. With a deep sigh, I decided to be honest. "I got in some trouble a few months ago. I'm just here to clean up my act."

His eyes grew wide, but he recovered quickly. With a simple shrug, Tommy smiled and relaxed more into his seat.

"Well, I'd hate to be the dumbass that got on your bad side."

I grinned, but I didn't comment.

We spent the rest of the lunch period going over the ins and outs of CSA. Already, it seemed much more entertaining than anything Laney High had to offer.

Toward the end of the day, I headed straight to the guidance counselor. Nobody was more confused by my presence here than she was, and she didn't hide it either. Pops had told me only a little about how he was able to swing my sudden acceptance here out of the blue. It was no small favor for the dean of admissions to allow me to be here.

I'd heard one too many stories about all the people who'd tried and failed to get in. Just by being here, I raised too many questions that went unanswered or explained. None of this made sense, and it wasn't fair. That much I could agree with.

"Here's your readjusted scheduled for the semester." Mrs. Collins slid a sheet of paper across her desk to me. She said the word "readjusted" like I was special in the head or something.

Her office was cramped and cold. I had to wedge myself into the stiff, wooden chair across from her desk.

"This is a lot," I noted. Not only was I expected to handle regular classes, but there were all kinds of music and dance courses listed on the schedule.

"These are the most basic courses. There'll be freshmen sitting next you in class."

Mrs. Collins didn't seem to understand. I was pointing out the nine different class changes I was expected to go through in one day, not the caliber of the classes themselves. It made me wonder how long the school days were here. As I glanced over the list one more time, I noticed a few more things that remained the same.

"Advanced visual arts II? Fashion and design?" I asked. Those weren't basic at all. They were listed as senior courses.

Mrs. Collins turned to her computer screen. Her nails clacked loudly against her keyboard as she searched for a shorter list of classes, I hoped.

"Hmph." She leaned into the screen. "It looks like you actually need to pass a few senior level courses to graduate."

I sighed. "Is there nothing else I could do?"

Mrs. Collins resumed her loud clacking for only a minute. When she finished, she turned the monitor toward me so I could see for myself.

"You could always try advanced musical composition, or maybe something in theater arts? We're pretty limited on what's available."

"Never mind, I'll keep what I have," I said as I rose from my seat. I didn't play an instrument, and theater was the wrong stage for me.

As I headed out of Mrs. Collins's office with my now-crumpled class schedule in hand, I thought of a whole new plan. If I could help it, I'd find a one-way ticket out of this school. I didn't belong here, that much was clear from the moment I walked through those doors. What difference would it make to pretend I had an ounce of artistic talent anyway?

I thought of all the ways I could get myself transferred back to Laney as I made my way to my locker. With a stubborn father, a sensitive mother, and a lawyer that made too much sense, my odds weren't looking good. It would take something drastic to make them change their minds, but I wasn't sure I was ready to take that risk just yet.

I rounded the corner to the rows of metal lockers that lined the hall, searching for mine. 238 was the bold number on the page Mrs. Collins gave me, but there was a girl already standing in front of that locker number. She turned at my arrival and graced me with a smile like she had been waiting on me all along.

The people at CSA were almost unbearably nosy. All day, my classmates found reasons to talk to me and ask me about my talents or my life before Cambridge. Outside of my circle at Laney, I'd never been that much of social guy. I didn't care to have my life's story all out in the open, but as a high-ranking fighter, privacy wasn't always a luxury.

"Hey," I said curtly as I came to a stop in front of her.

She was an art student, I could tell by the paint that coated her hands, arms, shoes, and her heavily decorated overalls. Her long black hair was pulled back into a low sitting ponytail. It swayed as she shifted the weight on her feet.

"Hey." The brown-skinned held her smile. It teemed with a sort of confidence that was admirable. Unlike the others who had approached me all day, this girl didn't shy away at my hostility. "Look, I know everybody's probably asked you a million questions today about your niche, and who you are, but that's not why I'm here."

"Okay." I went to open my locker door. It didn't look like she was moving anytime soon.

"I sit behind you in advanced visual arts II with Ms. Hazel."

"Yeah, I remember Ms. Hazel. What about it?"

"You sit right in front of the window that I usually stare of for inspiration, but today you blocked my view."

"Uh, sorry?"

"Oh, no, you don't have to apologize! I was coming to thank you, actually. It's because you blocked my view, that I was forced to stare at you the whole time. I kind of got inspired by you."

That brought me to a pause. I stuffed my last book into the locker and shut the door. She stood there, staring at me expectantly, but I didn't know what I was supposed to say to that.

"I wanted to ask you something," she went on, "and I hope it's not too weird."

I waited.

"Will you be my muse?"

If I was shocked at all by anything she said before, now I was completely thrown for a loop. I didn't know much about muses, but I thought they were supposed to be a deep, intimate type of thing. It definitely wasn't something that was brought into normal conversation.

"Maybe I should explain," she continued. "I'm working on this piece for the senior art show, and only the best art students get invited to show off their work. This could be a really big deal for me, so I need something absolutely amazing to win over the critics."

"And you want me to be that absolutely amazing thing?" I asked.

"Yes." She smiled.

Again, I waited for more, but none came.

"Um." I glanced around the busy hallway. "It's just my first day, and this isn't really my thing. You'd have better luck with some-body else."

"Probably, but I really need you."

First, it was Tommy at lunch with his concert, and now this girl came to me with the oddest request. I wasn't just a new student to them. I was an anomaly, something everybody wanted to figure out. And now, apparently, I was a muse too?

"Is it always like this here?" I asked.

"It depends on who you ask." She smiled again, exposing a hidden dimple in her right cheek.

I found myself smiling too as I held my hand out toward her. "I'm Jevon, by the way."

"Oh, I know. We have homeroom together too. Plus, you're all anybody can talk about." She rolled her eyes.

"Tired of me already?"

"Not at all."

She stared at me like I stared at her, full of curiosity. I wondered what was going through her head. Her eyes analyzed my face like an architect's would to a new building. What was it about me that *inspired* her?

"And your name is?" I asked when the silence became too loud.

"Oh, right, sorry. I'm Akilah" She shook my hand and soon she was looking away, probably realizing how she was staring.

"Nice to meet you, Akilah."

"You too, Jevon. I know this is a lot, but I promise it'll be worth your time. Just think about it, okay?"

"I don't need to think about it. I'm not an artist, or a muse, or any of that. You should really ask somebody el—"

"If it'll help you make up your mind . . ." Akilah reached for my arm and pulled up my sleeve. Before I could even react, she had already begun writing on me. "Here's my website. All the work that I've ever done is on there. Check it out, and then make your decision."

With that, she walked away, leaving me with the sharp memory of her pen grazing against my skin. The blue ink bled into my arm, dotted at the very end with a smiley face. One thing was for sure, this was bound to be an interesting year.

CHAPTER FOUR

Akilah

"You did not go up to that boy and ask him to be your muse!" Kayla gushed in disbelief as I told her about my run-in with the new boy.

We were upstairs in my room, listening to Jhene Aiko soulfully spill her heart out. It had almost been a week since I'd last talked to him, and I hadn't heard anything from him since that Monday.

"I did," I groaned as I fell back on the bed, "but I don't know if he even looked at my website. He hasn't said anything about it, and he just keeps to himself most of the time."

Aside from a few waves here and there in passing, Jevon remained a silent mystery. I wanted to give him time to decide, but time wasn't always on your side when opportunities were on the line.

"What did he say when you asked him?"

"I didn't give him a chance to say anything, but I could tell he really wanted to say no. Maybe I came on a little too strong."

"Or, maybe just give him some time to think about it. That's a pretty heavy question to put on somebody you just met."

She was right. It was a heavy question, one I hadn't put too much thought into before asking him. Jevon didn't know the kind of inspiration I got just from looking at him. I saw so much potential in what I could create with him that I'd blurted out the first thing that came to mind when I saw him.

Did I make a mistake in being so bold with the new boy? He did seem like a fish out of water on that first day, and he *did* say he wasn't an artist . . .

"If he says no, then—"

"He won't," she reassured me.

"It's a possibility, Kayla. I have to at least think about my options."

"You can't think like that. You're an amazing artist." Kayla stood up to look around my room.

My artwork was everywhere, literally bunched into any corner it would fit. She walked over to my vanity, where I stored a collection of paintings on the end. Absentmindedly, Kayla's fingers brushed against the tallest one in the middle.

"I mean, look at this!" She pulled it out for me to see.

On the canvas was an old project I'd worked on for an assignment at school. The painting was of a younger version of my mother at her dance studio. There was a photo of her hanging on the wall in my parents' room. I always stared at it whenever I was in there.

The picture was captured at the perfect moment, as Momma was in the midst of one of those pirouette spins ballerinas did. She was so graceful, like she defied every law of gravity in just one turn. Momma was truly beautiful.

"Okay," I admitted, "you might have a point."

"I know."

It did make me feel better to have my best friend's support. Maybe it *was* completely insane to take a risk with the new boy, but I would let my work speak for itself. The hard part would be forcing myself to relax while I waited for his answer. I was so eager to get started on something that it made me jumpy with an impatient kind of energy.

I left my bed and walked over to my dresser. Tucked deep into the back of the first drawer was a stash that I kept hidden in a small lock box. I pulled it out and punched in the code to lift the lid.

Four neatly rolled joints lay horizontally inside next to a lighter, a folded wad of saved allowance money, and a few sticks of incense. I took the lighter and one of the joints and stuffed it into my pocket. Closing the lid to my safe, I placed it back where it belonged.

My parents kept such a strict handle on just about everything I did that there was never any room to fully breathe. If they knew I smoked—even as seldom as I did—they'd never let me live it down.

A part of the reason I was so excited about senior year was because after graduating, I'd finally be on my own. I would be on my way to adulthood, free to make my own decisions.

"Are you down for a mall run?" I turned to Kayla.

A "mall run," was really code for "You wanna go smoke?" She must've seen me collecting the spliff, because she already had her bag in hand. I followed her lead, grabbing my own purse from the hook on my closet door.

Without another word, we left my room and headed for the staircase down the hall. My younger brother, CJ, peeked his head out of his room as we passed by. He wasn't that much younger than me, though in comparison, he looked like my older brother, not the other way around.

"You're going to the mall?" he asked.

"No, Clarence." I breezed past him. He hated his government name.

"You just said you were about to go."

"Yeah, but I didn't say you could come with me."

"Come on, AJ, I already told Natasha I would meet her there. Do you want to tell her dad I lied, or should I?"

Natasha lived down the street from us. Her friendship with CJ had always been questionable. There was a running bet on when they'd both eventually come out as a couple. I thought it was partly because CJ was afraid of Natasha's father.

Mr. Peters was Atlanta's Chief of Police. He liked to joke about locking CJ up if ever he broke his daughter's heart. Given the illegal activity Kayla and I were about to partake in, I didn't think it was wise to test those waters. For that reason only, I let my little brother come along.

"Okay, let's go, but you have to split when we get there."

"Cool. I don't want to be around you and your dusty-ass friends anyway."

"Watch your mouth, little boy!"

"You only got a year on me. I'm not a little boy. I'm a man." At that, CJ pushed up on Kayla, grabbing her by the waist and holding her there.

Kayla palmed him in the face, instantly halting his advances. "No."

"And you can't flirt with my friends," I added.

"Kayla's not a friend, she's like family."

"Ew, CJ. That's even worse."

From the dumbstruck look on CJ's face, he didn't understand where he went wrong. I let him think over it a little while longer before eventually giving up all hope. With those moves, there was no wonder he and Natasha hadn't gotten past the friendship phase of their relationship. CJ had no game.

Explaining to CJ why it wasn't okay to consider Kayla "like family" if he was going to flirt with her took almost the entire ride to the mall. My brother's looks did little to make up for his stupidity, but in his eyes he was the man, so I guess that counted for something.

Once we arrived to the mall, CJ was out of sight before Kayla and I could fully make our way inside. We took a lazy stroll up to the front, not in a real hurry to meet or see anybody there. The mall wasn't as packed as it normally was on Saturdays. With the start of the new school year, everyone began sticking to a stricter schedule.

"Are we meeting somebody at The Spot?" Kayla asked.

Behind the mall, up a trail that led to a gazebo hidden within the trees, was The Spot. It was known for the wildest after-school hook-ups, and was generally a meeting point for those extra secret rendezvous. Most importantly, The Spot was a place where a lot of teens went to smoke when they didn't want to be discovered. It was perfect.

"No, I don't think so. There's hardly anybody here today."

Kayla and I looked around the mall. It was practically empty inside with only a few other kids that went to different schools walking around. I turned to head out toward the back exit that led to the trail when I noticed Kayla staring ahead at a group clustered at the entrance to a store.

"You know them?" I asked, taking another look myself.

"No, but look who's with them."

My eyes followed the direction of her finger as she pointed to the person at the very center of the group. I blinked a few more times to make sure I was seeing straight.

And like that, what was meant to be a moment of lazy relaxation had suddenly morphed into pure dread. I was instantly ready to turn around and go back home.

Deshawn Evans.

My ex-boyfriend looked exactly the way I remembered him, just as cocky and blatantly unaware of his arrogance. I didn't have to be close to know that every word out of his mouth was a conceited attempt to make him seem better than he actually was. There was a time when I'd actually found that cute.

At first glance, Deshawn exuded confidence all around him. Thinking back, I couldn't believe I'd fallen for it. All the wasted time, effort, and tears I'd put into him only shined a light on the large sign stamped on my forehead. A sign that read "DUMMY."

"Come on." I tugged on Kayla's arm. "Let's go the other way around. I don't want to deal with him right now."

Kayla didn't move an inch. She stood firmly in place, eyeing me like I was a crazy person. N"o. You're not running from him. Hold your head up high and walk right past him. Show him what he missed out on."

I really wasn't in the mood to show him anything. The last place I wanted to be was on Deshawn's radar, but that seemed impossible with the way Kayla pushed me toward the exit.

Left with no other choice, I did as she instructed and kept my chin up as we walked by. All conversation lowered to a distinct hum when we were close enough to actually hear anything. Still, I kept my eyes on my destination, focused only on getting to the other side of the mall.

"See!" Kayla nearly shouted when the doors to the exit closed behind us. "How hard was that?"

She held her hand out for me to slap it in agreement, but I just looked at her.

"Why did you make me do that?"

"Because you needed it. You need to stop wallowing over him. Deshawn is clearly not missing out on any sleep over the breakup, and neither should you."

"I don't wallow over him."

"Yeah, okay. But, uh, you should fix your face when you lie. It might make you more believable."

To that, I had no comeback. Kayla snickered as she pointed to the frown I quickly tried to wipe from my face. This only made her laugh harder.

"You're not funny," I grumbled.

Kayla didn't argue with me further. She led the way up the trail to The Spot as her laughter slowly died down. I was thankful for the stash tucked away in my pocket.

In a few moments, nothing else would matter. Not Kayla and her teasing, my anxiousness over the new school year, Jevon's pending response to my very urgent request, or even Deshawn and his entire being. I planned to be high enough to get lost among the clouds. Maybe then my problems would fade to a soft whisper, just low enough for me to ignore.

We came to a stop at the end of the trail to find the gazebo empty, and Kayla and I took a seat on opposite sides of the long bench. I dug for the joint in my pocket while Kayla sparked a flame with her lighter. Leaning into her cupped hand over the flame, I inhaled deeply, holding there until the end sizzled away.

My head dipped back slowly to the post behind me. With my eyes closed, I parted my lips to let the smoke find its way out. The welcoming burn in my lungs signaled the countdown to my ascent into the clouds.

After a few more puffs, I passed the joint off to Kayla. She mirrored my movements, leaning back in the bench as the smoke billowed out through her nose. We kept up the rotation between us until the joint was about the size of a bean. Kayla soon squished the bud out on the bottom of her shoe and flicked it off to the side.

"Better?" she asked, her eyes all glazed over and red.

I nodded sluggishly. "Better."

We sat like that for a while, enjoying the breeze that blew by every so often. The sun shone brightly through the trees, illuminating every crevice of the gazebo around us. This was definitely better. My body felt light.

Even though I knew I was firmly planted in my seat, when I closed my eyes it felt like some part of me drifted away with the passing smoke, floating high up in the air. Nothing compared to the bliss I felt coursing through my veins.

"Do you ever think about life after CSA?" I asked.

Kayla tilted her head in my direction and cast her eyes up to the wooden roof while she thought. The trees cast shadowy patterns over her light brown skin, as her loose curls flowed with the gusts of wind that blew by.

"Yes and no," she said eventually.

"Why both?"

"Yes, because we get to live out our dreams in New York City. I submitted my application to Ivory Middleton last semester."

"And you got in?" I sat up in my seat. Ivory Middleton School of Visual Arts was my dream, but every time I went to apply I psyched myself out.

"I did." She grinned.

"Kayla, that's amazing! Why didn't you say anything?"

She shrugged and looked away. "Because I'm also not ready to leave yet. With me gone, my mom will be all alone."

Kayla didn't talk about her dad's death that much. It had happened years ago, but I knew it still affected her deeply. She stared off into the trees for a while, and we both went silent as a cool breeze blew through the gazebo. It ruffled the sleeves in my oversized T-shirt, bringing with it, a fresh wave of pine needles from the trees all around us.

"Sometimes I feel like I'll be stuck here," I admitted.

"Why would you say that?"

"I don't know." It was my turn to shrug. "Where I want to be and where I am now feels so far away from each other. There's too many missing pieces."

Kayla's brows scrunched together in confusion, so I took a deep breath as I tried to explain.

"I can't get into Ivory Middleton if I don't stand out in my application. You're lucky because you get to do fashion shows every year, but the senior art show is the only way for me get noticed, and I can't do that if I don't present something incredible. That's why I really need Jevon to agree to work with me. If he doesn't, then I don't know what I'm going to do."

I was talking so fast that my words had started running together.

"Now I get why you wanted to go to the mall." She chuckled. "You're stressing *me* out!"

I threw my head back against the post. "I can't help it!"

"What makes Jevon so special? You barely know him."

"A gut feeling." I sighed. "I feel like we can do great things together."

"Well, it sounds like you need to step your game up."

"How am I supposed to do that?" I asked. Jevon acted like didn't even want to be at CSA, he traipsed around school like a black sheep.

"Don't think too hard about it." She suddenly lowered her voice. "It might just come to you."

"Huh?"

"Akilah?" A deep voice called to my left.

I jumped at the sound, and my head whipped around to follow the voice and match it to a face. Jevon Williams walked up the few steps of the gazebo, ducking his head low to get inside.

"Speak of the devil," Kayla mumbled with a smile. She must've seen him coming.

"What are you doing here?" he asked, taking a seat across from us.

"The same thing you're here for."

He couldn't have found this place by accident. If he was here, then he knew exactly what this gazebo was used for.

Jevon quirked a brow. "I'm not here for that, actually. I was out for a run."

"In the middle of the woods?" Kayla asked.

"Yeah, there's another trail back that way." Jevon pointed to a slowly fading pathway covered in leaves and debris. I took a second glance at him and noticed the small sheen of sweat dotted around his tapeline. He breathed deep and evenly, like he had hardly done anything.

"Is running your *thing*?" I tried to ask innocently, but Jevon seemed to catch on quick. With a coy smile, he lifted the end of his shirt to swipe at the sweat before it could reach his eyes.

"No, it's not my niche, if that's what you're asking."

Kayla nudged my leg. Her eyes darted between Jevon and me like she was alerting me to something vitally important.

"Ask him!" she mouthed.

"H-have you thought about my offer? At all?" I let out.

"I saw your website."

I perked up. "You did?"

"She's dope, right?" Kayla asked.

Jevon nodded thoughtfully. "I just have one question."

"What's that?"

"If I do this, what's in it for me?"

I blinked, taken aback. "What do you mean?"

"You get your big break and all, but what do I get in return?"

I hadn't thought about what Jevon would be looking to get out of this experience. My mind had only focused on the limitless art I could create through him, and I realized suddenly I had nothing to offer him in return.

"Um . . . you'll be recognized by the most accredited companies in the art industry."

I meant it as a statement, but it came out like a question, almost as if I was unsure of the bargain myself.

Jevon shook his head. "That's not good enough for me."

"Do you want a payment or something?"

I wasn't sure how much I could really offer him. Daddy's credit card would only take me so far.

"No, I don't want your money."

I took a moment to think of something good. Kayla was right. I barely knew this boy, but I couldn't ignore that there was something special about him. Even now, as he sat there, I captured mental images of his features, the way his smooth brown skin contrasted with the glow of the sun, and the slowly changing trees around us. I wondered, not for the first time, what it would be like to draw him, to paint him as the living work of art that he was.

Kayla sighed loudly as she stood up to leave. "I'm going to get some food. Are you hungry?"

I shook my head no, even though I was dying to bite into a cheeseburger. The munchies had kicked in, but I needed to focus if I wanted to get Jevon on board. Kayla descended the steps and disappeared into the trees as she followed the trail out of the woods.

It was only Jevon and me, left to stare at each other through the awkward silence. Eventually, he came over to sit beside me, leaving a little space between us.

"What do you want out of this?" I asked.

"I want you to make it public, your artwork I mean."

"Wait, how does that benefit you?"

"Long story short, if the right people saw me in a different light, this could change my career too."

There was a hint of seriousness in his voice that made me lean in. I didn't know the meaning behind his words, but for a moment his mind seemed to go somewhere else entirely.

Before I could analyze his face too deeply, Jevon recovered, making me wonder if I was just seeing things. I didn't even know what his niche was, or if his interests were even remotely related to visual arts.

Whatever it was, he was vague enough to keep me guessing. I didn't press him for more, though. Instead, I held my hand out for him to shake.

"Okay, you got a deal."

Jevon shook my hand firmly, solidifying our agreement. It should've ended there, but I felt the sudden urge to go in for a hug. Something in his expression before gave me the impression that he needed it. However, in my high state of mind, I could've been very, very wrong.

Without thinking, I wrapped my arms around his shoulders and gave him a gentle squeeze. Jevon froze in place, seemingly equally as surprised by my actions as I suddenly was. What was I doing? I'd finally gotten him to agree to work with me, and now I was sure to scare him away just as fast.

Eventually, though, I felt Jevon move to reciprocate the gesture. He brought his hands up to pat me lightly on my back. Our hug was all kinds of stiff and awkward, but I didn't let it deter me. I guess, in a way, I needed it too.

CHAPTER FIVE

Jevon

All week, I'd thought of ways to cut my time at CSA short. I figured I could start a fight and get expelled. Or I could secretly re-enroll at Laney High. If I was really desperate, I could just drop out altogether.

Though the last option was the most appealing, I knew I'd never drop out of school. I wasn't a quitter. Plus, Pops would never take me serious as a high school dropout. For now, I was stuck at this snooty school with its weird curriculum and its even weirder student body.

On Friday, I had a meeting with Pops after school. He said we needed a game plan for the upcoming season, and I couldn't agree more.

"Your father's waiting for you," Ma said to me when I placed my bag down on the kitchen table. She was face-deep in a pile of paper work at the island. She didn't even glance up to make sure it was actually me and not some burglar with a gun.

"You work too much, Ma," I said as I passed by.

"You're one to talk." She grinned.

She had a point. I *was* on my way to a meeting about my career after a long day of school. Snagging an apple from the basket in front of her, I placed a kiss on her cheek and pushed a bar stool closer to her.

"At least get off your feet for a while."

Ma didn't argue. She claimed the seat and exhaled gratefully. My parents owned a real estate brokerage firm and most days they brought their work home with them. I guessed the hardworking gene was in my blood. As I headed to the back of the house, where Pops's office was, I knew he'd still be working too.

At the end of the hall, behind the staircase, I caught the blurred edges of his silhouette through the frosted glass. The familiar smell of peppermints and aged leather permeated through the crack in the door. His voice carried into the hallway, as he was in the midst of a business call.

I lightly tapped my knuckles against the glass and cracked the door open wider. With two fingers, Pops motioned for me to come inside. Not missing a beat, he rotated his chair to face the wall as he brought his call to an end.

"Yes, that should work," he said into the phone. "Make sure the case is closed by Monday and file it under expedited. Thanks."

When he was done, he turned to place the phone back on the receiver. I took a seat in the chair opposite of him. His desk was an organized mess of papers and plaques and beige file folders all stacked on top of each other.

"How was your first week?" he asked.

"It was hell."

"I doubt that. Cambridge is one of the best schools in the city."

"Pops, I don't belong there. You know I don't."

He leaned back in his swivel chair, rocking a little with the sudden movement. Pops took on that concentrated look I hated. The one that instantly let me know I wasn't going to get my way.

"Jevon, what has complaining ever gotten you?"

I turned my head with a deep sigh. I wasn't in the mood for a life lesson or some metaphor about my work ethic.

"Hmm?" he pressed.

"Nothing."

"Exactly, and it won't get you anywhere here either."

"Well, then, can you make it plain to me what I'm doing here? I'm confused. Looking good to the board will only get me so far. I need to change their minds."

"Now you're thinking," My father sat up in his seat. "The only question is: how? I got you in the door, son, but I can't do the work for you. Step one was taking you out of an environment you're comfortable with. You're never going to make any real change if nothing changes around you. Step two is up to you. You've got a world of opportunity at your fingertips. Use it. Find a way to make it work."

"You make it sound like it's so easy."

"It's not impossible."

I pushed away from his desk, fully prepared to head up to my room, but Pops stopped me with a snap of his fingers.

"Sit down."

I did as instructed.

"Since you're graduating soon, we need to consider your long-term goals."

"Is this about college?"

"Not today. The Olympic trials for your division have already begun."

"And?"

"And you won't qualify in time to compete."

"What?!" I shot up from my seat automatically. I wasn't sure where I was going, but I suddenly couldn't sit still. My feet paced the length of the office as my father's words settled into the air.

This couldn't be happening. My hands started to shake without permission, so I clenched them into fists to keep them still.

"Calm down, son."

How could I calm down? How could I feel any sort of calm when my world, my dreams were crumbling all around me?

"So, what? Now I have to wait another four years?" I was spiraling, pacing a hole into the floor as my mouth began to dry.

"Jevon!" he barked and I came to a standstill.

"Did you really think I would bring this up without having a plan in place?"

He was so sure of himself, so composed, that it eased a bit of the tension I felt building in my hands. They clenched and unclenched themselves as I unconsciously dug mini crescents into my palms. The pain from it was a welcoming presence. It kept me focused.

I took a deep, calming breath. "What's the plan?"

Pops heaved a big sigh. "The reason you don't qualify is because a decision hasn't been made yet from your last competition. The judges' final decision will tell us how you ended last season, but there's too much back and forth between them about right versus wrong and fairness versus aptitude. We should've had your paperwork for the trials turned in months ago, but again, we can't do that with your current standing in the league."

"Let me get this straight," I cut in. "We don't know my scores, and we don't know if or when I'll be able to compete in the Olympics? Is that what you're saying?"

"I did hope that by now we would've heard back, but these things take time. We will get you back in good standing, trust me. But, until then, Dave and I are working on something big for you. This goes beyond the judges or anything they could decide on."

"What is it? What are you working on?"

"I can't say now. I don't want to jinx it, but you'll know when the time is right. In the meantime, just remember what I said about this school. Find a way to make it worthwhile."

"But, Pops—"

He cut me off with the palm of his hand. "That's all for now, Jevon." He said nothing more as he diverted his attention back to the stack of papers in front of him.

The meeting was over and there was nothing more to be said. My limbs moved stiffly as I exited my father's office. I wished he trusted me more with information. Most of our meetings were the standard "Do as I say," or "Trust that I'll make it happen," type of vibe. It made me wonder if he treated me like a dimwit because I acted like one, or if that was the way most manager/talent relationships worked.

Maybe I didn't need all the details because at the end of the day, Pops always got the job done, no matter what. I trusted my father more than anybody, but if I wanted him to trust me, then I'd have to find a way to prove myself trustworthy.

I took the steps two at a time to get to my room, narrowly avoiding stepping on my dog, Cujo, on the way up. He yelped at our almost-collision and barked at me like it was playtime. I gave his head a good scratch and snuck into my room before he could catch up to me. Now wasn't the time for games. I had an idea.

As I took a seat at my desk and opened my laptop, I tried and failed to remember the name of the girl from Monday. I remembered her face clearly. I'd seen her almost every day for a week straight. But she said something about an art show, or was it a website? A museum?

I went straight to CSA's website which had a directory for all the students. I clicked on the senior class and scrolled through the list of names.

From the pictures, I didn't recognize anyone in particular. It was when I got to page three, all the way at the bottom, that I caught a face that came with a sudden memory.

Akilah Johnson.

It all came rushing back to me. She'd asked me to be her muse. I'd thought she was half-crazy then, but now as I looked at her picture, I realized I might've been the crazy one for turning her down. Pops had told me to make the most of my experience at CSA, and here was a girl that was ready and willing to turn me into a project. It was at least a step in the right direction.

I clicked on her photo and it suddenly enlarged. Forced to stare at her up close, I instantly noticed the differences in her picture on the directory from the way she looked on Monday. Her hair was different here. It was big and coily, hanging down to her shoulders. A few stray strands brushed against her clear brown skin, adding more volume to her slim face. The dimple in her right cheek was more prominent as she smiled sweetly at the camera. I didn't recall her being so pretty when we first met. I thought she was weird, quirky, and oddly confident in that weirdness.

Below her picture was a link to what I assumed was her website, and that was all I really needed. She'd asked me to view it before I made a decision.

So, that's what I did.

CHAPTER SIX

Akilah

After last weekend, I made it my mission to convince Jevon that I was worth working with. He had half-heartedly agreed to meet with me after school today. I think a part of him was still on the fence about this whole ordeal. I told myself that it wasn't me that weirded him out—unwarranted hugs and all. He'd said so himself; he wasn't an artist. Maybe he was skeptical?

I was anxious for the school day to be over with so I could finally get started on my piece. I had this vision in my head about what I could add to my bust to really make it shine. That one time in class, I had only been able to sculpt the contours of Jevon's back and I wasn't even sure if I got it right.

There were only so many times I could keep going back to the same drying mold of clay before it eventually cracked and ruined the entire frame of the sculpture, so I decided to start over. Everything had to be perfect.

I was in the middle of kneading a fresh block of clay when Jevon sauntered into the art studio. He seemed wary at first as he placed his things on the table across from me. Slowly, he pulled away from the station and walked the four steps over to me, standing there expectantly.

"Thanks for coming." I said, flipping a piece of hair out of my face as best as I could without actually touching it.

"No problem. What do you need me to do?" he asked, looking around the room with uncertainty.

I gestured with my head to the stool at the station across from us. He grabbed it and pulled it so that he was sitting right in front of me.

"I just need you to sit and pose on that stool for a while."

"How long is a while?" he asked, eyeing me funny.

"Since this is your first time doing something like this, I wasn't planning on making you stay for too long. Maybe like an hour to an hour and a half?"

His eyes widened. "What?"

Okay, so maybe I'd neglected to tell him all that would be required of him while we worked together. Most people couldn't sit still much longer than five minutes, let alone an hour. I understood his dilemma because I was one of those people too.

"Why can't you just take a picture of me posing and use that while you work?"

I rolled my eyes at his ignorance. People who didn't understand the complexities of true art would always assume a picture was as good as the real thing.

"Because I need to make this as realistic as possible. I can't do that with a two-dimensional photo. When sculpting someone, you have to make sure that the shadows are cast in exactly the same way you would see it in person. Pictures don't always represent the real thing."

Jevon seemed mildly impressed by my knowledge of what I was doing, but I didn't need his approval. All I needed was his time and willingness to cooperate. With a bored huff, he sat on the stool. Jevon looked off to the side and into the sunlight that shined through the window. It cast a halo across his dark skin. I wished more than ever that I could somehow replicate that effect in my bust. While he posed, so blatantly unaware to his allure, a thought occurred to me.

"Oh! One more thing."

He turned back to me, his brows raised.

"Do you mind taking your shirt off?" I asked.

I half expected him to look at me like he thought I was suggesting something, but he didn't. Instead, Jevon silently obliged and undid the buttons on his shirt. The first thing I noticed when his shirt disappeared was how much more defined his body was underneath his clothes. Jevon's muscles sort of blended into each other in a rippling effect that could only be accomplished by lots of dedication.

I wondered *again* where he could've come from. Of all the talents at CSA, I couldn't think of one that would require the amount of work needed to get ripped the way Jevon was. Not even the most principled dancers looked like that, and they practiced every single day. Whatever it was that Jevon actually did, it was clearly above any physical standards set by our school.

Jevon returned to his pose and I took that as my cue to begin. I figured it would be better to start with his torso and then work my way up. His face would be a whole other complication to deal with on another day. I wasn't sure Jevon could do much with his facial features beyond his constant brooding anyway.

Boredom mixed with a deeply seeded contempt were the only emotions he could seem to muster. If Jevon only knew how many people would lie, cheat, and steal just to have a seat in a classroom at Cambridge, maybe it'd change his outlook on where he was.

We worked in silence for a while, letting the music I had on a speaker fill in the awkwardness. Every now and then, I would catch him glancing over to see how far along I had gotten in the sculpture.

He didn't let on to what he was thinking, but there was no hiding his apparent curiosity.

"Are you always this quiet?" I asked when I caught him looking again. He'd barely said a word to me since he came in.

From his side profile, I caught the curve of his smirk as he turned back toward the window. I knew he was dying to look.

"I didn't know I *could* talk."

"You can talk."

I waited as I used my fingers to blend all the harsh lines and indents I made into the clay, but Jevon was silent. I glanced up at him. He seemed at ease while he posed, staring at nothing in particular out the window. Did he not like talking at all, or was it that he didn't want to talk to me?

"Nothing?" I challenged.

Jevon's smirk held as he shrugged. "There's not a lot to say."

There was a short silence again as I reached for a new tool in my pouch. I carved out the indent of his left clavicle and used my fingers to smooth over the harsh edges.

"If I asked you a question, would you answer it?"

"Depends on the question."

Challenge accepted.

I decided to start off easy. "What's your favorite color?"

"Black."

"Favorite movie?"

"*The Wood.*"

"Ah." I smiled. "So you like the classics? Me too."

He turned to me with a raised brow, almost daring me to compare.

"I love the movie *Bring It On* but only the first one."

Jevon snorted. "That's not a classic."

My hand paused over the base of the sculpture as my eyes snapped up to his. "Yes, it is."

"No." He shook his head stiffly in his pose. "It's not. It's a played-out cliché."

"And *The Wood* is boring!" I snapped.

We had mini stare down that lasted all of three seconds before we both lost our composure. I was the first to laugh and Jevon quickly followed suit. It helped to ease any remaining awkwardness still lingering in the air.

"We'll just have to agree to disagree," I offered.

"Deal."

Jevon drew in that same bored breath of air as he returned to his pose. I noticed his eyes briefly dance around the room in distaste while he waited. It was such a strange reaction that I blurted out the first thought to pop into my head.

"You don't like it here, do you?"

"No. I shouldn't even be here."

"Everybody thinks they don't belong at first. Just give it time."

"Sure," he said, but I could tell he didn't believe a word of it.

It wasn't that Jevon was self-conscious at all—no, I didn't get that vibe from him. He was too arrogant, like he thought he was better than this place. Who was this boy? And where did he come from? The questions burned on the crease of my lips, but I kept them to myself. It was nothing a good search on Google couldn't resolve.

As hard as he tried to keep still, the wait soon had Jevon shifting uncomfortably in his seat. His knee began to bounce on the stool with a slight impatience, and that's when I knew it was time for a break.

"You should stretch," I offered.

I took the time to flex out the tension in my fingers. My bones popped and cracked under the pressure, but it felt good to relieve the tautness in them. Jevon didn't hesitate to stand up and do a full stretch.

As if from memory, he started with his legs and worked his way up to his back, his arms, his neck, and even his fingers. I tried not to stare at the expanse of his muscles as he stretched them out. Jevon really was a living, breathing sculpture in his own right. His every move was fluid and calculated. He had a practiced kind of control over his entire body.

When he was done stretching, Jevon came over to my side of the station to get a closer look at what I had done. It was only the front half of his torso, but already it was an exact replica. His eyes skimmed over the details quietly, a small smile beginning to stretch across his face.

"Impressive."

"I know," I smirked.

I left him there to take it all in as I went over to the sink to wash what I could of the clay from my hands, considering I'd been elbow deep in the concoction. Sometimes I got so focused on my work that I didn't realize the mess it made. Thankfully, none of it had made its way beyond the overalls I was wearing.

The music in the background had suddenly morphed into something more upbeat, and I swayed my hips a little to the beat while I worked. It was a subconscious thing I normally did as I cleaned around my area. The music gave me the energy I needed to finish faster than if it were totally silent.

Jevon had started to loosen up a little, but I still got the feeling that he wanted this to be over as soon as humanly possible, so I did my best to work quickly for his benefit. When I looked over at him though, he didn't appear to be in too much of a hurry to leave. He was too busy looking at some of my other art pieces around the room.

In the past, I had done a few paintings for Ms. Hazel on her birthday and her one-year anniversary at the school. They hung on the wall behind her desk. Each painting was symbolic of the effect she had on my life since meeting her. Ms. Hazel had taught me the most important parts of being an artist. The parts that came from within.

"Like what you see?" I asked as I moved to stand beside Jevon.

His eyes remained locked on the artwork in front of him.

"You did this?" he asked.

"Yeah." I nodded, waiting for more, but Jevon said nothing else as he stared.

"What do you think?" I tried again.

"I think there's a lot of anger in your work."

Instantly, my eyebrows scrunched down in confusion. My work could be aggressive and bold, yes, but nobody had ever described it as angry.

"What makes you say that?"

Jevon brought his attention down to me then, clearly assuming I'd taken offense to his observation. I was just genuinely curious about his thoughts on it.

"It's really good. There's no question about that. It's just that it's not hard to tell that you were probably feeling some type of way when you were doing this."

I took his thoughts into consideration and looked at the paintings with new eyes. The first one was of the island country of Jamaica, where Ms. Hazel was from. The country itself was painted as a waving flag raised high in the air, with its people waving their fists in the air down below. The idea behind it was supposed to be symbolic of its independence from the United Kingdom. From this new perspective, the expressions on the faces of the people—who once looked happy and jubilant—now seemed angry and deeply oppressed. Behind the smiles, if you looked closely, you could see it written all over their faces.

Well, I'll be damned.

"You have a good eye," I conceded.

"Nah. I'm not into all this art stuff. I just pay attention."

"I'm sure that skill gets you out of a lot of trouble."

I suddenly thought of all the times I'd attempted to get my ex, Deshawn, to pay attention to me, or even remember one redeeming quality about me. His excuse was always that I expected too much from him. "I don't sweat the little things," he would always say.

There was no way Deshawn would be able to interpret the minor details of my work the way Jevon just had. Jevon questioned the meaning of my words with a look, but I decided to change the subject.

"Are you ever going to tell me what you meant when you said you needed the 'right people' to see you in a different light?" I asked him, remembering our conversation from the gazebo.

Jevon went rigid all of a sudden, and I realized I asked a question that dug too deep. There was a distinct tic in his jaw at the mention of that conversation. Our little game of questions was fun on the surface level, but clearly Jevon would only peel back so much of who he was. Still, I waited patiently for him to respond.

"It's a long story," he finally said.

By the way his teeth ground together, I felt it was probably smart to drop the subject altogether. I didn't know much about Jevon, but I knew then to back off. He didn't seem too open to sharing his story just yet, and I had this nagging feeling that it was a fresh wound to him. Whatever the case, I didn't want to antagonize him further.

"Well, we have the room for the next forty-five minutes. I want to get started on your back while we still have the time."

Being around Jevon was going to take some getting used to. I was learning that his silent brooding was a trait that was as much a part of him as the muscles on his body. Soon, I got to work on his back, making sure to duplicate all the dips and grooves in the structure of his bones. We worked in silence for the rest of our time in the studio, with only the sounds of my music surrounding us.

CHAPTER SEVEN

Jevon

My time at Cambridge had started off as a real pain in the ass. The constant staring and questioning was beginning to be more than a little irritating. I couldn't wait until the novelty of being the new student wore off. I wasn't as interesting as people painted me to be, and when I failed to give them any clue as to what my talent was, they all began to make up their own stories.

The rumors got so carried away some people believed I was a backup dancer. Others concluded I was a singer, or a musician. And those who didn't believe in all the hype just assumed I was some spoiled rich kid with connections to the admissions board. They were half right on the last part. I wasn't spoiled.

I thought it was funny watching them guess and assume. Of course there were those that discovered who I was from my competitions that were aired on TV, but my true identity was lost amongst the rumors instantly. It wasn't like I was trying to keep my talents a secret—I just didn't feel the need to divulge my whole life story for clout and popularity. It was all just a big popularity contest anyway.

Eventually, though, my opinion on CSA started to change. The rumors died down after some time, and people left me alone for the most part. I didn't really go out of my way to make new friends. They just sort of gravitated toward me of their own accord.

Tommy had a lot to do with my new status at Cambridge. He sat with me at lunch almost every day since that first day I'd met him. I learned quickly how well-known Tommy was throughout the school. Our classmates tended to go out of their way to be around him when he was in the room, so much so that it wasn't a surprise when some of his friends eventually followed his lead to sit with me at lunch.

What did come as a surprise to me was the people included on Tommy's list of friends. Akilah, Kayla, and Tommy's best friend Andre were the first to follow. They welcomed me to their group just as easily as Tommy did, with no nagging questions or scrutinizing stares.

"AJ, when are you going to get off your lazy ass and finish that design for my album cover?" Tommy asked playfully, throwing a fry in her direction.

We were sitting in the cafeteria at a table closer to the windows. This area gave a better view of the quad, and it was a good distance away from the rest of the students. Though there was plenty of room left at the table, the rest of our peers avoided our area like it was restricted to only us.

Akilah picked up the French fry and tossed it back at Tommy. It landed on the brim of his bucket hat then slowly fell back down to his tray. She then reached over to steal a fresh fry from his basket for added measure.

"When you pay me for all this extra time you think I have set aside for you?"

Akilah held her hand out expectantly, wiggling her fingers like he was already past due on his payment. Tommy analyzed her waiting hand for only a second before loudly smacking his hand against hers. The shock on her face was enough to get a few chuckles out of her friends. The longer she stared with her mouth open wide, the funnier her look became.

"What are you laughing at?" Akilah called me out.

She crossed her arms and sized me up. "Keep laughing, Jevon." She smirked. "I haven't gotten to your face yet on my sculpture."

"You better chill, Jay, before she has you out here looking like a toad!" Andre chimed in.

The attention at the table suddenly shifted my way as the laughter geared toward me. Everyone else had a joke to add in, but it felt more like my initiation into the group than anything else. It was Tommy who eventually came to my rescue. He brought it all back to Akilah, demanding a date on the release of his album cover. They bickered back and forth about it until the end of lunch. In the end, Akilah agreed to have the cover completed over the weekend, but only if Tommy promised to get her VIP tickets to his next show.

* * *

When lunch was over, I used my free period to go to the dojo. Being at Cambridge didn't give me a lot of freedom to do what I wanted. School lasted way longer at CSA than it ever did at Laney High. Free time was pretty touch-and-go these days, but with at least forty-five minutes to myself, I had enough time to get to the dojo and release a little bit of pent-up tension from the day.

I'd only been at CSA for four weeks, yet I found myself needing time at the dojo more and more. Word got around in the fighting community that I'd transferred to an art school. As expected, they took me for some chump.

Jao Shang had made it his personal mission to make me look weak to all the other competitors. "*Soft. Factory made. See you at the finals, Williams*," was the most recent addition to his Twitter page. Above the caption was a photo of me entering Cambridge School of Arts.

A part of me wondered if Shang had hired a PI to follow me around, but it made more sense to believe that I was already being followed by press and reporters. My incident at the last competition had inadvertently put me in the limelight, and not for good reasons. Though my real identity was already mixed up in all the fake assumptions about me at school, it was only a matter of time before they discovered who I *really* was.

I didn't consider myself famous by any stretch of the imagination, but every international competition was televised, including my fight with Shang in London. After last summer, it felt like my every move was being followed and marked down for future reference. If anything, I was infamous for my record of losing my temper in the ring. I couldn't mess up this time.

When I arrived at the dojo, my trainer, Nick, and his wife, Sasha, were already sparring in the ring. Sasha had him pinned to the ground with her legs wrapped tightly around his throat. She pulled Nick's arm so far back it looked like it would pop out of its socket.

On any other day, I was sure that was a position he'd gladly be in. Sasha might've looked sweet, but she was deadly nonetheless. Nick's face turned bright red as he attempted to maneuver out of her grip, but Sasha wouldn't let up. She was going to make him tap out.

When I first began training with them, I'd thought—just like everybody else did—that Nick would always let Sasha win. It only took a few rounds in the ring with her myself to realize the mistake in that assumption. Having been in Nick's position before, I knew that the hold Sasha had on him wasn't fun or easy to get out of. Sasha was a beast in the ring, with a respect she'd earned from kicking our asses with little to no effort on her part.

Nick brought his other hand up in a surprising move. He jabbed a finger in her belly button and gave it a mean twist. The surprise caught Sasha off guard, and that was all he needed to get her to loosen her grip. In seconds, Nick had his wife pinned beneath him with a goofy grin on his face.

"Cheater," she grumbled.

Sasha had a smile her face that matched the one on Nick's. Clearly, they hadn't noticed me come in. Neither of them made any attempt to move. They were so wrapped up in each other that if I didn't say something soon, I was sure they'd be getting down to business.

"That was definitely an illegal move, Nick," I spoke up.

Their heads snapped over to me, first in surprise and then in recognition.

"Don't you have school or something?" Nick shot back. It was evident that I'd ruined their moment, blocking him in the worst way.

"It's my free period. I need a room."

Nick didn't question me further. He knew just as well as anybody how much the competition could get in your head. Jao Shang wasn't quiet about our rivalry. Unlike me, he needed the whole world to know what he had planned for our next battle.

"That Shang kid still messing with you?" Sasha asked, coming out from under Nick.

"Yeah."

Deep down, I knew that I was expected to atone for all that I'd done to Shang. I'd beat him senseless, without a second thought, but it was hard to feel bad for him when he'd brought it all on himself. He'd provoked me constantly, pushed me past the point of control at our competition, and suddenly he got to be the victim?

Jao Shang wasn't anybody's victim. He was smart, calculated. He knew exactly what to do to get ahead, and like an idiot, I fell for it every. Single. Time.

My hands began to shake as I thought about it. Pops's advice was to ignore him while I focused on the plan to get myself back on good terms with the league. As hard as I tried to ignore Shang, certain things he said and did had a way of slipping through the cracks.

Without another word, both Sasha and Nick left the ring to unlock one of the private training rooms for me to begin. I quickly changed into my workout clothes and popped in my earbuds. In front of me was a punching bag and a sparring stand, both worn out from overuse. I'd be sure to make use of whatever I could in the few minutes I had to myself.

Repeatedly, I fed my fists into the punching bag, allowing the music to drown out all other thoughts in my mind. Nothing else mattered as my instincts guided me through each move.

The thing about fighting wasn't always in who was the strongest or the toughest. To me, it was about understanding your opponent, and anticipating their next move. Jao Shang was a skilled fighter. He had been trained in the arts since he was in diapers. Fighting was in his blood.

For him, the fight was about his inflated ego, but for me, the fight was my redemption. It was my safe haven. Odd as it was, I'd be lost without it. Without Silat, I was destined to be a spark of rebellion.

Eventually, I moved on to the sparring stand. It was a rock-solid padded structure in the floor with imitation arms and legs sticking out for training purposes. I named it Shang Jr. I practiced my kicks and reflexes on him.

There were a few dents in the foundation of the sparring stand. Most of them had come from me, in fits of anger or frustration. I didn't hesitate to add a few more in this session. The more power I added to a blow in practice, the better prepared I was for the real thing when the time came. And when the time came, I'd be more than ready.

Before I knew it, Nick was pulling me out of my session. Training classes for the kids were about to start, and the dojo was suddenly flooded with little people in their uniforms. They played tag, screaming and running around as Sasha tried to gain control of the room.

I trudged out to my car slowly. Though I had plenty of time to make it back to school, I decided to skip my design class. I truly doubted I'd miss anything important, so I headed to the locker rooms in the gym instead, to shower off my session at the dojo. There was a class already taking place, so no one would be in the lockers.

I washed quickly, both because the water was too damn cold, and because I didn't want to risk the chance of running into anybody. My new student royalties hadn't quite worn out yet, and I wasn't in the mood to get caught up in one of the other student's curiosity.

I finished up before the bell rang. As I left the locker room, my phone vibrated in my back pocket. Pops was calling me, which was weird because he was at work. My father never took or made personal calls while he was at work unless it was something serious. I wasn't sure if I was ready to hear more bad news, but I picked up the phone anyway.

"Hello?"

"Sorry to interrupt your classes, son. Are you able to talk for a minute?" He was being formal with me. This call was strictly business.

"Yeah, I can talk. What's up, Pops?"

"I just got off the phone with your lawyer."

"Dave? Did he find out what the judges plan to do about Shang?"

Jao Shang was known for playing dirty during competitions. He never fought fair, and he always got away with it. Though there was no way to prove he had provoked me past the point of recovery in our last battle together, my team had been working tirelessly to find something on him that would stick.

"No news on that yet, but there's something else I want you to consider."

"Okay."

"Do you remember what we talked about in our meeting last Friday? I told you Dave and I were working on something big for you, something that goes beyond the judges' control?"

"Yeah, I remember everything."

Pops paused for a moment, and I could hear papers shuffling on the other end. When he began to scribble something down, I felt an impatient excitement building inside me as my mind raced with all the possibilities. "We've been in communication with Shane Tithers for the past few weeks," Pops said. I turned the volume up on my phone make sure I'd heard him right. "Dave suggested the possibility of you going on tour with him this summer."

"Tour?" I repeated, dumbstruck. "With Shane Tithers?"

My father had never discussed bringing my career to this level before. Not only had my name been brought up in conversation with *the* Shane Tithers, but the thought of going on tour was almost as wild as the idea of me competing at the Olympics.

"Yes, Shane is good friends with Dave. They go way back. We've been discussing the idea of you joining the team he's building for his international fighting tour. I'm actually going through those papers as we speak. You have a contract on the table, Jevon. All you have to do is sign on the dotted line."

Shane Tithers was ranked third internationally. He was an undefeated champ, known all over the world as one of the greatest fighters of his generation. Shane must've owed Dave a debt or something. What else would make him so willing to take me on his tour? Granted I was good, but I wasn't *that* good. Shane could have anybody on his team.

"Wow," was all I could say.

"Wow is right, son. We'll talk more about it later. I'll see you when I get home."

Pops hung up, and I was left in shock, standing in the middle of the hallway. I was going on tour with Shane Tithers. The thought itself was unimaginable.

If things went well, maybe my dad would hold off on bugging me about college. Maybe then he could see the potential of my future in this industry. I let my mind wander through its own realm of possibilities as I made my way down the hall to my next class. This could be the start of something I had only ever dreamed of.

Olympian . . . world champion . . .

They were just words for now, thought bubbles that could still be popped. But as I repeated those words in my head over and over and over again, they started to feel more like promises to myself. Vows I intended to keep.

CHAPTER EIGHT

Akilah

Ms. Hazel's class always had a way of putting me in the right head space. As an artist, I felt that I was an open-minded, evolved individual, set apart from the rest of the world. But as a student—especially in Ms. Hazel's class—there was so much more that I had yet to understand.

She had a way of teaching that forced you to think outside the box. Technique and procedure didn't exist when she was around. They were only barriers of the mind in her eyes. Because of that viewpoint, Ms. Hazel often found other ways to pull creativity out of us.

Today, our assignment was to capture moving pieces in a drawing. Ms. Hazel played a children's cartoon on the TV at the front of the class, and it was our job to capture a moving moment from one of the characters on screen. I watched the show carefully, not really caring to pay attention to what was going on. It was one of those interactive shows that took long pauses to ask children the most obvious questions. I worked fast, using one of the pauses in the show to capture the previous moment.

"Focus class!" Ms. Hazel instructed. "It's not as easy as it looks, is it?"

She made her way around the classroom, checking on our work and giving advice where needed. For the most part, I was in the zone. I didn't need much help from Ms. Hazel as I easily transitioned to a whole new drawing before the others had finished the first.

Ms. Hazel made her way down our aisle where she stopped at the end of my station. I looked up to see what I had done wrong, but it wasn't me that she'd set her sights on. It was Jevon, who sat at the station before me.

He seemed at ease as he used a ruler to straighten out the lines in his drawing. He didn't notice Ms. Hazel trying to gain his attention, but it was only when she brought herself directly in front of him that he finally looked up at her.

"Capturing moving art does not require a ruler, Mr. Williams."

Ms. Hazel was all about the raw, unrestricted, uninhibited type of art. Her ideals granted us a lot of creative freedom. Though her viewpoints went far too deep for my tastes, I still respected them just the same.

For the rest of the class period, Ms. Hazel took the time to school Jevon on the limitlessness of his creative mind, while everybody else focused on the TV at the front of the class. The lesson on the ruler was one that we had all learned the hard way. In truth, I could've told him to put it away before Ms. Hazel locked him in on a lecture, but what would he have really learned?

A small part of me giggled on the inside as I watched him pretend to understand where she was going. Call it a little payback for him joining in on the laughs at lunch. It was clear that Ms. Hazel's words went right through him, yet still, he took what she said and applied the changes to a new page. It went on like that until he was all out of paper, and Ms. Hazel was all out of time.

When class was over, I nearly had to jog to catch up to Jevon as he exited the room. His long legs carried him at twice my speed. He headed straight his locker, which was convenient for me because my locker was close to his.

"I could've told you not to use a ruler in Ms. Hazel's class," I admitted when I was finally able to catch up to him.

"Why didn't you?"

"Hmm. I kind of like watching you squirm."

Jevon ignored my comment as he went to open his locker door. He exchanged the books in his hands for the math textbook all the way in the back. Once it was tucked safely away in his bag, he shut the door and faced me.

"You know I'll never get those thirty-five minutes of my life back, right?"

Ms. Hazel had left nothing unsaid in her lecture to Jevon. She'd even stopped a few times to repeat herself when she thought he wasn't getting it. I was almost sure she quizzed him on what he'd learned just before the bell rang. Thinking about it made me laugh a little.

"I can make it up to you," I offered, still laughing at his expense.

Jevon quirked a brow. "I'm listening."

"How about I warn you next time you run into a trap like that?"

He was shaking his head before I could even finish the offer.

"Well, what do you want?"

Now it was his turn to smile. For a moment, Jevon said nothing. He just looked at me.

"I'll take the I-O-U," he said finally. "It might come in handy someday."

Jevon smoothly breezed past me to head to his next class. The hallway began to fill with students going to and from their classes, but I was too caught up in the way he'd looked at me to move.

It almost made me forget the reason I'd followed him out of Ms. Hazel's class to begin with.

"Wait!" I caught him by the arm just as the bell started to ring. "Do you have plans after school?"

"Yeah, but not until later. Why?"

"I couldn't book the art studio for us this week. The sign-up sheet was all full, so I was wondering if you could come to my house to work on the sculpture."

"Today?"

I nodded.

Jevon, blew out a breath and briefly checked the time on his watch. "Uh, yeah okay."

We parted ways after promising to meet in the courtyard after the last bell. If I thought working with Jevon at school was awkward, I wondered what it'd be like to actually have him at my house. We were slowly becoming friends. That had to count for something. Maybe by the time school was over, the idea of us hanging out wouldn't feel so strange to me.

CHAPTER NINE

Jevon

I met up with Akilah in the courtyard after school. She had her hands full with a large box that seemed to weigh more than she did. Her struggle to keep it balanced on her knee was a juggling act beyond her talents. When I was close enough to see what she was carrying in the box, I realized it was the unfinished sculpture we were set to work on this afternoon.

I helped her carry the faceless mold out to her car. It looked like something out of a scary movie, but I tried not to judge it since there was more work to do. She strapped the box safely in her back seat, and I went to my car to follow her to our new destination. I expected Akilah to drive slow because of the art piece in the back seat, but she pulled out of the lot like a bandit.

Her small Honda Civic breezed through the flow of traffic, surprisingly making me to work to keep up in my Audi e-tron GT. There weren't many people I knew that drove faster than me. It took me four speeding tickets to realize that the purpose of the yellow light at a stop light was not to speed through before the light turned red. It made me wonder how many tickets she had under her belt. There had to have been at least one.

We took the next exit and drove down a suburban road for a while. The road went from pavement to dirt to pavement again until eventually we made it to a cul-de-sac at the very end. Akilah parked her car in the driveway, and I followed her lead. Her home was almost an exact replica of all the other houses around it, all beige and brown with white trimmings around the edges. I had a feeling that the inside would be different though. There had to be some sort of artistic touch inside, just because of who Akilah was.

When she got out of her car, I walked around to help her retrieve the box from her back seat. Surprisingly, it survived her wild driving. It didn't appear to have moved much from when we'd first set it there. Carefully, I unbuckled the seatbelt and lifted the box from the seat.

With the sculpture secured in my hands, Akilah headed up the steps of her porch to open the door for me, but someone beat her to it. A boy who couldn't have been much older than us peeked his head out from inside. He glanced at me briefly, acknowledging me with a nod of his head before turning his attention back to Akilah. I assumed he was her brother. He was tall and lanky with facial features similar to Akilah's. The resemblance was very evident with them so close together. He stood in front of the door with his arms crossed, blocking our entrance.

"What, CJ?" Akilah sighed.

"I need a ride."

"I just got home. Why can't one of your little girlfriends take you?"

CJ ran a hand down his face like he was already tired of explaining himself. "Natasha's trippin' hard today."

"What'd you do?"

"Nothing! Why do you always assume it's me?"

Akilah gave him a pointed look with a tilt of her head.

"I'm innocent, swear." CJ tried to keep a straight face but eventually he cracked and laughed. Akilah started laughing too, shaking her head as she did so.

"When are you gonna learn?"

"I'm trying. Look, just let me borrow your car since you're home now. I'll have it back before sundown."

At that, Akilah laughed harder. She tucked her keys deep into her pockets and barreled her way inside.

"Pass the driver's test first, and then we'll talk!" she called over her shoulder.

With no further introductions, I followed her lead and headed inside behind her. As expected, Akilah's art littered the walls of their home. Her paintings hung in the hallway entrance and even around the living room. It echoed with her presence.

Much like the work I saw hanging in Ms. Hazel's class, the paintings on the walls were attention grabbing. They invited you in for a closer look. Each piece, though different in every way, matched the color scheme of the entire house: beige, burgundy, and gold.

Akilah ran off somewhere upstairs. I didn't think it was appropriate for me to follow her, so I just placed the box on the kitchen table and dug out my phone while I waited. She didn't say how long this session would be, but I hoped we'd finish quick. I couldn't wait to hear more about my collab with Shane.

Eventually, CJ got the hint that she wasn't taking him anywhere, so he came inside and closed the door. It didn't seem like anyone else was home. There were no other cars parked outside, but I wondered briefly what her parents would think of me being here. Would they be okay with her bringing some random dude home from school, or were they chill about that sort of thing?

"Hey man, I'm CJ." Her brother came into the kitchen and extended his hand out to me.

"Jevon."

I shook his hand and stepped aside so he could get to the fridge. CJ rummaged around in there for a minute before coming out with a couple bottles of water and what I was assuming were leftovers from the night before.

"You want?" he asked, offering me a bottle of water.

I took it and unscrewed the cap to take a sip.

"So . . ." CJ walked over to place his food in the microwave. "You're the new boyfriend?"

"No, I'm just a friend from school."

He nodded, but it didn't seem like he believed me. If Akilah wanted to correct his assumption, then I was sure she would. CJ watched his food revolve around on the plate. He stared at the microwave until it dinged and then he brought the plate to the island to eat. The food smelled good. I couldn't tell what it was by the smell, but it looked more fancy than what I was expecting when he pulled it from the microwave.

"What do you do?" CJ asked, assuming like everybody else that I had a talent.

"I'm a fighter." I said with a shrug.

CJ didn't seem to care that much anyway, at least not like the people at school. He wasn't greedy for gossip or viewing me as his competition. He was just making small talk while he ate his food.

"Word?" He glanced up from his next bite, and a brief look of recognition suddenly crossed his features. "Wait, you're Jevon *Williams*! Right? The MMA fighter? Last year's MVP?"

I nodded.

"Oh." He dropped his fork. "That's—wow! I mean, that-that's cool, or whatever." He played it off.

"Thanks."

"So, you're with my sister now." He nodded slowly. "That's what's up. Not shocking, or anything."

"We're just friends."

"Right, yeah. But, since we're all friends now, if you ever have any spare tickets to one of your fights . . . you know, as a *friend*, I wouldn't mind taking some time out of my busy schedule to support."

I grinned. CJ was terrible at playing nonchalant, but he recovered quickly as his sister rejoined us. Akilah glided into the kitchen with her sock-covered feet. She'd gone upstairs to change into a pair of tights and an oversized T-shirt

"Mmm, that smells good." Akilah leaned over her brother's shoulder to see what he had.

She plucked a piece of meat off his plate and popped it into her mouth. Then she went over to the fridge to get some for herself. When she found nothing, she closed the door in irritation and faced her brother.

"Did you eat it all?"

"This was all that was left. There's other stuff in there!"

"You are so greedy."

He shrugged without a care and made his way out of the kitchen. Before leaving completely, CJ took a big bite of his food to rub it in, but Akilah ignored him. She grabbed a pair of scissors off the counter and cut into the box I'd placed on the table earlier.

"Sorry I took so long," she said as she opened the side of the box.

"It's cool. Where do you want me?"

"Umm, you can stay where you are, actually. I really want to get started on your face, so you don't have to pose today."

When the sculpture was released from the box, Akilah pulled it closer to her and took a deep breath. Whatever she saw in the clay instantly grabbed her attention as she stared deeply into the faceless creation. I liked watching Akilah work. She got so into what she was doing sometimes, I could see her lose herself in it. The art drew her in, but it was her mind that seemed to hold her captive.

Akilah looked over at me then, analyzing my features so she could replicate them in the clay. She started with my hairline, marking out the places where my forehead began and ended. Every now and then, she would come over to turn my face the slightest bit. The light hint of her perfume breezed over me every time she passed by. It kept me alert to all the changes.

There were so many minor details that went into a sculpture. Akilah wasn't comfortable moving on to the next thing until she'd perfected whatever it was she was working on. I knew this would take some time, and for the most part, I was okay with that. When she showcased her work to everyone, I wanted it to be perfect too. I wanted the judges, the spectators, and all the non-believers to see me in a better light.

"Are you hungry?" Akilah asked suddenly.

Her stomach growled loudly then, and she rubbed at it apologetically. She chuckled at the sound as another growl soon followed.

"Sure."

Akilah grabbed her phone and dialed a number she knew by heart. She put the phone on speaker while it rang as she went back to sculpting my face. Before she could get too far though, a thought occurred to her. Akilah ran to the kitchen counter, and looked through the drawers to pull out a menu. She slid it in front of me. I didn't really pay attention to the name, but the food listed on the menu looked very similar to what her brother, CJ had warmed up earlier.

"Thank you for calling Le Bleu! How may I direct your call?" a preppy voice answered.

I'd heard of Le Bleu before. It was a restaurant right in the middle of the city. My parents went there sometimes for special occasions and business dinners. At the mention of the restaurant I took another look at the menu. The food, the name, all of it definitely fit the type of place that my parents would frequent.

"Hey, Suzie. It's AJ. I want to place an order for delivery."

"Hey, AJ! Give me a sec, I'll put your dad on."

Suzie placed us on hold and classical music filtered through the phone. Akilah looked over at me expectantly. "Figured out what you want yet?"

"Um, no. I've never been here before."

"Oh, just pick anything. It's all really good."

"Hello?" Mr. Johnson picked up the phone. The sounds of sizzling pans and noisy pots clinging together could be heard in the background.

"Hey, Daddy! I wanted to place an order for delivery."

Her dad heaved an exasperated sigh. "I spoil you too much. What do you want, sweetheart?"

"I want the beef Wellington—you know the way I like it cooked—with a side of garlic-roasted potatoes and blistered green beans."

"Anything else?"

"Yes, my friend Jevon wants . . . ?" She looked over at me then, and I pointed to a picture on the menu that looked good. "He wants the roasted duck with your famous sauce and some pan-seared veggies."

"What about your brother?"

"He ate all the leftovers from last night. He should be fine."

"Okay, I'm putting your order in now. It'll be there soon."

"Thanks, Daddy!"

"Of course, baby girl. Now tell me, who the hell is Jevon?"

"He's a friend from school, Dad. We can talk about this when you get home."

Akilah rushed to take Mr. Johnson off speaker, as I'm sure he had a few choice words to say about me being there. She nodded along to whatever he was saying, even rolling her eyes a few times. Eventually, she hung up and turned back to me with a guilty smile.

"Everything okay?" I asked.

"Yeah, he's just being overprotective. The food should be here in about thirty minutes."

I reached for my wallet to pay for our food, but Akilah smacked my hand and shooed me away.

"No need," she said. "Daddy never makes me pay."

I squinted, but didn't argue her further. Instead, I went back to my position and watched Akilah get back to work on the sculpture. She took her time working on my eyes. She wanted everything to be perfect, so she kept starting over when something went wrong. Every now and then, she'd look up at me in frustration and take more clay away from what she had just created.

With a sculpting tool in her mouth, Akilah came over to reassess my features. She turned me so that I was facing her, placing both hands on the sides of my face. With her thumbs, she smoothed out the creases in my eyebrows. Akilah's fingers were soft and warm and surprisingly clean after working with the clay. She was so close I could feel her breath lightly fan over me when she exhaled. It blended in with the smell of her perfume.

"I swear you have this permanent angry face going on," she grumbled.

"What do you mean?"

"See!" she exclaimed as she rushed to rub her thumbs across my face again. "You do this thing with your brows. You scrunch them up and it makes you look all angry. Is that the way you want people to see you?"

Good point. I tried to rearrange my face to her liking, but I wasn't sure if it was working. I was well-known for having issues with my temper in the public eye. It didn't help to have that duplicated in art form.

Akilah went to work, apparently satisfied by the sudden changes in my facial expression. She stared at me for a while, comparing my face to the changes she'd just made. After a few more strokes of her sculpting tool, she used her fingers to blend them out.

I didn't know how long I sat there, watching her work, but when the doorbell rang, my legs were thankful for the break. Akilah ran over to get the food, thanking the driver before tipping him and closing the door.

"Come on, you deserve a break." Akilah waved me over.

We sat in the living room, and she turned on the TV. She flipped through a couple channels to find the one she liked before digging into the bag and separating my food from hers. My mouth watered just from the smell of it. I took the time to appreciate the way it looked, prepared exactly the way it appeared on the menu. At first, I didn't notice how Akilah took me in, gauging my reaction to my first bite. After a few more, I felt her lean in.

"Well?" she asked.

I nodded. "It's good. It's really good."

"Just good? Come on, Jevon. You can do better than that."

"Alright, your Pops is the greatest of all time." I admitted.

There was no denying it. Satisfied with my answer, Akilah leaned back in her seat, really getting into her show. We sat like that for a while, just eating and watching TV. I wasn't paying much attention to what was on. It was when the final commercial came on that Akilah suddenly sat up and looked at me.

"Can I ask you something?" She muted the TV and placed her food on the coffee table.

"What's up?"

"What brought you to Cambridge?"

My eyebrows shot up in slight surprise. I knew she wondered about my talents, but she had never asked me out right. I thought over the best way to answer the question as she took me in curiously. Akilah stared at me like I was some puzzle she couldn't crack.

"If I answer your question," I began, "then you have to have to answer one of mine."

I had a few questions of my own.

"O-okay," she agreed warily, surprised by my request.

"I didn't get into Cambridge because I wanted to. I got in because I needed to."

Akilah nodded, urging me to keep going.

"I made a mistake over the summer that's almost cost me everything I've worked so hard for."

"Which is . . . ?" Akilah motioned with her hands for me to keep going, but I wasn't having it.

"Nope. It's your turn," I grinned. "I answered your question, now you have to answer mine."

"You didn't even answer the question fully, so that shouldn't count."

"But it does."

Akilah scoffed. "Okay, if that's the way you want to play."

She got up to come and sit closer to me. Turning to face me, she sat cross-legged in the seat, her knees barely brushing against my leg. With her arms folded, Akilah waited for my question.

I thought of the some of the things I'd wanted to know since meeting her and asked the first thing that came to mind.

"Why did you ask me to be your muse?"

With a sheepish smile, Akilah relaxed her pose. "You're going to think it's corny."

"Tell me."

"When I first saw you, I couldn't stop staring at you," She paused for a second and looked away. "Not in a weird way, but in an artistic one. When I see you, I see what I could create with you."

I took a moment to mull over her words. When I thought about that first day at CSA, I couldn't remember a time I'd felt her staring, but it felt like everybody was staring that day.

"That's how you decided to turn me into clay?"

"Nope." Akilah shook her head, grinning widely. "Your turn."

I really should've seen that one coming.

"What was the mistake you made that's costing you so much?"

My jaw tensed. I'd never told anyone the full story behind my sudden appearance at CSA, but I guess if we were friends now, there shouldn't be a problem with me telling her what really happened last summer.

I took a deep breath.

"Have you really never heard of me before I came to CSA?" I genuinely wanted to know. She had to have done her research about me, like I did for her, or at least heard some of the rumors at school.

Akilah quirked a brow, eyeing me up and down. "Am I supposed to know who you are?"

I smiled. "No, I guess not."

"I'm a professional fighter." I went on. Akilah opened and shut her mouth like she wanted to say something, but thought better of it. "I lost control during an international competition last summer, and I broke the rules. Now, I'm paying for that mistake in the worst way. I don't even qualify for the Olympics anymore."

"They have an Olympic team for that?"

"Careful. That's another question." I flashed her a taunting smile.

Akilah made a motion to zip her lips and throw away the key.

"Silat is a violent sport, but we still have rules to follow. I hurt someone pretty bad, and there was a lot of fallout after the fight that really messed up my reputation. I had to make a choice. It was either switch up my image and attempt to change the way people see me, or do nothing and accept all the consequences. Being at Cambridge might honestly be a waste of time, but it's better than sitting around, waiting for something to change. So, in a way, I came to CSA to make a difference."

Akilah remained silent. She fiddled with the fraying threads on the couch for a while, too deep in thought to say anything. When she finally looked up at me, her expression was unreadable. I waited for her to say something, but she was quiet still.

After only a moment, Akilah reached up to wrap her arms around my neck in an embrace. I was taken by surprise. This was the second time she'd hugged me because she thought I needed comforting. It wasn't entirely uncomfortable—I just wasn't used to this affectionate display of friendship. It took me longer than it should've, but eventually, I hugged her back.

CHAPTER TEN

Akilah

This was a different side of Jevon. A part of me couldn't fully believe that he was opening up to me. The more I listened to his side of the story, the more I understood why he was so guarded and reserved. I soon found myself wanting to know more, but I tried not to push it with my questions. We were still playing the game, and suddenly it was my turn again.

"Why do you smoke weed?" he asked after a not-so light hearted discussion about the "weirdos" Jevon encountered at school . . . me included.

I hesitated. Up until then, Jevon's questions were more geared toward my art and our shared commitment to the sculpture. My eyes immediately shot up the staircase, where the sounds of CJ's video game could be heard playing gently in the background. I silently prayed he wasn't listening.

"Umm," I stalled, "because . . . "

"Because, what?"

"Because I'm an artist. It's a part of the job description."

Jevon made a face more similar to disdain than all-out judgment. He didn't say anything right away, but from the way he shook his head, he didn't have to. It shouldn't have mattered to me what he thought about what I did in my free time, but I was suddenly scouring my brain, searching for the right words to defend myself.

I narrowed my eyes. Who was he to judge me anyway? He'd just told me all about how he'd brutally assaulted someone a few months ago, and I'd hardly batted an eye, but smoking one blunt was suddenly beneath him?

"Are you seriously judging me now?"

"No, I'm not judging you, Akilah. I just didn't think you were that kind of girl."

"Exactly what kind of girl did you think I was?" I smiled, but it wasn't a happy smile. It was one of those nose-flaring, brow-arching, test-me-if-you're-bold kind of smiles that really illustrated my agitated spirit.

Jevon turned to me then, his eyes scanning over my face carefully. "All I'm saying is, I wouldn't have pegged you for a stoner."

"Is that supposed a bad thing?"

"How would I know?" The left corner of his mouth suddenly turned up in a self-satisfied smirk. "You didn't answer the question honestly."

I pushed away from him and sank back into my seat. Bringing my knees up close to me, I tilted my head back and stared up at the ceiling. If it was honesty he was after, then I guessed I owed him that. Jevon had no qualms about telling me his truth when I asked about his reasons for enrolling at CSA.

If I were being honest with myself though, I'd never actually thought too deeply into why I smoked. I just remembered there was a time that I didn't, and then suddenly I did.

I sighed. "I do it because it makes me feel good. And I know that sounds like an excuse, but I am being honest. Sometimes I get too caught up in my own head, and all I can think about is my future and where I want to be in life. But that just makes me feel bad about where I am now, so I smoke."

"What's so bad about where you are now?" Jevon's eyes danced around the living room like he was searching for the bad parts of my life. As if they would suddenly jump out of the walls or the curtains.

I chuckled. "My life outside of school is fine. I have no complaints, but you're still new to CSA. At Cambridge, people only focus on what's next for them. This is my last year to find *my* next thing, and all of my friends have it figured out. Tommy's going to get signed to a record label before we even graduate. I just know it. 'Dre got accepted to the School of Photography in Chicago, and Kayla"—I swallowed down a sudden wave of jealously—"Kayla's future is set. My future is stacked on top of 'maybes' and 'hopefullys.' I don't know what's next for me. I'm just stuck. "

"You're not stuck, believe me." Though he'd mumbled his response, it was the way he said it that made me wonder if there was more meaning behind his words. Did Jevon feel stuck too? But that didn't make any sense—Jevon was so sure of himself.

When he looked at me this time, I could've sworn I saw something different in his eyes. Respect? Understanding? Empathy?

I was all out of guesses because with a sudden blink, Jevon tore his gaze away. We got so caught up in our little game that we didn't notice the time. Before long, we heard keys jiggle in the front door and Daddy soon made his way inside.

"Kiki?! CJ?!" he yelled loudly from the corridor. I could hear him grunting as he took off his shoes in the foyer.

"In here!" I called back.

Daddy made his way into the living room. He looked tired and drained from the work day, but upon seeing Jevon, he straightened his posture and fixed his face with a smile.

"You must be Jevon." He extended his hand.

Jevon stood at almost the same height as my dad. Confidence exuded from his person without any effort.

"Yes, sir." He shook my father's hand firmly. "It's nice to meet you."

Daddy gave him a quick once over, probably wondering what he did at CSA. Jevon looked nothing like the other students. He was all beefed up and mannish.

"Akilah tells me you go to Cambridge with her. Are you an artist too?"

"Umm, kind of."

If you consider mixed martial arts an art form.

"Really? What's your focus?"

"Dad!" CJ suddenly yelled as he came barreling down the stairs. "Can I borrow the car for tonight?"

I was thankful for the distraction as I grabbed Jevon by the wrist and quickly led him back over to the kitchen. If Daddy saw us working, then he'd hopefully leave us alone for a while. We came to a stop at the half-finished sculpture on the kitchen table. I watched as he nodded in appreciation.

Jevon started to comment on our progress when his phone rang loudly. He looked down at the screen and swore underneath his breath. In a flash, Jevon retrieved his car keys from the counter.

"I actually have to go. I'm running late for something."

We gave each other a brisk goodbye as he speed-walked out the door.

* * *

Later that night, sleep evaded me. My thoughts replayed the conversation I had with Kayla at The Spot a few weeks ago. She had gotten into Ivory Middleton and I was supposed to be happy for her, but all I could think was what about me? What if she got in and

I didn't? What if I wasn't good enough? What if this sculpture with Jevon was only a waste of time in the end?

I blew out a frustrated breath as I rolled onto my back and forced my eyes shut. With deep, labored breaths, I willed sleep to come to me. After a few leg twitches, and eyes that fluttered with the pace of my racing thoughts, I peeled them open and immediately focused on the popcorn ceiling above me.

When I was younger, I would stare up there and try to find shapes or pictures within its depths. It helped to calm me down back then. I wondered if that was why I'd become an artist. In a way, art had always been my escape.

Now as I looked up, I discovered hands raised up in prayer, the face of a lion, and an old oak tree. I traced the figures with my fingers and made a mental note to replicate it on paper later.

My eyes danced around the room slowly, catching the moonlight shining through the blinds. I noticed my sketchbook perched on the edge of my vanity and sat up in bed. Without thinking too hard about it, I tiptoed over to my window and slid it open as quietly as I could.

There was an escape ladder hidden underneath my bed for "emergencies" such as this one. I chucked it over the sill and grabbed all of my valuables before making my escape. Tucking my sketch book under one arm and using my phone as a flashlight, I took the steps one at a time. The ladder swayed unsteadily beneath me, but I had enough practice in keeping my balance.

On the last step, I double-checked the windows to the left where CJ and my parents' rooms were. The lights were still off, so I took it as a good sign. When we were kids, CJ and I would play in the treehouse Daddy built in the only tree in our backyard. As we got older, CJ had no use for the small house. He was more into video games and running games on girls he knew he never had a chance with. I still used it from time to time for nights like this.

There were little steps nailed into the trunk of the tree that felt too small for my now seventeen-year-old feet, but I never missed a step. The multicolored Christmas lights that Momma thought she lost last year were strung up along the walls. I flicked them on as I settled into the bean bag chair in the corner of the room.

Digging into my pocket, I reached for the lighter and the joint that I tucked in there before I left. It was so late that even the moon shined a lazy hue down to the earth. With the rest of neighborhood sound asleep, I felt a risky kind of freedom wash over me.

In just three flicks of my lighter, the joint sparked to life between my fingers. Smoke began to fill the tiny treehouse, surrounding me with the promise of ascension. I breathed it in deeply and held it there for a while. It was instantly calming. My once-hectic thoughts had suddenly mellowed out into the silence of the night, giving me space to think, or imagine, or hell, even sleep. But sleep was the farthest thing from my mind.

My sketchbook was perched on my knees. The lighting from the small window wasn't so great, but it was enough for me to work with. I kind of liked the way the shadows danced between the multicolored lights. It cast different patterns on the page that gave me an idea.

The images from before, the figures I noticed on my ceiling, came to mind. The face of a lion struck out to me the most. I saw its fangs pierce through the shadows, and from there, I let my fingers and the pencil do all the work. They traced out a mane that billowed softly against the wind, fur that bristled across his prowling body, and whiskers that accented his feline face.

I spent so much time focusing on the details that I nearly forgot the joint in my hand fizzling away at the ends. Taking another big puff, I let the smoke blow out of my nose slowly. It captured me under a cloud for only a second before I swatted it away with my hands. Already, I felt my worries drift further and further away into non-existence.

The drawing kept me occupied for as long as I could stand it. Time meant little to me as I worked to finish, and the night began to fade into an early morning haze. Quickly, I cut the lights, flipped my sketch book closed, and descended the steps on the tree. With any luck, I'd get in a quick nap in before school, but the clock on my phone read 3:25 a.m.

CHAPTER ELEVEN

Jevon

When I left Akilah's house yesterday, Pops's good mood from earlier had turned sour by the time I got home. He had every right to be pissed at me. I should've told him I was meeting up with her, and I'd fully planned on doing that at some point during our session, but I forgot all of that after the food. Akilah and I had gotten so caught up in our game of questions that calling my dad never crossed my mind.

"It's late," Pops said when I finally made my way inside the house. He stood by the door with his arms crossed and a tired expression.

"Yeah, I know. I just got caught up."

"What was so important that you couldn't tell me where you were, son? We were supposed to discuss business today."

"I'm sorry. I was working on a project for school at a friend's house."

"A school project," he repeated, as if saying it to himself would somehow make my actions more believable.

"Yes. It won't happen again."

He took me in quietly, the stern expression never leaving his face.

"Shane Tithers was on the phone earlier. He wanted to set up a meeting to talk with you about the tour."

I kicked myself as I realized what being late had cost me. How could I have been so stupid?

"What did you tell him?" I asked.

Pops wasn't some big-shot lawyer like Dave, but talking a good game came along with his job. It was one of my father's best attributes. Whether I was there or not, I knew he'd be able to handle just about anything.

"I told him you were spending most of your time at the dojo . . . training." He threw in a disapproving side-eye. "He's agreed to meet with you in a few weeks, after your next match."

Even though Pops delivered the news to me sourly because he was annoyed, I still felt honored and grateful for the opportunity. As hard as I tried to fight it, the joy at my father's words caused me to smile. Shane Tithers was going to one of my matches to watch me fight.

Looking over at my father, I could see that even he was a little excited about the news. Soon, he was pulling me into a brief hug, and just as quickly, he let me go. Pops wasn't the emotional type, but neither was I. Just his simple grin was enough to tell me that he was satisfied.

"Stay focused, son," he warned, placing a hand on my shoulder. "This opportunity won't present itself again. I know I've been hard on you about your future, but right now you're exactly where you need to be."

I did a double take, "Really? Does this mean I won't have to apply to anymore colleges?"

"I didn't say all that. This is only a *summer* tour, and you haven't signed anything yet. The contract is still on my desk. Nothing is set in stone, son. You'd do well to remember that."

"But, you just said—"

"I know what I said. Now I'm telling you that college is still an option. We're not ruling that out until you're selling out your own stadiums."

I nodded, knowing then that conversation was over.

All of a sudden, Pops leaned into me, causing me to involuntarily lean back. He sniffed my shoulder twice, and then leaned back suspiciously. What was he on about?

"Who's this friend that you're working on the project with?" he asked with an arch of his brow.

"Just a girl from school, Pops. It's not like that."

"She smells . . . eccentric."

What did that even mean? I thought Akilah smelled good, sweet like coconuts and honey. Lifting my shirt up to my nose, I smelled the light hint of her that had somehow rubbed off on me.

"Stay focused," Pops said again, eyeing me seriously.

I didn't need the warning. I knew what was at stake.

* * *

School dragged on slowly, like most of the days here. On the plus side, I was starting to get used to my fully loaded schedule. It wasn't as daunting as it had seemed before. I even found time to hang out in the senior lounge between classes with Andre and Tommy and few of their other friends at the school.

They were in the midst of planning a party when Tommy suddenly blurted out, "This is a small get-together, ya'll. Don't invite the whole school."

"You say that every time," Andre chimed in, "but we always end up packed like a can of Vienna sausages."

"I'm serious this time. Twelve broke up the last party, and I swore to my parents that wouldn't happen again."

"Okay," 'Dre said in clear disbelief. He shook his head as he added the note to his notebook.

"You're mighty quiet, Jay. You coming tonight, or what?" Tommy asked.

I was in the middle of packing my bag to head back to class. The bell had rung only minutes ago, but it seemed I was the only one making a move.

"Umm, it's a school night. I don't know if I can."

That granted me a few chuckles.

"What, you got a curfew or something?" Tommy teased.

No, a curfew wasn't what I was worried about. If I was out training at the dojo, it wouldn't have mattered to my father what time I came home, but to waste my time at a party with so much on the line for me was too big of a risk.

Stay focused, son.

Even now, I could hear his words ringing in my ears. A part of me wished I could explain, but I knew they wouldn't understand.

"I'll think about it," I said instead.

"Don't think, just come! I'll be low-key offended if you don't show up."

I started to wonder how much I cared about Tommy's disappointment. He wasn't the one who had to answer to my Pops.

"I'm going to head to class." I threw my book bag over my shoulder and headed for the door.

"See you tonight!" Tommy called just before I made it out of the senior lounge.

I jogged down the steps to the second floor of the school. The hallways were emptying out as the second bell was about to ring. Ms. Hazel's class was all the way at the end of the hall, near the emergency exit. I had to wedge my way past a few slow-walking people in the middle of the walkway, and I finally burst through the door as the final bell rang out.

"Let's get started!" Ms. Hazel clapped her hands together excitedly.

We were doing group projects today, working in pairs. Everybody was already paired up, which left me standing partnerless by the doorway. Ms. Hazel instructed me to tack on to another group, so naturally, I made my way over to the far end of the classroom where Akilah was. She was partnered with Jessie, a guy who talked enough to bore a snail back into its shell. I watched as Akilah's eyes rolled over in genuine lack of interest.

"Oh, hey, Jevon." Akilah's voice was perky, but her eyes said "Help me!"

Jessie had his back turned, so he hadn't seen me approach them. Upon hearing my name, he whipped his head around quickly, looked me up and down, and then slowly backed away. With his seat now available, I claimed it and made myself comfortable. There wasn't really a lot of space at our station, so that moved Jessie down to the end.

"You don't mind, do you, Jessie?" Akilah asked sweetly.

Her words hinted more at a command than a simple request. Jessie got the hint quickly, understanding that she'd basically given him the boot. Wordlessly, he left to join another group.

"Thanks for that. I owe you one," she said.

"That's twice now, that you owe me." I grinned as I reached for an apron on the hook.

"Are you keeping a tally on me?"

I shrugged.

Akilah worked to hide a smile. She screwed up her lips and shook her head as a small chuckle escaped her. I noticed that she was in a pair of overalls with her hair pulled back into a ponytail. Akilah never wore an apron.

"We're working with watercolors," she said, balling up the piece of paper she was just painting. "One of us has to be the painter. The other one needs to pose."

"Well, it's only fair that I paint you," I said, reaching over to slide the painting materials toward me.

Akilah's hand shot out to stop me.

"That's okay." She shooed my hands away. "I got this."

"Have some faith, come on."

I gently pushed her fingers aside and grabbed the painting equipment once again. This time she didn't complain. With a sigh, she sat up in her stool and turned to face me. Akilah reached up to pull her hair out of its holder, but I stopped her.

"No, stay like that."

"This is graded, Jevon."

"So?" I shrugged.

"So, don't mess it up." She stuck out her tongue.

Akilah squirmed in her seat before finally settling on a pose. She pulled her long, wavy ponytail to the side and tilted her head slightly to her left. Fixing me with a fierce gaze, Akilah watched me intently while I worked.

It was odd being on the other side of the canvas. I could tell it was hard for Akilah to relinquish control of her craft, but I knew I'd feel the same way if it came to someone else's fighting skills being graded on my behalf.

I kept my focus on the page in front of me. Her outline was the easiest to scribble down, so long as she kept still. It was the details that threw me for a loop. Akilah's face was slim. Her ears were small, but they kind of stuck out with her hair tucked behind them. She had eyes that were sort of almond shaped, with thick lashes that curved up and out like feathers. Her lips were plump and slightly turned up into a snickering smile, thus exposing the dimple in her right cheek. Akilah had a button nose that wiggled in distaste every time she looked down to see what I had done.

I had just begun the sketching Akilah's hair when she broke her pose and looked over to assess my work. Her blank stare gave away nothing that she was thinking, but she was definitely thinking something because her stare became more and more critical.

"What?" I asked.

"Nothing." She bit back her words.

I went back to shaping the ends of her hair. It was hard trying to get it to look like anything more than just a few squiggly lines that curved around a circular head, but I did the best I could. When I finished, I searched for the color that best matched her skin tone—chestnut brown—and began painting. Every now and then Akilah would look over and give suggestions for adding more definition and detail, but then Ms. Hazel would catch her helping me and she had to stop.

I snuck glances her way to get a nod or a head shake on what I was doing. We kept up that routine until it was time to turn in our work. Akilah gave the painting a quick once over. If she found any flaws, she kept them to herself because at that point, it was too late.

"Next time, let me do the artwork. You stick to modeling," Akilah said when Ms. Hazel's class came to an end.

We were walking through the hall, back toward our lockers.

"It was not that bad."

"It was so bad Ms. Hazel had to put it in a separate pile. She's cool and all, but she grades like a villain."

I didn't care much about the grade. It couldn't've counted for much anyway. It wasn't like I was a real student. We came to a stop at our locker doors and there was a brief moment of silence as we both began to put our books away.

"Did you hear about the party?" she asked.

"Tommy's party?"

"Yeah, are you going?"

I sighed loudly. Why was it so important for me to be there? I doubted I'd miss out on anything special.

"Is that a no?"

"It's a maybe."

"Just come." She shut the door and turned the dial to lock it back in place. "It'll be fun!"

"Tell me something."

"What?"

"How wild do Tommy's parties get?"

After promising my father to stay on the straight and narrow, and knowing who Tommy was in such a short amount of time, I needed to know what I was walking into . . . *if* I decided to go.

"Umm..." Akilah hesitated.

"Am I going to regret coming?"

"Maybe." She grinned. "But you'll definitely have a good time. I mean, only if you manage to remember it all the next day, or avoid ending up in a jail cell."

I blinked.

"I'm kidding! Relax. I promise it's not as bad as you're thinking. It's a lot of fun, really."

"Your idea of fun comes with a warning label."

"Scared?" she challenged with an arch of her brow.

I only smirked in response. Then, I turned to loop my arms through my bag and headed in the opposite direction.

"What if I promise to keep you out of trouble?" Akilah called.

That got my attention. I turned around to face her.

"And how do you plan to do that?"

"I'll get creative. Just come to the party. I'm not taking 'no' for an answer." She seemed pretty determined to get her way, and for a moment, I wondered what she would do if I actually said no.

"Alright," I gave in reluctantly, "but only for a little while."

"I'll see you tonight."

She breezed past me and headed for the stairs. With her gone, I took a minute to really think about what I was getting myself into.

Earlier, Tommy had mentioned the police breaking up his other house party. The last thing I wanted was a run-in with the law.

Even though Akilah had promised to keep me out of trouble, I decided to invite my own friends. If things got really wild, and I hoped they didn't, Akilah would definitely need some help.

CHAPTER TWELVE

Akilah

I was a little excited about tonight. It had been a while since I'd gone out with my friends. Though we had the entire summer to let loose and go wild, it was our senior year! Somehow, it felt like a sacred duty to go out with a bang.

"Here, try this on." Kayla rummaged through our combined pile of clothes on my bed. After hours of gossiping and mindless scrolling through social media, we were forced to rush through our process of getting ready.

A sheer, lacy bralette hung from the tips of her fingers. It had spaghetti strap bands that crisscrossed in the back. Putting it on looked like more of a hassle than it was worth. Not only was it risqué and borderline lingerie, it was also entirely too small.

"No." I threw it back into the pile.

"You didn't even try it on."

"That's a see-through top, Kayla. *Everything* is going to show!"

Kayla rolled her eyes like I was being dramatic. She went to reclaim the flimsy piece of fabric. Holding it up to her chest, Kayla admired herself in my full-length mirror. On her, the bralette seemed to be the right size, small enough to look like a crop-top but large enough to actually cover everything.

With Kayla's slender frame, she could get away with just about any look. I had curves that turned mini skirts into waist bands; crop-tops into bralettes; and bralettes into...well, pure imagination.

"I would wear it, but my boobs aren't big enough." Kayla turned from side to side, and I wasn't sure if she was trying to convince herself or me.

"Do you honestly think I'd let you walk out the door looking crazy?" She went on after I made a face. "There's an inner lining right here. Nobody's going to see anything you don't want them to, AJ. You'll feel different about it if you try it on. Just humor me." Kayla dangled the piece in front of me like it was a prize.

I snatched it from her fingers. "Does it at least come with a shirt?"

She pointed to a black Kimono jacket with a belt dangling over my bed post. Wispy silver flowers decorated the back, going all the way down to a train at the very end. It was a beautiful silky material that was soft between my fingers.

The kimono hung loosely over my shoulders while the train swayed just past my calf muscles. Paired with low rise, boyfriend jeans and strappy, black heels, the look was fierce. It was edgy, and it was totally outside my comfort zone.

I gave myself a middle part and tucked my bangs behind my ears. My straightened hair flowed down to the center of my back. Like Kayla predicted, the bralette actually fit me. I was completely covered, and the more I stared at myself through the mirror, the more I thought I looked . . . sexy.

"You don't have to say it." Kayla appeared behind me in the mirror looking all smug and self-satisfied. "But it feels good to hear it." She cupped her hand around her ear.

* * *

We made it to Tommy's house by midnight, and the party was just getting started. Bodies were packed all throughout his home, both upstairs and downstairs. Some people sat comfortably on his couch, playing video games, while others poured drinks at the countertop in the kitchen.

I noticed a few familiar faces grinding to the music booming from his speakers, or talking in groups clustered around his front door and living room. When Tommy threw parties, word got around quickly and not just at school. Tommy had sort of created a small fan base in Atlanta's underground rap community. A lot of these people were strangers to me, but they were definitely fans of Tommy's.

"Over here!" Tommy broke through the crowd to meet us at the door.

He took Kayla by the hand and she quickly grabbed mine as we wedged our way through the crowd. Unfamiliar hands touched and groped me as I made my way through. Most of the lingering hands were merely trying to find their footing in the over-filled room, while others clung to me unnecessarily.

I held on to Kayla's hand tightly, as Tommy led us down into his basement. There weren't as many people down here, so the vibe was less chaotic. I instantly spotted our group of friends lounging on the couch, secluded from everybody else.

They made room for Kayla and I to squeeze in the middle. There was a steady conversation going on around me, but I tuned it out as I let my eyes dance around the room. It was almost the exact opposite of the scene upstairs. I knew just about everyone down here, and I was positive that they all knew each other.

"What did I tell you?!" Andre shouted over the music. He grinned at Tommy as his arms flailed out to emphasize his point.

Tommy sucked his teeth. "You didn't know it would turn out like this. I didn't invite all these people."

"This happens every time, T! Like a can of Vienna."

"It's not that bad, 'Dre."

"Give it time."

I had no clue what they were talking about, but I was only half listening. When my eyes landed on Jevon, lounging by the basement bar with a red Solo cup in his hands, my attention span drifted completely. He was talking to a group of people I assumed were friends he'd invited. I had never seen them before, and he looked oddly comfortable around them.

Two boys that were just as tall and almost as brawny as him and a girl around my height that stood in the middle of their little huddle garnered all of my attention. I stood up from the couch and left my group with a quick "I'll be right back" thrown over my shoulder.

Jevon saw me coming before I was even close enough to speak. He held the conversation with his friends easily, but his eyes were on me the entire time. I smiled.

"You came," I noted, coming to a stop before them.

Their conversation stopped as they all turned toward the intruder: me. They bore curious expressions while they stared. Jevon blessed me with an easy smile of his own.

"I told you I would."

He brought the Solo cup to his lips and took another sip. His friends exchanged looks.

"Hey, I'm Akilah." I introduced myself with a wave.

"I'm Trisha, but you can just call me Trish," the girl said as she extended her hand for me to shake.

Trish was very much a tomboy, but in a way that didn't take away from her girliness. She didn't wear a ton of makeup, and she seemed to like sticking to the T-shirt and jeans combo. She was very pretty with her pixie cut curls.

"It's nice to meet you, Trish."

"I'm Kent, and that's Darius," said the other guy in the group. He pointed to Darius, who had stepped away to play a round of beer pong even though he was already swaying on his feet. Kent was dangerously cute with his devilish green eyes and reddish-brown high fade. He gave Jevon a subtle nudge in my direction and they briefly exchanged a silent look.

"Watch him." Jevon pointed to Darius.

With his head, Jevon then gestured to the pool table by the wall. It was tucked away in a corner, dimly lit by a single light bulb that swayed with the vibration of the music. I led the way through small crowd in the basement and made myself comfortable on the table's green surface. Jevon came over and leaned on the edge beside me. We were almost the same height with him standing there.

"Are you having a good time?" I asked.

I wanted him to enjoy himself. Jevon was still new. It had to feel weird partying with a bunch of strangers.

"Yeah, I'm glad I came."

He suddenly scooted a little closer to me when someone tried to pass by him to get to the bar. I could smell his cologne as he brushed against me and couldn't help leaning in just a bit.

"Did anything wild happen before I got here?"

"No, but I think it's getting there."

He looked around the room at the slowly growing crowd. As more people filed into the basement, the room grew more chaotic. From the messy game of beer pong still going strong in the middle of the room, to a different game of strip poker played by the staircase, Tommy's party was well on its way to wild territory.

"Well, you better buckle up," I said as I caught Kayla making her way over, juggling three red cups in her hands. Jevon followed my line of vision and made room for her to squeeze through to the other side of me. "It's just getting started."

"Shots!" She passed us each a cup. "Come on!"

I made the mistake of sniffing the dark brown liquid inside. It was about as pungent as rubbing alcohol. Kayla tapped her cup on the table before raising it up and taking it to the head. Jevon and I followed suit, taking in the mouth full of liquor. On instinct, I waved my hand in front of my face to get it down and when I finished, Kayla took our cups to pour us another.

Already, I could feel a warmth building inside of me. I was in the mood for a good time, and the liquid that kept appearing at the bottom of my cup promised just that.

After the fourth shot, I ignored the pressure to take another. The buzz I felt had me swaying off-beat to the music, doing my best to keep my balance. It was Tommy who found us all huddled at the pool table. He nodded discreetly toward the sliding glass door that led outside to his backyard. Kayla and I knew in an instant that it was an unspoken invitation, and it didn't take a lot of convincing to get us to go with him.

Tommy freed up a trail to the door, pushing party goers aside as we made our way through. It was warm outside and oddly quiet compared to the blaring music in his home. There was a stillness in the night that brought a stark contrast to the party raging inside.

We found a few seats dotted around his patio. Kayla, Tommy, and I formed a half circle with the chairs as Tommy procured a small bag from his pocket. Carefully, he pulled out a pre-rolled joint and passed it to Kayla. In his other pocket was a lighter that he used to help her spark the end of it. Kayla expertly inhaled the smoke and slowly blew it out before passing it to me.

We kept up a rotation: from Kayla, to me, and then to Tommy. In just a few puffs, I was climbing on a high that kept a constant grin on my face. Tommy had us giggling, telling jokes with a freestyle he created to the faint beat of the music from inside. Between him and the steady rotation of the blunt, it was hard for me to catch my breath. I eventually had to tap out. My lungs couldn't take anymore and my buzz was quickly turning into a tipsy disposition.

I left Tommy and Kayla outside to finish the rest. Inside, the DJ was playing some of Tommy's old hits. It shifted the mood in the room and I shouted out the lyrics like everybody else, while finding my groove to the beat. Tommy was such a good musician. It was often hard to believe that I was friends with someone like him. Out of the four of us, Tommy was the one we'd all bet on making it after graduating from CSA. He didn't have to try. His talent was effortless.

I swayed back and forth to the music, caught up in my own little world. I was feeling good. Other people came to join me on the dance floor and it wasn't until I turned around that I noticed Jevon across the room. He stood by himself with a drink in hand, silently watching me. I wasn't sure if it was the alcohol, the few puffs of weed I'd just had, my own personal desire, or some combination of the three, but my legs carried me over to him.

All at once, the music morphed into something slower tempo. Jevon set his drink aside when I got close enough to reach out for his hand. He didn't hesitate or resist when I pulled us back to the dance floor. The crowd sort of dispersed on its own and everybody went back to what they were doing. The slow music killed the vibe for them, but it also made a clearing in the middle of the room.

"I'm cashing in on that favor." I smiled up at him

Jevon arched a brown, garnishing a smile of his own. "You mean the two that you already owe me?"

"You looked bored over there. Trust me, I'm doing you a favor."

I placed my hands on his shoulders at the same time that his arm encircled me. I could feel the warmth of his hands around my bare waist. My kimono jacket was very thin. It took little to no effort to move the train aside.

We rocked to the music from side to side. The smell of his cologne had me leaning in closer. He smelled so good I couldn't help placing my head on his chest. We stayed like that for a while, dancing like we were the only two in the room. Eventually, the track changed to a beat unfamiliar to me, yet Jevon seemed to know exactly what it was. He took my hand and spun me so my back was to him.

He bent down to whisper in my ear. "Follow my lead."

I nodded, too surprised to say anything.

My mother was classical dance instructor; it was the only style of dance she knew. When I was a kid, she'd take me to her studio and give me lessons in the hopes that I'd one day follow in her footsteps. I was pretty good at catching on to the basics: grace, agility, and discipline.

Though that last method never seemed to stick, I was a pretty good dancer in my own right. But I was suddenly questioning all of my skills with the way Jevon held my hips and moved us to the reggae beat. I did my best to keep up with him, but he had a rhythm that kept his front firmly pressed against my back. It was distracting to say the least.

Jevon's hands were so sure as they guided me to the next move. He was in complete control. One moment, I was leaning into him as he swayed us smoothly to the beat and in the next, something entirely new had come over me. I was so caught up in keeping up with Jevon, that I didn't notice all the eyes on us. It didn't even register to me that we were the only ones still dancing.

When he spun me back around, it was only him that I could focus on. The wandering eyes, the empty dance floor suddenly didn't matter. Jevon bit down on his lip, drawing my eyes directly to his mouth, and without thinking, I leaned up on my toes and pressed my lips to his. He froze for only a second before responding with a vigor that surprised me. His arms tightened around my waist and pulled me in to him.

"What the hell, Jevon?!" a high, shrieking voice cried.

Jevon and I were instantly ripped apart, separated by a girl who stared me down like I was in the wrong. As if *I* had somehow offended *her*. I didn't recognize the girl from any of my classes at Cambridge. She was tall, light-skinned, and slim, with a honey-colored bob that stopped just short of her shoulders. Her hazel eyes pierced through me as her long nails pointed between Jevon and me, like we were a problem that needed to be fixed.

I couldn't recall ever seeing her on campus at all, yet there she stood, sizing me up like she knew me personally. I held her gaze—unafraid, but it was when Jevon grabbed her by the arm and tugged her toward the door that I realized the connection.

CHAPTER THIRTEEN

Jevon

It took a lot less convincing to get my friends on board for a party. At Laney, we only partied for homecoming and winning football games. The kids at CSA threw parties just because it was Tuesday.

I had no clue what we'd be walking into, but the last thing I expected was a full on talent show in the middle of the room. Dancers took up space in Tommy's living room, moving in sync to a song performed by a wannabe pop star on the other side of the room.

Those who didn't go to CSA took it all in with amazement—my friends included. Darius stared wide-eyed at the singer, who put on her own show across the room, while Trisha joined the slow forming circle around the dancers.

"Is this what you meant when you said things might get a little crazy?" Kent asked. Like me, he scanned the room warily. This environment was new to us. We didn't have full-on performances at our parties. It was more laid back. We vibed to the music, and with the right kind of song, everybody would dance.

"No," I shouted over the music, "but we'll see."

We headed further into the room, away from the crowded living room, but close enough for us to keep an eye on Darius. He'd somehow managed to get a drink in his hand as the singer singled him out of the crowd with a beckoning finger. It didn't take much for him to follow along.

My eyes continued to scan the room, searching for a familiar face, or at least wherever Darius got his drink. This party felt more like an ordinary day at CSA. If that were the case, I wouldn't make it through the night.

Thankfully, I didn't have to search for long. I noticed Tommy juggling a case of beer and three different types of liquors from the kitchen. One of the bottles wobbled unsteadily on the edge of the beer case, and I jogged over to catch it before it could fall.

Tommy looked up in surprise. "Jay? What are you doing here?"

"You invited me."

"Yeah, but don't you got a bedtime." He laughed at his own joke.

"Not tonight."

"What made you change your mind?"

"Akilah." I said. She'd pestered me into saying yes.

Tommy face was almost doubtful. He cocked his head back and raised his brows. "AJ? Really?"

"Yeah. Why?"

With a smile, he shook his head like he was shaking away a thought he didn't want to say aloud.

"No reason. You wanna help me carry these downstairs?"

Tommy didn't wait for a response. He thrust the case of beer into my hands and piled one of the liquors on top. He then led the way down into the basement.

"Who's Akilah?" Kent asked as he followed us downstairs. I could hear the sarcasm dripping in his voice.

I sighed. "A friend."

"Jalissa's on the way here, right? You know how she is. Does she know about this *friend*?"

"Me and Jalissa broke up months ago. I can have *friends*."

At that, Kent laughed—a deep, belly laugh. It was like he knew something I didn't. Something I should've already known. Something that I could've probably prevented.

It took a while for me to realize my mistake. Dancing with Akilah was fun. It wasn't how I'd planned for my night to go, but she a way of getting what she wanted—making me do things I should say "no" to.

If I were being honest with myself though, Akilah made the night more bearable. Until she arrived, I'd spent the night looking after Darius—who was way past his limit—and turning down drinking game requests from Tommy and his friends.

Akilah came through looking completely different than she did at school. She looked *good* and she knew it. I wonder if that's why I couldn't say no. When we danced, I couldn't look away. I couldn't help it. Then we kissed, and...well.

* * *

I was able to get Jalissa outside before anything major happened. She never thought about the real consequences of her actions until the mess she created exploded right in her face.

"What are you doing, Jalissa?" I asked, frustration coating my tone.

"No, the real question is, "what are *you* doing?""

She was fuming, but for no good reason. Beyond our mutual group of friends and our strained friendship (at best), I had no other ties to Jalissa.

"We're not together anymore. Why are you tripping?"

"Is that what this is? You're mad because I dumped you, so you're acting out to get back at me? That's real childish, Jevon."

I would've laughed if not for the fact that she actually looked serious.

"You think I was trying make you jealous?" I actually did laugh—a knee-jerk reaction.

Jalissa crossed her arms and fixed me with a look that said "Well, weren't you?"

"This is what we do!" she went on, getting louder with each word. "Yeah, sometimes we need a break from each other, but we always come back."

Most times, we'd break up just for the promise of making up again. And making up was always the best part. Other times, we'd just be sick of each other. I was always busy, and Jalissa required way too much attention. When she couldn't get that attention from me, she found it elsewhere.

Jalissa had one thing right though, we always came back to each other. It was like clockwork. On, then off, then back on again. This time things were different. I was sick of the twisted games.

With a deep sigh, I looked her in the eyes so there was no misunderstanding. "I'm not coming back this time. I'm done."

I waited for the shock to register across her face. It was shortly followed by a look of hurt that, in the past, would've had me taking all my words back.

"So, that's it?" she asked, barely above a whisper. "You're choosing her over me?"

"I'm not *choosing* anybody. I'm just having fun. If anything, I'm choosing my future, and I guess I have you to thank for that."

If not for our breakup, I wouldn't have focused so hard on my training over the summer. I wouldn't have clung to it the way I did, and I definitely wouldn't have mastered the art of Silat in a way that gained Shane Tither's attention, of all people. Jalissa did me a favor. She'd cleared up space in my head for the thing that was most important to me.

"When you invited me to this party, I thought—"

"That I changed my mind?"

Jalissa nodded.

The way she looked at me, so full of hope in what I would say next made me almost feel bad for moving on. This was new for the both of us. Now that the cycle was broken, it felt weird.

"You should do what makes you happy, 'Lissa. I can't be the reason you act out like this."

"I guess I deserve that." She smiled bitterly.

"You deserve to be happy, just not with me."

With a defeated sigh, Jalissa turned to leave. There wasn't much else for us to say to each other. A part of me wanted to leave right behind her. It wasn't fair that she could walk away and leave me to clean up her mess. I tried not to think about it as I turned to head back inside.

I didn't have to go far to find Akilah. She stood at the bar amongst her friends, talking with them like normal. When she saw me, she took a long chug from her drink, handed the cup off to someone else, and then wedged her way through the crowd to get to me.

Akilah didn't stop once we were face to face. Instead she pinched the edge of my shirt and led us back out through the sliding door. Tommy's backyard was empty. I didn't notice before how the faint smell of cigarettes and weed smoke permeated the air. It added a different kind of weight to the already cloudy night. I went and sat on one of the lawn chairs Tommy had on his patio. Akilah preferred to stand. She leaned on the post at the corner of the patio with a smirk that couldn't be mistaken.

"So, I'm guessing that was a close *friend* of yours?" she asked.

"Not really."

"She seemed . . . friendly."

"Yeah, I'm sorry about that. It won't happen again."

"Hmph." She perked a brow. "Interesting."

"What?"

Akilah left the post and walked over to claim the seat in front of me. With her legs crossed, she placed an elbow on her knee and tucked her hand under her chin for support.

"It makes sense that you'd like them feisty like that."

"Why? Because I'm a fighter?"

"Maybe." Akilah turned her head to stare out at the rows of trees lining Tommy's backyard. With her hand, she tried to hide a smile that seemed more like an inside joke to her.

"What's so funny?"

"Nothing." She pressed her lips together, but a small laugh eventually escaped. "It's just, I have this idea in my head of who I think you are, but you constantly prove me wrong. You're just very surprising, that's all."

I didn't know if that was good or bad, or how I was supposed to take that, but it suddenly made me curious.

"Who do you think I am?"

"Honestly?" She turned back to face me. "A mystery. Sometimes you come across very jaded and detached from everything around you, like you'd rather be anywhere else and other times, like right now, you're different."

I snorted out a bitter laugh, "What if I told you there was no mystery, that it's all in your head? What if I'm just a regular dude with shitty luck and a bad temper? What then?"

She paused. "Is that a warning?"

"No." I looked away. "It's just a thought."

Silence fell over us. The cicadas were somewhere in the distance, kicking up a tune much louder than the muffled music playing inside. I hadn't meant to kill the mood, but Akilah had all these wild assumptions that just didn't make any sense. There was nothing mysterious about me, not even close.

"Wanna know what I think?" Akilah suddenly stood up.

I was almost hesitant to ask, but with the renewed smile on her face, I felt the mood shifting again.

"I think you should get up and dance with me." She extended a hand to me, wiggling her fingers impatiently. "We never got to finish our song."

"We have a song now?"

"Yes, and it's playing again. Come on!"

I could faintly hear the beat to "No Letting Go" by Wayne Wonder playing on the other side of the sliding glass doors. Akilah took hold of my hand and did her best to yank me up from my seat. I let her drag me back inside, right to the middle of the dance floor, where a space had cleared up for us.

I blamed my mother's West Indian roots for what was about to happen. Dancing was a skill that I never tapped into, but it was in my blood, and music like this brought it out of me.

CHAPTER FOURTEEN

Akilah

At school the next morning, gossip hovered over the hallways like a heat wave. Anybody who wasn't at the party last night either wished that they were, or pretended to be. As I breezed through a huddle of sophomore girls all claiming to have a juicy story of their own, I did my best to ignore the babble.

I'd heard every story: from the guy who got so drunk he puked all over the stereo system, to the group that went streaking up the street on a dare. They were all exaggerated truths—that much I knew—but there was something about hearing your own name slip through the lips of someone you didn't know that piqued your interest.

I was at my locker, searching for the spare bottle of scented lotion I kept in the back for a rainy day. My knuckles were dry and slowing forming a little ashy business between my fingers. That's when a new huddle of gossip came to a stop a few doors down from me.

"Did you hear about the fight last night?" one girl whispered loud enough for me to hear.

"There was a fight?" Another more eager girl chimed in. "When? With who?"

"The new boy. What's his name—"

"Jevon?" the third girl added.

"Yeah, him. I heard he hooked up with AJ at the party and his girlfriend from his old school walked in on it." The story-teller waited for the oohs and ahhs from her peanut gallery before continuing. My face was hidden by my open locker door, but I tucked some hair behind my ear so I could hear them better.

"She went right up to AJ, and smacked her clean across the face! I heard she gave her a black eye and everything."

From the tiny mirror stuck to my locker door, I examined my perfectly clear, brown skin. Other than the slight smudge of my mascara on my lower lids—which I quickly fixed with my finger—my face and my makeup was flawless.

"Can you blame the girlfriend, though?" Thing #2 asked, "Have you *seen* Jevon? I'd go crazy behind him too. Shoot, if it was me, I would—"

I suddenly slammed my locker door shut, having heard enough of the lies. At the sound, all three girls jumped and turned around to face me. It was then that I noticed Netta standing in the middle of it all. I should've known it was her from the beginning. Somehow, she was always the first to know everything, and if Netta knew something, it was basically public knowledge by now.

"AJ, hey." Thing #2—who I now realized was Netta's friend, Crystal—smiled brightly. "I didn't see you standing there."

"Sure," I said doubtfully. "And you didn't see a fight last night either. None of that's true."

"We didn't mean to..." Netta chimed in. "I mean, I'm just saying what I heard."

"Well, you heard wrong."

Just in time, the bell rang as the hallway filled with people going to class. I tucked my small bottle of lotion in the side part of my bag and slung it over my shoulder. With nothing left to say, I bristled my way through the grapevine, bumping shoulders with two of the girls, and headed for my first class.

* * *

The day dragged on painfully slow. By midday, I hoped that the rumors would die down, but I had no such luck. All day, people examined my face much closer than necessary. It could've all been in my head, but I just knew they were looking for the black eye that didn't exist.

Damn Netta and her big, lying mouth.

After lunch, I made a beeline for Ms. Hazel's class. It was the only place I could really relax without all the curious stares and intrusive questions about last night. The familiar smell of dried paint and pencil shavings was soothing in a way I couldn't explain.

As I slipped on my overalls to prepare for class, I heard the stool beside me shift. On instinct, my head turned toward the intruder. I was in no mood to deal with anymore gossip about Tommy's party.

"Hey." Jevon nodded to me casually as if he and I weren't the talk of the school.

"Hey." I finally settled into my seat.

My leg bounced restlessly as I spared glances in his direction every so often. He seemed calm, like he hadn't heard all the rumors. Or, if he had, he just didn't care. Jevon must've sensed me staring because by the fourth glance, he turned to give me an odd look.

"What's wrong?"

"Didn't you hear?" I shrugged. "Your girlfriend gave me a black eye last night."

His brows lifted in surprise. There was a brief pause as what I said fully registered to him. Then, he laughed. It started out as a chuckle he couldn't hide, but then he couldn't help himself. Jevon laughed so hard we got a few head turns from the people in front of us.

"It's not funny!" I whisper-yelled.

When he finally sobered up, he looked me in the eye, like people had all day, examining my face for any bruises.

He squinted. "I can't even tell."

"Be serious."

Jevon grinned, but I could tell the jokes were over. "We both know that's not true, so it doesn't matter what they're saying."

I tried to be comforted by his words, but there was one other thing I couldn't let go of.

"So, *none* of it was true?" I asked, hoping he could read between the lines.

Though he didn't comment right away, I had a feeling Jevon knew exactly what I was hinting at. He gave me a knowing look as he waited for me to say more, but I wasn't bold enough to explain what I was really asking for.

"Just ask me," he said, his voice low.

"What?"

"What you really want to know."

I took a deep breath and decided to just get it over with.

"That girl, is she your girlfriend?"

He shook his head. "Jalissa's my ex. She just gets really jealous sometimes."

I tried not to show how valuable this new insight was to me.

"Does that happen a lot? The jealousy thing?"

"No. Not like last night. That was mostly because of you."

"The kiss?" I asked. We'd never actually acknowledged our kiss until now. In the middle of Ms. Hazel's class was the last place I would've wanted to talk about this, but I suddenly had to know all the whys and hows surrounding it.

"Yeah. That too."

What does that even mean?

Jevon turned back toward Ms. Hazel. She placed stacks of papers on the first two stations. Each person took one and passed it back.

"These are your midterm study guides," Ms. Hazel announced to the class. "I want you go over the materials carefully because you should all know by now that my tests are not easy."

When the stack got to us, Jevon plucked a thick pamphlet from the top and passed one over to me before sending it back to the station behind us. I knew then that our discussion was over for now. Ms. Hazel was going over her lesson plan, and that left no more room for talking.

I flipped through my study guide, both satisfied with what I'd learned and annoyed that it wasn't enough.

CHAPTER FIFTEEN

Jevon

My next match was coming up in a few days. I was constantly reminded by Sasha, Nick, and my Pops just how important this meet was. Not only was this the first fight of the season—the fight that would ultimately set the tone for me and my team, but Shane Tithers would be watching.

I wondered how long it would take for that to finally sink in. Every member at the Hard Knocks Dojo was hyped over Shane's arrival. It wasn't so much of a shock that he would be in Atlanta—this was his hometown. What had everyone so excited was the fact that he'd chosen to visit our dojo.

Nick and Sasha had built their company from the ground up. They had a pretty rough start in the beginning because they'd built the dojo in a rougher part of town. Little black and brown kids weren't really interested in martial arts at first, but when Sasha reached out to the community, she gathered kids of all ages and gave them all a free membership for a year. It was crazy to think that Nick and Sasha had started off so small, and now their dojo would host *the* Shane Tithers, a world champion.

"Again!" Nick tussled with me on the floor mat.

We had been going over the same move for the last hour, and I just couldn't seem to get it right. I usually caught on fast to new techniques, but I was having trouble with a simple move. All I had to do was find the pressure point in Nick's shoulder blade and hit him there sharply and swiftly, rendering his arm useless.

Of course, he made the task harder by dodging every one of my blows. Though he wasn't as good as his wife when it came to sparring, Nick was more than a worthy opponent. On a better day, I'd typically have more luck in the ring with him. Today though, I found it hard to get out of my own head.

Frustrated, I shook off the pain in my arm from Nick's defensive blow. It went momentarily numb from the impact. He was showing me firsthand how it easy it was to strike a pressure point, yet still I fumbled through a round with him.

"Come on, Jay!" Nick yelled "What's up with you today?"

In some ways, Nick and Sasha were like a second set of parents. They were just as proud as my own parents when they'd heard about my opportunity with Shane. When Nick yelled at me, I knew it was his own way of showing that he cared.

After another failed attempt at perfecting the move, Nick instructed me to take a break. He left to go work with his other students while I found a seat on the bleachers to chug my water.

"Nervous?" Sasha asked, suddenly appearing beside me.

"No. I just need some more practice."

"Look, I know we've put a lot of pressure on you with Shane, and coming back strong from last season. Plus, starting this new school can't be easy for you. It's okay to feel a little overwhelmed, Jevon."

"I'm not, though."

One bad practice didn't suddenly mean I couldn't handle the stress. I was ready for this. I was made for this.

Sasha sighed as she scooted closer to me. This time she lowered her voice so only I could hear her. "You've been missing out on a few of your usual training days since you started this new school. I haven't said anything because I figured you were still adjusting, but now I'm wondering if that's the reason you're not performing like you should."

True, I had missed a couple days of practice, but I always made up for it on the weekends. I knew she was hinting at the time I'd been spending with Akilah, working on our sculpture. Pops had told me to make the most out of my time at CSA. That's what I thought I was doing, through Akilah's art, yet Sasha was certain that it was the problem.

"You haven't said anything to my Pops, have you?"

"Not yet." She folded her arms. "But I will if I have to. I'm worried about you. You're better than this."

"I have more responsibilities at this school. It's different than Laney."

"I get that, but you also have responsibilities here. If it's too much for you to handle, then—"

"I can handle it!" I didn't mean to snap, but I was tired of people assuming the worst of me before I could prove myself better.

With a tight-lipped smile and a soft pat on my shoulder, Sasha rose from her seat.

"Balance," was all she said, before she turned to go to her office.

The thing was, I didn't mix my school of arts world into my fighting world. The two just didn't blend well. Finding a balance between school and Silat would be a problem for another day . . . that was, if Sasha didn't snitch on me before I could figure it out. There was no reason to get Pops involved in anything that didn't cost him money, or required him to clean up my mess.

I waited until Sasha was all the way inside her office to fix the tape that had started rolling down from my hand wrap. In my rush to get on the fighting floor, I'd never double-checked to make sure it was secure. When I pulled at it, the whole wrap fell apart, so I just decided to redo it.

Nick was busy showing a few of my teammates the same move I'd struggled with earlier. I watched them carefully, studying their footwork and the precise way they executed the move. More than a few times, my teammates targeted the nerve endings in Nick's arms and his sides.

It was such a simple move, maybe Sasha was right to be worried.

* * *

At school, I spent my time memorizing pressure points and target areas. Practice this morning was embarrassing. With so little time until my first match, I needed to get it together, and fast.

Sooner or later, Pops would be on my back again about colleges, adding to my already full plate. In his eyes, it was education before everything unless a better opportunity came along. If I couldn't prove to him that I could actually make this work—the new fighting season, my training sessions, and CSA—then I could kiss the tour goodbye.

More than anything, I knew my father would rather ship me off to the nearest business school so I could one day run the family business. To him, a businessman was more respectable than a fighter. A part of me always wondered if that's why he didn't take me seriously when I tried to have more of a say in my career. Maybe it'd be less embarrassing if I failed out of the spotlight. It would be way easier to sweep my mess under the rug.

"I need volunteers!" Kayla loudly addressed everyone at our lunch table. She had a clipboard in hand, effectively snapping me out of my thoughts.

"For what?" Dre asked.

"The fashion show!" she squealed, "It's going to happen during spring semester, but I need volunteers now, or else I won't be able to sign up."

"Count me out!" Tommy said, striking his hand across his neck.

"What? Why?"

"Last year you tried to make me walk out in a thong."

"I was going with the theme." Kayla rolled her eyes. "And we walked away with grand prize in the end."

"Whatever," Tommy mumbled. "I'm not going out like that again."

"Wait." I butted in. "You walked out in a thong, Tommy?" I couldn't hold back a laugh.

"Chill, Jay. It's for the culture."

"Nah," Andre added holding back a laugh, "it's for the puss—"

"Man, shut up!" Tommy growled from across the table.

He threw a water bottle at Andre to stop him from finishing his sentence. 'Dre dodged the blow and chuckled quietly to himself.

"What about you, Jevon?" Kayla stared at me expectantly, her pen poised to mark a "yes" by my name on her sign-up sheet.

"I'm not a model."

"You don't have to be a model to be in the show, silly."

"He's saying that he doesn't want to be in the show," 'Dre said.

"Basically," I agreed, stifling a laugh.

"Well, you don't have a choice because I already put your names down."

"So why did you even ask?" he retorted.

Kayla shrugged. "Out of courtesy."

"You don't have us all wrapped around your finger like Tommy, Kayla." He smirked. "That's not going to work on us."

Kayla turned her attention to Akilah. They both shared a look and smiled a secretive smile. With a quick wink, Akilah then turned to Andre.

"Please?" Akilah smiled sweetly, instantly drawing him in under her spell. Suddenly, whatever argument that had formed on the tip of Andre's lips died off as he stared helplessly back at her.

He was a goner for sure. Akilah eventually joined in on the laughs around us, not noticing the damage she was doing to his ego. Akilah was toying with the guy. I almost felt bad for him.

"Alright, I'll do it," 'Dre said suddenly, looking as if he'd come up with the idea himself. "It's for the culture, you know?"

"Riiight," Kayla said.

Girls could be cruel sometimes.

CHAPTER SIXTEEN

Akilah

On Saturday, Kayla and I took a well-deserved trip to the mall—a real trip this time. Unlike the last time we were here, the mall was full of life. People drifted in and out of stores, swaying their bags as they merged into the crowded walkways.

We passed by a few shoe stores that had lines curved out the door. There must've been a sale or some new brand that everybody wanted. The sweet smell of cinnamon and fresh-baked cookies wafted in the air as we crossed through broken lines at the Cinnabon and Mrs. Fields stands near the escalators.

"I hope it's not this packed upstairs," Kayla complained as we found a spot on the escalator platform.

I gestured to all the people on the escalator with us. "It's Saturday. What do you expect?"

"A short line at the makeup counter," she offered. "A black card with no limit, and a big, strong man to carry all my bags. Is that too much to ask for?"

So far, Kayla only had two small bags, and neither of us had the luxury of owning a black card, but since we were being dramatic, I played into her delusions.

"It's so hard being us."

"Too hard!"

I laughed because she was serious. Kayla towed her two bags like they already weighed too much.

"One of your other lives is showing," I muttered as we made it to the second floor.

We always joked that in a past life, she was definitely a princess. I was an explorer. Out of the two of us, I was most likely to wander off, either in real life or in my own head. My parents called me a dreamer, while CJ joked that I was just slow.

"Here ye, hear ye!" she exclaimed, strutting off the escalator's platform and right into the MAC store.

I followed behind her less enthusiastically. We were starting to get a few looks from the strangers around us, and not the good kind. As expected, the MAC store was full of customers, but thankfully there wasn't a line forming outside.

I grabbed a black bag from the hook at the front of the store and made my way to the lipsticks. Their fall colors had arrived and I wanted to get a good selection before they were gone. Seeing how full the store already was made me anxious to get a head start.

"Is there anything I can help you with today?" A tall woman with pasty skin, fiery red hair, and bright red lipstick came to stand next to me.

I hated that question. It was always followed by overly helpful suggestions and a lack of personal space. I politely declined and moved over to put a little distance between us. My fingers had only lightly grazed over the color Media when the woman resumed her earlier position.

"Honey, with your warm, neutral tones, I think you'd look great in Rebel or Velvet Teddy."

I worked hard to control whatever look I knew was displayed on my face before turning around. Again, I slid to my right, hoping she'd catch the hint.

"Thanks, Heather," I read her name tag. "But I'm okay. I'll let you know if I need help."

"Hmm." She examined my features like she hadn't even heard me. "Maybe Chili, or—ooh, what about Diva?! You strike me as the glamorous type."

This time, I didn't hide my irritation. I could feel my lip curl of its own volition, and that's when Heather finally got the hint. She gave me a toothless smile as she moved on to help another customer.

At the tiny mirror on the end of the aisle, I tried on a few different shades. The dark brown and deep red colors paired beautifully with my dark skin. Already, I imagined tons of different looks I could create.

"There you are! I was looking everywhere for you." An out of breath Kayla suddenly appeared beside me.

I leaned back to double-check where she'd come from. "At the back of the store?"

"I had to grab these." She held up her goodies. "This old lady tried to fight me for them."

"A glitter kit?" I really tried not to laugh because, again, Kayla was absolutely serious. The package was all dented and covered in loose glitter, adding weight to her already ridiculous story.

"It's for the fashion show."

"Kayla, the fashion show is in the spring."

"So?" Kayla shrugged. "You know the saying: stay ready so you don't have to—"

"Get ready," I finished with her.

"Exactly." She smiled proudly.

I tossed my items into the black bag and we both wedged our way through the narrow aisles to get checked out. The cashier took her time jotting down my email and promising me all the coupons a girl could never ask for, until finally, we were able to leave.

Kayla and I headed for the escalators, back toward the food court on first floor. I could smell the blend of teriyaki chicken, fresh hot pizza, and Italian subs from all the way up here. It made my mouth water.

When we got to the food court, we searched for an empty table away from the fountain. Little kids were splashing puddles and swiping coins from the bottom, and their parents were nowhere to be found.

"Here, take this." I handed my bag to Kayla so she could hold my spot at the table we'd snagged. I had my eyes set on the "Hot" sign glowing over the pizza stand.

"What can I get for you?" the boy behind the counter asked. He waved his hand toward the huge pizza slices that were still steaming under the heat lamps. I pointed to the slice of plain cheese in the middle and waited patiently for him to box it up.

The box was so hot I had to make a barrier with a stack of napkins, so I didn't burn my hands. After paying, I briskly walked back to our table and nearly threw the pizza down to get the heat off my hands.

"Mmm. That smells good. What'd you get?" Before even waiting for a response, Kayla reached over to lift the lid and steal a string of cheese from the corner. She must've scorched her tongue trying to eat it, but it didn't stop her from going back to take a larger chunk.

"Okay, that's enough!" I closed the lid.

Satisfied, she leaned back and set her mouth ablaze as she munched on her stolen piece of pizza.

"Did you really fight an old lady for that thing?" Her dented glitter kit was tucked close under her arm, as if the lady might come back for round two.

With a sly smirk, Kayla popped the last bite of pizza in her mouth. "Only if you can prove it."

"You're evil!" I choked on a laugh.

"Call it what you want," she shrugged carelessly.

"Akilah?"

Both our heads snapped toward the interruption as a girl approached our table. She gave us a wave when she came to a stop.

"Trisha?" I almost didn't recognize her in her black and white striped uniform. Her pixie cut curls were hidden under a white cap, but it was her golden, bamboo earrings that were a dead giveaway. They had her name embossed across the middle.

"I didn't know you worked here," I said, noticing the Foot Locker logo on the sleeve of her shirt.

"Yeah, I just got off. I was going to head out, but I saw you sitting here, and I thought it would be weird to just walk right past you."

"Do you want to sit with us?"

I made room for Trisha to claim the seat beside me, pushing our things onto the tabletop.

"Trisha, this is my best friend, Kayla. Kayla, Trisha is friends with Jevon."

"Oh, yeah. I think I saw you at the party the other night."

"Yeah, it was . . ." Trisha searched for the right word.

"Wild?" I offered.

"Crazy?" Kayla suggested. "Doing too much?"

"I was going to say fun." She chuckled. "I'm glad I went."

"If you thought that was fun, just wait until the next one."

Trisha sighed. "Jay is so lucky. I should've been the one to transfer."

"Are you into the arts?" Kayla asked.

Trisha arched a brow as if to say "what do you think?"

"No." She snorted. "But I'm definitely here for the parties. Laney could never."

Trisha checked the time on her phone then. I doubted she was in a rush to be somewhere else because she suddenly found something more interesting on her screen. Now that my pizza had cooled down to a more measurable degree, I lifted the lid and took a bite.

"How long have you known Jevon?" Kayla asked.

"Since we were in diapers." Trisha grinned, barely glancing up from her phone. "He used to live in my neighborhood. We called him Bougie Boots because he always had the newest stuff. Me and my cousins would get jealous and beat him up, but then he learned how to fight and the rest is history."

I tried to picture a younger Jevon getting beat up by Trisha and her cousins. I even laughed a little as my imagination got the best of me. Trisha seemed nice and all, but behind her bamboo earrings, short black acrylic nails, and the myriad of chunky rings on her fingers, it wasn't hard to believe that what she was saying was true.

Trisha gasped all of a sudden, staring deeply at the screen. "Is this for real?"

"What?" I leaned over to get a peek. She was on Twitter, scrolling through a trending topic that didn't make a lot of sense to me at first.

#TAKEHIMOUT littered the screen as Trisha scrolled past all sorts of GIFs and hate comments. People were outraged and offended. I even noticed a few popular blogs retweeting quotes and images, but why? It was when her finger landed on an edited photo of Jevon with black X's scribbled over his eyes that it suddenly clicked for me.

"What's going on?" Kayla asked.

"I should go check on him." Trisha got up and collected her things.

"Wait." I stood up too. "We'll come with you."

"Really?"

"Yeah, Jevon's our friend too."

"This is about Jevon?" Kayla tried again. "What happened?"

"Okay, I'll meet you in the parking lot. You can follow my car." Trisha left without another word, placing her phone to her ear to make a call on her way out.

"Do *you* want to tell me what's going on?" Kayla stared me down, annoyed that she'd been ignored.

"I'll tell you in the car." I grabbed my MAC bag and my purse, and headed for the exit.

"Hey, Dora!" Kayla called as she struggled to keep up. She waited until I came to a full stop so she could catch up to me. "One of your lives is showing."

* * *

It took us forty-five minutes to make it to the gated community on the Northside. We passed through acres and acres of large homes, all intricately built. I followed close behind Trisha as she led us to the far end of the community.

Two lefts and a right, and we finally came to a stop at a huge gray house cut straight out of a magazine. Stone brick columns accented the gray siding that covered the entire home. There were white rose bushes dotted around the property, standing strong against the slowly changing season. It was beautiful. The driveway opened to a three-car garage, where there was more than enough room to park my car.

Following Trisha's lead, Kayla and I walked up the stone steps and waited. The doorbell rang four times before we heard a click on the other side. I actively ignored the sudden leap in my heart at the thought of seeing him. It was a good thing I did because it wasn't Jevon that opened the door. Kent greeted us on the other side, slightly confused by mine and Kayla's presence, but he didn't comment on it.

"Have you seen this?" Trisha thrust her phone into his face.

"Uh, hey to you too." He squinted away from the brightness.

"Hey." She sighed impatiently. "Jay's trending online. Have you seen it?"

"Yeah, we all saw."

"Where is he?"

"In the back."

Kent opened the door wider and welcomed us all in. The house was drafty at first, but I got used to the coolness as we stepped inside. Jevon's home was even more impressive on the inside. I tried not to stare, but there were certain things that drew me in, like the spiral crystal chandelier dangling over the dining room table; or the wall mounted TV hovering over an electric fireplace with color-changing flames.

"I wouldn't bother him," Darius warned from the couch. He was watching a game, muttering plays under his breath. "He's in one of his moods."

Trisha ignored the warning and marched her way through to the backyard. Jevon stood on the other side of a wide pool. He was in the middle of punching a red bag. He hit it with so much force the metal stand vibrated violently against the concrete surface.

I could faintly hear music playing from his headphones, so he didn't notice her approach him at first. Trisha was dangerously close to one of his targeted swings at the bag. Even I jumped a little from the impact and I was nowhere near him.

"Jay!" she yelled over his music, but he didn't hear.

"Jevon!" She poked his arm, though she probably shouldn't have done that.

"What?!" he exploded, towering over her as he breathed heavily from his workout. Trisha didn't even flinch.

She held her phone up as evidence. "Why aren't you responding?"

Jevon tilted his head back and heaved a big, exasperated sigh.

"Why are you just letting this happen?"

"You know why."

"What? Poppa Williams got your tongue?"

At that, Jevon removed his headphones, breezed past her and headed back toward the house. When he saw me standing near the door, he gave me the same quizzical look that Kent did earlier. I suddenly felt very stupid for coming. Jevon was my friend—I thought . . . especially after that kiss—but were we close enough for me to just show up uninvited like this? *Doubtful.*

"Hey." I waved.

His features softened a little, which instantly made me feel a little less awkward. "Hey."

"We ran into Trisha at the mall," I felt the need to explain, "and we saw the hashtags. Are you okay?"

Jevon breathed out through his nose. His jaw flexed as his fingers curled in and out of tightly bound fists. "I'm fine."

Jevon led the way back inside, right to the leather couch where Darius hogged up the most space. He plopped down on the end, dipped his head low, and rubbed at his temples. Kayla and I stood back, heading Darius's warning for real this time.

Then, Trisha came back into the room, already tapping urgently at her screen. "Look, if you don't respond to this, I will."

Jevon's head snapped up. "Don't."

"Some of these are death threats, Jevon. We're supposed to just let people say all these things about you?"

"Yes, you are."

"Why?"

"Because I'm asking you to! Let it go, Trish."

Trish dropped the argument. She claimed a spot between the boys and tuned in to the football game. The silence that followed was loud and uncomfortable. Only the sounds of the commentator on the TV screen and Darius's constant muttering throughout the game could be heard in the room.

I felt a nudge on my elbow and turned to see Kayla gesturing to the sudden change in atmosphere. Her eyes pleaded for understanding.

"What are we doing here?" she mouthed.

"He's our friend," I whispered.

"No, he's your crush. We should go."

I took another look at Jevon. He stared blankly at the TV without really seeing what was on the screen. Though he seemed calm, his fists were clenched so tight I could see the skin stretch thin over his knuckles. It instantly brought me back to that night at Tommy's party.

What if I told you there was no mystery, that it's all in your head? What if I'm just a regular dude with shitty luck and a bad temper?

Even then, he'd hinted at something terrible happening. Maybe not this exact scenario. I mean, who could predict themselves trending online for all the wrong reasons? I hardly even knew why Jevon was suddenly a target for people on the internet, but Jevon didn't seem surprised. He was acting like he'd expected this, or maybe—somewhere deep down—he thought he deserved it.

"Wait, pause that for a sec." I heard Kent before I saw him barreling back into the room. He had a look of unmistakable shock and pity for his for his friend as he handed Jevon his phone. "Someone posted a video."

"What video?" Darius muted the game as we all leaned in to get a better view.

"I don't know. It's some kind of unreleased footage of the fight in London. It's already viral, and I think it's the reason you're trending."

Jevon pressed play, and we all collectively held in a breath as we waited. The video was blurry and unsteady, but we could hear the audio loud and clear. On stage, we saw a huddle of bodies all crammed together at the center, four men in black shirts, and three in yellow.

There was a frantic struggle between them as they yelled things like "grab him!," and "that's a foul!," or even "we need a medic! He's bleeding!" A whistle blared non-stop in the distance as the crowd booed and ahhed at the action.

When the camera man finally found the right angle, we caught a glimpse of Jevon and Jao Shang. Jevon was straddling him, beating Jao Shang senseless. The camera man zoomed in, and we could clearly see Jao Shang bleeding from his mouth and nose. His eyes were bruised and swollen shut. They fluttered like he was losing consciousness, but he spewed blood in Jevon's face as he said things that made him more angry.

We couldn't hear what he said over the sound of the crowd, but I had a pretty good imagination. Security struggled to restrain Jevon; he was out of control. At some point, Jao Shang stopped struggling. His arms went limp and his face had started to slack. I feared the worst until a man in yellow tackled Jevon to the floor.

Then the screen went black.

"Whoa," Kayla muttered under her breath.

Slowly, Jevon returned Kent's phone and rose from his seat. His face was blank, but his stance was so rigid I thought I heard his bones pop into place.

"What are you gonna do?" Kent asked.

"Nothing."

"Are you seri—" Trisha started to argue, but Jevon held up a hand to stop her in her tracks.

"Let it go," was all Jevon said before he turned on his heels and headed straight for the front door.

CHAPTER SEVENTEEN

Jevon

There wasn't a lot I had to say about the video. It was actually the first time I saw myself in action since last season. I didn't remember there being so much blood, or even how they got me away from Shang.

The last thing I remembered from that fight was how sore my knuckles were the next morning. Pops filled me in later on what I had done, and I don't think either of us expected how much I'd have to pay for that mistake.

The unreleased footage was posted anonymously, but I knew exactly who was behind it. I had to give Shang much more credit; he was a clever bastard. Jao Shang was an incredible fighter. At any moment toward the end of that fight, he could've maneuvered his way out of that position.

He could've easily defended himself against me, but he didn't. He'd wanted me to lose control. I was his biggest competition, and what better way to take me out for good than to label me the bad guy? Shang was a coward.

Pops had already prepared me for the day I became public enemy number one. I knew better than to respond or say anything to defend myself. What I did was wrong; I knew that much. People had a right to be angry, but a small part of me wondered if I would've gotten more respect had I bit Shang's ear off instead.

My friends, though loyal but misguided, made it hard for me to stick to the original plan. I saw everything people were saying about me. I received every death threat and impassioned hate comment.

If I could, I'd yell 'til I was blue in face about how much I'd changed or how much I'd learned from my past mistakes. But my past wasn't completely behind me—it was staring me right in the face, blasted all over the internet.

Being in that house, surrounded by their looks of pity and their urge to help, was suffocating. There was nothing I could do, not yet anyway. Pops and I had a plan.

In a week or two, this would be old news. Someone else would do something stupid, and they'd forget all about me. With any luck, Shane Tithers would still have a contract waiting for me to sign when this all blew over.

I headed for my car and started the engine without really thinking about it. Where would I even go? My name was a trending topic and my face was everywhere by now. I just needed a moment to breathe, to get away. I needed to *not* be me . . . for just a little while.

Three sharp raps on my window suddenly brought my attention to the passenger side. It was Akilah. She motioned to the door handle, and I reluctantly unlocked it.

"You were just going to leave without saying anything?" she asked.

"I was thinking about it."

Without waiting for an invitation, Akilah claimed the passenger seat and buckled herself in. Oblivious to my desire to be alone, she fiddled with the radio.

"What are you doing?"

"I know a place where we can go."

"We?" I challenged.

"Yes." She smiled. "This is my last favor to you. You're welcome."

"I didn't ask."

"You didn't have to."

I sighed deeply. This was turning into a very long day.

"Thirty minutes. That's all I need. Then you can go hit a punching bag, or run through the woods, or do whatever it is you do when you're alone."

Akilah seemed intent on staying put, and given the option to remain here with my overly opinionated friends, leaving with Akilah didn't seem like a horrible choice.

"Where is this place?" I asked

"It's not far."

I put my car into gear and backed out of the long driveway. Akilah's radio station bumped softly in the background, filling in the silence between us. I tried to imagine where she was taking me and how I could possibly say "no" in a way that she would understand. The last place I needed to be was in public. It was too much of a risk to chance the wrong person noticing me, considering all the people who now wanted me dead.

"Slow down," Akilah said. "You're going to make a left up here. Do you see that sign?"

The dark green sign was nearly hidden in the cover of the overgrown bushes. As we neared closer to my turn, I could fully read the sign.

"Tanyard Creek?" I almost pumped the brakes. "That's on the BeltLine."

The BeltLine was the busiest trail in the entire city. It was connected to just about every restaurant, venue, and in-city neighborhood downtown, and on a Saturday, it was hell. I wanted to be away from the public, and Akilah had led me right to it.

"Just trust me," she said confidently. "There's a parking spot right there."

Akilah pointed to an open space on the curb. I parked parallel to the sidewalk, but I was slow to cut my engine. As expected, there were crowds of people all headed in different directions. There was some kind of music festival about to happen, as I noticed a stage being put together in a clearing across the street. The smell of grilled food wafted into the car, and I knew I'd made a mistake.

"Thirty minutes," Akilah reminded me. She opened her door and waited patiently for me to join her.

No. It was just one word, one syllable. It wasn't hard to say at all, so what was my problem?

I cut the engine and pocketed my keys. With a deep, regretful sigh, I left my car and joined Akilah on the walkway. We blended into the passing crowd as we headed in the opposite direction of the music festival.

"Don't look so nervous." Akilah chuckled. "You act like I'm walking you into a trap."

"It feels like a trap."

I unintentionally made eye contact with a few people we passed. There were only a couple looks of recognition from wide-eyed strangers, but they said nothing.

"We're almost there." She rolled her eyes.

We came up to an old bridge that opened into a woodsy area. The wood creaked beneath our feet as the moist, swamp-like air almost overpowered my senses. There must've been a river or lake nearby. I could hear running water in the distance, and I hoped we weren't headed that way.

At the end of the bridge, Akilah turned right, and suddenly it was like we'd walked into a whole new territory. We were fenced in by trees and open fields on both sides. Every now and then, we'd pass by small monuments or scattered jungle gyms, but for the most part, we relied only the long stretch of the trail to guide us through.

"This is where I go when I need a real escape," Akilah admitted.

It was quiet here, peaceful even. The sounds of the city were like a distant memory. If peace was the goal, then I was positive she'd find it here.

"How often do you come here?"

She shrugged. "Often enough."

Akilah made a full stop at a wooden bench. It was tucked under the shade of a willow tree. I claimed the spot beside her, and for a while, we watched the geese fight over crumbs left behind by passing strangers.

As peaceful as this place seemed to be, it wasn't enough to make me forget. How was it possible that I did everything right, and somehow it still wasn't good enough? Already, I was disqualified from competing as an Olympian, my scores were still up in the air from last season, and I was forced to attend an arts school for shits and giggles. *Haven't I been punished enough?*

"Do you want to talk about it?" Akilah asked quietly.

I shook my head. Talking about it would only make me more angry because I couldn't actually do anything about it.

"Well, can I?" she persisted. "I'm curious."

"Of course you are," I muttered. "Go ahead."

"Is this what you meant when you said you had bad luck?"

I took a second to think about it and came to a quick realization, "This ain't got nothing to do with luck. This is karma."

"You don't really think you deserve all this, do you?"

"You saw the video. What do you think?"

Akilah's eyes roamed over my face, probably reading much more than I wanted her to. She didn't say anything for a while, but she pursed her lips as she thought over her next words.

"I think"—her eyes cast down to her feet, which were swinging back and forth over the neatly trimmed grass—"that I wasn't there, so I can't judge."

I barked a sarcastic laugh. "You can be honest, Akilah. I've pretty much heard it all."

"I am being honest. I mean, the video was hard to watch. If I didn't know you, I would definitely think the worst of you too. I can't even imagine what would've happened if nobody stopped you, but they *did* stop you."

"Doesn't change the fact that I did it."

"Right. But it also doesn't mean you deserve to be punished by everybody with an opinion."

"What's your opinion?"

Akilah surprised me with a laugh. "Haven't you had enough of people telling you what they think about you?"

That was true. I'd read through enough hate comments to last me a lifetime. I knew what the world thought of me, but I wanted to know what she thought, or if she felt the same.

"One more won't hurt," I said.

"Okay. I think that the person I saw in that video wasn't you. The Jevon I know is way too serious and brooding . . . like all the time! But you're actually a nice guy, even though you don't always show it. Surprisingly, you're a really good dancer, and—" Akilah stopped short, as if she suddenly realized what she was saying.

"What? Say it."

"Nothing. It's a short list, but that's what I think of you."

I could tell there was more she wanted to say, but I didn't push it.

"Thanks," I said instead.

"You're welcome."

The geese suddenly squawked at us as a few of them invaded our space. Their gaggle was moving on to find more scattered food, taking all the noise with them.

Akilah sighed as she rose from her seat. "That was thirty minutes. It wasn't that bad, was it?"

"Well, it wasn't a trap."

She squinted her eyes at my comment. "Give me thirty more minutes, and I bet you'll take that back."

I started to smile at the serious expression on her face. What was she trying to prove?

"Deal?" She stuck a hand out for me to shake.

I stared at her outstretched hand.

"What happens if I don't take it back?"

Akilah grinned so wide it made her giggle. "Then I'll tell you what I was really going to say earlier."

"Deal." I answered quickly.

Akilah led the way back toward the car. I trailed behind as I realized one very impressive thing: she had just done the impossible. She'd successfully shifted me out of my bad mood without violence, and I wasn't sure how to feel about that.

CHAPTER EIGHTEEN

Akilah

I convinced Jevon to take us to the family-owned diner in midtown: Shack Daddy's. It was the best place in the city to get a good cheese-burger. Jevon and I were sitting at a booth across from the entrance. It was my favorite spot in the diner because it was closest to the jukebox, and I got a pretty good view of the spray painted murals on the buildings that lined the street. I always hoped I'd see my art decorating a building one day. I thought it was an amazing honor.

While we waited for our server to come and take our orders, I took the time to think about how I'd even gotten here. At first, I'd felt very stupid for barging my way into Jevon's house uninvited. Although we had become friends, it wasn't really my place to show up for him in that way.

When he'd stormed out of the house, Jevon's friends were quick to point fingers.

"Why would you show him that video?" Trisha went in on Kent. "Are you trying to make him feel worse?"

"Me? What about you? Miss, 'Respond! Respond! These are death threats!'" He mimicked her voice.

"I do not sound like that."

"Yes, you do, and you don't know how to shut up."

"Both of ya'll need to shut up!" Darius boomed.

They bickered for a while. I hardly paid attention to them. My eyes lingered on the door he'd slammed shut as exited the room.

There was something in his eyes that I just couldn't put my finger on. It was like a sadness that nobody else seemed to notice.

Kayla blocked my view of the door. "Tell me you're not thinking about going after him."

I gave her a guilty smile. "Would you be mad if I did?"

I was Kayla's ride, and she'd hinted at wanting to leave earlier. If I went to check on Jevon, then I'd ultimately leave her stranded here.

"No, but I don't think you should. It didn't seem like he wanted the company."

"He needs a friend right now."

"Are you sure about that?"

For that, I had no answer.

"AJ, I just don't want you to get your feelings hurt."

"I don't think I will."

She rolled her eyes. "Okay go, but leave your keys with me."

I dug my car keys out of my purse and placed them in her waiting hand.

"Good luck," she said.

"Thanks."

Now, as I sat across from him in the brightly colored booth, I couldn't sense any of the sadness or anger from before. Jevon's habitually quiet brooding was normally cute and kind of mysterious, but this was different. He seemed unguarded, almost comfortable here with me.

"Have you been here before?" I asked.

He'd been staring at the menu for a while, flipping the laminated page over to the back for other options. I knew what I wanted before I'd even walked through the door.

"No, I haven't."

"You don't get out much, do you?" I was only joking, but Jevon smiled sheepishly down at the table.

"Actually, I don't. There's not a lot of free time outside of work."

"Really?"

He nodded.

Until now, I hadn't realized that fighting was like a job for him. I'd never worked a day in my life, and I couldn't imagine having responsibilities outside of school. CSA on its own was like a true nine to five, with all the class work and constant competition.

"Wow," I breathed, "that must get really tiring."

Jevon shrugged. "It's the life I chose."

A slim, lanky guy with freckles approached our booth then. He bore an overworked smile as he pulled out a pad and pen.

"Hi, my name is Franklin, and I'll be your server toda—" His eyes drifted over to Jevon, who was busy scanning the menu. Franklin's face instantly froze in shock. "Whoa, you're Jevon Williams!"

For a small sliver of a second, I had forgotten all about Jevon's infamy. He was a prized fighter after all, and he was currently the number one trending topic on Twitter.

"What are *you* doing here?" Franklin asked in awe. You would've thought he'd come face to face with his idol.

"Hi, Franklin," Jevon drew a very charming smile. Was this how he was with his fans? "I'm just here to eat."

"Bro, can I please get a picture?" Franklin begged. "My brother's never gonna believe this! We watch you all the time!"

"Sure, but after you take our orders."

Jevon winked at me, purposefully bringing me into the conversation. Why did that simple gesture make my ears all hot? Jevon's ultimatum did little to deter Franklin's excitement.

"What would you like?" Franklin asked Jevon.

Jevon brought the attention back to me. "Akilah?"

With a disappointed sigh, Franklin turned to face me. "What would you like?"

I kept my attitude at bay as I gave him my order. Daddy always taught me to respect the people making and/or serving my food, mostly because I didn't want to discover spit on my plate. When I was finished, Franklin turned back to Jevon.

"Make that two of whatever she's having," Jevon said quickly.

Franklin rushed to collect our menus and pull out his phone. In his excitement, he nearly tripped over the chair behind him. Jevon was patient as he stood and waited for Franklin to get a good angle. With Jevon's height, it was hard to get them both in the frame on selfie mode, so Franklin thrust his phone into my hands.

He held the biggest grin as he posed beside Jevon with both thumbs in the air. I took a couple snapshots of the two and returned his phone. Franklin smiled proudly as he pocketed his device.

"Hey, don't worry about the haters," he said to Jevon. "You deserve that title. I stand with you."

"Um, thank you."

"No problem. I'll be back with your drinks soon."

Franklin headed back toward the kitchen and I developed a sudden staring problem.

"What?" Jevon asked.

"You didn't tell me you were *that* famous."

Jevon snorted. "I'm not *that* famous."

"So, we didn't just meet your number one fan?"

"That doesn't count. I've been viral all day. You didn't know who I was when you met me."

"True, but my little brother did. CJ told me how nice you were to him. He's convinced you're like best friends now."

Jevon smiled, but he didn't comment. It was starting to make much more sense why Jevon was the way he was. I wondered if this kind of thing happened a lot, strangers fawning over him and asking for pictures. Could that be another reason he didn't get out much?

As promised, Franklin came back quickly with our milkshakes. He placed them carefully in front of us as they overflowed with whipped cream and cookie crumbles. I'd asked for a cookies and cream milkshake with three cherries on top, my favorite. We sipped our shakes slowly, savoring their sweetness.

"Speaking of best friends," I grinned, "Trisha told me how she used to beat you up when you were kids."

Jevon made a face. "She's gotta stop telling that story."

"So, it's true?"

"Trish likes to exaggerate. She probably told you half the truth."

"I don't think so." I was starting to crack up before I could even finish. "Bougie Boots."

Jevon deadpanned. The look on his face, only made me laugh harder. He had no idea he'd be known as Bougie Boots from now on. I took another sip of my shake. It was starting to liquify and become easier to pull through my straw.

"Well, well, well," a voice boomed across the diner.

Our heads snapped toward the entrance where a small group had emerged. A man in a sleeveless muscle shirt approached our booth. He looked young, but much older than us. Maybe in his mid-twenties. He was flanked by two others who smiled at us like their day had just gotten better.

At first, I thought they were more fans of Jevon's. They appeared both surprised and excited to be in his presence, but in a way that was unlike Franklin's reaction.

It was when muscle shirt pulled up a chair from the table beside us, and sat at the end of our booth that I knew something was off. The man quickly made himself comfortable as he propped his elbows on the table, invading our limited space. My eyes swiftly darted over to Jevon to gauge his reaction, but he was eerily calm.

That was odd.

"You've got a lot of nerve," the man said to Jevon. "After what you did, you should be in jail."

"You cheated!" the man's entourage backed him up.

By now, Jevon's face was a well-rehearsed mask of tranquility. He didn't appear hostile, but I noticed the subtle twitch in his eye as he addressed the men.

"I get it. You're fans of Jao Shang. That's fine, but I'm just here to eat, alright? I'm not looking for trouble."

"They should've never let you get away with that," muscle shirt went on. "You wouldn't last one round with me."

At this, Jevon laughed. It wasn't a humorous laugh, but one that I was sure kept him from losing it. He looked the man directly in his eyes, while simultaneously addressing all three of them.

"Look, I'm only going to say this one more time, and I really hope it clicks. I'm not looking for a fight, so let's not do something we'll all regret."

There was no malice in Jevon's voice. In fact, if I didn't know any better, I would've thought he was being polite. Jevon smiled that rare handsome smile of his, but unlike any other time, all hints of friendliness were gone. He was like the calm before the storm.

The man hesitated, as if he'd expected a different response. Left with no comeback, and no other choice really, he rose from his seat and returned the chair. He puffed out his chest like he was unafraid, but he seemed to comply with Jevon's request. I didn't fully trust it, but their group started to head back the way they'd come. Muscle shirt trailed behind slower, and he kept his eyes on Jevon the whole way to his table.

"That was weird," I whispered when I was sure they were gone.

"No." Jevon shook his head. "That was the trap."

I was confused.

"You lost." He smirked, seemingly unaffected by his almost-altercation.

Then it hit me. The bet we'd made at the park.

"Technically, it's been more than thirty minutes," I argued.

Jevon glanced at the watch on his wrist. "Oh, yeah, you're right."

All of a sudden, he flagged down our server, and Franklin was at our booth in no time.

"Can we get our order to go?" Jevon asked.

"Sure thing!"

Did he really just . . . ?

"What are you doing?" I asked.

"Time's up."

CHAPTER NINETEEN

Jevon

"We didn't have to leave," Akilah grumbled as I pulled out of the narrow parking spot.

"Yes, we did."

If I had stayed there any longer, I would've eventually broken every rule I had ever learned. As a professional trained in the arts, it was highly frowned upon to engage in any physical altercation outside the dojo; especially with a noncombatant.

I had to force myself to ease my foot off the gas pedal. It took a lot of effort for me to walk away from a guy begging for a fight. I should've been proud of myself, but all I could feel was more anger building and growing inside me.

I felt so stupid. From the start, it didn't feel right being out in the open after all the backlash I'd received from the video. People online had basically painted a target on my back, and I'd made it all too easy for them.

My phone rang then, halting all the music because it was connected to the Bluetooth in the car. It was an unsaved number, but I had long since memorized my parents' office number. I picked up on the third ring.

"Hello?" My father's voice vibrated through the speakers.

I turned him down a little before responding, "Hey, Pops."

"I'm glad I caught you, son. Is now a good time?"

I glanced at Akilah in the passenger seat. She had our food in her lap as she gazed out the window. I wasn't worried about Pops revealing something confidential, but I doubted that he'd respect having listening ears on a business conversation. Even my mother was left out of most of our meetings.

"Not really," I answered. "Is it important?"

"If I'm calling you from the office, you should always assume it's important."

I slowed to a stop as we got caught up in the line of slow-moving traffic.

Pops took my silence as his cue to go on. "Dave is working to get the video removed, but there's no guarantee. The internet is forever, and we know how that goes. For now, we're working on a cease and desist letter for the original post and any blog that continues to run articles on it."

"Okay, that's good." I sighed. "Bad news?"

Knowing my father, for every ounce of good news he had to offer, there was always a little bad news to go along with it.

"Well, this video coming to light doesn't help your case. Any move the judges were making on your final decision could be delayed by now. Now that the public has shared their viewpoint, it's not just about merits and technicalities. It's about appealing to their viewers, and a lot of them are standing against you. This may not go in your favor, Jevon. You should prepare for that."

All I ever did was prepare for the worst. What else was new? In my peripheral, I could see Akilah watching me. She probably held the same look of pity I was trying to escape from earlier.

"But you don't need to worry about that right now," Pops continued. "Aside from training, all I need you to focus on is your education."

I heaved a very audible sigh, knowing exactly where this was going.

"I know this isn't your favorite topic, but like I told you before, college isn't off the table."

"Not yet," I added.

"Net yet," he agreed. "Still, a few of my old colleagues are faculty members at my alma mater, Emory University. All it takes is a phone call and a good recommendation letter. Your future is set either way."

Was it really my future if it was crafted at the hands of my father? Emory University was as close to Ivy League as I would ever hope to get. It was a pretty high-ranking school, a school I knew I had no chance of getting into on my own.

Maybe I should've been grateful. Even with all the odds stacked against me, Pops was trying to make a way for me to succeed. Although, if I couldn't make it as a fighter, and I was forced into college, then I'd only ever feel like a failure.

"I'll think about it," I said. It wasn't a no, but it definitely wasn't what Pops wanted to hear. He paused again, this time to grumble a few choice words away from the phone.

"Was there anything else?" I asked.

"Yes, just one last thing. Your mother and I will be home late, so you're on your own for dinner. I want you to take a look at the contract in the blue folder on my desk. I highlighted a few areas I think we can negotiate, but other than that, it's pretty much ready for you to sign."

"Alright, I'll check it later."

"Great, I'll see you at home."

When he hung up, the music started back up instantly. I fully intended to zone out as we inched our way through the traffic. We had barely moved a foot since merging onto the freeway. Akilah had other ideas, though. She turned down the music and shifted in her seat.

"That was your dad?"

"Yeah." I nodded.

"Why didn't you tell him what happened at the diner? It seems like he could help."

"Help with what? Nothing happened."

"Something *almost* happened."

"I had it under control." Pops was a very busy man. If I told him about every little thing that went wrong, then how would he ever trust me to handle more responsibility in my own career?

Akilah gave me an indignant look. Her brows scrunched together like she was worried, but she screwed up her lips like she was thinking of something she'd rather not say aloud. Then, she scoffed and shook her head.

"What now?" I asked.

"You have it so good, and you don't even appreciate it."

"Are you for real?" I nearly slammed on the brakes. "After everything you saw today? You listen to one phone call, and you think I got it good now?"

"I know you do."

"You don't know a damn thing."

Everybody had an opinion, and they always assumed the wrong things. Akilah wasn't backing down, though. She looped one of her arms out of the seatbelt's hold and turned her body fully to face me.

"I know you have options after you graduate," she went on. "I know you have a fully involved parent who's willing to help you reach your goals. To some people, that's everything."

"You mean you? What, because you think you're stuck? You're not stuck, and you don't need help, you just need to try."

It was no secret that Akilah was playing catch up with all of her friends. She'd told me as much the day I came over to work on the sculpture. She had no plans for her future, and not because she couldn't, but because she didn't try.

"So, now I'm lazy because I actually have to work to get into a good school? Is that what you think?"

"I think you make things harder than they have to be."

"You're one to talk."

"Maybe." I shrugged. "Or maybe I'm just telling you the truth."

"Or, maybe *you* don't know a damn thing."

Akilah folded her arms and turned back toward the road. Her knee bounced lightly as she scowled at the windshield. Her silence was a welcomed change, but it was also condemning, and very effective.

I merged into the far left lane as soon as there was a break in the flow of traffic. It wasn't much better, but we at least weren't moving at a snail's pace anymore.

"I'm sorry," I said. "I shouldn't have said that. You are half right, though. I do have it better than most and I don't take that for granted, but it's still not easy for me and I think you know that."

She only glanced at me from the corner of her eyes, but I could see her features begin to soften.

"I do," she said softly.

The road cleared up more as the sun began to set. Akilah lived closer to the east side, which was a good distance away from where I lived in north Atlanta. The drive was long, but it wasn't terrible.

After a while, we had even started a safer conversation, one that strayed away from college and the future. But Akilah was too curious for her own good.

"What happens if you're not able to fight anymore?" Akilah asked when she grew bored of talking about spirit week at school.

"What do you mean?"

"I mean, it sounds like you don't want to go to college," she paused, waiting to see if I'd object—I didn't, "so if worse comes to worse, and you can't fight because of that video, what's your next step?"

"Like a backup plan?"

She nodded.

"College is supposed to be my backup plan. My dad's got it in his head that I'm gonna run the family business one day, champion or not."

Akilah chuckled. "That sounds familiar."

"Really?"

"I think my parents secretly hope that visual art is just a phase for me. They're always saying I should major in something more practical, like business, or marketing, or literally anything that would get me a job in the next four years. I haven't applied to anywhere because . . . I don't know, I just don't want to make the wrong choice, you know?"

I didn't know.

I didn't know that Akilah was second-guessing her future. I didn't know what it was like to *not* know what I wanted. Fighting had been my goal for so long that I couldn't imagine wanting anything else.

"You're going to have to choose soon," I said.

"Yeah, I know, but what about you?" She suddenly perked up. "If fighting was off the table and you didn't have to run the family business, what would you do? Who would you be?"

"I don't know."

I wasn't good at anything else. What else could I be? I wasn't a scholar, I definitely wasn't an artist, and other sports bored me. My imagination wasn't strong enough to conjure up a life outside of Silat. It didn't exist.

"You didn't even try." She laughed.

"What would you do?" I asked instead, "Who would Akilah be if she wasn't an artist?"

A small, almost shy smile came over her face. I tried to think of some other talent Akilah could possess and came up empty. Akilah *was* art.

"I've always been interested in archaeology." She shrugged as if it were no big deal. Her answer was something I never would've guessed. "All my life, I've been in and out of museums. When I wasn't lost somewhere in an art museum, my mom would force me to go to historic museums. I just remember being excited to see all the artifacts from ancient Egypt, Greece, and Rome. If I become an archaeologist, I feel like I could be touching history, and that somehow makes me become a part of it."

It was then that I realized Akilah saw the world in color. By default, I felt blind in her presence.

"Oh, it's right here." Akilah pointed to her neighborhood's entrance. I didn't realize I was staring until I almost missed the turn.

I made a right and followed the path all way to the end at the cul-de-sac. Parking near her curb, I waited for her to gather her things. When she had everything, she opened her door but paused before getting out.

"Do you want to have dinner with us? You don't have to eat alone. My dad's cooking tonight, and I promise it'll be better than this." Akilah gestured to the bag of food in her hands.

"I would, but—"

"It's okay," she interrupted. "I just thought I would put it out there."

"Thank you."

Akilah hopped out of the passenger seat and turned to face me.

"Before I forget, since I lost the bet, what I was going to say at the park was: Surprisingly, you're a really good dancer, and . . . you're not a bad kisser either."

Without meaning to, my eyes drifted down to her lips. Akilah chewed lightly on her bottom lip, and I suddenly couldn't look away.

"Well, good night," Akilah said before closing the door and heading inside.

Before that, I thought I had said something similar to "um," or "okay," but I wasn't sure. What the hell was wrong with me?

CHAPTER TWENTY

Akilah

On Sunday, I went to the High Museum of Art. It wasn't exactly planned, but I found myself thinking more about college after overhearing a conversation Momma had with her friends.

I heard her bragging about CJ and his recent tour of the Morehouse campus. She went on and on to her friends as they took turns telling each other how proud they were of their kids. When asked about me, she said, "Kiki is still doing her art thing. She's so talented, but I'm hoping she'll branch out more at a well-rounded school. Vicky, you know this world can be cruel to artists."

For Momma, well-rounded meant traditional, boring. She was a dancer, for crying out loud! Just because she never graced the stage as an Alvin Ailey performer didn't mean my dreams would be crushed too. I couldn't picture myself in a cubical, pushing papers and staring at a computer screen all day.

That wasn't living! I wanted more, so much more, out of life and my future. Art gave me vision, it promised possibilities. It was exactly what I wanted . . . but if I was being honest, I had to admit I was a little scared.

Besides the late greats in the history books, I didn't know many successful artists. I hardly knew any that looked like me. In a way, Momma was right: the world was cruel to artists. If I let that fear take away my dream, though, I didn't know if I could ever forgive myself.

I hoped that by visiting the High Museum of Art, I would remember why I fell in love with the arts. Maybe I would get the push I needed to make a choice and stand by it, regardless of what my mother said.

I headed up the steps to the building, following behind a family that was obviously visiting from out of town. They walked slowly, taking the time to stop and read up on every visual we passed by.

When we made it through the hallway, I breezed past them in a hurry. There was nowhere for me to be, but the building was huge. I was sure I'd stumble upon something new and interesting.

The stairs led me up to the first exhibit. I didn't stay there long. It was a Sunday, so the museum wasn't that busy, but there were too many tourists hovering around the pieces. I found a separate set of stairs and headed up to the third floor.

There was a group set up in the middle. Their chairs formed a wide circle near the windows at one corner of the floor. At the center of the group was an all too familiar face.

"Ms. Hazel?" I asked when I was close enough for her to see me.

She looked up in surprise. "AJ, Hi!"

"What are you doing here?"

"I teach classes for the teen art program on the weekends." She gestured to her class, "Class, this is one of my students at Cambridge School of Arts. Akilah, meet the Teen Team."

I gave them all a wave. I couldn't be sure, but I had a feeling I was the oldest "Teen" in the room.

"I didn't know you were part of the art program," Ms. Hazel went on. "Grab a seat."

"I'm not." I didn't even know there was a program for teens, but I did as instructed. "I came for the inspiration."

"Well, you just found it! I was going to be the live model for this group to practice their freehand, but I think you can take it from here."

"Ms. Hazel, really?" I complained. I never liked being on the other side of the canvas.

"Do you want extra credit on the midterm, or not?" She bribed me.

My jaw dropped in surprise and her students giggled at my reaction. Ms. Hazel pulled an empty chair into the center of the circle and waited for me to take the seat.

I trudged over and plopped down as I settled on a pose I thought would be easy for them. With my feet one foot apart, I straightened my posture and placed both hands on my knees. They got to work quickly, glancing up to stare at everything from my hair, down to the laces in my sneakers.

Being a model was uncomfortable work. Having people notice every single detail in your features, every flaw, was not ideal. I sat still as stone as I watched Ms. Hazel go around the circle, giving advice and pointers.

Everyone was staring, but when Ms. Hazel stared at me, I could tell she was glad it was me sitting here and not her. I couldn't see what anyone was doing, but from the two students sitting in front of me, I had a feeling they were doing okay. Ms. Hazel hardly stopped to make any corrections for them. She even nodded in approval every so often.

After a while, I felt a kink being to build at the base of my neck. I kept still though, praying she would give me a break soon. A few students left their seats to get a closer look, and I tried not to flinch at their proximity.

"May I?" a girl no older than thirteen asked to adjust my left hand. I nodded and she spread my fingers out over my knee. When she was satisfied with her changes, she moved back to her seat and got to sketching.

"Thirty more seconds," Ms. Hazel warned them, taking another stroll around the circle.

I counted down in my head, but Ms. Hazel counted slower. By the time she said, "Pencils down!" It had already been a full minute.

"Pass your clipboards up to the front, and you can all head over to the next activity," Ms. Hazel instructed.

One by one, her class placed the clipboards in her hands as they dispersed to other parts of the building. When they were all gone, she turned to me with a smile.

"Thanks for volunteering, AJ. You didn't have to do that."

"Anytime," I said sarcastically.

Ms. Hazel came over and placed a few clipboards in my hands. Without warning, or any sort of notice, I had suddenly become her helper.

"What do you think?" she asked, passing me four out of the ten clipboards in her hands.

Since it was freehand drawing, everyone's style was completely unique to them. It wasn't as neat as it could have been, given the short time limit, but I was honestly impressed with how quickly they were able to capture my frame and a few minor details.

"These look good." I juggled the different clipboards. "The only critique I have is they could use a little more work on facial expressions. I look like a cartoon character here." I pointed to the drawing and Ms. Hazel took down my note.

"That's something we can work on next weekend."

I hoped that by "we" she meant her and the art program. My volunteered time was just enough to get me a good grade on the midterm.

"Come with me. We'll take these to my office. I've been on my feet all day."

Ms. Hazel led the way through a brand new exhibit that was still being put together. She walked brusquely, like she wasn't fascinated by all the colorful sculptures being put together. I stared at everything as we passed through, making a mental reminder to comeback someday when it was finished.

Down the hall, Ms. Hazel came to a stop at door 322. It was unlocked and she held the door open for me to come inside. Her office was cold. It had a peculiar scent of red Georgia clay and epoxy resin.

"You can put those clipboards on my desk."

I placed them neatly into the wire bin at the corner. Ms. Hazel did the same and finally took a seat at an empty chair near her unfinished project. She sighed gratefully.

"It was so good to see you today, AJ. You should come more often."

"I don't know, Ms. Hazel. I'm not really into the—"

"It's not just about drawing in circles. There's plenty of opportunities for you to volunteer and reach out to the community." I opened my mouth to shut her down again, but Ms. Hazel was relentless. "There's even a summer internship program that would look great on a college application. How is that going by the way?"

"Um, it's going okay," I lied.

"Just okay?" Ms. Hazel did that thing that all teachers did when they were about to pry for more information. She leaned back in her seat, crossing her legs at the ankles as she clasped her hands together in her lap.

"Yeah, it's still early, so I haven't heard anything back yet."

"AJ, it's almost October. Usually, they send out responses within two weeks. When did you start applying?"

"Uh . . ." I pretended to count back the days in my head. "Not that long ago."

Ms. Hazel arched a brow, unimpressed and unamused by my performance.

"What's going on? Is everything okay?"

"Mmhmm." I nodded, looking away so she couldn't continue to read me.

"That sounded believable." She chuckled.

I took a deep breath and held it there for a while. When I let it go, I turned back to face her. Ms. Hazel seemed genuinely concerned.

"Okay, if I ask you a question, can you promise to answer it honestly?" I asked.

"I can try."

Good enough.

"Do you really think it's worth it to pursue art after high school? I mean, realistically speaking?"

"Where is this coming from?"

"It's something I've been thinking about lately. I don't want to be stuck because I made the wrong choice."

"Akilah, I don't understand. This doesn't sound like you at all. Are you feeling overwhelmed about the senior art show? Is there a way I can help?"

"No, my sculpture is almost finished."

"Well, did something happen?"

"No." I prayed she didn't hear the crack in my voice. "I was just wondering."

Whether or not Ms. Hazel believed me, she didn't show it. She appeared thoughtful as she tapped her clasped fingers against her knuckles.

"To be honest, I can't tell you if it's worth it to pursue your passion. That's for you to discover. Every dream comes with some level of difficulty. If it were easy, then it would never be worthy enough to be called a dream.

"What I *can* tell you is I wouldn't be who I am today if I never went after mine. Believe me, it was hard, but I wouldn't change a thing. I made the most of every opportunity that came my way." She gave me a pointed stare. "And who knows? Maybe one of these days, we'll walk past *my* exhibit, on the way to *my* office, in *this* very building."

It wasn't until the end that I started putting the pieces together.

I gasped. "Ms. Hazel, is that your exhibit being put together out there?"

She didn't give me a direct answer, but she smiled . . . so I knew.

"Like I said." She stood. "I wouldn't change a thing."

I stood too. We both heard the sounds of multiple footsteps all headed in the same direction up the hall. They must've been her students because she headed for the door and I followed suit.

"I hope that answered your question," Ms. Hazel said as we followed the sounds of the footsteps.

"It did, thank you." She had no idea how helpful that was.

It felt like a weight had been lifted off my chest. My options didn't seem so black and white anymore. I wasn't condemning myself to failure if I went after my passion, and I could still be true to myself even if I was unsure of the journey.

"Think about what I said earlier," she paused at the staircase, "about those opportunities."

"Is this you offering me the summer internship?"

She snorted out a laugh. "No, you'll have to apply and interview for that. You should consider volunteering on the weekends, though. These kids could learn a lot from you. You're one of my best students."

"I'll think about it," I said, and I would. I had more than enough to think about. "Thank you, Ms. Hazel."

"See you at school, AJ."

Ms. Hazel turned in the opposite direction, leaving me at the stairs. I descended them slowly, taking the time to stare at her work being put together. I guess now I knew one successful artist who looked like me.

CHAPTER TWENTY-ONE

Jevon

My first match of the season was Tuesday. Tomorrow. I had one day to get my shit together.

Ever since last week, when I'd struggled to target Nick's pressure point, Sasha watched me like a hawk. I stayed late most days, working until I was sore and aching by the time I left. That satisfied Sasha enough to keep her promise not tell Pops on me. The last thing I needed was for him to show up at the dojo just to see for himself.

Today, I sparred with Sasha right before school. She trained me harder this morning than she had in weeks. I knew she was anxious about Shane Tithers visiting, but she seemed to get some kind of pleasure out of kicking my ass.

I quickly ducked low to the floor to dodge one of Sasha's brutal roundhouse kicks. Her strikes were always swift and powerful. Because of her size, she maneuvered easily around my defenses. It was impossible to land a good blow on her.

"Too slow." Sasha scorned as I scarcely avoided a mean lift kick.

"Sasha," I groaned, struggling to catch my breath.

I normally wasn't much of a complainer, but today was different.

"Get up, Jevon," she said, going over to the weaponry podium.

After rummaging through all the practice weapons, Sasha pulled out a Tongkat—a fighting stick used in Silat—and threw it my way. I caught it and skillfully twirled the staff in my hands as I prepared for the onset of her attack.

Sasha was a master in the art of Silat. She knew the ins and outs of every weapon, fighting stance, and move I could muster. It was best to play it safe with her, especially with the mood she was in.

Quick like lightning, I could hear the whoosh of her swing as her Tongkat came down to clash against mine. I had barely enough time to bring mine up in answer to her strike before she expertly swung her weapon in the air again, only inches from my face.

"Tighten up your defense, Jay," Nick coached from the sidelines.

He wasn't as hard on me as Sasha was, but he was nervous about tomorrow too. This left no room for error my part. I had to be great. I lifted the Tongkat high above my head and spun it into an offensive position. Playing defense with Sasha wasn't working. It pretty much made me her target, so I thought I'd try something else.

Sasha stood confidently, ready to answer my next move with one of her own. As I observed her, I noticed a slight opening for attack in her stance. It was barely noticeable, but it was there. In two swift moves, I let my staff smack against hers. Just as quickly, I brought the stick back up and swept it under her left ankle, causing her to lose her balance.

Sasha landed hard on her back, but she recovered instantly. Arching her back away from the floor, she flipped herself up into a standing position. I gave her time to catch her breath, but that was a mistake. Sasha whipped her staff in a crisscross maneuver that forced me to back away.

She struck me once on the side of my face, then again in the arm. The sting of her blows felt like sharp pens and needles jabbing at my skin. When Sasha struck at me a third time, I caught her Tongkat in my hand mid-swing, and pulled it with enough force to bring her barreling into me. As she came closer, I lifted my leg into a side-kick, effectively knocking her back down to the ground.

Her weapon was mine now, but I threw it off to the side. Sasha quickly rolled out of the way just as I prepared to take another swing. She dodged most of my hits, but the few that I landed slowed her down just enough for me to have the upper hand in this fight.

Nick threw a rag onto the floor mat, signaling us to break. Sasha got up sluggishly, but she came over and tapped her knuckles against mine, a proud grin spreading across her face.

"Nice work. Do that tomorrow, and you're golden, baby!"

I smiled too. It felt good to get one thing right.

"That's it for today, Jevon." Nick called over his shoulder as he led Sasha down the hall to his office.

* * *

School started off kind of strange. At first, I didn't notice the way people went out of their way to give me space when I walked by or made a sudden move. I thought they'd be used to me being at CSA by now, but maybe I was wrong.

After the third dude nearly jogged out of my way when I headed into my English class, I discreetly sniffed my shirt to make sure there wasn't another reason my classmates were acting so funny. I caught the light hint of my soap, and I knew that wasn't the issue.

That's when the staring began.

It started with a couple of my classmates at the front, who whispered to each other when our English teacher, Mrs. Parker, turned her back. Soon after, they turned to me and stared, their eyes wide in wonder.

I did my best to ignore it, but their eyes suddenly fell on me like a domino effect, one after another. Whispered conversations became much more audible with half the class joining in. I didn't have to guess to know why they were staring. That video was still up, and I was still trending.

"Excuse me, class!" Mrs. Parker clapped her hands with each syllable to bring everybody's attention back to her.

Her eyes landed on me, just like everybody else, but she looked confused. Either she hadn't seen the video, or she did a poor job of acting like it. Mrs. Parker continued on with class anyway, as if it hadn't been interrupted.

It wasn't so much of an issue that people were staring at me, it was the way they looked at me that rubbed me the wrong way. They acted like I would lose control at any moment. If I had to endure this all day, then maybe it was good for them to stay away.

CHAPTER TWENTY-TWO

Akilah

After school on Monday, I met up with Ms. Hazel to get her critiques on my piece for the upcoming exhibit. I'd told her before that I was almost finished, but the truth was I kept changing my ideas on how I wanted to present it.

We were standing in the art studio with my sculpture on my station. Ms. Hazel observed my piece with the utmost scrutiny. She had her reading glasses perched loosely on the bridge of her nose as she examined every line, indent, and crease I'd made into the clay.

Ms. Hazel was brutally honest, but she was always helpful. I valued her opinion deeply. If Ms. Hazel loved it, then the art critics would too.

"When do you expect to be finished?" she asked.

"Soon. I want to paint it all black when I'm done."

Her eyes snapped up to me sharply like I was crazy. "Don't paint it."

"Okay." I waited as she took another stroll around the station, but she was taking too long to say anything. "So, what do you think?"

"I think you should finish it," she came to a stop beside me, "because this may be one of the best visuals you've ever created. I can't wait to see the finished product."

I released the breath I didn't know I was holding. Ms. Hazel picked up a carving tool and marked off the areas that needed to be cleaned up. She wasn't one to give too much praise, so for her to compliment my work meant a lot to me.

Weeks from now, my work would go in front of the most important people I'd ever meet, and I'd already gotten approval from one of the toughest critics I knew. All this time I'd spent worrying about whether I was good enough, all the nights I'd spent wondering if my dreams were even worth it, and suddenly, they felt more real, more tangible, within my reach.

"I shouldn't tell you this." Ms. Hazel continued to mark up my sculpture. "But I've been bragging about you."

"Really? To who?"

She shook her head. "Just know I'm not the only one looking forward to this."

"Can I guess?"

"You can try."

Ms. Hazel was well-connected in the industry. She knew professionals all over the east coast. If she wanted, she could help me get into just about any school on the east through word of mouth alone.

"Will there be anybody from Ivory Middleton at the senior art show?" I asked instead.

"Oh." She raised her brows in surprise. "You're interested Ivory Middleton?"

She couldn't have been more surprised if I'd said I planned to go to a law school. Okay, true, Ivory Middleton School of Visual Arts was like the Juilliard of fine arts schools. Getting in was a one in a million shot.

"It's my top school."

"Why didn't you tell me about this yesterday?"

"Because of your reaction just now. You don't think I can get in."

It wasn't a question.

"I didn't say that."

You didn't have to.

Ms. Hazel dropped the sculpting tool and went to grab the blue file accordion from her desk. She opened the pouch on the station across from me and thumbed through the different files for a while.

"To answer your first question . . ." She pulled out single sheets of papers one at a time. "No, I don't know anybody connected to Ivory Middleton, but I did invite administrators from other schools in New York."

I busied myself with cleaning up the areas Ms. Hazel had marked off. There were a few uneven spots in the arms of my bust that I scraped away and smoothed down with my fingers. Next, I deepened the creases of Jevon's chest and added more detail to the surface of his skin. With a wet sponge, I dabbed at the impressions left behind by my fingerprints.

"Ivory Middleton is a tough school to get into. They won't accept just anybody."

I sighed. "I know that."

"What I'm saying is, you have to be more than just talented for them to notice you, AJ. Of course you have the talent, but what sets you apart from everybody else? Why should they pick you over any other artist?"

"I don't know." I shrugged. "I don't have a sob story to give these people."

"Who says they're looking for a sob story?"

"They're always looking for a sob story! You just said so yourself—they don't care about how talented I am or how good my grades are. All these colleges want to know is how much more pitiful my life is compared to everybody else's."

I hated to admit it; I hated myself for even thinking it, but a part of me believed that Kayla was so easily accepted into Ivory Middleton because of her own tear-jerking story. A father that passed away from brain cancer and a single mother who'd be devastated when she left. I'd never be able to top that.

Ms. Hazel chuckled, and I instantly stopped what I was doing.

"Did I say something funny?"

She wasn't affected at all by my tone. Instead, she collected the short stack of papers she got from the file accordion and walked back over to my station.

"Yes, you did. It's funny that you think you have to be pitiful to get into a great school."

"Well, I can't be great either, can I ?" I mumbled.

"I know this all sounds very complicated, but it's not. It is true that the saddest stories get the most attention, but that doesn't always mean they'll be accepted. Most colleges want to know if you can be beneficial to them, as much as they're beneficial to you."

"What does that even mean?"

Ms. Hazel spread the pages out in front of me. My hands were dirty from the clay, so I used my elbow to pull one toward me. In bold letters, the top of the page read "Summer Internship Application." It was for the High Museum of Art, the same program Ms. Hazel tried to recruit me for yesterday.

"How does this benefit Ivory Middleton?" I asked. From where I stood, interning at the museum only benefitted Ms. Hazel. The whole time I was there, she'd used me like I was her personal assistant.

"Because doing this means that you're not just an artist. It means you're capable of caring about something other than yourself."

She pointed to another page that highlighted community service and something about a Big Sister, Little Sister painting class.

"How do you want to present yourself to one of the best schools in the country? Do you want to be someone who's good at art? Or, do you want to be someone who does great things and just so happens to be a really talented artist?"

When she put it that way, there wasn't an argument good enough for a comeback. Without another word, Ms. Hazel returned the file accordion back to her desk and left the studio shortly after. The silence she left behind brought a ringing to my ears that felt exactly like a wakeup call.

CHAPTER TWENTY-THREE

Jevon

Tuesday. Fight Day. A good day.

It was like a chant that kept up a rhythm in my head. I woke up feeling better than I had since starting at Cambridge. Even Pops, who was normally all business on fight days, seemed excited for today.

Pops treated MMA like most Americans treated football or basketball. He imagined me being roped in with some of the greats like Muhammad Ali or Quinton Jackson. I didn't know if I was that great, but only time would tell.

Before I left for school, Pops surprisingly skipped his speech about the importance of my performance. He didn't drill me about some interview or meeting I needed to prepare for afterward. Instead, he gave me a clap on the back and a reassuring smile.

"It's going to be a good day, son."

My mother, on the other hand, never liked to see me fight. She was way too sensitive and worried about me getting hurt, so she showed her support in other ways.

"You should invite your friends and teammates over later," Ma said as I packed my book bag at the kitchen table. "We'll host the celebration dinner here."

"Celebration dinner? Ma, I didn't win anything yet."

"You will, and when you do, you're going to want to celebrate with your friends."

I appreciated her confidence in me, but I couldn't remember the last time we'd hosted a celebration dinner for my first match of the season. I also couldn't recall the last time Pops let me walk away without so much as a "Stay focused, son." I was willing to bet this all had more to do the Shane Tithers than anything else.

"Shane's coming over tonight," I guessed. It was the only explanation that made sense. Why else were my parents acting so weird?

"Yes, he is, so tell your friends there's a dress code."

In my family, a dress code only meant one thing.

"Is this a celebration dinner or a business dinner?"

"It's a dinner party, sweetie," Ma answered simply. "There's room for both." She didn't elaborate as she neatly wrapped a breakfast sandwich and shoved it into my hands. "Have a great day at school."

* * *

I spent most of the school day in a daze. All I could seem to think about was how good it would feel to finally be back in the ring. Sparring with Nick and Sasha was nothing compared to adrenaline rush I got from competing. The packed bleachers, the roaring crowd, and that antsy, exhilarating feeling I got just before the whistle blew, were some of the best parts of a fighting match.

Tonight would be a lot different from my other fights in the past seasons, though. There was a lot I had to prove. First, was that I actually had some level self-control. Despite what everybody saw in that video of me losing it on Shang, I usually had a better grasp on my temper.

Second, Shane Tithers had everybody on edge, waiting for his arrival. There wasn't one part of the entire day that went without mentioning him. He was coming to see me fight, and I should've been excited, or nervous, or anxious even, but as the day slowly came to an end, all I felt was numb. My trainers, my parents, and my teammates were all so excited *and* anxious *and* nervous that there wasn't enough left for me to feel.

And lastly, I wanted to start this season off so well that maybe, just maybe, people would forget how badly I'd ended last season.

"Yo, Jevon." A hand suddenly waved back and forth in front of my face. "You alright, man?"

I blinked. Tommy was trying to get my attention. We were having lunch outside near the quad and, for the most part, I had tuned everybody out. There were three separate conversations going on around the table, but Tommy suddenly had everybody focusing on me.

"Yeah, I'm good."

"How come you didn't tell us about the fight?" he asked.

I hesitated. For a moment, I wondered which fight he was talking about, the viral one or the new one.

"Tonight," he explained. "It's fight night, right?"

"Oh, yeah, right." I nodded.

"You don't sound that excited about it," Kayla chimed in.

"I am, I'm just . . . " *Very numb at the moment.* "Tired."

"What time is the fight?" 'Drc asked.

"It starts at eight," I said, and then I thought about what my mother said right before I left for school, "and afterward, we're doing something at my house."

"What, like an afterparty?"

"Not really."

"So, a *party* party?" Tommy bopped to the music in his head like the party had already started.

"No, there's a dress code."

"What?" It was like a record had screeched to a halt for Tommy. He stopped dancing and stared at me like I was suddenly the oddball.

"Damn, Bougie Boots!" He shook his head. "Just when we thought you were loosening up, you go and hit us with a suit and tie formal."

That cracked everybody up. I set my sights directly on Akilah. She was the only person that knew about that nick name. She sat across from me, covering a smile that should've been full of guilt. Instead, she winked at me and laughed a little harder.

"Ya'll don't have to come," I said.

"Whoa, whoa." Tommy simmered down. "I ain't say all that. I mean, a party is a party."

"We'll be there, Jay. We're just messing with you," Andre added.

"Yeah, we'll come," Kayla said.

Akilah remained silent. She picked at her food like it was suddenly more interesting.

"Akilah?" I called.

"Yes?"

"Are you coming?"

"I don't know." She played coy, staring at the invisible dirt under her nails. "I've been kinda busy lately."

Tommy sucked his teeth. "Doing what?"

"Minding my business, for one."

"That's code for 'nothing'!" Tommy cracked up again. "She'll be there."

With no objection from Akilah, I took that as a yes. Ma would be happy to host so many people. She loved throwing dinner parties, usually for people her own age because she liked to show off. For now, things were slowly falling into place.

All that was left for me to do was win.

CHAPTER TWENTY-FOUR

Akilah

Jevon said the fight would start at eight o'clock, but he should've told us to get there early.

By 7:45 p.m., the parking lot was so full we had to park two and a half blocks away. This fight brought in a crowd I wasn't expecting. There were so many people lined up outside the building that I double-checked the address a few times just to make sure we had the right place.

Had I underestimated how important Jevon really was? Was he the reason all these people seemed so excited to burst their way inside?

We made it to the end of the line just as the doors opened, and the line moved fast as people bumped into each other just to get in. I wanted to be as excited as everyone around me, and to a certain extent, I was. I had never seen Jevon fight in person, so I was very excited to see that part of him. But this, the way people tripped over themselves with glee, was a fandom I wasn't accustomed to.

As we passed through the entrance, the rush of AC hit me like a gust of cold wind. I shivered involuntarily at the sudden drop in temperature, hugging my arms close to my sides for warmth. 'Dre led the way to a set of bleachers on the far side of the room. They were filling up fast, and we all wanted the best seats. We had to push our way through a few people that crowded around the concessions, but it was worth it because 'Dre located a space big enough for the four of us in the middle row.

"Do you see him?" Kayla asked once we were settled.

"No." I shook my head. My eyes danced around the room briefly, but there were so many people, it was impossible to tell.

On the floor, in the middle of the room, was a green mat large enough to cover the entire area between both sets of bleachers. There was a big white circle at the center of the mat. I assumed that was where the fighting would take place.

A whistle suddenly blew loud and clear, bringing the room to total silence for a split second. Then the lights dimmed, and everybody else quickly made their way to an empty seat. That's when the fighters all emerged from somewhere in the back. They separated based on the colors of their uniforms and disperse to different sides of the room.

There were four groups of fighters. The group on the left wore red uniforms with golden dragons embroidered on their chests. They stretched in groups of two as they waited for the fight to begin.

Right next to them was a team in navy blue with white belts. I knew from watching old kung fu movies that white belts meant that they were beginners, but this didn't quite look like their first rodeo.

The white belts all looked fierce and disciplined. They stared straight ahead with their hands firmly clasped behind their backs. They didn't even say a word to each other while they waited.

On the right were the next two teams. The first was a group of fighters in all white uniforms with belts varying from red to black tied around their waists. They also stretched while they waited.

Finally, in a reserved section of the floor, stood the Hard Knocks team. In their black and silver uniforms, they looked similar to the white belts, all professional and polished.

I immediately noticed Jevon standing in the middle. His facial expression did not match the looks of most of the other fighters in the room. He was at ease, taking in the scenery around him. His competitors, on the other hand, had mean mugs that made me look the other way.

I suddenly realized why Jevon always looked so mean. It was very much a part of his talent.

"Hello everyone," a man addressed the audience, his microphone in hand. "Welcome to the Hard Knocks Dojo!" His voice filtered through the speakers all around the room. "I know you're all excited to get the competition started, but I want to make a quick announcement. We have a special guest here tonight, and before I bring him to the floor, I want to give a big thanks to everyone for coming out tonight. None of this would be possible without you.

"This man truly needs no introduction, but he's come all the way from Los Angeles to see this fight, and we're very excited to have him here. Without further ado . . ."

The man nodded to someone on the first row. I couldn't see who it was from here, but he handed the mic off to them, and that's when the screaming began. It started at the bottom of the bleachers where people could see more clearly what was going on. I heard a few people shouting, "Oh my God, it's really him!" from below us as the screaming intensified.

"Who is that?" I asked, craning my neck, hoping one of my friends had a better view.

Kayla shrugged. "I don't know."

When he finally came into view at the center of the white circle, my eyes went wide. Though he wore dark shades and a low-sitting baseball cap, I recognized him instantly. Shane . . . something. His underwear ad commercials played on TV all the time. He smiled as he waited for the screaming to die down.

"Thanks, Nick. I'm glad to be here," Shane said. "I'm especially glad to be back home in my city. Tonight, I'm here to tell everybody about my World Tour this summer. We're hitting twelve countries in twelve weeks, and I'm looking for a few champions to join my team."

Fighters exchanged looks of surprise. They turned to each other with questions all over their faces. The only team that didn't seem surprised by this news was the Hard Knocks team. They kept their composure, looking straight ahead.

Shane turned toward the fighters. "Give it your all tonight. Impress me. Fight like there's a check waiting for you at the end of this."

The last part got him a few chuckles. Nick returned to the center of the circle and reclaimed the mic. The applause for Shane was so loud I had to plug one of my ears.

"Let's begin!"

At once, a horn was blown and the fighters seemed to know exactly where to go and who would go first. The first round was The Golden Dragons vs. The White Belts. As promised by Jevon, this fighting style was very brutal. It had barely even started and already a boy from the Golden Dragons' team was swiping away at a bloody nose he got from a kick to the face.

I found myself scooting up to the edge of my seat while I watched. There was so much going on, it was almost hard to keep track. I didn't know the rules, but if I had to guess, I'd say the white circle kept the fight in play.

Every now and then, I noticed the White Belt trying to force the Golden Dragon out of the ring. By the extreme way the Golden Dragon avoided the outside of the circle, I figured if he left the circle, the fight would end and he would lose.

"My money's on the dude with the ponytail," I heard 'Dre say to Tommy.

"Nah, that's the obvious choice." Tommy shook his head. "I rooting for the underdog. Look at him! He's down there fighting with a broken nose and everything."

"He's an underdog for a reason, Tommy. He's losing!" Kayla said.

"Maybe that's what he wants you to think. He could turn this whole thing around in the end."

"You want to put money on it?" I asked. Tommy was so gullible when it came to taking bets. I wasn't seriously going to put money on this fight, but it was too easy to get him riled up.

"Bet!" He reached for his wallet, but then a whistle blew, calling an end to the fight.

When we turned back to the floor, it was the Golden Dragon who'd fallen outside the circle and the White Belt waving his arm in the air.

"On the next one," Tommy muttered.

The next few fights came and went just as quickly as the first. On each round, I waited to see Jevon come up to the center, but it wasn't his turn yet. All the teams had at least one round inside the circle, and so far the White Belts were taking the lead.

The Hard Knocks Dojo came up as a close second with just a couple points behind the White Belts, and I waited patiently to see Jevon bring his team up to the top. There had to be a reason they were saving him for last.

"Oh, there he is!" Tommy pointed, and sure enough we caught Jevon walking toward the wide circle. He wasn't overly cocky like some of the others before him, and he didn't try to intimidate his competitor when they were brought face to face. Instead, they bowed to each other with their right fists positioned in front of their left palms.

The referee blew his whistle and then they began. The White Belt, I think they said his name was Kaseem, was instantly on the offense. He thrust his leg out in a side-kick, but Jevon was quick to respond as he held his arms out in an X shape to block his blow.

Kaseem recovered quickly as he spun around to dodge Jevon's defensive strikes. In an instant, Kaseem took his hand and thrust it into Jevon's side really hard. Jevon staggered back from the impact, inching toward the edge of the circle, but Kaseem didn't stop there.

He aimed at Jevon's chest, hitting him in the same spot, right below his collar bone, over and over again. Even I winced away because it looked like it hurt. Each blow brought Jevon closer to that boundary line.

"Come on, Jevon!" I stood up, too anxious to continue sitting.

Even as far away from the action as we were, I could see Jevon's lip curl up in annoyance. Kaseem was pissing him off. This time, when Kaseem reached out to strike, Jevon was ready. With his left hand, Jevon was able to grab hold of Kaseem's arm and bend it all the way back. Kaseem let out a painful cry as Jevon sharply twisted that same arm, which caused Kaseem to involuntarily flip over.

Kaseem landed hard on his back, and he immediately clutched his arm close to his chest. The crowd went silent while we waited for Kaseem to recover. He took his time rising to a standing position, and a few people clapped for him.

The referee came over to check on him, but Kaseem shook his head to whatever the man had said. Another whistle blew to signal the fight going back into play, and Kaseem dropped his arm to continue.

Now that Jevon had given Kaseem a weakness—his arm—I figured the battle was over. Jevon was now on the offense as he attacked Kaseem on his right side. In just three sharp pokes to Kaseem's shoulder, arm, and chest region, his entire right arm went limp. It swung loosely at his side as he tried to regain his composure.

Kaseem was left to fight with only his left arm in full use. He dodged Jevon's jabs easily, but he was defenseless without the use of his other arm. Jevon continued to jab at Kaseem, pushing him closer to the edge of the large white circle around them. In one final move, Jevon dropped low to the floor and swept his foot out beneath Kaseem, effectively knocking him over. Kaseem's head hit the floor mat outside the circle at the same time that the referee threw the towel on the floor.

The battle was officially over and Jevon was the winner.

CHAPTER TWENTY-FIVE

Jevon

I felt good.

No, I felt more than good. I felt great.

I wasn't going to lie, Kaseem had me in the first half of the fight. He came at me harder than I'd expected, but I should've known better. The White Ribbon Martial Arts Academy—where Kaseem trained—was known for their speed. They had the ability to end a fight quickly and efficiently with little to no flair or hesitation.

That ability was what kept them at the top of the charts for a while . . . until me. I wasn't intimidated by the White Ribbon Academy. They were legacy kids who thought they knew everything there was to know about martial arts.

"Good fight." I felt a clap on my back from my teammate, Lincoln, as I left the circle and rejoined my team.

I smacked my fist against his. "Bring us home."

Lincoln was one of the bests at the Hard Knocks Dojo, but he wasn't very competitive. He had no desire to go pro or take his fighting much beyond the dojo. To him, this was all in good fun, but I often wondered how good he would be if he actually took himself seriously.

Maybe with Shane Tithers watching, he would take it up a notch, especially since he was our anchor. I brought us to the top of the scoreboard from my win with Kaseem, but it was now up to Lincoln to make sure we stayed there in the final round.

I didn't stay to watch the last fight. My chest was sore and burning from all the hits I took right below my collar bone. If I didn't ice it soon, I was sure to have bruises by tomorrow morning. As I headed to the locker room in the back, I undid the belt to my uniform shirt. My skin was hot to the touch, so the cool air felt good against my chest.

The locker room was empty when I got there. I headed straight for the medicine cabinet on the wall. The door was already open with aspirin packets and unraveled rolls of gauze hanging over the side. I reached for the cold packs in the back and grabbed two of them.

My shoulder was starting to ache a little too, but it wasn't that bad. Placing my shirt on the hook in my locker, I broke the pack in with a few clicks. When I draped it over my shoulder, and the ice hit my collar bone, I let out a low hissing sound as the cold pack did its job. My head fell back against the locker doors and my eyes closed on their own. I slid down to the bench released a deep sigh of contentment.

It wasn't long before I heard the distinctive clack of my father's Oxford loafers on the tiled floor. He made his way inside like he was in a rush.

"Jevon?"

"Over here."

I adjusted the cold pack on my should and waved my other arm until he saw me. Pops held a proud smile as he leaned on the lockers across from me.

"Good work, son. I knew you could do it. How do you feel?" He pointed to the cold pack on my shoulder.

"Sore, but I'm okay."

"Good. Get dressed, your team just won. Let's get out of here. Your mother needs help setting up."

On any other day, Pops would make me stick around after a fight to greet people and take pictures. With Shane here, you'd think he would want to stick around for a while, but since we would see him at the dinner party later, I guessed it didn't matter.

I let the cold pack sag down to my hand and grabbed my uniform shirt from the hook in my locker.

* * *

At home, Ma put us to work along with the people she'd hired to be here. Pops and I were tasked with clearing up space for all the cocktail tables she was setting up. We took separate ends of the long couch in the living room and turned it sideways so we could move it into his office behind the staircase.

Halfway through the move, I got a painful kink my shoulder and nearly dropped the couch on the floor.

"Pops, wait." I winced. My chest was starting burn again.

"What happened?" He put his end down gently so he could see me.

I rotated my arm a few times, but it was only making it worse. When he realized what made me stop, Pops snapped his fingers at the nearest server with a black vest on and made him switch places with me.

"Go take an aspirin and fix your tie. We got it from here."

Ma had forced me to get ready in such hurry when I got home that my tie was all crooked. Even now, she was so busy bossing every-body around that she didn't notice me slip past her. I yanked at the loose end on the way upstairs, and it came undone completely.

Nobody was here yet, but I felt a ball of nerves settle deep in my stomach. I wasn't sure if it was because I was meeting Shane Tithers for the first time, or playing host to everyone I knew, but I took a few deep breaths to calm myself.

The hard part was over. I won the fight, and that should've been enough to impress Shane. Pops gave me no feedback afterward, so I took that as a good sign.

In the bathroom, I found the bottle of Tylenol and dry-swallowed two gel caps. When I was sure I wouldn't choke, I flipped my collar and redid my tie—over, under, and through the loop.

I looked good.

After another deep breath, I left the bathroom and headed back downstairs. Ma had completely transformed our house into a Williams-worthy event. The cocktail tables were set up, decorated, and spread throughout the living room. There was food lined up in metal trays at the kitchen island, and a bartender was stationed where the kitchen table used to be.

"We're almost done, honey. Can you help me pin this up?" I caught Ma bossing Pops around. They were tying the ends of a table cloth to the legs of the dining room table. She was the only person who could get him to do any kind of labor. He darted his head around, urgently looking for a server or anybody to come and replace him as she moved them on to the next task.

When the doorbell rang, he was the first to say, "I got it!" but I beat him to the punch. I opened the door to complete strangers. They were an older couple that smiled at me like they knew me.

"John, Sheila," Pops bellowed from behind me, "come on in!"

I opened the door wider for them.

"You remember Jevon," he went on as he took their coats and passed them off to someone wearing a black vest.

"I remember him being much smaller," Sheila said. "The last time we saw you, you were snaggletoothed and scrawny."

They shared a laugh over the memory. Pops led them deeper into the house, picking up an easy conversation about mergers and acquisitions.

I stayed by the door, hoping that someone my age would walk through soon. The idea of spending the entire night reminiscing over childhood memories with people I didn't know, or pretending to understand what a merger was, had me thinking of escape plans.

Thankfully, I didn't have to wait for long. More people started arriving after John and Sheila. They brought the house to life, and my parents right along with them.

There was no sign of Shane yet, and I was honestly glad. I didn't know what to say to him. I guessed I could start with "Thank you," but I didn't think much beyond that. What did you say to someone who had the power to give you a once-in-a-lifetime experience? "Thank you", wasn't enough.

"What are you thinking so hard about?" I was standing at a cocktail table near the wall, thinking of how my conversation with Shane would go, when Darius joined me. He had a tiny plate of food spilling over onto the table. Kent and Trisha followed close behind him.

"Nothing. When'd ya'll get here?"

"Just now," Trish said. "Parking was a bitch. Why are there so many people here?"

The house was filling up quickly with unfamiliar faces.

"You know how ma is," I said.

"Yeah, I know, but this is . . . a lot."

"I don't know, I kinda like it." Kent snuck a drink from the tray of a passing server.

"Me too." Darius clinked his glass against Kent's.

"When did you even—" I started to ask. I didn't see Darius grab a drink too. "You know what? Never mind." I really didn't care.

I almost wished I could join them, but I needed a clear head for tonight.

"Oh, look! There goes your girl." Trisha nudged my arm. "And she brought friends."

We all turned at the same time to see Akilah and her friends making their way inside. They huddled near the kitchen, unaware that they were being watched.

"Wait, for real? That's you?" Darius seemed surprised. He stared at her like he thought Trish was making it all up.

"I was wondering why she showed up out of the blue the other day," Kent added. "Now it all makes sense."

"Nah, we're just friends."

"Friends, my ass!" Darius snorted. "Ya'll left at the same time and never came back."

"Nothing happened, D. It's not like that."

"But you want it to be," Trisha stated matter-of-factly.

I blinked. "I didn't say that."

"No, but your face did. You gonna just stare at her all night? Go say something!"

Trisha gave me a rough shove in Akilah's direction. I didn't have to prove anything to my friends. As a host, it was my job to make everybody feel welcomed. At least, that was what I told myself when I was close enough for her to notice me.

Akilah's dimpled smile had me grinning involuntarily. She took me in like she was excited to see me, and I found it hard not to stare at her in her long burgundy dress. She was...gorgeous. Her hair was different. She now had braids that fell down her back, almost matching the color of the dress exactly.

"Hey," I said to her.

"Hey."

"So, you weren't that busy."

Akilah shrugged. "I made some time in my schedule."

"And?"

"And it was worth it. I'm a fan."

"Really?"

"Do we take pictures now?" she teased. "Or, do I get your autograph? How does this work?"

"You're a terrible fan," I played along. "You're way too calm."

"Am I supposed to be screaming? Because I'll do it."

She had the kind of challenge in her eyes that I didn't want to push too far, not here.

"No, don't do that."

"Hey, Jevon." Tommy suddenly wedged his way into the conversation. "Do we say good game or . . . what do you normally say after a fight?"

"Good game is fine."

"Well, good game!" He paused and looked around the room like he was missing something. "So, uh, when does the party get started?"

"It already did."

He shared a look with 'Dre and they held a silent conversation with their eyes.

"Can you at least act like you've been somewhere before?" Kayla interrupted

Tommy tugged at his tie. "I'm trying, but it's real stiff up in here."

"Just go, both of you." She snapped her fingers toward the cocktail tables. "Nice party, Jevon. Congratulations!"

The three of them left Akilah and me standing there. It was better that way because Trish kept looking over, giving me a thumbs up every time Akilah wasn't looking.

"You look really nice, by the way."

"Just nice?" She arched a brow like she knew she looked good.

Again, I tried not to stare at the way her dress hugged every curve I didn't know she had. As if that wasn't hard enough, she bit down on her lip, drawing attention to the lipstick that also matched the color of her dress.

It took some effort, but I focused on her eyes when I said, "I meant beautiful."

She held my stare for a short while, until her smile shifted to something more shy, almost hesitant. Then her eyes fell to my chest.

"Your tie is crooked."

"Again?" I followed her line of vision, already yanking at the fabric.

Akilah suddenly placed her fingers over mine. "Let me help you."

When she leaned in, the sweet smell of coconuts and honey followed. She was gentle as she tugged on the knot around my neck. With one final pull, she smoothed my tie against my shirt and leaned back to check out her work.

"Perfect."

"Thank you."

"Don't thank me yet." She chuckled. "Because now you finally owe me one."

"Hold that thought." Pops saw me at the same time I saw him, heading into the kitchen. He walked straight toward us, waving me down before he came to a full stop.

"Son, where have you been? I've been looking everywhere."

"Pops, this is Akilah." I ignored the urgency in his voice, and he caught on quickly. My father plastered on the same posed smile he'd used all night.

"Ah, yes, the artist." He shook her hand. "I've heard a lot about you."

"You have?" Akilah glanced from me, to Pops, then back to me.

"Yes, Jevon's told me about the project you two are working on."

"Oh, yeah, he's my muse."

Pops did a double take. He turned to me for a better understanding, but I didn't have one...that would make sense to him, anyway.

"I just meant that he inspired the piece," she explained.

"Well, I can't wait to see what you come up with." He said to her, then to me, "I hate to steal you away, Jevon, but we need to go. He's here."

There went those nerves again.

"Don't go anywhere," I told her, "I'll be right back."

Pops led the way to the den. It wasn't decorated for the party, but it was crowded with cameras and people who blocked our way inside. He cleared up a path for me to squeeze through to the other side, and there was Shane, sitting on the sofa. He had an entourage with him. They snapped pictures of every moment.

"Jevon Williams." He stood to shake my hand for the cameras. He was shorter than I'd imagined, standing at just a head under me. "It's nice to finally meet you."

"Thank you."

Shane made room for me to sit in the limited space we had. People crowded around us like they were waiting for their turn.

"Congratulations on the win. That was very impressive. I wasn't even half that good when I was your age."

There were a few chuckles from our audience.

"So, tell me about yourself," he said.

"Uh." I racked my brain for something, anything other than the first thought to cross my mind, "I, um . . ." drew a blank.

Though I couldn't see my father standing somewhere behind me in the room, I could feel his stare burning a hole into the back of my head. We rehearsed different interview methods all the time. It shouldn't have been this hard for me to talk about myself, but after everything that had happened leading up to this moment, I couldn't think of anything good enough to overlook it all.

"You know what?" Shane gestured to the crowded room. "Can we have the room?"

Nobody questioned him. They formed a short line as they all drifted out of the den. Pops lingered by the entryway, looking more nervous than I was.

"We'll be out in just a few minutes," Shane reassured him.

With a final nod in my direction, Pops left the room too.

"Relax." He leaned back in his seat. "It's not an interview. I just spent so much time talking to Michael Williams these past few weeks that I wanted to get to know the person I'm adding to my tour."

"Okay." I nodded.

"So, what do you like? What do you do outside of fighting?" He tried again, but since this was informal, and there were no cameras around, there was one thing I needed to get out of the way.

"Actually, can we talk about something else?" I asked.

"Sure."

I took a deep breath. "I know you saw that video of me from last season, and—"

"Is that what you're tripping on?" He barked a laugh. "Oh, man, I don't care about that stuff. I've had so many scandals, I couldn't tell you the last time I *wasn't* making headlines."

I blinked. Shane brushed it off like it was nothing.

"Look, your dad and I talked about everything. That's just a part of the job that'll never go away. I've been threatened by the league, old opponents, and people who swear they're so perfect they never once made a mistake. That's just how it is.

"I want you to be a part of this tour because I've seen what you can do. You were a beast out there today, and that's something I can get behind. That's what I want representing me worldwide. You're a star, kid. It's time you start acting like it."

Maybe he was right. Maybe I was looking at it all wrong. All this time, I'd accepted the consequences of my actions like they were a punishment. And yeah, to a certain extent, I guess I deserved it, but I was done wallowing about it. I deserved this too, and it was time I started acting like it.

CHAPTER TWENTY-SIX

Akilah

I spent the next hour trying to convince myself to stay. As much as I wanted to disagree with Tommy, he did have a point earlier. This "party" was more of a networking event than anything remotely close to what I considered a party.

There were more business suits and bowties in one room than I had seen in my entire life. The food, though elegant and tasty, wasn't enough to keep us entertained. For a while we spent time with Jevon's friends from Laney High. They weren't surprised at all by the dull atmosphere that surrounded us. Unlike us, this wasn't their first event at the Williams house.

It was Trisha's idea for us all to escape near the pool in the back-yard, and it was the best thing she could've said because at least here we didn't have to pretend like we were having a good time.

Darius found a deck of cards from a drawer in the kitchen, and the guys played Tonk at the table by the sliding glass door. I slipped off my heels and dipped my feet in the water. It was nice outside. The moon was full. There was a soft breeze in the air that made the water feel icy against my skin.

"Aren't you cold?" Kayla shivered beside me. She sat a little distance away from the water, crossing her legs in a way that showed off the slit in her shimmery pink dress.

"Not really." It wasn't all the way a lie. The water was cold, but my feet adjusted to the temperature the longer they stayed there.

"I should've brought my Bluetooth speaker. These things run kind of long," Trish said as she came over to join me at the pool. She rolled her pants up, stuck her feet in, and swung her legs back and forth.

"Won't they hear your music?"

"Yeah, but they won't care. Half of them are just as bored as we are."

I laughed a little as I imagined the type of music Trish would play, and the reaction to it from the people inside.

"Do you guys normally stay the whole time?" Kayla asked.

"Usually Jevon is out here with us, and we all just suffer through it together." Her foot splashed water into the deep end. "But he's in there doing God knows what with all of Corporate America."

"I think I'm leaving after I win this game," Kent boasted. We turned to see him slam a card down on the table, and the immediate disappointment at what it was.

"You mean, after *I* win this game." 'Dre lined up his cards and spread them out so we all could see. "Yeah, just like that."

"Shuffle 'em again." Kent rounded up all the cards. "One more game."

"Why? So you can lose again?" Trisha teased him.

"I'm going to forget you said that when you ask me for a ride home later."

To that, she had no comeback.

"Anyway," she turned back to Kayla and me, "I don't think I'll be leaving anytime soon."

"Well, I have to go." Kayla stood. "My mom's working a late shift at the hospital. I need to get the car back to her before she starts calling me."

"Do you want me to walk you out?" I asked, already searching for my heels.

"No, stay. I'll text you when I get home."

I was going to argue, but Tommy stood to open the door for her. He walked with her to the front door, and I instantly felt better about her leaving so late by herself.

Kayla's mom was a nurse at Piedmont Hospital. She worked so many late shifts that Kayla was used to being the first to leave. It used to annoy her when her older sisters had to pick her up without notice every time we went out. She'd complain that she never got to have any fun. Now, I guessed it didn't bother her so much.

"What about you?" Trisha asked.

"Huh?"

"How long are you staying?"

"I don't know." I shrugged. "Probably long enough to let Jevon know I'm leaving."

"He'll understand. Trust me, it won't get any better than this."

"I can wait."

"Hmph." She smiled to herself as she stared at her feet swaying slowly in the water.

"What?"

"You like him, don't you?"

"W-what?" I shook off a nervous giggle.

"You heard me."

I did hear her.

"Is it that obvious?"

"Yeah, it is."

I didn't know what to say to that. She caught me. I liked Jevon. I *really* liked Jevon, but I didn't know what to do about it and I didn't know if he felt the same.

"I think he likes you too." She brushed her shoulder against mine.

"He told you that?"

"No, but I see the way he is around you. The other day, when that video went viral, you went after him but you didn't come back. That's when I knew."

"Wait, we didn't—"

"I know, he told us." She cut me off. "When Jay gets angry, he's a different person. He likes to distance himself when he gets that way, and most of the time it's better for everybody, but he let you in."

I thought back to that day and remembered it a little differently now.

"So, even if he doesn't say it," she went on, "he likes you."

Suddenly, I couldn't stop myself from smiling. I had to turn my head so Trish couldn't see how goofy I looked.

"What am I supposed to do with that information?" I asked.

Even if what she said was true, Jevon and I had already kissed once before, and we'd never really talked about it. If I told Jevon how I felt, and he didn't feel the same . . . ugh, the embarrassment.

"I would tell you." She cast her eyes over my shoulder. "But we have company."

My head whipped around so fast I made myself a little dizzy. Jevon was walking toward us, and the closer he got to me, the more my heartbeat sped in tempo. He looked like he'd stepped off the page of a GQ magazine.

"Jay." Trisha beamed. "We were just talking about you."

He squinted his eyes at her while mine doubled in size.

"I'm going to go see if Kent is still willing to give me that ride." She got up like she hadn't just exposed the both of us and led a trail of watery footprints to the table where the boys played their game.

Jevon took her place beside me, but he didn't stick his feet in. He placed his elbows on his knees as his shiny shoes stuck out over the edge. He smelled like an odd mix of soap and . . . cigar smoke? There was a light hint of it that lingered on his clothes.

"What'd she tell you?" Jevon asked when we were all alone. The table was clear, and we were the only two outside.

I played it cool. "She just told me how bored she was."

"I bet." He clearly didn't believe a word I'd said, but he didn't push for more.

My feet swayed with the flow of the water as the soft breeze came back.

"You told your dad about me?" I asked. The question had been burning on the tip of my tongue since the moment I found out.

"Yeah, I told my trainers about you too."

"I don't know if I should be flattered or concerned." I was only half joking.

He grinned. "I missed some training sessions because of you. They had to know why."

"Oh. Why didn't you just tell me?"

"Because I had it under control."

"You're always saying that."

"And, I'm always right."

Cocky.

"I guess this means I'll have to find a new muse now."

Jevon was offended. "Why would you say that?"

"Because, look around. Things are going good for you now. You don't need me anymore."

"Yeah, you got the first part right, but we're not done yet. I still need you, and you still need me."

The phrasing of those words together did something to the inside of my chest. It didn't help that he looked me directly in the eyes when he said it.

"Why?"

Jevon took a moment to think about it, staring at my feet while he concentrated.

"When I started at Cambridge, I hated it. I didn't want to be there, but it was too late to take it back. Pops told me to make the most of my time there. He wanted me to make it worthwhile, but I think that was just a clever way for him to keep me busy.

"So, I agreed to work with you. And now that I think about it, the sculpture really won't make that much of a difference for me, but I'm okay with that."

I took offense to that last part, and it showed all over my face.

"That came out wrong." He chuckled at my expression. "What I meant was even if nothing changes at the end of this, it was worthwhile, Akilah."

I didn't realize I was holding my breath until it all came out of me at once.

"I'm listening," I urged him to keep going.

"Without the sculpture, I would've never met you and all your friends. I would never know how annoyingly curious you are, how you can't seem to ever take 'no' for an answer, and how you're always in the right place at the *wrong* time."

Jevon listed off the most horrible qualities he saw in me, the type to make any sane person run the other way. But he said them with a smile, like they meant something different to him. I stared at him, unable to think of a response, and he stared back. When his eyes drifted down to my lips, I acted on the sudden impulse to kiss him.

Jevon froze in surprise, and I immediately stopped.

"Sorry," I whispered. "I read that all wrong, didn't I?"

Damnit, Trish!

I lifted my feet out of the water and looked around for my shoes. They were bunched under the chair Kayla had sat in. As I bent down to grab them, Jevon caught me by the arm, gently pulling me back toward him.

He cupped a hand under my chin and made sure I saw him lean in before pressing his lips to mine. Jevon's lips were soft and warm, unlike the weather. I shivered for the first time since being outside. It could've been the breeze that felt more brisk now that my feet were out of the water, or the way he snaked an arm around my waist to pull me in closer. I wasn't sure, but I didn't spend too much time questioning it either. His lips parted slightly, inviting me in, and I lifted up on my toes to deepen the kiss.

Wounding my arms around his neck, I grazed my fingertips over the waves that rippled down the back of his head. He made a humming sound at the tender movement of my fingers, and it caused another involuntary shiver to run through me. He smiled and I did too.

Another gust of wind blew through the back yard, almost making me sway on my feet, but Jevon held me firmly in place. I wished I could stay there. I wished I didn't have to leave, but it was suddenly very cold and very, very late. With a sigh, I broke the kiss.

"I have to go," I whispered so low I hoped he didn't hear me.

He did though.

Jevon nodded, and then wordlessly, he took me by the hand and led me back out to my car.

CHAPTER TWENTY-SEVEN

Jevon

If I had to describe what it was like to have everything fall apart just to come back stronger, I'd never find the words.

Last night was like nothing I expected. Meeting Shane was easier than I'd thought it would be. He treated me like a person, not just a fighter, or a brand to help build his business.

After our talk, Pops conveniently found a way to include himself in the conversation. He got the contract from his office and brought up all the highlighted points he wanted to negotiate. Shane was very patient with us. He answered any question we had about everything from my salary to the new team I'd be joining on the tour.

I checked out halfway through the new contract proposal. Pops started throwing around words like licensing, sponsorships, and worker's compensation, and my brain turned to mush. I was glad to be there though because it was the first time Pops had involved me in the business aspect of my career.

He asked the hard-hitting questions, the ones that made Shane clear his throat before he answered. Like when he asked for a twenty thousand dollar boost to my already solid salary, in exchange for exclusive rights to my brand. Pops didn't stutter or hesitate. He stared Shane clear in his eyes until he got the answer he wanted.

Then, my father pulled out a polished box of cigars that somehow smelled old and new at the same time. The secondhand smoke from them was so strong I left wheezing midway through their session.

Then there was Akilah.

At first, when I saw Trish talking to her by the pool, a lot of different things went through my head. Trish was a wild card. She spoke her mind, and she never apologized for it. The last thing I wanted was for her to try and play matchmaker just because she thought she could.

I liked Akilah. I didn't realize how much until I was confessing how she made my time at CSA worthwhile. The way she looked at me afterward made me think I said too much, or maybe that I'd said the wrong thing, but then she'd kissed me. If Trish knew what had happened after she left, she'd never let me hear the end of it.

Though Akilah came very close to being the best part of the night, I thought of the ways my night could've ended differently as I made my way to school. I didn't have a lot of complaints, but if I could change one thing, then it would be the way I'd introduced myself to Shane. I hated that I let my nerves get to me. It had never been that bad before, and I was positive Pops would grill me about it later.

Overall though, the meeting had ended on a good note. Pops always said that the last impression you left with someone would be the one they remembered the most. I think we all remembered my signature scribbled across that dotted line in the end.

At school, nobody stared at me like they did on Monday. They must've found something more interesting to talk about because I quickly went back to being ignored. I didn't care to know why, but I hoped it stayed that way. I didn't like being at the center of attention any more than I had to be.

I took advantage of my new found obscurity as I headed up to the senior lounge during my free period. After staying up for most of the night, all I really wanted was an extra hour of sleep. There were multi-colored beanbag chairs huddled in one corner of the room. I snagged one and ducked off to the back where it was usually empty.

. . . and there she was again. Right place, wrong time. Same as always.

Akilah sat on the floor with her back against a shelf that was stacked to the brim with used textbooks. She was by herself, and she had her sketchbook perched on her knees while she worked on a new drawing.

Her burgundy braids fell over her shoulder as she leaned down to scribble something else. Akilah was so focused that she only saw me when she reach for the white eraser next to her foot. Her hand paused on the carpet as her eyes trailed up to my face.

"Let me guess." She straightened her legs. "You were looking for somewhere to hide?"

"What gave it away?"

Akilah swiped a finger on one of the shelves behind her. "Do you see all the dust on these books? Nobody comes back here."

"So, why are you here?"

"I needed a place to think. I'm working on something new and I couldn't concentrate out there."

On the other side of the room, more seniors crowded the space up front. They weren't loud, but I could see how the subtle buzz of their voices was distracting.

"Can I see?"

"Only if you share that seat with me."

I didn't think the beanbag chair was big enough for the both of us, but Akilah helped me push it against the wall and we both sat on the ends. Gravity, however, sank us both toward the middle, pressing us together. If she were any closer, she'd be in my lap.

"It's just a rough sketch for now," she explained, pressing the book close to her chest, "so don't judge."

"I won't."

Akilah sighed deeply before revealing her drawing to me. She smoothed the page down with her hand and turned it so I could see.

A large pair of eyes stared back at me. They were so detailed and realistic; I almost questioned if she drew them with just the pencil she had in her hand. The eyes had no pupils or irises, but in their place, Akilah had drawn separate images over the whites of the eye.

On the right, I saw a field of flowers that had yet to bloom. The buds stood tall in the overgrown grass, stuck in a stage of permanent underdevelopment. The left eye was just a fuzzy computer screen that glowed in the darkness that surrounded it. A single tear fell from that eye, running all the way down to the end of the page.

"*This* is a rough sketch?" I asked.

"It's not finished. I don't even know if I'm keeping it. I just needed to get it down on paper."

Never had I doubted what Akilah could do, but if this was what she considered unfinished work then I had severely under-estimated her.

"What's it about?"

"Me." She took the book back and started erasing the smudges around the edges. "It's two versions of my future. I could either choose to be complacent and boring for the rest of my life, or I could water my own seed and see what grows. I'm calling it 'Seeing Double', or maybe 'Double Vision.'"

I thought back to the conversation we had last weekend in my car. Akilah couldn't decide what to study in college, but it shouldn't have been a question what she would choose to do. She was a talented artist—anything else just wouldn't make sense.

"What?" she asked. "What's that face?"

I tried to think of a nicer way to phrase what was going through my head.

"Just say it. I can take it," she persisted.

"I think it'd be a waste of the last four years if you do anything other than this." I tapped the open page of her sketchbook. "This is who you are, Akilah. You're not struggling to decide what to do. You're struggling to believe what you already know."

She bit down on her lip and gently closed the sketchbook in her lap. Akilah turned so that she was facing me, but the sudden movement brought her much closer. Her knees brushed against mine in a way that had our legs tangling together.

"There you go again, making it sound like it's so easy."

"It shouldn't be that hard."

Akilah nodded like she was agreeing with me, but then she cocked her head to the side and stared at me through squinted eyes.

"You know what else shouldn't be hard? Figuring you out."

I questioned her with a look.

"We never talked about that kiss—last night or at Tommy's party. I'm not that good at pretending, so what are we doing?"

Her accusing tone made me smile a little. She seemed more frustrated than angry. It was the little dip between her brows, and the way she chewed on the inner corner of mouth that made it hard for me to take her seriously. She was cute when she was upset.

"So, don't pretend," I didn't back down. "I'm not good at it either."

"You're better than you think."

Just sitting near her, breathing in the scent of coco butter that wafted from her skin was enough to bring the memories rushing back to me. Akilah had it all wrong. I didn't forget anything.

"I like you, okay?" I admitted. "I can't fake that."

"Prove it."

She dared me with a smile. Akilah leaned in at the same time I did. Our knees, lips, and legs collided together all at once on the slippery surface of the beanbag chair. Akilah grabbed a hand full of my shirt, bringing me down with her as we sank deeper into the middle. Her fingers were stained from the residue of her drawing, but I didn't care.

It was like we picked up right where we left off by the pool. She wrapped her arms around my neck, closing the little bit of distance between us and I liked having her pressed so close to me. Akilah's lips tasted sweet, like cherry-flavored candy. It lingered on my tongue.

When her foot shifted all of a sudden, she lost her balance and we both tumbled down to the floor. We knocked a few textbooks down with us. The sound of our fall caused the whole senior lounge to go quiet for a split second.

Eventually, I couldn't hold it in anymore. I laughed—unintentionally giving us both away—but I couldn't help it. It was the look of shock and pure embarrassment on her face that did me in. She joined in on the laughter, but only long enough to fix her hair and straighten her shirt.

"Are you okay?" I asked. She took the brunt of the fall and she seemed fine, but she started rubbing at her elbow like it hurt.

"I would be better if you stopped laughing at me."

I covered my laugh with a cough and it helped me be more serious.

She cradled her elbow. "The next time we do something like this, please don't let me fall like that again."

"Next time?" I questioned.

"Or not?"

"No, that's not what I meant. I just—" I took a deep breath and tried again. "What are you doing on Saturday?"

Akilah made an apologetic face.

"Do not say you're busy."

"No, I really am this time." She laughed. "I signed up to volunteer at the High Museum of Art this weekend. It's for my application to Ivory Middleton."

That was good for her; it was definitely more important than what I had in mind.

"But, you should come with me! I mean, I won't be there all day. Plus, Ms. Hazel will give you extra credit on the midterm for helping out."

"Umm . . ." I had the strongest urge to say no. What was I supposed to do at a museum?

"You owe me one," she leveraged.

"Barely."

She had only fixed my tie that one time. That wasn't enough to make me excited to spend the day at the museum.

Without warning, Akilah placed a hand on my cheek and kissed me softly. Her cherry lip gloss invaded my senses long enough to make me forget why I was even resisting, but then she pulled away with that dimpled smile.

"What about now?"

CHAPTER TWENTY-EIGHT

Akilah

I spent the entire night before Saturday thinking of an idea that would be fun to the kids I was helping. Though Ms. Hazel was teaching them real skills in the drawing circle, it was honestly dull and boring. I couldn't imagine having to sit through that again, even for Ivory Middleton.

When I thought of volunteering at the museum, I figured it would be the same as last weekend. It was easy to sort through drawings and rate the work of the kids in the program, but to teach my own session was a little nerve wracking.

Ms. Hazel had sprung it on me at the last minute. Her exhibit was still in the building stages, so it took a lot of her attention away from the program. I was in charge for one activity, but thankfully I had help.

Collecting my bags, I headed downstairs where I could smell bacon and butter biscuits coming fresh out of the oven. Daddy had left for work already, so it was Momma I saw at the kitchen counter, making three plates of food.

"Where are you going?" she asked, nodding toward the large duffle bag I carried on my shoulder.

"Momma, I told you was volunteering at the museum today."

"That's today?"

I nodded. I was positive I'd mentioned it to her at least once when she'd asked me how my day was at school last week.

"Oh." She turned around to press the off switch on the oven and then she pushed a finished plate toward me at the end of the counter. "I made plans for us to tour some colleges. We took CJ last weekend, and I thought it might be helpful for you too because I know you haven't applied anywhere yet."

I worked to fix the irritated look on my face as I dropped my bag and took a seat at the stool on the other side of the counter. The food looked just as good as it smelled: cheese grits, scrambled eggs, a few slices of crispy bacon, and a freshly buttered biscuit that glistened under the steam rising from the plate.

"I've seen all the colleges in Atlanta, Momma. I'm not going to school here."

Just like CJ, my parents took me on a tour of almost every college campus in the city when I was a junior. I'd seen everything from Georgia State University to the Art Institute of Atlanta. All the schools I'd visited shared a common theme: a focus on anything but a good visual arts program.

"You don't have a lot of time to make up your mind, Kiki. You're way past some of the deadlines for fall semester next year, and I just don't want you to get left behind. This could be good for you. You might find something you like at these schools that you didn't notice before and—"

"Ma!" I cut her off. "All you ever do is tell me how hard it's going to be to become a successful artist. You make it seem like it's so impossible to be who I want to be. I'm not going to find something I like at a traditional school. I won't notice something new at Spelman or Georgia Tech. I'm an artist! Why is it so hard for you to believe in me?"

"I do believe in you, baby." Her tone softened, despite the way I'd just yelled at her. "I believe in you so much that your father and I spend over ten thousand dollars a semester on your tuition at Cambridge. I never said you wouldn't be successful, Kiki, but I know the industry, and I know how heartbroken I was when everything I wanted didn't magically come true for me."

I'm not you! I was only brave enough to scream the words in my head.

"All I've ever asked is that you make a wise decision about your future. You don't have to put all your eggs in one basket. You can still study the arts, but think about learning a new skill along the way."

"In case I fail, right?" I finished her thought. Those were the words she didn't want to say aloud.

Momma heaved a big sigh and shook her head like she'd given up on the conversation.

"Go tell you brother to come down for breakfast."

I scarfed down a few more bites of my food and snagged my biscuit before reaching down to get my duffle bag. At the foot of the stairs, I yelled for my little brother to come down. He turned off his video game and slowly made his way down the steps. When I was sure he was all the way in the kitchen, I left the house without another word.

Quickly, I hopped in my car and slammed the door shut. I tried not to think too hard on what Momma said about broken dreams and having options. Ms. Hazel was living proof that it could all work out, and she believed in me without hesitation. I was going to get into Ivory Middleton, and I'd be damned if I needed a backup plan just to do it.

As I made my way up to the Northside, where Jevon lived, I thought about what it would be like to spend the whole day with him. Could it be considered a date if it wasn't planned or thought out? I mean, we were doing what we were already going to do today, but together.

I guessed it didn't really matter because just the thought of being alone with him for any extended period of time made my stomach dip in the most unnatural way. My little baby crush on Jevon had sprouted wings. They flapped against my belly whenever I was near him. I prayed I would be able to get that under control before I saw him.

He agreed to let me pick him up this time, but there was an ultimatum for his willingness to volunteer. Jevon would show up at the museum, but only if I came to the dojo with him afterward. His logic was that watching him train would be just as boring for me as the idea of volunteering at the museum was for him.

If his training was anything like the way he'd fought on Tuesday, then he was definitely mistaken. I liked seeing Jevon fight; it was exciting. To be behind the scenes, watching him prepare for the next one was something I looked forward to, mostly because I wanted to know how he did that pressure point thing. Three pokes on the shoulder and Jevon made someone's arm go limp! If I could do that to my little brother then maybe it would keep him out of my stash when he thought I wasn't paying attention.

Eventually, I pulled into the long driveway of Jevon's house. I'd never get over how beautiful his home was. It looked like the type of house that was the *after* to some home makeover show. It was too clean, too new-looking, too perfect.

Jevon walked through door, carrying a black and silver gym bag on his shoulder, looking just as perfect as his surroundings. He sported a pair of shades that made him look like he was in hiding. I doubted anyone would notice him at the museum, but I guess you could never be too sure.

As he opened the passenger door, those imaginary wings waged war with the butterflies in my stomach and I took a deep breath to settle them. He tossed his bag in the back seat and quickly buckled himself in.

For just a split second, we were both confused. Do we kiss? Do we hug? How were we supposed to greet each other now?

"Hey," he settled with a regular one.

"Hey." I tried not to show how disappointed I was that he didn't at least attempt to tongue me down . . . just a little bit.

I put my car into gear and backed out of his driveway. The museum was closer to where he lived, so it wouldn't be that long of a drive.

"Are you excited?" I asked

"No." he answered honestly. "Who do you know gets excited about community service?"

"It's not community service. What do you think we're going to be doing today?"

"I don't know. With Ms. Hazel, she might have us doing something crazy, like painting all the bricks on the wall one by one."

I laughed at that. Ms. Hazel's methods were odd sometimes, but she always had a good reason behind what she did.

"What if I told you I was in charge today?"

"Are you?"

I grinned. "Excited now?"

Instead of answering right away, he adjusted his shades, pushing them up the bridge of his nose to cover his eyes completely.

"We're about to find out," he muttered.

I backed into a parking spot near the front of the building. It was busier today than the last time I was here. There was a short line at the entrance, but since we were volunteering, we had the option to skip it. With our badges looped around our necks, nobody questioned us as we breezed past the growing line.

The materials in my duffle bag felt heavier and heavier as we headed up toward the third floor. I spent a lot of time thinking of an activity good enough to compare to what they were used to doing with Ms. Hazel. Her activities were boring, but she was amazing teacher.

"Is this the museum you used to visit when you were little?" Jevon asked. Even with the sunglasses on, I could see him staring hard at some of the art pieces we walked by.

"One of them, yeah."

We were passing through the African American art collections when Jevon slowed to a stop, taking in the different pictures on the walls. They were all highly expressive with deep and symbolic meaning.

The Civil and Human Rights section was close by, and from experience, I knew if we stayed long enough, we'd get wrapped in every single piece. It was like treading through heavy water; hard to ignore, but even harder to stay.

"Come on." I gently tugged on his arm. "We can always come back later."

Jevon gazed a little longer, but eventually he came with me. We trekked up the last set of steps to the top floor and straight to Ms. Hazel's office. Her door was wide open. We found her on the floor, sorting through metal placards.

"Ms. Hazel?" I called. Her curly fro bounced from side to side as she frantically searched for a missing piece.

"It's right there." Jevon pointed to the small metal piece sticking out from under her desk.

"Oh." she sighed in relief, "Thank you!"

Ms. Hazel collected all the cards and stacked them neatly on the edge of her desk.

"You're here early," she noted with a smile. "Are you ready for this?"

I nodded. "I think so."

"Good! The other teens should be here soon, so that gives you a little bit of time to get set up. I'll be in and out every few minutes to check on you, but you got this."

"Um, where do I set up again?"

"There's an empty room down the hall that we normally use for technical classes, but feel free to take up any space that's available."

"Okay. Thanks, Ms. Hazel."

"Oh, and Jevon?" She stopped us as we headed into the hall. "Lose the shades. This isn't a night club."

I hid a smile as Jevon slowly pocketed his Ray-Bans. When she was satisfied with his new appearance, Ms. Hazel shooed us away and we went in search of a good place to get started. There was an open area by the floor to ceiling windows where the chairs were arranged in a circle already. It wasn't what I had in mind, but it was less work for us. I dropped my duffle bag by the nearest chair and plopped down to the floor in the middle of the circle.

"Now what?" Jevon asked.

"Now, we wait."

"For how long?"

"I don't know, five, maybe ten minutes?"

Jevon was too impatient. He went over to the bag and pulled the zipper back. The small, eight by ten canvases spilled out onto the floor. He picked one up and stared at it.

"You're making us paint?"

"Yes, but it'll be fun." *I hope.*

Jevon was unconvinced. He made a face as he stuffed the materials back into my bag. When he finished, he came over to sit beside me in the middle of the circle. His arm brushed against mine in the process and I leaned into him without thinking.

I knew he didn't mind because he wrapped his arm around me, pulling me in a little closer. This was a much better interaction than our initial greeting. I liked being close to him, wrapped up in his arms.

Moments like this were often fleeting or rushed, but I wanted to make the most of this one. My head rested on his shoulder while we waited, and I caught the light hint of fresh linen on his clothes. He smelled clean. I nuzzled in a little closer, discreetly inhaling the scent of him. It was becoming more familiar to me now.

I peeked up at him as he stared out the long windows. From this angle, his jaw line was more defined. It made him look older, more mature, not that he needed any help in the looks department.

Jevon was handsome in a way that was so obvious, he had to know. He had to know the power he wielded with just a simple smile. He had to know how the feeling of his hand on my shoulder—his thumb rubbing soothing circles near my neck—could quite literally drive a girl insane. He had to know the affect he had on me!

When he turned to catch me staring, my heart did palpitations in my chest. His lip-biting smile definitely wasn't helping, but I smiled back on instinct.

"What?" He asked.

"Nothing." I stared at all of him. "You just reminded me why you're my muse."

Jevon seemed surprised by my words. He started to say something, but he was cut off by the sounds footsteps coming toward us near the stairs. Jevon and I separated as we stood to greet the Teen Team. I waved my hand when I notice the first two girls looking around in confusion.

"Over here!" I beckoned them over to the circle of foldable chairs.

They were still confused, but they came to me anyway. The rest of them trailed behind a little slower, and I counted the heads to make sure we had all ten.

"Where's Ms. Hazel?" the first girl asked.

"She's a little busy right now, so you're stuck with me for the first activity."

"I remember you!" another girl said. "We had to draw you last time."

I smiled. "Yeah, that was me, but we're going to do something a little different today. If you don't remember, my name is Akilah, and this is Jevon. We go to Cambridge School of Arts together."

I pulled the duffle bag toward me and had Jevon help me pass out all the canvases. We gave them each three different colored paint markers and a pencil.

"Who here knows what concept art is?" I asked the group.

At first, they stared at me like I was speaking another language. I started to wonder if my idea was too advanced for them. Then, a boy no older than thirteen or fourteen raised his hand to answer.

"It's like drawing video game characters or cartoons."

"Close." I nodded. "Concept art is like the blueprint to animation. It's the idea behind what a character or a video game could look like."

"We're making cartoons?" he asked.

"You're creating your own ideas. This activity is going to challenge your creative thinking skills. I want you to make something you haven't seen before, something that you could see re-made into a cartoon, or a movie, or even a video game."

They got started before I could even finish explaining, and I smiled at their sudden excitement. Ms. Hazel chose that moment to check in on us. She quietly made her way around the circle, checking what Jevon and I couldn't see in their work.

"You're doing well," she came over to whisper to me, "but conceptual art is more than just cartoons and video games, AJ. You know that."

"Yes, I know, but look at how much fun they're having."

We watched as they traded ideas around the circle, swapping paint markers and half-finished canvases.

"What do you think, Jevon?" she asked him.

"I think it's a good idea," he said simply.

"Do you have anything to add, or were you planning to stand there the whole time?"

"Hey, you." He suddenly pointed to the girl closest to him. She looked up from her painting in surprise. "Good job."

Jevon gave the girl a thumbs up and she blushed a little before returning to her work. With a smile, he turned back to Ms. Hazel like he had just contributed the most valuable information.

"Okay." Ms. Hazel shook her head. "I'm going to head back to the exhibit. I'll be close by if you need anything."

She left us to go back to her own section of the third floor. With her gone, Jevon seemed to relax a little more. He even grabbed a canvas and joined the circle with his own creation.

This felt good. Looking at all the concentrated faces made me realize that maybe Ms. Hazel was right before. Maybe I *could* make a difference here.

CHAPTER TWENTY-NINE

Jevon

Volunteering at the museum wasn't as bad as I'd thought it would be. I definitely wouldn't sign myself up for it again, but it was interesting to see that side of Akilah. She was good with the Teen Team. They asked her questions that I wouldn't even know where to begin with. Most of them wanted to know what it was like at CSA, while the rest just wanted advice on their ideas.

I bided my time in silence. There wasn't much I could add anyway. When Ms. Hazel came back around for the final time, she took over and thankfully let us go.

"You have to admit, that was kind of fun," Akilah said as she led the way back down to the exit.

"It was okay." The only fun part was watching Ms. Hazel get all flustered over every little thing.

"Well, next time—"

"No." I shook my head. "You're not tricking me into that again."

"I never tricked you."

"Akilah." I gave her a pointed look.

"Jevon." She stared back.

Akilah knew exactly what she did to get me here, and as much as I'd liked it, I wasn't falling for it again.

"My debt is paid." I grinned, "I'm not coming back next time, but good luck with that."

"You should be saying 'thank you.' It's because of me you got extra credit on Ms. Hazel's midterm."

Ms. Hazel couldn't stand me, and according to Akilah, she graded like a villain. Extra credit would most likely save my grade.

"Thank you."

"You're welcome."

When we got to her car, I buckled in and double-checked to make sure it was secure. Akilah drove like she was above the law, or better yet, like she didn't know any. The speed limit didn't seem to matter to her, and her brakes were so worn out they screeched with resistance every time she slammed her foot on them to avoid a near collision on the freeway.

By the time we got to the dojo, I had to peel my fingers off the door handle.

"You're being dramatic." Akilah rolled her eyes.

"Tell that to the dude you cut off when you pulled in."

"We could've walked here faster than he was driving!"

"Akilah, with you behind the wheel, we could crash going slow."

"But did you die though?"

I grabbed my gym bag from the floor of her backseat. She drove so wildly, it had fallen from the seat and landed facedown under the passenger seat.

"Exactly," she answered her own question.

I looped the bag over my shoulder and closed the door as we headed toward the building.

"Let me see your keys." I held out my hand.

"Why?"

"I think I have that same key chain."

Akilah held up her car keys to see what I was talking about, and quicker than she could've anticipated, I snatched them from her hand and stuffed them in my pocket without warning or explanation.

"What are you doing?"

"You can have these back later." *After I drive myself home.*

"Really?"

"Yup."

I held the door open for her to go inside first. The dojo was slowly emptying out as the earlier sessions were coming to an end.

"You excited?" I threw her previous question back on her.

"I am actually." She smiled proudly.

"Why? You're just going to be watching."

"You can learn a lot from watching."

I was going to ask what she meant by that, but I was suddenly caught off guard by the round of applause I received when I came into the room. My teammates and all the trainers at the Hard Knocks Dojo clapped for me. It wasn't because of anything I did at the match last Tuesday.

Ever since I'd signed the contract to join Shane in his world tour, my team gave me flack for it when they could. They were mostly upset that I was leaving the team soon after I graduated. With Akilah here as their audience, I made it too easy for them to tease me.

"Hey, superstar!" Sasha greeted me with a light punch in the shoulder.

I sighed. "Hey, Sasha."

"Who's this?"

"Sasha, Akilah, Akilah, Sasha."

"Hi." Akilah waved.

"Hi, are you joining us today, or . . ."

"No, I'm just watching."

Sasha stared between Akilah and me in confusion, a range of different questions in her eyes.

"Akilah goes to CSA with me," I said, hoping that would be enough for Sasha to catch the hint.

"Oh, the artist?"

"Yes."

"Ah." Sasha stared between us for a completely different reason now, smiling like she'd finally caught on to a secret we'd never shared. "Okay, well, have a seat, Akilah. I'll see you on the floor in ten, Jevon. Go get changed."

I headed to the locker room to change into my workout gear. A few of my teammates were packing up to leave when I came inside. They immediately stopped what they were doing when they saw me and clapped so loud their echo bounced off the walls.

"Alright, I get it!" I waved them down. "Ya'll can chill out now!"

"Woo!" Marc and Theo kept it up.

There was a roll of wrap tape on the bench next to my locker. I picked it up and chucked it as hard as I could in their direction.

I hit Marc in the leg. "Ow! Man, what the hell?"

I laughed when he started to rub at his shin.

"You better be glad I'm leaving, Williams." He threatened, but he wasn't serious. I knew because he dapped me up on the way out.

I got changed quickly and was back on the floor in no time. Sasha was ready for me when I got there. She was practicing air strikes with a Tongkat as she skillfully maneuvered around the mat. Her ponytail whipped wildly around her while she worked. I went to the weaponry podium and grabbed my own fighting stick before joining her on the mat.

Sasha didn't stop when she saw me. She didn't give me time to warm up or stretch as she aimed her next strike at my face. I brought my Tongkat up just in time to clash against hers. It vibrated in my hands from the force of her swing.

"Good anticipation, Jevon!"

Sasha whipped her staff around her body defensively, waiting for me to return her first move. I watched her footwork closely. She inched toward me slowly while leaning back on her right foot. That told me she was planning to lead the next strike with her left foot then dodge and move with the right.

In two easy strikes to her staff, I broke up the defensive rotation she was spinning. She lost her grip on her Tongkat, but it didn't fall. Still, I used that to my advantage. It left her entire front open for me to follow back with another strike. Taking the butt end of my Tongkat, I jammed it into her midsection. Sasha stumbled backward, but she caught her balance quickly.

"Whew, that one hurt." She made a T with her hands to signal a time-out. After a few deep breaths and a mouth full of water, she gave me a single nod, and we were back.

This time, Sasha came back harder. She swung her staff at me with a vengeance, not allowing me a second to recover. I blocked the first swing, but the next two hit me hard enough to pause the blood flow in my right arm. It stung like hell, but I kept moving, dodging what I could as she came at me.

"Watch your defense, Jay." She snapped her fingers. "Pick it up."

All of a sudden I bent back as far as I could go. It was more of a natural instinct, than anything I did on purpose because Sasha's Tongkat came barreling at my head out of nowhere.

"Whoo!" I whistled at how close I'd come to a possible concussion.

"Nice." She casually took another swing.

"Let's go, Jevon! Finish it!" Nick encouraged me from the sideline.

I almost wished we could trade places. Sasha was too fast. Left with no other options, I planted my Tongkat into the floor and used it as a base to support my weight as I gave myself a short running start into a powerful kick-spin. When she was close enough to make contact again, I kicked out with my legs, sending Sasha's body pummeling down to the floor with a heavy thud. She grunted on impact, releasing a small cry of pain as she stared up at the ceiling.

It took Sasha a little longer to get up than any of the other times I was lucky enough to knock her down. For a moment, I thought I had seriously hurt her—until she rolled over onto all fours. Using her Tongkat to help her up, Sasha rubbed away the pain in her mid-section with her hand.

"Are you okay?" I asked. I'd never had to ask her that before.

She shook her head no. "You knocked the wind out of me that's for sure, but I've taken worse whoopings than you, kid."

"Let's take a break, and then we'll run that move again." Nick suddenly joined us on the mat. "That was quick thinking, Jevon. If we clean it up a little and work on your control, you'll be damn near unstoppable."

He helped his wife over to the nearest first aid cabinet. They broke in an ice pack and placed it on her stomach. I left my Tongkat on the mat and joined a wide-eyed Akilah on the bleachers. She stared at me with her mouth open in disbelief.

"What?" I asked.

"That's how you train?"

"Yeah, why?"

"You could've killed each other!"

That made me chuckle.

"What's funny about that? She almost put you in a coma."

"We're professionals, Akilah. How'd you think this was going to go?"

"I don't know, but I wasn't expecting that."

"Still excited?"

"Oh, yeah." She answered that one easily. "But now I'm a little nervous for you."

"I'm offended." Didn't she see how I'd just ended the fight? I knocked Sasha off her feet . . . Sasha!

Akilah smiled. "Just don't get knocked out, okay? I have to get you back home in one piece."

"That's real cute." I added sardonically.

Now she was the one laughing. When she got her fill, she leaned in to kiss me on the cheek.

"What was that for?" I asked.

"For luck. Now go, superstar."

* * *

Later that day, after training was over, I made good on my promise to drive myself back home. Akilah's car should've been grateful to have me behind the wheel because she nearly blew her engine every time she hit the freeway.

"I had a really good time with you today," she said when we were safely in my driveway.

"Me too."

"We should do it again."

"But without the museum," I added.

"And, the dojo," she countered.

"Okay, so a date?"

"A real one."

"Deal."

"Swear on it," she demanded. Akilah held out her pinky finger expectantly.

"You want me to pinky swear?"

"Yeah." She smiled sheepishly. "Is that weird?"

It was a little weird in general for me to pinky swear on anything, but for Akilah, I hooked my pinky with hers. She leaned in and kissed her thumb to seal the promise. When she was done, I leaned in to kiss her cherry-flavored lips.

"I'll see you later," I told her.

"Bye, Jevon."

CHAPTER THIRTY

Akilah

That night, I took a chance and decided to finally work on my application to Ivory Middleton. After everything my mother said about keeping my options open. I felt like I needed to do this, not only for myself, but to prove a point.

Momma would never admit it—not even to herself—but there was a part of her that secretly doubted me. Maybe, in her own way, she was trying to protect me. Maybe she really thought she was helping, but to me, every time Momma opened her mouth to talk about college, or my future, all I ever heard was "you'll never be good enough."

It was *her* voice that I heard in the back of my head whenever I thought about my future. *She* was the reason I was behind in my applications, and if I were being honest with myself, it was because of *her* that I was so afraid to be stuck here. Because then she would be right, and I would be forced to believe every doubt that swarmed my mind.

I said a silent prayer as I logged into my laptop. Ivory Middleton's website had been saved as a bookmark on my computer for so long, but now I actually had the courage to apply. The candid photos of the students on campus, in their dorm rooms, and even in class was enough to make me want to physically be there. I wanted so badly to be a part of this institution, yet as I stared at the big, green button that said "Apply," I couldn't seem to fully shake that voice. *Momma's* voice.

... I know how heartbroken I was when everything I wanted didn't magically come true for me.

Ivory Middleton students were amazingly talented and from all over the world; kids who had been labeled artistic geniuses at such young ages. I took the time to mull over my portfolio. Pages and pages of work I'd completed since the day I started at CSA. From cover to cover, all of my heavily critiqued artwork littered the glossy pages. Funny how what was once a perfect creation to me was now covered in flaws when it came to attaching them to my application.

...You don't have to put all your eggs in one basket.

Maybe it would be better if I worked my way up to the Ivory Middleton application.

That way, I could get at least a few backup schools in place. It was smarter to have a backup plan, than no plan at all. I was stubborn, not stupid.

I opened a new tab and pulled up a list of art schools that were far away from home. It wasn't that I was trying to escape my family, but more distance somehow made me feel more successful in my journey to becoming a true artist.

These applications seemed easier; they asked for less information with lowered expectations. Some of my work almost seemed too good, too polished for schools that just didn't hold up in comparison. Still, I submitted my applications without hesitation.

After the third backup school I applied to, I went back to the Ivory Middleton screen. An "Are You Still There?" popup brought me to a pause. Once again, I flipped through the pages of my portfolio. I stared at the glossy film of each page for so long that it started to dull in my eyes.

With a frustrated groan, I roughly shoved my laptop toward the foot of my bed. It was getting late, and my thoughts were working against me. There was no point in trying to complete it tonight. I went to the dresser by the door and opened the top drawer. Hidden behind a mound of socks and underwear, was my lockbox.

I punched in the four digit code and waited for the click to open it. Pushing aside the sticks of incense and the wad of saved allowance, I grabbed a perfectly pre-rolled joint. There was a lighter tucked somewhere in the treehouse, so I didn't bother trying to find another one in my room.

My lockbox went right back to its hiding spot and I tiptoed over to the window. The house was quiet, but if I listened hard enough, I could hear the faint sounds of CJ's TV playing softly in his room. I took extra care opening my window and throwing the escape ladder over the sill. Sometimes it liked to sway against the side of the house, causing more noise than if I had just walked out the back door.

From practice, I easily descended the swaying ladder without losing my balance. When I made it to ground, I double-checked to make sure everyone was still asleep. My parents' room lights were off, and as expected, I caught the blue glow of the TV reflecting in CJ's window. His lights were off too, so I was hoping he'd just fallen asleep with the TV on.

The only light unaccounted for was the treehouse. The multi-colored Christmas lights lit up the small box, and for a moment, I wondered if I'd forgot to turn them off the last time I was there. I was high when I'd left, so the possibility of me leaving them on were also . . . high.

In the dark, I normally had to feel my way around for the tiny steps nailed into the tree, but with the Christmas lights illuminating everything, I made it up the steps much quicker this time.

A voice greeted me before I was all the way inside. "It's about time you showed up."

I lost my footing on the last step, and I would've dropped to the ground if a hand hadn't reached out to catch me. My eyes followed that hand up to a face, too wary to trust it to pull me up.

"CJ?!" The shock made my voice squeak.

"Shh!" My brother yanked me up with all his strength. "You trying to wake the whole neighborhood up?"

"What are you doing here?"

"It's my treehouse too."

"Yeah, but you don't come here. Why are you here now?"

CJ claimed the spot I normally sat in. He made himself comfortable as he stretched out his long legs and rested his hands on the back of his head.

"I was waiting for you."

"Come again?"

"You're not as slick as you think you are, Ki. I know what you do up here." He paused to sniff the air. "And you brought the loud pack with you this time."

My hands flew to my pocket, like that would help to cover the stench. He'd caught me, and I had no defense. The best I could do was give him my most menacing stare, but it really had no effect on him.

"Chill, I won't tell on you." He grinned. "*If* you share with me."

"No." I didn't even have to think about the answer.

"Do you really want to play this game?" CJ dared me.

I crossed my arms and matched his audacious stare. It took only a few blinks to realize he clearly wasn't going to give in, so I tried to level with him.

With a sigh, I claimed the seat beside him. "Why are you trying to smoke all of a sudden? What's going on?"

CJ shrugged and I was starting to think that was the only answer he would give me when he looked me straight in the face and asked, "Why do you do it?"

There was that question again. Was this a test? Were he and Jevon in cahoots now?

"Because I'm grown," I said matter-of-factly. It was the same "do as I say, and not as I do" answer we often got from our parents.

"You're seventeen."

"Almost grown!"

"I'm going to be a senior next year. How do you know I'm not doing it already?"

"Are you?" My stash was getting lighter every time I checked, and it couldn't have been our parents going through my stuff.

Again, CJ shrugged. "I tried it."

"And?"

He hid an embarrassing smile, but then he started laughing at himself.

"I was wheezing after the first puff."

I laughed with him, remembering the first time I'd tried it, and how embarrassing it was when I coughed so much I couldn't catch my breath.

"I'm glad you told me, CJ, but I really don't like the idea of you smoking." CJ started to argue, but I cut him off. "I know I sound like a hypocrite, but you're my baby brother. Just because I do it, doesn't mean it's okay."

"Just because I want to do it, doesn't mean it's a bad thing. People use it all the time for medicinal reasons and other stuff."

"Other stuff like what?"

"Like anxiety and stress."

CJ made a face at the last part. I would've asked what he had to stress about, or what he could possibly feel anxious for, but then I realized it was none of my business. He'd told me enough, and I was glad he did.

There was a deeper reason my little brother was in this tree-house with me. Maybe we shared the same overwhelming feelings of doubt and uncertainty when it came to our futures, or maybe I had it all wrong. Maybe there was something else that brought him here, something that just simply sharing a blunt with his big sister would solve.

Either way, I didn't question him further. I dug the spliff out of my pocket and reached for the red lighter stuffed under the rug. In two sparks, it lit a flame, and my brother and I shared more with each other than we had in a really long time.

CHAPTER THIRTY-ONE

Jevon

Monday started off early for me. I trained with Nick right before school, and today was all about endurance. He took me on a jog around the nearest neighborhood to the dojo, which really felt more like a marathon. We were up so early the only signs of life in the area were the birds chirping up in the sky.

We ran on the back roads of the city. They were surrounded by mainly trees, grassy fields, and suburban homes. The humid air was coated in a morning dew so thick it was foggy outside.

Nick kept up a good pace beside me, breathing as easily as if he were taking a lazy stride. This was a typical morning for him and Sasha, while I struggled to keep my breathing even. It wasn't hard to keep up with the pace we were going, but knowing Nick, he'd kick up the speed at any moment.

"Breathe, Jevon." He modeled the way I was supposed to do it. "In through your nose, out through your mouth."

I followed his example, doing my best to gain control of my lungs.

Nick laughed at my attempt. "We're just getting started. If you can't keep up, let me know now."

Nick was in his mid-thirties, about to out-run me, an eighteen-year-old. He was testing me.

"I can keep up," I managed to get out between jagged breaths.

"Good."

Nick smiled like I had no clue what I'd just asked for. Without another word, he took off, kicking up small rocks and dust behind him. My reaction time was way too slow. By the time I had even managed to follow his lead, Nick was already at the end of the road, waiting at the stop sign for the cars to pass by.

He jogged in place to keep his heart rate up, but he was really just showing off. I chugged the bottle of water I had on hand while we had a short break. I knew that as soon as the next two cars passed by, my break would be over and Nick would leave me to eat his dust again. If he could do it, then I could too. He just made it look easier.

Like a flash, Nick was off again. He gave no warning or indication that we were about to run. He was gone before the last car could drive fully past us. At this point, it felt more like a race than a jog for training.

With my long legs, I was able to make up for distance where I lacked in speed. We ran all the way up to a trail that was just as brutal as a hike through the Arkaquah Trail in north Georgia. Nick effortlessly ran through the brush of trees, low hanging branches, and the occasional slippery incline of fallen leaves over the hidden, rocky earth beneath.

By the time we made it the through to the end of the trail, I was drenched in sweat and completely out of breath. I tried to place my hands above my head to slow my breathing, like Nick said, but that wasn't working. I hadn't run that far and that fast in a very long time. Meanwhile, Nick seemed only a little winded, ready to take on another expedition.

"How are we getting back?" I asked. We were at least a good six and a half miles from where we'd started.

"The same way we got here."

Nick stretched his calf muscles, pulling his legs back one at a time by the toe of his sneakers. I checked the time on my watch. The sun had just begun to peek through the clouds, bringing with it a slow rising heat that would settle throughout the day. I had hardly enough time to run back, get showered, and changed to be ready for school.

"I have to be to school in the next hour, Nick. We won't make it back in time."

"Well, you better run fast, kid."

I looked around at the trees, the dirt, and the bare, empty road ahead. There was no way he'd make me run through the same trail that had me breathing like a chain smoker already. Nick wasn't really the joking type, but there had to be a punch line or something.

"Ready?" he asked, already jogging in place to prepare himself.

Do I have a choice?

Nick took off into the maze of trees. He disappeared quickly, running as fast as I should've been if I wanted to make it to school on time. It was like he got a boost of energy out of nowhere. I took one last swig of water, gulping down a mouthful before daring to following after him.

* * *

Of course I was late.

I showed up to school by second period. As hard as I tried, I couldn't catch up to Nick. Halfway through coming back, I had to take a break going downhill. My lungs felt like sand paper scraping against my chest. It would take a lot more training before I was able to do a twelve-mile run every morning, and Nick knocked it out like it was his warm up.

By the time I came into class, Mrs. Parker, my English teacher, was in the middle of a lesson. She paused for a moment, giving me a bored stare all the way to my desk. I was kinda sore from the marathon I just had to run, so I walked slowly.

My feet dragged across the floor like cinder blocks. Eventually, she went back to her lesson, talking about the same things she always did. She joked that she was the "grammatical ninja, coming to chop away at all the errors." Nobody laughed.

All the way in the back of the classroom, I busied myself with my phone. There was a recent update to the rankings of fighters. It was posted on the league's national website today. Pops had warned me that my scores would be delayed because of that viral video, and the judges had finally come to a decision.

I was anxious to know if my rankings had changed. After my fight last week, I was hoping to go back to my original status, or somewhere close to it. Before my summer brawl with Jao Shang, I was third in the nation overall in my division, and fifth internationally. I couldn't even remember the last time I'd checked my status. It was never something I had to worry about. Now, I couldn't stop my leg from jumping under my desk as I waited for the page to load.

Regardless of where I stood, Shane Tithers had already given me a deal. He knew what happened all those months ago and he'd still decided to work with me. It shouldn't have mattered where I stood, but it did to me.

Finally, the page came into focus as it refreshed for the last time. The scores were up for the world to see. I typed my name into the search bar, too impatient to scroll down the list. My profile popped up instantly, showcasing all of my victories and losses.

Where there used to be the word "Champion" underneath my name, it was now left blank. Like Pops predicted, my rankings had dropped. No longer was I third in the nation, or fifth internationally. Despite my recent win last week, and my overflow of wins from previous seasons, I was brought down to twelfth place overall in the nation.

I checked the numbers from my last fight of the prior season in London. In all three rounds, I lost to Shang by a 10-5 margin. A 10-8 margin was a rare score, because that meant the loser—who ended up with 8 out of 10 total points—had lost by such a large difference that it wasn't considered an even fight. 10-5 was unheard of.

Mrs. Parker showed up beside me suddenly, zeroing in on my screen. "I don't think I put my lesson plan on your phone, Mr. Williams."

I was quick to flip my phone over and tuck it up under my notebook, but Mrs. Parker had already seen it. She held her hand out expectantly. I knew the rules against phones, but I wasn't in the mood to comply. My title had been stripped away like it was nothing. All my hard work was suddenly reduced to a below average score.

"Jevon," she tried again with a sharp, authoritative tone in her voice.

All eyes turned on me and Mrs. Parker as she placed a hand on her hip in expectation. "Either you give me your phone, or you can leave my classroom."

If those were my only options, then my choice was easy. I grabbed my book bag from the floor and stood up to leave. I ignored the whispers and comments my classmates made as I walked by. They would gossip about this for the rest of the week, I was sure.

With my bag over my shoulder, I made my way out into the hall. It was empty, except for a few students with different class schedules. I didn't intend on ditching school today, but I found myself walking past my locker, past the principal's office, and right out through the front door.

Right now, nothing else mattered to me but the scores I'd just received. There had to have been worst battles in MMA history than the likes of me and Jao Shang. The judges could swipe my scores, drop my rankings, and drag my name through the mud if they wanted; but to take my title, the one thing I had truly earned, felt like more than just a punishment. It was a sentencing, a criminal conviction in its own right.

I wondered if Pops knew. What would he say when he found out? An "I told you so," would be too cruel, but he had to have a plan. There was no way he'd lie down and accept this as my fate. I couldn't.

I got in my car and stuck the key in the ignition. Without thinking too deeply about the consequences, I put it in gear and drove out of the school's parking lot. There was nowhere for me to go. I couldn't go to the dojo, I had just finished a session with Nick, and I definitely couldn't go home. The security cameras would alert my parents the moment I stepped through the door.

So, I just drove. I drove until the urge to punch something slowly faded away. I drove until I was calm enough to ease my foot off the gas pedal. I drove until all I saw was open road and fields of trees. I drove until my phone started vibrating in my pocket with an urgency that was all too familiar.

"Pops." I picked up on the second ring.

"Where are you?" He didn't sound upset, but he was out of patience.

I must've taken too long to answer because he said, "Don't lie to me, Jevon. I got a call from your school."

"I'm driving."

"How far are you from the office?"

My parents' office was all the way in Buckhead, in the middle of the city. I didn't know exactly where I was, but I knew I had driven myself outside the city limits. For miles, all I could see was open fields of grass.

"Not that far." I lied. "I'm on my way."

"Good. I'll see you soon."

Pops hung up swiftly. Soon for him, often meant immediately. I flipped a U-turn in the middle of the road and gunned it back toward the direction I'd come from.

Now that the shock had worn off from me losing my title, I could think a little more rationally. This didn't have to be the end-all-be-all for my career, but it definitely took a massive hit at all my achievements. Who was I if I wasn't the champion I'd worked so hard to become? Who would I be if I never got the chance to reclaim my title?

I made it to my parents' office building before Pops had to call again. By the time I got up to the ninth floor, he and Dave were locked in a deep discussion. Their heads snapped up the moment I entered the room.

"Jevon," Pops addressed me, "come sit."

I took the chair opposite of him, right next to Dave. My dad had this look in his face that I couldn't really read. He tapped his finger-tips together in front of him as he leaned back in his chair. Dave seemed a little bit wary too, but not of my father. He was watching me, like he was waiting for something.

"What do you want most of out your career right now?" Pops asked.

I was confused. He already knew what I wanted.

"Short term," he clarified. "What do you want most out of your career in the short term."

"To raise my rank and get my title back."

Pops nodded, his face void of any emotion. "That's an obstacle, son, not a goal. Think hard. What have you wanted more than any-thing recently?"

I wished he would just tell me what it was. I wasn't in the mood for a quiz. The one thing I'd always wanted in my career was to be an Olympian. To me, it didn't get much bigger than that, but he wanted me to think short term. What could I really want bad enough right now?

I took a minute to think about my life in rewind, going back a few days first, then a few weeks, a few months. When I broke it down that way, there was one common theme I noticed replaying in my past. The one thing I'd craved the most out of everything was: redemption.

"Jao Shang." My jaw clenched. I didn't need to explain.

Pops sat up in his seat, a satisfied grin taking over his face. He looked to Dave, who had been silent this whole time. Dave seemed satisfied by my answer too. He reached over to pull out a thick stack of papers from his briefcase. They were held together by a bulging clip at the top.

"What if I told you there was an opportunity for a rematch?" Dave finally spoke up. He had that lawyer smirk on his face that told me he already had something in the works. "Something small and out of the public eye?"

"If you told me I had the opportunity to go up against Shang again, all I'd need to know is what time to be there."

"I'm glad you said that, son." Pops stood from his seat and walked over to his door before turning back to me. "Now, I need you to remain very calm."

"Why?" I was suddenly anything *but* calm. He was acting strange.

"Jevon, I need you to trust me." He gave me a hard glare, his hand going rigid around the door handle. "Do not leave that seat, and don't you dare do something you can't take back."

I turned my entire body toward him—the chair included. Something wasn't right.

"Dad," I kept my voice as calm as I could manage, "what's going on?"

Pops didn't answer. Instead, he opened the door to welcome in new guests. When I saw who was on the other side of that door, I stood up so fast the chair fell back behind me.

"Pops, what the hell is this?"

Jao Shang drew a cunning smile from the other side of the room. He winked at me when Pops' back was turned.

"Jevon!" Pops barked at me, then to Jao Shang and his PR team, he posed a political smile. "Thank you all for coming. Please, have a seat."

Dave ushered them to suede couch in the corner of the room. He brought his stack of papers with him, passing out the copies while they talked. Pops was in my face before I knew it. He lowered his voice so only I could hear.

"You need to get yourself under control, now! You are not in the fighting ring. This is about business, and we will conduct ourselves like gentlemen. Do you understand me?"

"This was an ambush," I matched his tone. "You could've told me that—"

"I don't have to tell you anything! You get over there and you nod your head 'yes' and shake your head 'no' when you're supposed to. On the fighting floor, that's your territory, you can do what you want. But here, in *my* office, we handle business with our words, not our fists. Remember who you are."

Without another word, my father joined the other men at the couches. He turned on the charm as he brought life to the conversation. My fists were balled so tight I felt the veins shift painfully over my knuckles.

I took the biggest, deepest, calming breath I could muster, and imitated my father. The smile I plastered on my face wasn't only good enough for photo ops and interviews. Claiming the seat next to my father, I paid close attention as Dave went over the details in the contract he'd drafted up.

He took the time to make sure there was a clear understanding on both sides that we were repealing the judges' scores from the finals last season. Shang agreed all too easily. He had way more to lose in this fight than I did, but I didn't care why he wanted the rematch. I needed this.

When it was all said and done, Shang and I were forced to shake hands across the table. All smiles were gone as an unspoken retribution was declared. I'd see him in the ring in just a few days.

CHAPTER THIRTY-TWO

Akilah

Monday went by without a word from Jevon. It was like he disappeared or ghosted me or something. I heard all about him walking out of class, but I figured he would be back on Tuesday.

I didn't want to pry even though there was nothing but radio silence from him since Saturday. Maybe he was suspended for skipping school, or in trouble at home. Either way, he wasn't here, and I was honestly worried about him.

Kayla and I were in the Senior Lounge upstairs. It was our free period, and she had her books out, pretending to study, but that only lasted about ten minutes until her phone lit up. Her earbuds were tucked in her ears as her head bopped to the music.

I tugged on the notebook she had out closest to me and started doodling between the lines to pass the time. I started off with swirls, just to get a feel for the glittery purple pen I'd grabbed from my bag. The swirls got bigger and bigger as they slowly formed into long-stemmed roses.

Doodling gave me an easy distraction. What I really wanted was to escape to the back of the lounge where Jevon and I had kissed for the third time. That hidden section of the room was now ours, but he wasn't here.

My ring finger smudged out a shading pattern into the bud of the roses. The glitter stained my fingers like crazy, but it was worth it to see my picture come to life. I let a few petals fall from one rose to cover up the swirls that just didn't make the cut.

"Oh my God!" Kayla gasped.

Her mouth hung open as she switched her phone to her left hand for a better grip. She scrolled up the page to reread what she saw and gasped again, "OH MY GOD!"

"What?" I finally asked.

"Did you know about this?"

Kayla slid her phone my way, pointing to a flyer from a post she found on Twitter. In big, bold letters, it read:

PRIVATE WATCH PARTY. TONIGHT. A REMATCH YOU DON'T WANT TO MISS.

Under the letters were two separate photos of both Jevon and his opponent, Jao Shang. They were cut out to fit the flyer like they were facing each other. They both squared up across from one another, sporting mean mugs that seemed personal.

I scrolled down to see if this was real. Words like 'exclusive', and 'restricted access' stood out to me as I read through the fans' disappointed complaints. This was an invite-only kind of thing.

"Well? Did you know?" Kayla pressed, an eager smile on her face.

I returned her phone and brought my attention back down to my drawing. "No, I wasn't invited."

"Really? He didn't tell you?"

"Nope."

I focused on the roses blooming on the page. They sparkled in the light with each movement of the notebook paper.

"Why don't you just ask him?" She shrugged like it was the obvious solution.

"Kayla, if he wanted us there, then he would've told us about it."

I didn't mean to snap at her, but it was a little frustrating that I hadn't seen or heard from Jevon since Saturday and suddenly he had this big event that no one knew about. Kayla ignored my tone. She took her phone back and read over the flyer again like she would spot something new on the page.

"Look." She pointed to the fine print. "It's at the same place from the last fight. You were there last weekend. They know you!"

I took another look at the flyer. The address was familiar, but there was something else I noticed this time, something I'd over-looked before.

Jevon Williams VS Jao Shang. Tonight.

Jao Shang.

I remembered that name. He was Jevon's biggest rival. This was the boy that taunted Jevon online. The same boy from the video that was all over the Internet.

"Woah, Kayla, this might be something big."

"That's exactly why we should be there."

Whatever was going on with Jevon's absence, I bet it had a lot to do with this fight.

"Okay, I'm willing to try to get us in, but I can't make any promises."

The last fight was open to the public, but this was different. This was a private event with restricted access. My limited familiarity could only get me so far.

"Only one way to find out." Kayla smiled.

* * *

After school, I drove us to the Hard Knocks Dojo by memory. I chose to drown out my own subconscious, which told me to stay home. The closer we got to that side of town, the faster my heart began to beat. If this fight was really as legendary as it was advertised to be, then it would come as no surprise if we were turned right back around at the door.

When we finally made it there, I found a parking spot easily, only because the parking lot was nearly empty. There weren't as many people as I thought there would be.

"Are you sure this is the right place?" Kayla asked.

"Yeah, it's what the post said."

Kayla and I headed to entrance of the building. Two security guards were at the door with their arms crossed tightly against their chests. So, that was what they mean by restricted access.

"Name?" the first one asked, pulling out a clipboard from his podium to check.

My eyes briefly drifted to Kayla. She knew just as well as I did that our names were not on the list, yet she garnished a confident smile that said otherwise.

"We know the owners," she said as she attempted to make her way into the building.

Her movements were instantly halted by the other security guard who blocked our entry with his arm planted firmly in front of the door.

"I didn't ask who you knew. What's your name, ma'am?"

"Akilah Johnson," I butted in. "Is Akilah on the list?"

Security guard number one breathed heavily as he took the time to scroll through the list, even flipping over to the second page. His head was already shaking 'no' before he could give us a verdict. I knew it was a bad idea to come. There was no way they would let us in without our names somehow magically appearing on their lists.

I began searching for my keys in one of my jacket pockets, but Kayla stopped me. She pointed to the entrance where Sasha was suddenly leaving. Her arms were full to the brim with two boxes of trash and leftover decorations from setting up.

She couldn't see us with the way the boxes were positioned in front of her face, but she watched her steps from underneath. Kayla nudged me forward with an elbow to my spine, and my feet stumbled closer to where she was as I nearly ran into her.

"Let me help you," I offered, reaching for one of the boxes in her hands.

Sasha looked up in surprise, angling her head to see who was talking to her. She lowered the boxes for me to grab the one on top and I gave a little wave.

"Akilah? Hey!"

"Hey, Sasha."

"You came to see the fight?" She nodded her head toward the dojo.

"I did."

We walked in silence as I thought of a way to bring up the fact that I wasn't actually invited. There was a very good possibility that she would let us in, but they'd hired security for a reason. I threw the box into the dumpster bin once we made it over to the side of the building.

"This is a really important night for Jevon," she boasted proudly. "I'm glad you came. He'll need the support."

I couldn't imagine Jevon needing my support. He was just so okay with going about this whole ordeal without saying a word.

As we rounded the corner to the main entrance of the dojo, Sasha breezed past security easily. She walked straight into the building without looking back, expecting me to follow behind. I did try to catch up to her, only when I got to the door, security guard number two caught me by the arm and pulled me back.

"I'm with her!" I pointed at Sasha, who finally turned around.

"What's going on here?" she asked.

"Ma'am, this girl is not on the list. We're not authorized to let her in."

"Well, consider this your authorization." Sasha said with a little force. "Let her go."

The security guard released my arm, and I quickly took Kayla by the hand. We rushed to follow Sasha inside the building. The familiar rush of air conditioning almost stopped me cold in my tracks with its briskness, but I shook it off. We were finally in and that was all that mattered.

The dojo looked almost the same as the last time I was there. The large floor mat was gone. There was now a stage that took up the center of the room with a circle that covered everything but the edges of the stage.

People lined the bleachers like before, except there was something strikingly different about the crowd this time around. They all stared at the fighting floor with a suspense that made my stomach flop.

The fighting hadn't even happened yet, but the air around us was already charged with an intense kind of expectation. These people weren't just fans of the sport—they looked more official than Kayla or I had even anticipated.

Sasha walked us over to the back where her office was. She sighed deeply as she unlocked the door to let us in. Quickly, she reached over her desk to grab the stack of bright red wristbands before ripping off two for Kayla and me.

"Sorry about all the security. You have to understand how important this is."

"It's okay, I get it. Thanks for letting us in."

Sasha seemed confused for a moment as she peeled off the back sticker to wrap the band around my wrist.

"Your name really wasn't on the list?"

"No, it wasn't."

"Hmm, that's weird. Jevon should've added you."

Yeah, he should've.

Sasha moved over to place a wristband on Kayla and ushered us out of her office. The lights started to dim, so we quickened our pace to find a seat in the bleachers. I didn't want to miss a thing.

Upfront, Sasha made it to the stage just in time to get the show started. She adjusted the mic stand to her height as Nick slipped in to join her. He wrapped his arm around her waist in support.

"Welcome back, ladies and gentlemen, to the Hard Knocks Dojo!" Sasha said. "This is the rematch that you all made possible through your continued support and love for these two incredibly talented fighters. This is not only about fairness in judgment, but this is a fight for the title of champion in this past season."

Sasha paused as we all erupted into applause. Now I knew why this battle was so important. Jevon was fighting for his title, his respect—two things I knew he took very seriously.

"Without further ado, I would like to invite both Jevon Williams and Jao Shang to the fighting floor."

The two rose up from wherever they were hiding within the crowd and met each other halfway on either side of Nick and Sasha. Jevon's face was a blank wall, void of emotion. He stared right through Jao Shang, unaffected by his intimidation tactics.

Shang took to flexing his muscles and smacking himself across the chest and face with his fists. His beige skin turned slightly red under the impact, but he looked like he didn't even feel it. Jao Shang bounced lightly on his feet as if he couldn't wait for the fighting to begin.

Sasha and Nick stated a few mandatory rules and regulations before ushering them to shake hands. Jao Shang smacked his hand so hard against Jevon's I could see their conjoined clasp quiver. The crowd got a rise out of this as many people started to lean over in their seats. Jevon and his opponent were separated instantly and held in place until they were given the signal to begin.

In comparison, Jao Shang was much slimmer than Jevon. His muscles were compact and tightly wound around his arms, legs, and chest. I stared at the both of them, noting all the ways they were different from each other. As two champions fighting for the same title, there was no telling how this could all end.

Before we knew it, Sasha and Nick were leaving the stage. The room went silent as the fight was set to begin. Jevon and Jao Shang took to circling each other within the fighting area. Neither one of them made a move as both boys intently watched the other.

I couldn't hear from all the way up in the stands, but I could see Jao Shang spouting words to Jevon. He smiled like what he said was funny, but I could see that Jevon didn't think the same. In fact, whatever was said caused Jevon to break stride in their circling tactic. He had suddenly brought himself on the offense as he reached out to strike Shang clean across the face.

Shang's head whipped to the side forcefully, knocking him back a few steps. This did nothing to wipe the grin off of his face; he was loving this. He bounced lightly on his feet from side to side as he prepared to take on more of Jevon's hits. Shang gave Jevon the signal to bring it on and my hands clasped together tightly in anticipation.

Jevon wasted no time in striking Jao Shang again and again. He went for the jugular, aiming to take him out cold with a tooth clenching jab to the throat, but Jao Shang was quicker. He easily dodged Jevon's blow and returned a few of his own. With lightning speed, Shang repeatedly struck Jevon's side so brutally it caused Jevon to double over in pain.

"Come on, Jevon," I mumbled—mostly to myself—over and over again.

Jao Shang was full of energy as he was now on the offense. In a high jump-kick maneuver, Shang whipped his foot out sharply, making contact with Jevon's chest. Jevon tumbled backward and almost fell over, but he caught himself just in time. Thankfully, he recovered quickly. Jevon was up on his feet and he was angry now, really angry. I could see Jevon flex his muscles, shaking off the pain of Jao Shang's hits as best as he could.

One thing that became very clear as I watched this whole encounter was that Jao Shang was incredibly cocky. Every hit he was able to land on Jevon seemed to give him more energy to fuel a reaction out of the people in the crowd. He waved his fists victoriously like he had already won, and the fight had barely even begun.

Jevon held his hands in a defensive position, ready to take on whatever Shang had coming. Shang's movements were sharp and jerky. For a minute there, he moved too fast for me to keep up. Luckily, Jevon was able to match his pace. He deftly blocked Jao Shang's hits as they slowly inched toward the edge of the circle.

Both boys struggled to gain the upper hand, jabbing and kicking at each other until somebody showed pain. Any chance that he could, Shang attacked Jevon in that same spot on his side. Over and over again, Jevon took hits to his left side, causing him to wince in pain.

When Shang got close enough, Jevon was better able to defend himself. He was somehow able to lock Jao Shang in a hold that kept him down and out of the way for a while. Kayla and I inched closer in our seats like the rest of the audience as we watched Jao Shang struggle against him. After seeing how arrogant he was before, I kind of liked watching him squirm.

"Yes!" I shouted.

I wanted Jevon to hold him there longer, or push him over the edge, or choke him out, or something! They were so close to the edge of the circle, all Jevon needed to do was kick him out. But of course, it wasn't as easy as it looked from up here. Jao Shang fought against Jevon like everything depended on it, and everything did depend on it.

All too soon, Shang broke free of his hold with a sharp elbow to Jevon's rib cage. Even I gasped at the way Jevon curled over from the brunt of the hit. It brought me up from my seat as I stood to get a better view of what was going on. Shang had still somehow managed to do damage to Jevon's already bruised side.

The referee threw a white towel in the circle to end all fighting. He rushed over to check on Jevon, but Jevon was already standing up. After a few deep breaths, Jevon was able to regain his defensive position. The crowd went wild with applause. He was clearly in pain, but he'd chosen to fight through it. Though I was sure my voice got lost within the mix, I hoped he heard me cheering him on anyway.

Before the ref could finish blowing his whistle to continue the fight, Shang was already on to his next move. In a very sneaky motion, Jao Shang ducked low to the floor, quicker than anybody anticipated, and swept his foot out beneath Jevon. Jevon's knees buckled under the impact and he went tumbling down to the floor, outside the circle.

There was a brief moment of silence where we all took in what had just happened. One side of the room exploded with applause as they cheered on Jao Shang for his victory in this round. Jevon remained where he was, staring up at the ceiling in disbelief.

It wasn't until his trainers came back up to the stage that he rolled over and pulled himself up. My eyes focused on him intently as he stormed past the stage, past the crowd of people, and back somewhere deep within the building.

I probably shouldn't have, but I found myself following after him. He moved so fast I had to jog to keep up.

Jevon quickly ducked into the boy's locker room and disappeared. I was hesitant to follow, but my feet slowly carried me there anyway. I couldn't see him at first; he was hidden within the maze of single-tier lockers that lined the floors. It was when I heard a locker door slam shut with a force that should've broken it that I knew where he was.

Jevon sat on the bench with his head tilted all the way back. His eyes were closed and his breathing was heavy. I stared at him quietly, waiting for him to calm down just a little before approaching him.

As if he could sense me standing there, Jevon's eyes opened suddenly and connected directly with mine. He paused, confused by my presence there, but he didn't say anything. Slowly, I walked the few steps it took to get to him and sat down on the bench beside him.

Jevon wasn't in his normal uniform. Like Shang, he wore only a pair of shorts that went down to just above his knees. They clung to him like glue. He kept his left arm tucked close to his side to compress the pain.

"I'll go find you some ice," was the only thing I could think to say.

What did you say to someone who'd just lost a battle against their arch-nemesis? It was only round one, but Jevon was already hurt pretty bad.

"Don't," he urged, trying to get up from the bench.

"No, you sit. I got this."

I walked over to the nearest medicine cabinet. It was next to the first aid. There had to be something in here that would help him. Once I was able to locate a cold pack, I broke it in to activate the cold and went back to where he was sitting. When I tried to bring the cold pack close to his bruise, Jevon flinched away.

"Stay still!" I fussed.

"No, Akilah. I don't need that, and I don't need you here right now."

I blinked at his tone. Normally, I would stay away from where I was unwanted, but one look at the suddenly blueish/purple tint around his rib cage brought me to a pause.

"That looks really bad, Jevon. Just let me help you, and I'll go."

"How about you just leave now and call it a day?"

Trish's words that day at the pool suddenly came back to me.

When Jay gets angry, he's a different person. He likes to distance himself when he gets that way.

That should've been my first warning to stay away. I should've got up and left him right then and there, but when I looked at him now, I saw more than just an angry boy lashing out at me. Jevon's whole body was shaking. His breath was short and labored, like it hurt for him to breathe. He was in a lot of pain.

Against my better judgment, I went in again with the cold pack. Jevon's nostrils flared as his lip curled up in annoyance. This time he stood up and walked away from me.

He headed out toward the back exit. I could hear the door slam shut and loudly ring throughout the locker room. For a moment, I had to collect myself.

It didn't take long for me to realize how stupid it was for me to still be here. I dropped the cold pack on the bench and turned to go back to the front. With any luck, Kayla wouldn't question why I was in such a hurry to leave.

Suddenly, a loud crashing sound and a cry of pain stopped me in my tracks. I knew it was him before I even turned around.

It was either really dumb, or very brave of me, but either way, I was foolish enough to go after him again. I snagged the cold pack and jogged through the exit where I saw him leave. He was crouched in front of a tree with his back to me. Jevon had knocked over a metal trashcan, probably punched it with his hand.

Very carefully, I leaned down to his level. Jevon didn't look at me right away, he cursed at the ground as he took a few swings at the trunk of the tree. Pieces of tree bark chipped away under his assault.

I wasn't sure what to do. I'd never seen him so furious, so out of control. After a final swing, he let his arms fall to his sides. His body was still quivering, but he managed to stay upright.

With a shaky hand, I touched his shoulder. He was hot to the touch, sticky with sweat. Jevon didn't jerk away from my fingers. I doubted he even noticed.

It took a while, but when he stood, I stood too. On instinct, I backed away—unsure how he would react. He wasn't hostile, but he wasn't calm either. I stared up at him without fear, ignoring the frustrated dip in his brows.

"Akilah, I don't—"

He started, but he didn't get to finish because I took the cold pack and pressed it to his injured side.

"Ahh!" Jevon winced and recoiled from my touch, but I wouldn't let up.

I kept the pack close to his skin, allowing him to feel the coolness from it. He clamped his mouth shut and clenched his teeth together to keep from expressing how much it hurt. Jevon stood rigidly still, like the compression from my hand kept him frozen in place.

He panted out short, jagged breaths until eventually his body relaxed against me as the cold pack began to do its job. He hung his head low and allowed his breathing to slow. I didn't dare move an inch from where I was. Jevon was just starting to calm down, and even if he didn't say it, I knew he was grateful that I was able to ease his pain a little.

His head sank down lower until his forehead connected to mine, and I suddenly felt trapped in a completely different way. I chanced a glance up into his eyes, but they were closed like he was concentrating.

We stayed like that for a while, quiet and motionless, until the cold pack no longer felt cold between my fingers. I was the first to move, taking my hand and pressing it softly to his face.

Patiently, I waited for his eyes to open, and when they did, he surprised me with the vulnerability hidden within them. There was a subtle tenderness in his eyes.

"You're a champion." I said, believing every word. "A damn good one, so go prove it."

Jevon took me in like I'd said everything he didn't know he needed to hear. With that, I broke away from him and went back inside. He didn't follow or say anything as I left, and I thought it was better that way. After all of that, I wanted nothing more than to give Jevon exactly what he wanted.

I left.

CHAPTER THIRTY-THREE

Jevon

I felt hot all over—mad as hell and frustrated about it. Every time, every single time I went up against Shang, he found a way to get in my head. In some cases, that was how he'd win, but this couldn't be one of those cases.

All the training and practice and patience I was forced to exercise led me right to this moment, and for what? Jao Shang talked a big game, which was mostly for the fans that ate it up, but he'd just proven he could back it up. What was the point in ignoring him if I was just going to fall short when it came time to perform?

I had to remind myself that this wasn't over. There were two more rounds to get through and I was already forced to fight with basically one hand tied behind my back. My left side was done for; I knew it before I'd even walked off the stage. It hurt to breathe hard or even put too much pressure on that side.

Shang was very skilled, he knew precisely where to target me that would leave me open and defenseless to him. It was more difficult to guard your side than it was to guard your front, so it was wickedly smart of him to make that move. He'd planned to take me out from the very beginning.

The smart thing for me to do at that moment would've been to talk to Sasha or Nick about my next move in round two, but if they knew how bad I was really hurt, they'd put a stop to this whole thing and I'd be damned if I gave up that easily.

They would have to roll me out of the dojo on a stretcher before I let Shang take my title from me again. It wasn't long before Pops came barreling outside to find me. He had Nick on his flank, looking just as surprised and disappointed as Pops was.

"What the hell, Jevon?! We've been looking everywhere for you! The next round is about to start!" Pops was the first to speak.

"Get your head in the game, Jay. It was only the first round. It's not worth losing your head over." Nick said.

Their words went in one ear and straight out the other. They didn't know Jao Shang the way I did. He was a cocky bastard on the outside, but deep down, he was more devious and underhanded than anybody gave him credit for.

Shang would do anything to win, even if it meant destroying everything in his path just to get there. That was how we'd become rivals in the first place. Pops had suddenly brought himself in close view, invading all of my personal space.

"You need to get your shit together, son, and kick it into second gear. If you're not in that ring in the next few minutes, it'll be considered a forfeit."

Pops had orchestrated this whole thing. He was more than pissed at me; he was embarrassed by my performance.

"Now, let's go!"

I followed after him, back into the building. Sasha was on stage, stalling for time. I could hear her through the speakers as we all rushed down the hall to the main room.

Eyes followed my every move. Wherever I looked, there was somebody there staring back at me, wondering what I would do next. Pops made his way back to his seat, doing his best to hide his own frustrations, and Nick came with me to the stage. He took the mic from Sasha as she ran over to prep me for the second round.

"You got this, Jevon. You hear me?" Sasha said, placing her hands on my shoulders so that all I could see was her.

I nodded.

"This is the spicy round. You get to use a weapon. It's just like we practiced. You move quickly and you think on your feet. Do not give him an opportunity to gain the upper hand."

I nodded again.

"How does your side feel? He got you good, right in the soft spot. I'm surprised you bounced back the way you did."

"I'm fine, Sasha."

"Are you sure?"

"I'm ready."

At that, she gave me a proud pat on my shoulder and backed away. There weren't many weapons in Silat that could be made legal in competition. It was such a dangerous art form that the most we could legally use on each other in the ring were a Tongkat or a pair of nun chucks.

Sasha tossed me a fighting stick and I caught it just in time for the bell to ding. This was different from the Tongkat we usually trained with. This was sleek and polished, carved right out of the tree.

Jao Shang, who had chosen to fight with a pair of nun chucks, suddenly changed his mind when he saw me approach the center of the circle with my Tongkat. He grinned like he had something to prove, and that was good because I did I too. Shang grabbed his own fighting stick and took his place within the circle.

"You came back?" He laughed, twirling the staff expertly around himself to warm up. "I'll tell you what, Williams, you've got courage. I like that about you. You should spare yourself the embarrassment and walk away now. It's only going to be downhill from here."

I got a feel for the smooth new Tongkat I was holding. It was light, yet strong and very durable. My hands whipped the staff around me with movements that had long since been committed to muscle memory. This was one of my strengths. I was ready.

The bell dinged again, signaling the start of round two. The time for talking was over and that was also good because there was nothing left to say. I would say all I needed to say at the end.

"Suit yourself." Jao Shang shrugged.

In seconds, he was bringing his staff down to clash against mine. Heeding Sasha's advice, I was quick on my feet, thrusting my Tongkat up and back in an attempt to loosen Shang's grip on his, but he had a grip on his stick so tight that the movement caused him to lose his footing as he came barreling toward me right along with it.

This provided the perfect opportunity for me to double back and swipe my staff hard across his mid-section. Shang nearly flipped over from the brunt of the hit. At the speed he was going, I was sure that I'd knocked the wind out of him too.

He fell facedown to the floor with his Tongkat still in hand, which he used as a crutch to help him up. Shang took a minute to collect himself. One glance up at the audience had him turning back to me with a snarl.

He was mad. Good.

In the next breath, he was aiming for my head with a deadly swing of his staff. I spun out of the way just in time, causing him to miss by only a hair. As expected, he stumbled past me from the force of his swing, bringing himself closer to the edge of the circle.

With him left momentarily defenseless, I took the butt end of my stick and thrust it into his back. Again, Shang face-planted onto the floor. Though he'd somehow managed to stay within the circle, I could tell the fall had slowed him down.

As he pulled himself up for the second time, I prepped myself for the move I'd perfected with Sasha. My side burned with a vengeance, but I ignored it. This was my only shot, so I had to take it.

I gave myself a brief running start and slammed my Tongkat into the floor. Using all the strength I could muster on my right side, I propelled myself forward with a jump-kick so strong, it sent Shang flying off his feet outside the circle.

And it was over.

The crowd went wild, cheering loud enough to make my ears ring. Shang stormed off the stage and threw his Tongkat off to the side. It clashed to the floor, knocking over a few chairs in the process.

I didn't let the fact that I'd won the second round get in my head too much. There was still one more to go and it was anybody's game at this point. When I left the stage, I headed straight for the locker room. The muscles in my left side felt raw and overworked from all the soreness. I needed to ice it again before it got worse.

Grabbing another cold pack from the medicine cabinet, I broke it in and gently pressed it to my side. I half expected Akilah to pop up around the corner again like before, but she didn't.

After that first round, I was pissed, I was ashamed, and most of all I was shocked that I had let that happen to me. When I left the building, I figured she would go back to the stands, but what surprised me the most was that she'd stayed. She'd catered to my wound even though I didn't deserve it and left like it never happened.

Clapping suddenly drew me from my thoughts. The sound came from the entrance, slowly building until it was right in front of me.

"Well done, son. Now that's how you make a comeback!"

"It's not over yet, Pops."

I couldn't share his enthusiasm, especially with a bum left side and a whole other round to win. Right now, we were tied, which brought us right back to where we started. It was all or nothing, and I wanted it all.

"You should've seen the way the judges were watching you," my dad went on. "I mean, it took you less time to take Jao Shang out than it did for him to win the first round. That ought to count for something."

"It won't count for anything, if I don't win again."

Pops stopped whatever he was going to say next to take a look at me. He was so caught up in the possibilities of what came after I won.

"I don't like this defeated attitude, Jevon. It doesn't fit you."

"I'm not defeated. I just don't want to focus on that right now. You told me to get my head in the game, so that's what I'm trying to do."

Pops nodded slowly, absorbing my words. Then, as if I had asked him to leave, he walked out of the locker room without another word. I had no idea if he was mad or not, but I didn't really have the capacity to care.

This last round would be more hand-to-hand combat, but unlike the first round, we were being judged on technique, dominance, and overall fitness in the sport.

Round three was always the hardest because you were either wiped out from the first two rounds or forced to fight through a semi-injury like me. I would throw it all out there in this final round. This was for my title, my respect, my return to the big leagues. I had to win.

I felt the cold pack begin to lose its coolness as it sagged down to the bench, now too warm from my body heat. Not that it was much help anyway. But it did the job in prepping me for my last go with Shang.

My side still felt a little raw, but it was now numb to the soreness. I could hear the crowd suddenly break out into applause and I knew it was time to head back.

My feet felt heavy as I made my way back up to the stage. The pressure of possibly re-writing history weighed them down with each step I took.

Shang's hateful gaze stared me down all the way up to the front. He stretched the muscles in his neck and arms, popping every knuckle in his hands. He was ready, and so was I. Nick came into view, giving me the last bit of advice I was going to get.

"Stay low, guard your face, and make sure to follow through with every move."

I nodded.

"Give him hell, Jay." Nick patted my shoulder and ushered me into the circle.

The bell dinged twice and everything else instantly faded away. I got my feet moving, bouncing lightly in place. It was easier to be quick on your feet once they were already moving.

Shang had chosen to take defense as he held his position across from me. I watched him closely, searching for an opening that he couldn't easily block. Whatever I threw at him, had to be good enough to knock him off his game.

My eyes zeroed in on his stance. He stood with his legs more than shoulder width apart. His knees were bent at odd angles because of this, and that gave me an idea.

Attacking him head-on was too predictable. With the way he guarded himself, it was what he was prepared for. I played it cool as my feet kicked up speed. Shang was oblivious to what I was really doing.

As quick as I could, I spun on my heels and kicked out with my right foot, slamming it into his knee. Jao Shang let out a loud yelp as his knee locked in place where he stood.

He hit the floor with a thud, curving his body over his knee to protect it. The crowd gave a collective gasp of surprise as they took it all in.

"Time-out! Time-out! Excessive force!" The ref ran to the center, blowing his whistle and waving his hands.

He then ran over to assess Jao Shang while people leaned up in their seats to get a better view. From what I could see, he shook his head no to every question asked by the ref. That meant that he didn't want medical attention, and he wanted to stay in the fight. The ref helped Shang up to his feet and brought him back over to the center of the circle.

Shang flexed and stretched his knee out a few times to test it. Whether he was truly hurt or not, he would never show it. I knew that move would knock me down a few half points, but it was worth it to see him in so much pain. The crowd applauded him as he went back to his position.

I did notice the way most of his weight shifted from his right leg to his left.

Now we're even.

"You're gonna pay for that, Williams," Jao Shang spat.

"Hurts, don't it?" I smiled.

That seemed to piss him off more as he nearly growled in response. The bell dinged for us to continue fighting and I kept my guard up, expecting anything. Shang swung out wildly, trying to make contact any way he could. I was able to dodge most of his blows, but the ones I couldn't, hit me hard and with purpose.

We danced around the circle out of rhythm. It was tit for tat for the most part. Blow for blow, Shang and I were pretty tied in the amount of damage we were able to do to each other. My side felt like it would cave in from the throbbing pain just below my rib cage and Shang was one misstep away from giving himself a bad limp.

Suddenly he was coming at me, whipping his non-injured leg out in a poorly executed axe kick. His right leg wobbled from the effort of holding up his weight. I was able to block his hit, but in the next second, his foot came swinging back to make contact with my chin, forcing my teeth to click abruptly together.

I stumbled back to catch my balance, wincing at the familiar taste of copper that spilled from my tongue and perched on the crease of my lip. I was bleeding.

With the back of my hand, I swiped at the blood and gave it a look. It wasn't a lot, but it was enough to piss me off. This caused Shang to laugh really hard just before he dipped low into a butterfly kick.

This time, I refused to give him another opportunity to strike me with his foot. Before he could stick the landing and swing his other foot back to make a hit, I caught Shang's left leg mid-swing. He fell forward and I dragged him closer to me by that same leg.

Shang twisted himself around so that his back was to the floor, but his left leg was still trapped in my hold. I was briefly tempted to break this leg in too, but the fight wasn't quite over yet.

I watched him struggle to wriggle free, thinking of all the things that could disqualify me. My hand squeezed around his ankle so hard, I felt a vein shift from the pressure. Because nothing else was working, Jao Shang reached up to try and pry my fingers from his leg.

With his face so close, I didn't think. I swung on him with my free hand and let Shang's head whip sharply to the side. A few people "ooo'd" in the audience.

In one final attempt, Shang was able to free himself and scoot away from me. When he got back on his feet, he took a moment to massage his jaw where I'd hit him. All the energy he had when we first began was now gone. I was tiring him out.

Shang stood ready across from me, breathing deeply to catch his breath. Then, in the next instant, he was charging at me head-on. He ran at me full speed, tackling me down to the floor.

I felt the impact of the fall course through every sore part of my body. The wind flew out of me like a cough I couldn't catch.

"Hurts, don't it?" Shang mocked as he hovered over me to place his hands around my throat.

I could hear the ref blowing his whistle in the background, calling a foul on Shang's play. But Jao Shang wasn't letting up. Maybe it was hysteria from the lack of blood flow to my brain, but I started to laugh. Shang and I had completely switched positions from where we were last summer.

Now, *he* was the one out of control. *He* was breaking the rules, and *I* was the victim. He was suddenly everything they tried to make me out to be. It finally made sense to me why he'd agreed to this rematch. This wasn't just about revenge, or retribution. It was pride.

Jao Shang's hands tightened around my neck, pressing his thumbs deep into my trachea to cut off any sort of airflow. My laugh was cut short and my vision started to blur around the edges.

It wasn't until I found the soft spot behind his armpit and dug my knuckles in, that Shang loosened his grip. I was grateful for the immediate rush of breath that followed after. I had to end this. Time was running out and Shang was getting desperate.

With my father yelling "Come on, son!" loud enough for me to hear on one side of the room, and the dreadful thought of me losing to Jao Shang again, I rolled over and sprung up to my feet. The fall had brought me dangerously close to the edge of the circle. I needed to time my next move just right to end this for good.

In a quick crossover maneuver, I was suddenly on the other side of Shang. Before he could even think to make another move, I kicked out with my foot as hard as I possibly could. Shang stumbled over, clutching his knee from the resistance. He was now closer to the edge than I was.

Without thinking, or even giving myself time to come up with another plan, I spun fast on my heels, just like before. Shang was still assessing his bad knee when my foot whipped out and made contact with his face.

He let out an ear-splitting howl as he fell down to the floor like a crumpled piece of paper. His knee gave out beneath him, and the pain had him rocking from side to side. I stared at him for a while, just appreciating his misery.

Then, I looped my arms under his in an effort to help him up. Only when I was sure that he was steady on his feet, did I kick out once again with the all the force I could muster. Shang fell back hard, hitting his head on the floor of the stage outside the circle.

Half the crowd, who had just begun to applaud me for my flawed sportsmanship, started to boo on Jao Shang's behalf. The other half rejoiced in my victory.

CHAPTER THIRTY-FOUR

Akilah

I wasn't surprised that Jevon was missing from school the next two days. From what I heard, he'd won the championship rematch, but I wasn't there to see it. Kayla and I left halfway through the second round, much to her dismay.

I had joked about being a fan of Jevon's before, but Kayla was a true fan. She wanted to watch the rest of the fight, and she would've gladly stayed behind if her mother hadn't called to let her know she was taking another late shift at the hospital.

School went on like normal for the most part. People gossiped about Jevon even more now that he was trending again. This time, it was for something good. He'd won, he got his title back, and almost everybody assumed that was the reason he wasn't in class.

At other schools, when someone stopped showing up, you'd assume they had dropped out or they were kicked out. Here, at CSA, we believed differently. There were only a few times I could remember that someone never made it to graduation for reasons *other* than being discovered.

I didn't know if that was the case for Jevon, but I tried not to think about it too much. I also tried not to think about the last real conversation we had, where we'd promised to have a real date. The way things were going now, I didn't know if that would even happen anymore.

On Thursday, I texted to see if he was okay, but there was no response. He'd never even opened it. For now, he was gone, and I had to be okay with that.

After school, Momma made more of an effort to show her "support." Her longtime friend from college—my uncle—was sitting on the couch when I came home. He greeted me with a big smile and a bear hug.

"Hey, Uncle Christian!" I loved it when he came to visit. Momma was a different person when he was around. She was nicer, less judgy.

"Hey, my beautiful niece!" He let me go but held onto my hand as I joined him on the couch. "How are you? How is everything?"

A part of me wanted to be honest with him. If we were alone, I would've told him all about my struggle to apply to Ivory Middleton and even confessed to him how I felt about Jevon. Uncle Christian gave the best advice. He was honest, but in a way that didn't make you feel completely stupid. At least he was funny when he judged.

With Momma coming back into the living room, carrying a tray of sweet tea and cookies, I kept my true thoughts to myself.

"I'm doing good," *liar.* "Everything's good."

"You mother tells me you have an art show coming up?"

"Yeah, I do."

He suddenly crossed his legs like my tea was more interesting than the glass of tea in his hand. "Who's the piece—I mean, what's the new piece you're working on? CJ told me all about the boy from school you're working with? "

"Uncle Chris!" My eyes darted from him to my mother. She was suddenly more interested in the conversation than I wanted her to be.

He laughed. "You are working on a sculpture, right?"

"Yes."

"How much is it worth? Maybe we can mark it up and sell it on my site after the show?"

Uncle Chris was an art auctioneer. He could sell almost anything that claimed to be art. I once saw him market a piece of pre-chewed gum as the 'Jewel of Halitosis'. It sold for over two hundred dollars.

"It's for school. It's not for sale."

He waved my comment away with a sly look. "Oh, honey, you can sell anything for the right price."

"Chris!" Momma scolded.

"I'm talking about art, Gina."

Momma cleared her throat as she quickly changed the subject.

"Sweetie, Chris is here because he needs a favor, and we think you can help him."

"What do you need?" I asked.

Uncle Christian sighed. "I booked a venue this weekend for a massive sale, and the artist I had on hand dropped out at the last minute. Do you think you could—"

"Yes!" I was too excited to let him finish.

This whole time, I was waiting for the senior art show to be that one big thing—the wow factor—that would make me look good in my application to Ivory Middleton. With Uncle Chris selling my work there was no more room for second-guessing.

He was my ticket in.

CHAPTER THIRTY-FIVE

Jevon

Fighting Jao Shang was one of the biggest challenges I had faced thus far in my career, in more ways than one.

After the fight, an ice bath wasn't enough to help me bounce back like I usually did. I had never been so spent beyond natural recovery before. By the next morning, the pain had intensified. Even just breathing felt like an exerted effort.

One trip to the doctor and a few X-rays later, we came to realize that I fractured a rib on my left side. It wasn't as serious as it sounded, but it was serious enough for Nick and Sasha to force me to sit out of future matches with my team.

I was glad I'd won the battle with Shang. My title, my redemption, the respect I thought I deserved, had finally returned to me, but at what cost? My team would continue the season without me, and it was only a matter of time before my title was challenged again.

Would it always be this way—gaining one thing, just to lose another in return? Was I fighting for all the wrong things, or were some things worth the sacrifice? I didn't have all the answers, but with my injury, I had more than enough time to think about them.

I decided to go to school on Friday. Though my parents and my trainers insisted that I needed to rest, I had to leave the house. I couldn't sit and stare at the four walls of my room for one more day. It would drive me crazy. But I must've been halfway crazy already to *want* to go to back to Cambridge. Even with all the staring and the questions, it was better than staying home waiting to get better.

I went through the day like normal, trying not to let my injury slow me down. For the most part, it wasn't that bad. I ran into Tommy after my first period. He stopped me in the hallway to congratulate me on my win, but really he just wanted to pester me with more questions about the rematch.

"Tommy, why do you choose now to bug me with this?" I asked. I was headed toward the second floor and my side was starting to burn.

"I'm just giving the people what they want." He shrugged. "Everybody else is scared of you."

"And you're not?"

Tommy looked me up and down, sizing me up. "Ain't nobody scared of you, Jay."

He looked so serious it made me laugh, but that was a big mistake. The sharp pain traveled up to my chest, bringing me to an immediate pause. I gritted my teeth at the pain but I kept walking.

"If I invite you to the next match, will you cool it with the questions?" I asked.

"Say less," Tommy agreed.

He walked away, and I could thankfully go about my day in peace. The one thing missing from my normal routine was Akilah. I had barely seen her since the fight, and she was nowhere to be found outside of class.

During free period, she wasn't in the senior lounge like I'd hoped. I was starting to wonder if she was avoiding me, until I thought to check the art studio. It was usually empty around this time, but not today.

I noticed Akilah right away. Her hair was different. It was straightened and flowing down her back in dark waves. She had her back turned to me, standing in front of an easel that held up a brand new painting.

When she saw me, she only stared for a moment and then returned her attention back to her painting.

"Really?" I asked. "You plan to ignore me forever?"

"I wasn't planning on it," she said with her back still turned, "but since you're here, what do you want?"

"I want to apologize . . . to your face if that's okay."

Akilah sighed and put her paintbrush down before turning around to face me. I took a moment to study her face. She looked like she always did, pretty without effort. Today, however, her eyes took me in like a bad aftertaste.

"I'm sorry, Akilah. I didn't mean to snap at you the other day. There was just a lot going on, but that's no excuse. You didn't deserve that."

Akilah's face gave away nothing that she was thinking. She took a deep breath as she began to nod.

"Thanks for the apology. And . . . congratulations."

The air around us was all stiff and unforgiving. She said nothing else as she went to pick up her paintbrush.

"That's it? We're good?"

Akilah shrugged.

"You're not going to make this easy are you?"

"Did you?" She finally cracked a smile.

To that, I had nothing to say, but I could feel the mood shift to a more comfortable degree. It was progress.

"What's this for?" I asked.

"I'm hosting an art show this weekend."

How much had I missed? I was only out for three days.

"This is big for you, right?"

"It's mostly just a favor for a family friend, but yeah, it kind of is."

Akilah held back her excitement, but why? Just a few days ago, she was mulling over what choice to make for her future, and now she was going to host her own show.

"Are we good enough for me to come to the show?" I asked.

Akilah's brush paused on the stroke of blue she was making.

"Don't tell me you're into all this art stuff now," she joked.

I wasn't, but "I'm into you," I said. "Does that count?"

Akilah started to smile, but then she suddenly stopped herself.

"Saturday, seven thirty. Don't be late."

CHAPTER THIRTY-SIX

Akilah

It was Saturday.

The day of my art show. It felt good to be back, to get the chance to see people take in and really appreciate the work I'd put into crafting the perfect masterpiece.

Even though tonight was originally intended for another artist, I felt proud to get to show off my work. Maybe this time, Momma could really see my potential. She always hung on the borderline between being supportive and overly critical.

Hopefully, tonight would get her to take me more seriously. This wasn't only an impromptu art show; I was putting out my best work. If the response to my art was good enough, I would use it to submit to Ivory Middleton.

I wore a gold dress for luck and good fortune, though I didn't need luck since Uncle Chris had offered to auction off my pieces. With him, I'd walk away with enough money to pay for at least a semester's worth of tuition at Ivory Middleton.

My dress had sleeves that feathered out like petals on my shoulders with shimmery fabric that gleamed in the light. Kayla, of course, was able to whip something up for me on such short notice.

Her hands were touched by angels because I looked and felt blessed in this dress.

I styled my hair with big barrel curls that flowed over my shoulders. My pointy heels pinched my toes together at the end, but I didn't care. I grabbed my purse and all the final pieces I could carry downstairs, and CJ helped me get the rest. We loaded it all in Daddy's SUV and strapped in to go to my show. Everybody had dressed up for the occasion.

Daddy wore a suit with a tie I'd bought him for Father's Day last year. CJ wore one of his old football formal suits. Momma was wearing a royal-blue dress. She had her hair styled in a low bun that was swooped to the side and intricately pinned up. Momma was pretty, and she was being nice, so that was already a good start to my night.

We arrived thirty minutes early. I needed to make the finishing touches, and my family was thankfully there to help. I put CJ in charge of hanging my black and white paintings in one corner of the room. Ma carefully carried my abstract work to another room while Daddy helped me hang the colored paintings up in the front.

"Who's gonna take all this down?" CJ complained when we were done.

He had taken his jacket off to air out his armpits. Nobody paid him any attention because he knew the answer to that question.

"Put your jacket back on!" Momma nagged with a snap as the first few people started arriving at the door.

Uncle Christian braced the people with a big, friendly smile as he opened the door to let them in.

"Welcome! Welcome! Go and have a seat right over there." He pointed to the small makeshift stage at the very back of the main room.

My heart picked up speed as I took in the number of people lining up at the door. It was a little more than I was expecting, but I felt charged with a nervous kind of energy. The good kind of nervous, like that gut drop feeling right before you knew you were going to do something big.

I wiped my dewy palms on the skirt of my dress and went to greet the guests at the door with Uncle Chris. They shook my hand warmly, holding it firmly between both of theirs before moving on to have a seat. Most artists were very deep and emotional, even in the simplest interactions. I was surrounded by my people, and it instantly made me feel a little less awkward and jumpy.

A small crowd was already starting to form as the line flowed in. I watched as people snuck peeks of the surrounding art. When their eyes lingered on certain pieces, my eyes lingered on them, gauging their reaction to what they saw. So far, they all seemed to want to search for more with the few minutes we had left before the show.

"Tsk, tsk, tsk, no peeking!" Uncle Chris chastised a few rule-breakers as he led them over to their seats.

I stayed by the door to greet the last few attendees making their way inside. A light buzz of chatter coated the room, bringing it alive with all the different conversations. Anxiously, I swayed from foot to foot, waiting for the one person I was really hoping to see.

It was 7:27 p.m., and when the doors closed, they wouldn't open again until after my speech. I peeked my head out the door, checking both ways to see if he was there, but the sidewalks were empty, and the show was starting soon.

"Alright, I think that's it," Uncle Christian said. He reached for the handle on the door and used the industrial key to lock it from the outside. I stared through the glass in the door like the image outside would suddenly change.

"Ki, what's wrong?" he asked, gently rubbing my arm. "Are you nervous?"

"I was just waiting for somebody, but I don't think he's coming."

"Oh, sweetie." Uncle Chris smirked. He had that all-knowing 'I've-been-there-done-that' look on his face. "If we spent all our time waiting around for men, the only thing we'd gain is a new set of nerves."

I didn't fully understand what that meant, but I let him lead me back toward the stage. That was, until the urgent tapping on the glass door forced us to turn around.

"Is that him?" Uncle Chris arched a brow.

I nodded.

"He's handsome! But what are they putting in the water these days? That boy is jacked up like a hammer."

I chuckled. Even in his gray suit, Jevon looked bulky and strong.

"Should we keep him waiting?" My uncle twirled the keys around his finger, leaving the power in my hands.

"No, let him in." Though it was very tempting to make Jevon wait, I still had a room full of people ready for me to start the show.

Uncle Chris pushed the handle to the door and held it open for Jevon to come in. He smiled at me like he wasn't the reason we were suddenly behind.

"You're late," was my only greeting.

"Traffic," he explained as his smile quickly turned apologetic. "But I got you these."

A large bouquet of autumn roses appeared from behind his back. He placed them in my hands, and I suddenly couldn't help the smile that surfaced because of it. They smelled fresh and they were absolutely beautiful. I chanced a glance back up at Jevon and he was smiling down at me. He stared at my hair, my dress—all of me, apparently pleased with what he saw.

"This is very sweet." Uncle Chris broke up the moment. "But you need to get up on that stage, young lady. I'll walk your boyfriend to his seat."

"Uncle Chris!" My eyes went wide, but Jevon only smiled.

"Go!" He shooed me away.

I did as I was told and headed back toward the audience. My heels clacked loudly against the linoleum, and heads turned toward me as I made my way up to the stage. My heart did excited leaps in my chest with each step I took. The crowd applauded me loud and clear when I came to a stop at the mic. I put the bouquet on the nearest stool, took a deep breath, and let it out slowly as I glanced over the entire audience.

"Thank you, thank you," I said as I waited for the clapping to settle down. "I know that most of you came out tonight to see another artist, and I may not be everything that you expect, but I promise to be everything you didn't know you needed. I put together every perfect creation I've ever made, and I don't use that word lightly.

"When you view my collection tonight, you'll see bits and pieces of every part of me: the good, the bad, and the all-out ugly. I laid it all out in the open for you. It's perfect because it's not. I believe that imperfections set the foundation for creativity, and it's because of those imperfections that I'm able to present my collection: *Beautiful Dilemma*, to you tonight. Enjoy."

The room erupted in applause once again, which made my nervous smile bloom into a full-on grin. I gave a small bow and left the stage. Daddy was the first to hug me. He squeezed me tight, hiding a tear he thought nobody could see. Next was Momma, who didn't attempt to hide the indescribable emotion in her face. CJ had already left, but he gave me a genuine smile and nod before going his own way.

I floated around the room, listening in on conversations and debates about the meanings behind my work. It felt good to see how they reacted. So far, I overheard positive remarks on my paintings, especially the ones in color. They got the most attention.

Then, there was Jevon. He gave me a slow golf clap that built in speed the closer he got to me.

"*Beautiful Dilemma*." He tasted the words on his tongue. "It's catchy."

"It's me." I clutched a hand to my chest.

Jevon nodded. "It is you."

I looked away. My nerves were already hyped up on excited energy, and Jevon would only add fuel to the fire.

"Excuse me?" An older woman approached us with a smile. "Miss, Akilah? Do you mind if I steal her away for a moment?" she asked Jevon, who graciously stepped out of the way.

The woman held her hands out for me and I followed her over to one of my oil paintings. It was of a two-sided window with two very different views outside. One side was of a light rainy day that looked out onto an old country porch. It held wind chimes that blew lightly in the wind. I tried to capture the realness of each raindrop, the wispy sway of the chimes blowing in the wind, and the peculiar way that wood glistened when it was wet.

The other side of the window was of the same porch, in the midst of a raging thunderstorm. The wind chimes had broken apart from the force of the wind, and rain chipped away at the fresh coat of paint on the wooden porch. Lightning struck the sky so brightly it lit up the night like God himself left the flash on his camera. I called this piece *The Calm Before the Storm*.

"What provoked the idea behind this piece?" she asked, studying it like a scholar.

I broke down the meaning behind my painting as best as I could. The woman had so many questions that a small line had started to form behind her with people that wanted my attention.

"I'm so sorry, Mrs. Everett, I'm being rude to my other guests. If you want to talk more after the show, I would be glad to tell you more about it."

I took the time to get to everybody that stopped me. They all wanted to pick my brain for clues and meanings, but much like beauty, art was in the eye of the beholder. The viewer's interpretation was just as important.

After a while, I found myself moderating on the debates. A young couple went back and forth with an older couple over the symbolism in my brush strokes. They took turns discussing the pain and fear I must've felt when creating the piece I called *End-divisible*.

End-divisible was a bleeding heart split evenly down the middle. The two pieces of the heart were bound together by a rope of harsh words that cut deeper into the heart's flesh. It was definitely the most dramatic piece I had ever created as it came to life shortly after my breakup with Deshawn last year.

I almost wished I had put that painting in the "No!" pile because the couples soon turned the conversation into a psychological exploration of my mind. It was starting to become too much, so I left them to their own devices as quickly as humanly possible.

All around the building people talked about me, or made guesses about my work that kept a smile firmly planted on my face. After making a full round, I caught Jevon standing near the stage. I went over and took him by the hand.

He came with me into another room where my mom had set up my abstract art. Most of it wasn't really abstract in the real sense of the word. It was anything I'd created that wasn't a painting but still made you feel something.

I went through a phase my sophomore year at Cambridge where I'd only worked with candle wax. I made tons of candle wax sculptures that year. They all carried a unique scent that was special to each sculpture.

Jevon quietly gazed at all the different variations of my art. Everything from clay sculptures to interactive pieces that made the viewer see light in ways they never thought of.

"You're really something else," Jevon noted as his eyes danced around my work.

He stared at the black and white paintings we were headed toward. My hand tightened in his a little as I led him to one of my favorite black and whites. It was of a pair of well-manicured feet planted firmly in a cumulus cloud that hovered just above a small city. I called it *Higher than Life*.

Jevon hardly glanced at it. His attention went straight a self-portrait I had done so long ago that I'd forgotten all about it. It was strung up a few rows down.

"Is this for sale?" He raised our conjoined hands to point to the painting.

"It's not even supposed to be here, so no." CJ clearly wasn't paying attention to my "No!" pile.

"There's a tag on it."

"Jevon." I hid a smile. "I'm kind of expensive. You don't have to buy a painting from me, just ask."

Jevon looked from me to the painting on the wall. Without another word, he reached up to take it down. The tag read: $569.42. Jevon didn't seem to be alarmed by the price. He shrugged easily as he allowed it to be carted off to the side by the handlers. They would box it up for him before he left.

"Seriously, you don't have to do that." I tried again. "that's a lot of money! We're good, I promise."

"It's already done. You're worth it."

I clutched Jevon's hand a little tighter, unsure of what to say. He'd just spent more than what I had saved up in a year in my lock box at home. It shouldn't have been that surprising, considering where he lived. Plus, Jevon was like a superstar—of course he could afford my work!

"Ahh yes." Uncle Chris joined us, flanked by my parents on either side. He clapped his hands excitedly. "You bought the self-portrait. I was eyeing that one myself, young man. You're lucky I wasn't here to snag it first."

"Maybe next time," Jevon joked.

"You willing to bet on that?" Christian teased.

"Careful, young blood," Daddy warned Jevon. "Chris here is a professional auctioneer. He'll take you for all you've got."

That much was definitely true. Christian was more than a professional; he was an expert.

Suddenly, Christian brought his attention to me, a warm smile on his face. "How is my talented niece? Are you enjoying the show?"

"This is way more than I expected. Thank you for letting me do this."

"No, thank you for stepping in! I owe you one, sweetheart. Whatever you want, it's all on your Uncle Chris."

He thought I was doing him the favor, but really, it was the other way around. This night was so much more than a last-minute fixer upper. If things continued to go as well as they were, I wouldn't need to apply to another backup school.

My dad and Jevon struck up a conversation that seemed to be going well. Momma viewed the surrounding work, seeming to appreciate most of what she saw. I didn't expose my family to everything I did, so some of my work was new to them too. My mom appreciated the craft in a philosophical sense, but she still had her reservations about me choosing this as my career path.

"Ma," I began, catching her gaze linger on some of my older black and white paintings, "what do you think?"

"You're very talented, baby. You should see if Uncle Chris can get you an internship this summer auctioning off some of these paintings. Art auctioneers make a great living, honey, and the market is in their favor right now."

Was she serious?

"You do realize that auctioneers make a living off of artists like me, right?"

"Yes, but how many artists do you know that have consistent connections with professionals in the industry? It's such a topsy-turvy world, Kiki. It wouldn't hurt to learn all the parts of it, that's all I'm saying."

"But that's not all you're saying, Momma. Look at all this! This is my world, topsy-turvy and all. I don't need to learn all the parts of it because this is what I want to do."

I didn't realize, until my mother's eyes darted to my father, that my voice was loud enough to catch other people's attention. Daddy gave me a look that warned me to cool it while Momma walked away to go mingle with some of her other friends. I was embarrassing her, and she would rather act like I didn't exist than hear anything I had to say.

Watching her walk away from me like I was a childish nuisance she would rather not deal with made an unwanted tear pool in the corner of my eye. I blinked it away before it could fall, but the curious stares from people around me weren't helping.

It'd be a cold day in hell before I let a room full of strangers see me crack, especially today. I turned my head just as a stubborn tear bubbled over my bottom lid. Momma was living it up with her old college friends, laughing and talking like everything was fine, but everything wasn't fine.

I left them all behind as I made my way to the front door. That pesky little tear felt like it was becoming more than just a tear as I fought to swallow the golf-ball sized lump in my throat. I just needed to escape, if only for a minute, so I could collect myself and pretend just like Momma did.

It was windy outside. The street lights led a trail down to a few benches just at the end of the road. I was already wiping at my face before I even made it to the seat.

It sucked that she didn't believe in me the way I wanted her to, and it was even worse that she had to fake like she was proud of me just so we didn't argue over the same thing for the thousandth time.

When I made to the end of the road, I plopped down on the nearest bench. I didn't care that I was wearing a silk dress. I pulled my feet up on the seat and wrapped my arms around my knees. I gave up on wiping the tears from my face. They fell freely down my cheeks, and I sniffled quietly so as to blend into the night.

CHAPTER THIRTY-SEVEN

Jevon

Akilah disappeared.

She left us standing there, questioning what had happened. It was obvious that something was said between Akilah and her mother. They both walked away at the same time, but Akilah was the only one upset enough to leave the building.

"That girl is always at war with her mother." Mr. Johnson grumbled under his breath. "I just don't get it."

"Clarence, now is not the time." Christian snapped. "You'd better go check Gina before I do. She is my best friend, and I love her, but so help me!"

Christian didn't finish his threat, but he didn't have to. Mr. Johnson hurried over to his wife.

"Hey." Two snaps had me facing a visibly upset Christian. "Why are you still standing here? Go check on my niece and bring her back here."

I didn't have a problem following those instructions. I left just as Christian grumbled on a rant about the "so-called men" nowadays. It was chillier tonight that it had been in weeks. The wind blew at the bushes that lined the sidewalk, rattling the leaves something fierce.

Akilah couldn't have gone that far in weather like this. I followed the trail of streetlights in the direction she went, and eventually I saw her gold dress gleaming in the darkness.

She was sitting on a bench with her knees tucked close under her chin. Akilah stared straight ahead as tears streamed silently down her face. I took the spot beside her as I tried to think of the right thing to say. Usually, she was the one trying to comfort me. Now, our roles were reversed.

"Do you want to talk about it?" I asked.

Akilah sniffled then lightly shook her head.

"Well, can I?" I used her earlier words against her. "I'm curious."

This made her wipe away the tears and face me. Her nose was starting to turn red, and her cheeks were a little puffy but that could've also been because of the cold. She was still pretty, even while crying.

"Go ahead."

"What just happened?"

"Nothing happened—nothing that surprised me anyway."

"Okay." I waited, but that was all she would say. "Can you be more specific?"

Akilah sighed. "I asked my mom a question that I already knew the answer to, but I was hoping for a different response."

"What was the question?"

"No." She shook her head vigorously as she stood from the bench. "Let's just go back. I'm ready to get this over with."

I caught her by the wrist before she could walk away. "Akilah, that's not fair."

"What?"

"The day that video went viral and you brought us to that park, you asked me all those questions about Shang, and the league, and what was going through my head. I answered all of them. Now that it's me asking the questions, you shut down. How is that fair?"

Akilah's eyes shifted between mine, and I watched as her resolve started to crumble. With a deep, shaky breath, she reclaimed her spot on the bench.

"Do you remember when I told you that my parents secretly wish I'll study something new in college?"

"Yeah." I nodded.

"Well, it's not a secret. I asked my mom what she thought about my art, and she basically told me I had a better chance at selling art than creating it."

"She said that to you?" Who would say something like that to their daughter?

"Not those exact words, but in her own way, yeah." Akilah picked at a fallen leaf that was all brown and crusted. "She's always telling me how unpredictable the art industry is. Momma's an entertainer, so she thinks she knows more about it than I do."

"That doesn't mean she's right."

"But what if she is? What if she's just trying to protect me from the truth?"

"The truth about what?"

"The truth that maybe," she stopped to wipe at another tear before it could fall, "maybe I'm really not as good as I think I am. It would hurt a lot less to get that now, than to spend the next four years chasing a dream that'll never come true."

I couldn't help making a face at the last part. It was weird to me that Akilah would so easily disregard all the work she'd put into getting to this point because of a few words of doubt from someone who didn't understand.

She had a building full of people throwing money at her art, telling her how amazing she was. It was so strange that her mother had the power to make her see it differently.

Hearing her explain brought me back to when she'd asked if I ever thought of a backup plan. Akilah's mom made her believe she needed something else to make her successful, but she had to know how good she was.

This was so unlike her; I couldn't stand to see her this way. I took both her hands, and brought her up to her feet. She was shaking, and her hands were wet from wiping her tears. Akilah stared into my eyes; searching, questioning.

"If all it takes is one person's lack of faith to make you second guess yourself," I took a step closer, eliminating the space between us, "then let me make this very clear: you're amazing, talented, and your work is going to go far. It's too good to be doubted by you."

She gasped quietly.

My honesty brought on an intensity neither of us expected. As I looked at her, though, I couldn't bring myself to look away. It was the way she clung to my words that brought me to an absolute standstill, trapped there in her gaze.

"Thank you," Akilah said finally.

The wind blew again, sending a crisp wave of chills down my spine. Akilah wrapped her bare arms around herself and shivered violently against the sudden drop in temperature.

"We should get back inside." I wrapped an arm around her shoulders, providing what little warm I could as I steered us back toward the building.

Akilah leaned into me and we made a brisk walk back up the sidewalk. At the door, she fixed her face with a smile and held her head high before going in. Immediately, the art lovers crowded around her.

"Akilah, darling." A woman with a thick French accent strolled over to greet her. "I need your Calming of the Storm."

What she said made no sense at all to me, but Akilah seemed to know exactly what she was talking about. The woman pointed to a painting of a window. She looked at it like she already had it hanging up somewhere in her home.

"Oh, I'm sorry, Jacquelyn, but Mrs. Everett had her eyes on that one too. You may have to outbid her tonight."

Jacquelyn almost looked offended, "That will be no problem, child. Let the games begin!"

Jacquelyn rushed off to her seat just as dramatically as she had come to us. Then CJ came into view.

He placed a hand on his sister's shoulder. "You okay?"

"Yeah."

"Okay, good because I'm keeping this and I'm not paying for it." CJ held up a candle wax figure that was molded to the shape of a woman. The candle woman was naked, with her eyes closed and her mouth opened. In her hands was a bouquet of flowers that hardly covered her body.

"I don't care, CJ. You can have what you want."

"Wait." He did a double take. "Are you really okay? Because I just said I'm *not* paying for this."

"Just take it." Akilah shrugged.

CJ looked to me with unasked questions all over his face. I gave him a nod to let him know she was fine . . . for now at least. That was enough for him to shrug away with his new item.

The auction was about to start. Her uncle had just finished placing the materials that everybody wanted up front and center: three paintings, a clay sculpture, and a centerpiece that had me puzzled on where it started and ended.

Christian addressed everybody with a wide smile as he placed the first painting on an easel. Already people were sitting up in their seats to make their bids.

"We're going to start this piece off at two hundred dollars, ladies and gentlemen."

Someone waved the fan high in the air.

"Two hundred! Do I see two fifty?"

Another hand shot up to make a bid.

It went on like that for a few minutes until finally, someone settled on a price that nobody else wanted to top. Akilah's painting ended up going for $735.

Christian got through all the pieces in no time. It was odd watching this game of luck and strategy. Even the highest bidders had a stopping point, and the lowest bidders had the better bluff.

"I hope you all have enjoyed your time with us here tonight," Christian spoke into the mic. "I'd like to leave the closing remarks to the brightest shining start."

He handed the microphone to Akilah, who stood with a smile.

"Thank you once again to everyone that came out to support." She cleared her throat. "I hope that tonight was just as much of an eye opener for you, as it was for me. And if I could inspire just one of you to find beauty in every dilemma presented to you, then I accomplished exactly what I wanted. Good night."

The applause that followed was clipped and sophisticated, different than the screaming crowds I was used to. Everybody got up from their seats to either take one more look at the art that was for sale or exit altogether. I blended into the flow of people that decided to leave, and waited patiently for Akilah on the other side of the door.

She was one of the lasts to exit as she made sure to thank very single person individually. When she was done, she came right over to me with a smile.

"Did you drive?" I asked.

"No, I came with my family."

"Let me take you home."

"Okay."

We walked back over to where I was parked, and she quickly ducked into the passenger seat to strap herself in. I turned the heat up as high as it would go and we both thrust our hands into the vents for warmth.

"I'm really glad you came," Akilah said.

"Me too."

"Even though you were late."

"By half a minute," I argued. "I didn't miss anything. I wouldn't have."

Akilah had no response to that, but she did tuck a strand of hair behind her ear as she turned to stare out the window. She hid a dimpled smile that I only saw because of her reflection in the window.

Assuming she was in no real rush to get home, I took the scenic route to Akilah's house. We ran into more red lights, stop signs, and slower traffic than usual, but I was okay with that. I wasn't ready for the night to be over yet.

"How is your side feeling by the way?" she asked when we came to a stop at the next light.

It burned like hell, and it hurt even worse when I thought about it too much.

"I fractured a rib," I admitted.

"Really?" Her brows shot up in surprise. "You got hit that hard?"

"That's the price of a champion. The harder the hit, the greater the victory."

"Well then, you must feel pretty damn victorious."

I smiled. "I do, actually."

Akilah turned her body to face me, and I did the same.

"I almost wish I was there when you won so I could say 'I told you so' and then make you watch me walk away."

Was that supposed to be a punishment for me? Watching her walk away? That was the best part of saying goodbye.

"You didn't have to leave, Akilah."

"Would it have mattered if I stayed?"

Probably not, but I kept that answer to myself. It wouldn't have mattered much to me who was there, not in the heat of the moment, anyway.

Akilah took my silence as her answer, as she thought of a new question.

"How does it feel now?"

"How does what feel?"

"To be you?" She asked. "Do you still feel unlucky?"

Right at that moment, I felt the exact opposite. I felt like I was lucky to be near her. I felt lucky to experience this night with her, as flawed and imperfect as it was. In fact, I felt so lucky that there was a part of me that wanted to take a chance.

"I do still think I have bad luck," I answered honestly, "but that's mostly because of who I used to be. I don't feel unlucky when I'm with you, though."

"So, what you're saying is, I'm your good luck charm." It wasn't a question. She stated it like it was a fact she'd just discovered.

"Why don't you just be my girlfriend instead?"

CHAPTER THIRTY-EIGHT

Akilah

Girlfriend.

I tried the term out over and over in my head. It felt just as funny as it sounded. Saturday night, Jevon had asked me to be his girlfriend. It caught me so off guard that at first, I didn't know how to respond. But it didn't take long for me to find the right answer. The "yes" fell from my lips before it even registered to my brain.

Why don't you just be my girlfriend instead?

The words replayed in my head like a record I had broken on purpose. I didn't need music on the way to school Monday morning. I played my broken record over, and over, and over again. By the time I made it to the parking lot it had become my favorite song.

I glided through the hallways much more chipper than I should've been on a Monday morning. Physically, I was present at school, but mentally, I was wrapped up in what it would be like when I finally saw him today. Unlike like the last time, there would be no confusion on how we greeted each other. At least, I hoped not.

I didn't have to wonder for long because there, standing in all his tall, beautifully dark-skinned glory, was my boyfriend. Granted, our lockers weren't that far apart, it still made me smile to see him standing there like he was waiting on me.

He was just finishing putting his books away when I got close enough for him to see me. Then, as if he sensed my presence, he lifted his head at my arrival.

"Hey, boyfriend." It felt weird every time I said it, but I was intent on saying it until it felt right. Jevon scrunched his brows up at the word. He shook his head with a breathy laugh which instantly made my smile fall. "You're supposed to say it back."

Jevon took me in for the first time. He started with my hair—which I'd washed and finger curled the night before—then slowly made his way down to my eyes and finally my lips. He shut his locker door and brought himself in front of me. With how close he was, I was forced to look up at him.

Jevon cupped my chin between his thumb and the crook of index finger. Gently, he tilted my head back so he could kiss me once, twice, holding on the third time. He pulled away then, but only by so much.

"Hey, baby," his voice dropped an octave, causing my knees to slightly tremble.

This slip up didn't go past Jevon's notice. He placed a hand on my side to help steady me, and I gripped his bicep to further catch my balance.

"Yup." I rubbed my lips together. "That's exactly how I want to be greeted from now on."

Jevon and I walked hand in hand to my next class. With a promise to meet up at free period, he dropped me off at my math class, the same class I shared with Kayla. She caught our entire interaction from her seat across from the door, and by the look on her face, I knew she'd have tons of questions.

"Good morning, Kayla," I started off casually when I got to my seat.

"No, none of that!" Kayla wasn't having it. "Talk."

"Can I get ready for class first?"

"No, what's up with you two?"

I felt my smile stretch even wider as I thought back over the last few days. A lot had happened, too much to even get into before class began.

"Last Saturday, Jevon showed up to my collection viewing."

"He did?"

I nodded. "He bought a painting too."

Kayla gave a small clap of approval.

"Not bad! So how did—"

"Good morning, class!" Our teacher, Mr. Levi, interrupted.

I was thankful for the interruption. There were listening ears all around us and they all seemed just as eager to squeeze information out of me as Kayla was. For now, I had a break from all the questions and I decided to focus in on the lesson Mr. Levi had prepared.

That lasted long enough for Kayla to scribble me a note on a piece of paper when he turned around to write on the board. The note landed on my desk, and I waited for Mr. Levi's attention to go to the other side of the room before opening it.

So how did you go from selling him a painting to giving up the goods in all of two days? No judgment, I'm just curious.

I stopped to roll my eyes at her assumption. Kayla never shied away from what she wanted, so it made sense for her to jump to that conclusion.

I didn't give up the goods. He asked me to be his girlfriend.

When Mr. Levi went to get something from the drawer in his desk, I used the opportunity to fold the note back up neatly and slide it over on her desk. Kayla's eyes doubled in size as she read the words on the page.

"He WHAT?!" she whisper-yelled, too surprised to even write it down.

Unfortunately, in all her excitement, Kayla caught the attention of Mr. Levi, who poked his head up from under his desk to see what the commotion was. Kayla and I tried to play it cool, staring real hard at the board like we were concentrating on the equation he'd given us to solve.

"Ms. Jones," Mr. Levi called out. "Is there something you would like to share with the rest of the class?"

Kayla shook her head coolly. "Nope, I was just frustrated that X is so hard to find."

He squinted his eyes disbelievingly, but with no evidence to show that she was lying, he huffed out a frustrated breath.

"If you have a question, Ms. Jones, raise your hand. We don't blurt out our frustrations in the middle of class."

"Noted." She nodded.

Kayla went back to pretending to work on the complicated math problem, but really I could see that she was writing me another note. From then on, she kept her reactions down to a minimum, and the rest of the class went on without interruption.

* * *

At free period, I waited in the back of the senior lounge for Jevon to show up. This time I was prepared. I found the two largest bean bag chairs at the front and took turns pushing them both to the back. Nobody seemed to notice what I was doing, and I was glad because it looked very suspicious.

While I waited, I decided to re-stock all the textbooks we'd knocked over the last time we were back here. The dust they carried had me pinching my nose until I was finished. It was disgusting.

I felt a pair of hands slide across my waist as I added the last textbook to the shelf. It made me whip around so fast I dropped the book in the process. Jevon smiled at my clumsiness.

"You scared me," I whispered.

He leaned in to place a gentle kiss on my lips. "Sorry," he whispered back.

We plopped down on the beanbag chairs, and I instantly noticed Jevon wince on the impact. His hand made fists as he settled in his seat.

"What's wrong?" I asked.

"Nothing, it's fine."

"It's not nothing."

Without asking for permission, I lifted his shirt to check the damage. I gasped. The bruise had grown since the last time I saw it. The blueish-purple color over his dark-brown skin had changed. It was darker now, almost black with flecks of red around the edges. It had started a slow spread over to his abs.

"Jevon, that looks worse."

He sighed in annoyance as pulled his shirt back down to cover himself.

"It's the healing process. Sometimes it gets worse before it gets better."

"I've never heard of that before."

"It's not my first injury."

That much I could believe. I decided to let it go and move to a different topic. I could tell that it was making him uncomfortable to talk about the bruises.

"What took you so long to get here?" I asked. "Did they let you out late?"

"No." He looked away, almost like he was embarrassed. "I was checking my scores."

"From last week?"

He nodded

"But you won, right? Why do you need to check on it?"

"They didn't update the site. My title is still missing, so I'm not officially recognized as a champion. I need to know if it's because of my scores or some kind of glitch in the system."

"Jevon, you are a champion. You just proved it to the world last week. You don't need scores to tell you that."

He smiled. "If you think that's how this works, then you don't know much about the league."

He was right. I knew absolutely nothing about the league, but I was sure of one thing: Jevon was the best I had ever seen. On and off the fighting floor, he handled himself like a truly skilled professional. I couldn't imagine him not being rewarded for that.

CHAPTER THIRTY-NINE

Jevon

When school was over, I took Akilah with me to the dojo. She insisted on watching me struggle through a session with Sasha. Since I was still healing from my match with Jao Shang, I wasn't technically even allowed to train, but I needed to do something to keep my mind off my scores. It felt like I'd go crazy if I didn't see a change soon.

"Hey, Jay," Nick greeted us as we made our way inside. "Hey, Akilah! Nice to see you two."

Akilah waved back and took a seat on the bleachers next to some of the younger kids that were training. They took her in like a substitute teacher, questioning her presence with curious stares.

"Are you sure you're ready for this?" Sasha asked me as she finished up her hand wrap. "I'm not going easy on you."

"I don't expect you to."

Sasha smirked. "Why don't you stretch first. How's your side feeling?"

"A lot better. It feels like I'm healed."

"Jevon, you don't heal from a fractured rib cage in a week. It takes at least three to six weeks at a minimum for you to be back in real fighting condition."

"It's been almost two weeks, and I feel fine. I don't have three to six weeks to hold out. I'm ready to fight now."

"We'll see about that, hot-shot. Just warm up for now."

I pulled my shirt up over my head and quickly discarded it to the side. If I were being honest, my side still felt a little sore when I moved too quickly or over-extended my reach. It was nothing compared to the aching, breath-tightening pain that came when my bruise was fresher. This was more of a dull, slowly fading pain, and I could work through it so long as I was careful.

When I finished stretching, Sasha took her place across from me, bearing a smirk that should've made me nervous. Automatically, I guarded my side by turning to my left.

Since we were starting with hand-to-hand combat, I paid extra attention to her movements. Sasha spun quickly on her heels. She whipped her hand out in a shuto strike, aiming for my neck.

With the right precision and enough force, Sasha could easily strike a nerve that would disable me completely. I was a little rusty, but I could thankfully block her hit. Sasha really had no intentions of going soft on me as she hardly gave me enough time to recover before striking me again on the other side.

We sparred like that for a while, her attacking me like I'd never left while I did my best to keep up. Over and over again, she assaulted me at every opening she could find in my defenses.

Eventually, I was forced to tap out. Sasha had me pinned to the mat with my arm bent at an awkward angle. When she let me go, I rolled over and coughed out my next breath. My lungs felt like sandpaper scraping against the inner-lining of my chest, and my side burned so bad, I was sure that steam would rise from it soon.

"Here." Sasha thrust a bottle of water at me.

I took the water and gulped it down before I could even finish my next breath. It soothed the growing ache in my side as I turned to lie on my back.

She came to squat beside me. "You're not ready. Don't rush it."

"One more round." I bargained.

Sasha chuckled, shaking her head like I'd never learn. Instead of giving in to my request, she stood up to walk over to the bleachers where Akilah was. She then leaned down to whisper something in her ear. Whatever it was, it caused Akilah to look down at me with a smile she tried to hide.

"Okay, Jevon, you want one more round?" Sasha asked.

I quickly stood to my feet and tried to regain control of my breathing. With a nod, I went back to my first position, but Sasha shook her head no.

"Oh, no, see you won't be fighting me." She grinned, motioning for my girlfriend to stand. "You'll have to work your way back up to me."

I couldn't help it. I laughed. "So, what? You want me to fight Akilah?"

"Scared?" Akilah taunted, crossing her arms across her chest.

"Sasha, you can't be serious."

"Why wouldn't I be?"

All at once, she ushered Akilah onto the mat, right across from me. Akilah discarded her shoes and pulled all her hair up into a high bun. Her curls spilled out almost immediately after, but she didn't notice.

"Come on!" I looked between them.

"Take your first positions." Sasha ignored me, snapping us into attention.

As if Akilah even knew what that meant, she took her place across from me. With her feet shoulder width apart and her fists out in front of her, she stood ready. I was stuck in place.

"Here's the deal, kid. If you can get through Akilah, then I'll allow you to fight next week. If not, then you wait the full amount of time to heal. I'm not letting you on my fighting floor when you're not at one hundred percent. But since you can't seem to take no for an answer, we'll put it to a test."

"So, if I win, I can fight?" That was all I heard.

"Yes, but if you lose, then you do as I say and wait."

"Akilah's not even—never mind."

There was no point in arguing a winning battle. Whatever Sasha thought she was doing was clearly a misguided attempt. I wanted to fight, and if Akilah was the key to that, then I'd make my way through her.

"Ready?" Sasha asked.

We both nodded. I couldn't wipe the grin from my face. This was ridiculous. What could Akilah do to me that would make a real difference? She popped her knuckles and flexed her neck, smiling like she knew something I didn't.

Before I knew it, Akilah was charging at me full speed. With her arms out wide, she aimed to take me down. The move might've actually worked if she were a little faster and a lot heavier.

Granted, I could've moved out of the way in plenty of time, but I let her have an attempt. When she collided into me, we hardly moved. Her arms wrapped around my waist, squeezing as tight as she could, and nothing happened.

At this point, I wondered if this was a real joke. I didn't want to hurt Akilah, but aside from pulling her off of me, the only way out of this move was to get her to loosen her grip. I'd have to target a weak point.

Akilah looked over to Sasha for help, and that's when Sasha nodded. "Just like I said."

That was all the confirmation Akilah needed to hear. She kept her grip on me and lifted her feet up off the floor. The sudden shift made her drop, and it forced me to bear her full weight.

This wouldn't have been a problem if she weren't pulling on the tender muscles that had just begun to heal on my left side. It felt like she was re-opening a wound that had already been stitched up.

I sucked in a sharp breath. "Ahh, shit!"

Without permission, my knees buckled beneath me and we both crumpled down to the floor. Instantly, Akilah let go and wriggled her way out from under me. I stayed in place, unwilling to move too suddenly for fear that I might really tear a muscle.

"I'm sorry," Akilah whispered in my ear, placing a soft kiss on my cheek. "Are you okay?"

"He's fine," Sasha answered for me. She stood over us with my shirt in one hand and another bottle of water in the other. It took some effort, but after a few deep breaths, I was able to roll over and lift myself up into a sitting position. "Take this and go home, Jevon. I'm serious. You need to give yourself time to heal."

I accepted her offering and slowly got up from the floor. Sasha took the time to assess me, pressing her hand firmly into my side for good measure. I winced away from the pressure of her fingers, but she kept digging.

"It feels tender, but definitely not broken." She said to me. "Make sure he ices it and gets some rest." She added the last part for Akilah.

We left the dojo then and headed out to the car. I could feel Akilah staring at me the whole way there. It wasn't until we were inside the car and headed down the road that I finally gave in.

"What?" I asked.

"Are you really okay?"

"I'm fine. I'm just pissed that I won't be able to fight for another two weeks."

"It could take longer than that. You didn't just scrape a knee, Jevon. You fractured a rib. That's gonna take time to heal."

I sighed. "You're not helping right now."

She sounded just like Sasha. I didn't need another nagging reminder about my healing process. I knew it could take longer. I knew how bad my injury was, but I chose to be optimistic about it.

I chose to believe that I could bounce back in enough time to be ready for my next match. I had to believe in something other than the very real possibility of me striking myself out of the league altogether.

"What's the worst that could happen?" Akilah asked.

We were stopped at the light, and Akilah took the opportunity to face me full on.

"What kind of question is that?" I was doing my best not to think about that. What made her think I wanted to talk about the worst-case scenario?

"You're so hell-bent on proving something to the world that you won't even stop and give yourself a break. Why do you need to fight so bad? You have a serious injury, Jevon, one that can only get worse if you put yourself back out there too soon.

"So, what's the worst that could happen if you don't fight next week? Or the week after that? Or the week after that? I'm sure that by now the whole world knows your name. What more do you have to prove?"

I scoffed. "You don't even know what you're talking about."

"I don't know anything because you won't tell me anything. What am I missing? Tell me because I'm just trying to help—"

"But you're not helping! So, can you just drop it? Please?"

Akilah sighed heavily and said nothing else. She brought her attention back to the front, staring out the windshield the entire way home. The silence in the car felt thick and heavy with tense energy.

Neither of us said a word, but Akilah didn't have to say anything for me to have an idea of what she was thinking. Her facial expression said it all.

I was so frustrated and I couldn't even handle that frustration like I normally would. It was like a thorn pricking at my skin on repeat, constantly reminding me of what held me back.

By the time I pulled into my driveway, Akilah had all but stared a burning hole into the frame of the windshield. I cut the engine and took a deep breath before facing her.

"I'm not in it for the fame," I said finally. "That's not why I go so hard."

Akilah kept her glare straight ahead, but I kept going, "I don't really care about the world knowing my name, Akilah. It's just . . . fighting started off as an outlet for me. I never expected to get this far, and now that I'm here it's not a hobby anymore. It's my life. It's all I know, and it's all I want to do.

"I've worked so hard to get to where I am, but I just lost my title and my rank. You have no idea how far that set me back. It feels like any little thing can take it all away, all my hard work, all the training, all the effort I put in. It's like it doesn't even matter, like *I* don't matter.

"You asked me if I still felt unlucky, but this is all the proof you need. I'm not trying to prove anything to the world. I'm too busy trying to prove to myself and my Pops that I'm not just a screw up, that I can be cable of good things too."

Slowly, I could see Akilah begin to soften up. When she faced me this time, her eyes peered deep into mine, searching. The more she stared, the more it felt like her gaze had the potential to unravel me right before her.

I was left exposed under her scrutiny, so much so that I had to look away. Akilah wasn't having it. She cupped my cheek with the palm of her hand, forcing me to give her my full attention.

"Of course you matter," she said softly. "Everything that you've done matters. And if it means anything to you at all, I believe in you. I may not know everything about your world, but I know you.

I know you're not a screw up. I know you're more than capable of good things. It makes me so mad that I should have to tell you this, but you're so much better than you think you are, and that's enough for me to believe in."

Her words stilled me. Akilah didn't know how bad the odds were stacked against me. She didn't know how far away I was from my end goal—thanks to my injury—but that didn't seem to matter to her. She believed in me.

I couldn't even think to form a response. My lips were already on hers before my mind had the chance to catch up. She kissed me back without hesitation, wrapping her arms around my neck to pull me in.

Her lips responded to mine automatically, slowly building in intensity until she had somehow made her way into my lap on the driver's side. Akilah's hair soon fell down from its bun, cascading over us with sweet smells of tropical fruits. Our earlier argument was quickly forgotten as I was totally and completely wrapped up in her. Only when I shifted to make more room did I notice the time.

I pulled away. "It's getting late. I should take you home."

"Just a little bit longer? I'm supposed to make sure you get ice."

I couldn't say no to her, and I had a feeling she knew it too. Akilah opened the door and slid off my lap. She waited as I led the way inside.

We climbed the steps to my room, and I watched Akilah's face intently every step of the way. She kept her thoughts to herself, and I wondered if it was because she realized we were completely alone.

When we got there, I had to usher Cujo out. He got way too excited to see me, and he jumped on Akilah in the process. With just the two of us, Akilah looked around my room, inspecting it with the same level of curiosity she always seemed to have.

She went over to my medals and trophies that were arranged neatly in their display case. Akilah took her time reading over every award. Her eyes lingered on the pictures from a few of my very first competitions.

"Wow," I heard her mumble.

I stood there silently, watching her observe my things. Her curiosity drove her directly to the head of my bed, where I had recently strung up her self-portrait. She stared at it strangely, tilting her head to the side.

"You actually kept this?" she turned to ask.

"Yeah, I bought it. What else was I supposed to do with it?"

Akilah smiled sheepishly. "I guess I didn't expect to see it hung up already."

I took the necessary steps that brought me right beside her. "When you're some big fancy artist one day, I can re-sell it and make a fortune."

She squinted her eyes at that last part. With a huff, Akilah went over to my desk in search of something. When she found whatever it was she was looking for, she came back with determination.

"What's that for?" I asked.

She had a pen in her hand, aiming right for the painting.

"Making sure you can't sell it."

In the bottom, right-hand corner, just above her signature, she wrote my name.

Jevon Williams
&
Akilah Johnson

Joke or not, Akilah made it very clear that selling her work was not an option. Honestly, I didn't think I'd want to let it go. Aside from the person painted on it, I genuinely liked the piece.

Akilah's self-portrait gave off serenity-like vibes. She had a way of capturing peace and tranquility with just a few strokes of her brush. If I weren't careful, I could easily find myself getting lost in it.

CHAPTER FORTY

Akilah

Standing so close to Jevon's bed was like a danger zone. One minute, we were talking about the painting, and the next we were sitting on the edge of the bed. Jevon licked his lips, stilling my train of thought.

My eyes zeroed in on my target as I slowly brought myself closer to him. He met me in the middle, and we both fell back in unison. My legs tangled with his as the kiss deepened, sending me on a wave of excitement. Jevon's arms encircled me, pulling me closer to him and I happily obliged. When Jevon and I kissed, it was electrifying.

This kiss was different than the ones before it. In comparison, our first kiss was sloppy and drunken and all over the place while our last kiss seemed almost hesitant. This was . . . perfect, or as close to perfection as we could possibly achieve.

I worked to keep up with Jevon as he skillfully moved his lips across mine. His hands had their way with the bare skin underneath my shirt as they traveled up and down the length of my back. Every now and then, his hand would brush up against the curve of my butt. And each time I lit up inside with tingles that made my body shiver. Jevon smiled against my lips; he liked that reaction.

My arms wound around his neck as I let my fingers reach up to graze along with the flow of his waves at the base of his head. We were so close; it left no room for escape. Before I knew it, we were rolling over and I was pulled on top of him, straddling his lap.

My hair cascaded over us like a curtain, shielding us from everything that didn't fit within our little bubble. Jevon's hands led a trail of fire down to my thighs which rested on each side of him.

I took the opportunity to briefly come up for air, but it was short-lived because soon Jevon was pulling me back down to him, capturing me in a kiss that made me hot all over again. His shirt had risen up in the midst of our session, exposing just a peek of his incredibly toned abdomen.

As if he were able to read my mind, Jevon lifted up and took his shirt off, throwing it somewhere over to the side of the bed. Even with his bruise, his body was sculpted and cut from the purest form of onyx. He was truly beautiful.

I was putty in his very capable hands. Our eyes connected for a sliver of a second, and that's when I lost all sense and reason.

"I love you," I whispered to him before I had the chance to catch it, or even realize what I was saying.

Everything stopped. Like a splash of ice-cold water straight to our faces, we froze. Even though I'd whispered it, those three little words echoed around the room as if I had shouted them from the rooftop.

I hid my face behind my hands with a groan, too embarrassed to even look at him. "Did I just say that out loud?"

Jevon didn't say anything, but I could feel his quiet, breathy laughter shake the bed. His silence was making it worse. I was so embarrassed. If I could, I'd take the words back and bite down hard on my tongue so I wouldn't slip up like that again.

Gently, he pried my fingers from my face, tugging one finger at a time until I was forced to meet his gaze. I realized then that he wasn't laughing *at* me. He seemed...genuinely happy, pleased with my unintentional honesty. It made me feel all warm again, but in a completely new kind of way.

We heard a door slam shut from downstairs.

Jevon sprung into action. He got up to peer out his window, and what he saw had him turning back with a very serious expression. Gone was his giddy smile; it was replaced with pinched brows and slightly flared nostrils.

"Who was—"

"Jevon?" his mom called from downstairs, answering my unfinished question.

"Son?" That was his dad. "Where are you? We have some good news."

"Come on." Jevon reached for me, but I was considering hiding for the time being. "Akilah, it's fine. Just come on."

It felt like a trap, but I took his hand anyway and followed him out of the room. I held onto him like he was my lifeline, squeezing his hand so tight he had to readjust.

We met his parents in the kitchen. They were bringing suitcases in from the car but stopped short at the sight of us. It was late, and Jevon's shirt was on backward. I could only imagine what it looked like we were doing.

"Hey, son." Mr. Williams took in our conjoined hands and our appearance with a strong look of disapproval. "Miss, Akilah."

"Hi, Mr. and Mrs. Williams." I waved, feeling more than a little awkward. His mom's gaze had yet to leave my face. I was almost tempted to wipe at it for fear that there was something on it.

"Hey Ma, Pops. You're home early." Jevon was too casual. Couldn't he see the shift in mood when we came downstairs?

"The conference ended early." Mrs. Williams said.

"Oh, okay. So, what's the news?"

Mr. Williams shared a look with his wife. "Honey, why don't you go get settled in? I'll bring the bags up in a minute."

Without another word, Mrs. Williams headed up to her room, throwing a lingering glare of disdain my way when she walked by.

"What's up, Pops?" Jevon tried again.

Mr. Williams heaved a tired sigh. "Do you remember our agreement, son?"

"Yeah, I remember everything."

"Then you remember us discussing your priorities and those distractions getting in the way."

I didn't miss the way Mr. Williams's eyes drifted over to me at the word "distractions." He didn't hide his apparent contempt for me. It was clear all in his posture and face. Jevon's dad was cold to me, uninviting. It made me want to shrink in on myself and hide behind Jevon, but I didn't give him the satisfaction.

"Yes, I remember, but—"

"Jevon." His Dad held up a hand to stop him in his tracks, with his other hand, he gestured between the two of us. "I'm just going to assume that you haven't been to the dojo all day."

"I did go to the dojo! Sasha kicked me out."

"And why is that?"

Was he serious? What kind of question was that?

"Dad, you know I'm still healing from a fractured rib. She's not going to let me on the floor like this."

"You understand that learning is not just about doing, correct?"

"Yes."

"You also understand, that you're on the brink of a pivotal moment in your career right now, correct?"

Mr. Williams's tone went from fatherly to drill sergeant in a matter of seconds. He was in straight-up business mode with no room for excuses or wasted time.

Jevon cleared his throat. "Yes."

"Then, I don't see how you think it's okay for you to skip out on training because you're 'healing'. I don't care if you have to ride the bleachers and take notes for the next few weeks; there is still more for you to learn. Because, see, while you're busy playing house, your opponents are training and getting better every day. You thought it was over because you finally beat Jao Shang?"

Jevon could only stare at his father. He didn't like where this was going, and I didn't either. I wasn't the one being yelled at, but this was too much to even watch.

"I asked you a question."

Jevon took a deep breath. I could almost hear his teeth grind together when he said, "No, I didn't think it was over."

"Good. Don't get too comfortable, Jevon. The ink hasn't dried on your deal with Shane Tithers yet. There's always more work for you to do."

I could see the distaste for his father's words settle on his face. They both shared a look, a wordless encounter between them that only they knew meaning behind. It was so clear to me now why Jevon stressed over every little detail, like his scores and his image when it came to his fighting. His Dad drilled it into him so heavily, how could he forget?

"Please show your guest out. We have business to discuss."

His cold dismissal had me reeling back in disbelief. It was the complete opposite to how he was when I'd first met him at the dinner party. Now, I realized I was an unwelcome guest in their home and in their son's life.

Jevon made no attempt to do what his father said. He stayed put defiantly, squeezing my hand, like *he* somehow needed *my* support. Mr. Williams stared us down with thinning patience.

"No need," I said, finding my voice. "I know the way out."

I snatched my hand away from Jevon's and grabbed my shoes by the door. The disrespect from both Mr. and Mrs. Williams made me more mad than sad, really. It had my whole body shaking with it.

I tried to compose myself, forcing down the lump that had suddenly formed in my throat. A tear threatened to pool in the corner of my eyes, and I blinked it away fiercely. They could not see me break.

"Akilah, wait!"

I was already out of the house and walking down the long driveway when he caught up to me. I didn't have my car, but I would walk just to be away from them. Not only was I embarrassed by everything that had happened just before his parents arrived, but it hurt to know how they truly felt about me. I had never been so belittled—so disregarded in my entire life, and his father could do that to me with just a look.

"Hold up!" Jevon grabbed my wrist to keep me in place. "Please, just . . . don't leave like this."

"Let me go." My voice was even, but there was a storm raging inside me.

"You have every right to be mad. I don't blame you. Just let me take you home."

"Jevon." I looked him in the eyes. "Let go of me."

He dropped my wrist.

"Look, it's late. I'm not going to let you walk home."

"I already called an Uber," I lied.

"Akilah, don't do this," his whisper came out like plea.

His voice broke, and I almost cracked right there, but Mr. Williams stood in the doorway behind us. He stared at our interaction with an impatience that made me feel unimportant and insignificant. It was what gave me the strength to say, "It's already done."

By some pure stroke of luck, a bright yellow cab drove past the property. I waved it down with my hand and when it stopped, I hopped inside and begged the driver to speed away.

CHAPTER FORTY-ONE

Jevon

I'd never known my Pops to act so irrational toward someone other than me. It was over the top and uncalled for. He had every intention of making her leave for good.

After she sped off in the taxi, I stayed in the driveway, unable to move, unable to think. I don't know what kept me there, but the house was the last place I wanted to be. Going back inside was like accepting that it was over, like the last thirty seconds were more real than I wanted them to be.

"It's for the best, son." Pops suddenly appeared beside me, clasping a hand on my shoulder. "Come on back inside. We have a lot to go over."

There was a certain level of rage I kept deeply repressed inside me. I never willingly acted on it, and I never, *ever* expected to have it directed at my own father. But when he touched me, I suddenly couldn't hear the voice of reason that warned to settle down.

"Pops, I need you to get your hands off me." My voice didn't sound likely own. It was too calm, too deep to belong to me.

"Excuse me?"

"You heard me."

He glanced at my slow forming fists, and the realization had him taking a few steps back. I backed away too because there was more I had to say, and I didn't want to be close enough to make a mistake I couldn't take back.

"You know, sometimes I really don't get you." I stared at him through squinted eyes. "I followed all the rules. I changed schools. I applied to college. I checked everything off of your stupid little list, and that still wasn't good enough for you."

"Jevon, what I do is only—"

"You didn't do that for me! I risked everything on that rematch with Shang!" I lifted my shirt to expose my wound. "This is going to keep me out of the game for weeks, maybe months, based on a decision that *you* orchestrated!"

I barked out a humorless laugh. "You don't care about what I want. You don't give a damn about what's good for me. The one thing, the one person that I—" I couldn't finish, and it didn't matter because he didn't care. "If you cared about anything other than my brand or the family business, you would've never done that."

"Son, there's a lot of things you don't understand right now, but you will in time. I'll give you space to cool down, and when you're ready, we can talk like gentlemen."

He walked away, and I sank down to the ground. I sat there on the cold hard pavement of our driveway, staring at noting, but thinking about everything. And for a short while, I wasn't Jevon Williams—international champion; or Jevon Williams—heir to the Williams Real Estate Brokerage Firm.

I was just a regular dude with shitty luck and a bad temper.

* * *

Akilah wasn't answering my phone calls or texts. I knew it was pointless to keep trying, but I just wanted to talk to her, to see her. I needed to hear her voice, to watch her face as I explained myself.

I would've gone to her house, but I held back like a coward. It was crazy to me because I wasn't afraid of anything, except apparently facing the girl that told me she loved me.

At school, Akilah avoided me like the plague. She switched seats in all of our shared classes to completely different sides of the room. When lunch came around, she was nowhere to be found.

Nobody asked questions, but you had to be blind not to notice the distance between us. We went from a new couple to total strangers in the matter of a day.

On Wednesday, I'd just about had enough of the silence. Akilah wasn't a stranger to me, and I couldn't keep pretending like she was. I waited until school was over to make a move. It was the only way for me to get her alone long enough to talk to me.

Lately, every day after school, Akilah spent time in the art studio, going over her work. I never knew how long she stayed, but I was willing to take that risk today.

I saw her sitting at the table we used to share in Ms. Hazel's class. She concentrated solely on the clay version of me in front of her. It looked different from the last time I saw it. It was more lifelike, better looking than me.

When I entered the room, Akilah acted as if she didn't see me. Instead, she turned to switch tools from her pouch and went back to what she was doing.

"Hey," I said, taking a seat on the stool across from her.

Crickets.

"You have to talk to me at some point."

"Does your manager know you're here?" she asked, finally sparing me a glance. "Shouldn't you be training, or taking notes or something?"

I guessed I deserved that.

"No, not today. I stopped training on Wednesdays when I started working with you."

"Well, I don't need you here anymore. Right now, you're just in the way."

"Look, what my Dad said was . . . he's just—" I paused. There was no way I could defend him. Not after what he did.

"Rude? Controlling? Disrespectful?" Akilah finished for me. "I can keep going. Just let me know when you find the right word."

"That's okay. I know he was wrong. That shouldn't have happened. I'm sorry it did."

Akilah shrugged. "It's not your fault. You can't control what other people do."

Despite her words, there didn't seem to be a difference between us. It felt off, like she was still unreachable. Akilah went to grab for the pouch that held all her sculpting tools, but I beat her to the punch. I snatched it up off the table before she could.

That got her attention. She threw me a vicious look as she tried to get them back.

"Jevon, I really don't have time for this."

"And I really don't need a lot of your time."

We had a stare down. Akilah held so much rage and resentment in the way she looked at me that it was almost hard to believe I had her in my bed only days ago. The silence that stretched on held more than unspoken words between us.

The more I stared at her, the more I could see her anger waver. It flittered in and out of a pain that she worked hard to conceal and a tiredness that weighed heavy on her shoulders. On impulse, I reached across the table to touch her hand and she let me.

"Tell me how to fix this," I pleaded.

"You can't."

"Why not?"

"Because, Jevon," Akilah cast her eyes down to my hand over hers, "Your dad said a lot of stuff that hurt, and it didn't make sense to me at the time. But the more I thought about it, I realized something."

I waited.

"You and me, we could never work. We're in two completely different places in life. You're this big, famous fighter and I'm just an artist. Everything you do is monitored and recorded, whether it's good or bad.

"One slip up could affect your whole future, and your Dad controls every part of your life for that reason. You can't do anything he doesn't approve of, and he won't ever approve of me. You know that, don't you?"

It was a rhetorical question because Akilah wasn't done. She slipped her hand out from under mine as a sad look came over her.

"You can't fix something that was broken from the start. So, it was probably a good idea for us to end it before we got too deep."

Her voice cracked at the very end. A tear bubbled up on the lid of her eye, but she turned to wipe it away before I could see it fall.

I wanted more than ever to just hold her and erase all the ridiculous thoughts in her head, but I thought better of it. Akilah kept a good distance from me. She wouldn't let me get that close to her again.

"Akilah, you don't believe that. I don't believe that. You're not making sense right now."

She seemed to give up on her previous argument as she propped her elbows on the table and leaned in. "Okay, so let's be real then."

"Finally." I leaned in too.

"If we stay together, what happens after we graduate? I want to go to school and study art in New York. Where will you be? Traveling the world, am I right?"

"That's the plan."

"And when you're done traveling, what then? Am I in those plans? Do you honestly think we would even make it that far?"

"We're just teenagers. Do you hear how you sound? We don't need to have our whole lives figured out to be together."

"That would be true—if your whole life wasn't already figured out by somebody else."

"You mean my dad?" There was no reason to beat around the bush.

"Yeah, your dad, your manager, your decision maker. Whatever you wanna call it."

"But he didn't make this decision, you just did!"

"Can I have my tools back please? I only have two more weeks to work on this. It's really important to me."

I could see her fighting back another tear as she waited for me to give her back her materials. A stubborn part of me wanted to stay and ride this wave with her. I wanted to remain where I was until I made her see reason, but a stronger, more reasonable side of me realized then that it was a lost cause to argue it further.

There was nothing I could say or do in that moment to make her change her mind. I slid the pouch back over to her and got up to leave. For now, it was over, and I just had to accept that.

I headed straight for the dojo, hell-bent on getting lost in my own distraction. I didn't care if I had to take notes, mop the floors, or run errands for Nick and Sasha, I just needed to do something.

"Hey, Jay," Nick greeted me at the front. "Riding solo today?"

"Did you talk to my dad?" I ignored his greeting and his question.

"Yeah I did, and we're not making you take notes, kid. That's just ridiculous, but we can get you started on some moderate exercises. Nothing too strenuous. So that means no heavy lifting, no over the top cardio, and absolutely no sparring whatsoever."

"Okay, so what can I do?" He didn't give me many options to work with.

"You can start by stretching first, and then we'll work up to some light cardio and see how you feel after that."

I went over to the few machines dotted around the dojo. Looking at everybody else train with their coaches was like a direct slap in the face. If I could, I'd switch places with any one of them and fight until my knuckles were sore, or until they bled, whichever came first.

I stretched quickly, looking forward to what came next. Nick came over after a while and let me jog on the treadmill at a snail's pace. I didn't like being treated like such a delicate flower, but I popped in my earbuds and did as instructed.

If I could prove that I could handle this, then maybe he'd let me take it up a notch. Blaring my music as loud as it would go, I kept up a good pace and increased the speed a little with every full lap.

So far, I was doing pretty good. My breathing was even and my side didn't bother me at all. After the twelfth lap on the treadmill, Nick let me off and moved me over to some makeshift obstacle course he'd created outside.

"Okay." He clapped his hands together. "You're doing pretty good. Now we're gonna try and test your reflexes and endurance. Think you're up for it?"

"Yup, I'm ready."

From there, Nick took me through the course. It took about twenty minutes to get through the whole thing by myself. But with him pushing me through each round, I was able to get my time down bit by bit.

It wasn't my best, but it was all I could do not to agitate my side too much. Eventually, I felt a sharp pain beginning to stab at me on my left. It brought me to a complete standstill. It had me panting to catch my breath.

"You okay?" Nick jogged over to check on me.

"Yeah, I just need to catch my breath."

"Here, take some water." He handed me a bottle, and I chugged it down. "You're done for the day. Go home."

"No, I'm good, Nick. Just give me a second."

"Does it hurt? Don't lie to me."

"A little, but it's not bad."

"Then you're done for today, Jay. Come back tomorrow and we'll try again."

He left without another word. I stared after him, completely defeated. Here I was, trying to do at least one thing right in my life, but it felt like every step I took forward only brought me thirty steps back. If I couldn't train and I couldn't even get through a simple exercise, then what more could I possibly do?

It was a while before I followed Nick back inside to get my things. I took deep breaths all the way to my car, ignoring the slowly fading pain in my side. It was a constant reminder of all that I'd lost. When I got in the car, I decided to call the only person who wouldn't treat me like a wounded bird.

"Hey," she answered on the first ring.

"Hey, Trisha."

"What's up?"

"Are you home?"

"Yeah, you actually called at the perfect time because I'm bored out of my mind. Kent and Darius are at football practice, and I was this close to calling the wicked witch of the south, just to have something to do."

"I'm on my way."

"Alright, see you soon."

We hung up, and I headed toward Trish's house. She lived pretty far outside the city, but it was worth the drive today. Since I couldn't fight out my frustrations, she was the only person I'd want to talk to about it.

Darius wouldn't take me seriously, and Kent would only give me a reality check that nobody wanted to hear. It took me a while, but eventually I made it to her doorstep and gave it a good knock. I could hear her shuffling her way to the front door just before she opened it.

"Hey." She pulled me in for a hug.

"Long day?" I don't know what she saw on my face, but after a brief examination, she tugged on my arm to pull me inside.

Trish led the way past the living room and down the hall to her bedroom, where it looked like she was in the middle of folding clothes. Trisha pushed the pile of unfolded clothes to the side so I could have somewhere to sit. She then went back to her routine of separating and folding her clothes.

"What's going on? Why do you look so down?" she asked, not even looking up from what she was doing.

I leaned back, laying on top of the pile of clothes like a pillow. They were still warm, and they smelled fresh.

"Hey! I just cleaned those, move! You look like you just got done working out. And if they smell like sweat, Jevon, I swear I'm going to make you wash them again."

I sighed and pushed them closer to her so they were completely out of my way.

"Okay, talk to me." She threw a pair of bundled socks at me. "I know that's why you're here. You look like a sad puppy."

"Do I really?" I asked.

"Yeah, you do, so tell me what's going on. The suspense is killing me."

"A lot is going on, Trish. I can't train, I can't really workout because of my injury. Oh, and Pops kicked Akilah out of the house the other day."

"What?!" Trisha dropped everything she was doing. She even paused her TV and came to sit next to me on her bed. "Why didn't you lead with that? What happened? Wait—Akilah was at your house? Are ya'll together? Like, *together* together?Why didn't you tell me—"

"Trish." She rambled on with too many questions.

"Why am I always the last to know everything?" She went on like I hadn't said anything.

"Trish, please."

She took a breath. "Right, sorry. Start from the beginning."

"We are together—or were. But it's over before it even really started. My parents came home early from a conference and saw us together. Pops started talking about what I should be doing and what I should be focused on. Then he just dismissed her like it was nothing."

"Wow. Mr. Williams is tough. I don't think I've ever seen that man so much as smile."

"He smiles, just not without a reason." He never did anything without a reason.

"How did Akilah take it? I don't know what I would've done in her shoes. Your dad's hella intimidating."

"She left."

"She just left? That's it? Is she okay? Are you?"

"No, we broke up."

"Did you try talking to her?"

"Yeah, but that didn't go so good either."

I filled Trish in on our conversation after school. I told her how Akilah let Pops get into her head. She had completely convinced herself that we would never work. All the "what-if" questions that I didn't have the answers to, and the complicated future possibilities made her so sure that she was right. I vented a lot to Trish, even telling her about the moment just before my parents came home.

"Wait." Trisha's mouth fell open. "She told you she loved you and you didn't say anything back? Are you dumb?"

"There was a lot going on at the time."

"Do you have any idea how big this is?"

"What do you mean?"

"Akilah gave you the three biggest words a girl could ever say to a guy, and she said it first. Does she even know how you feel?"

"She should." I shrugged. "It's not like it's a secret."

"Yes, but did you tell her that? When you talked to her today, did you get a chance to tell her how you feel?"

"There was no point. She already had her mind made up."

"Jevon," she sighed tiredly, "you should know this by now. Girls are complicated creatures. You can't just assume that we know how you feel."

When she put it like that, it kind of put Akilah's wild assumptions about the future into perspective. The "what if" questions would definitely fall into that category of complicated.

"Telling her how you feel might make a big difference," Trisha continued.

"Or, it might not make a difference at all. It could just be a waste of time."

Trisha wasn't there. Akilah wasn't hearing me. There was nothing I could say or do to get us back to where we were.

"You never know until you try. Don't just give up without her knowing the truth, you need to tell her."

"And how am I supposed to do that when she won't talk to me?"

Trisha took a minute to think about it. After all of a minute, she shrugged.

"I don't know, but we'll figure something out. I got your back."

"Thanks."

"After this, you owe me."

"It's got to work first, Trish."

"It will. Trust me."

She seemed so confident, even without a plan. I wasn't sure if it would work out, but I would try it her way. At this rate, what more did I have to lose?

CHAPTER FORTY-TWO

Akilah

I kept myself busy as often as I could. It was all I could do not to think about him, and I thought about him all the time. When I wasn't working on my sculpture after school with Ms. Hazel, I spent extra time volunteering at the museum.

On Monday, in my rush to get home, the last thing I expected when I got there was for Momma to be home early from the dance studio. All it took was one look at me for her to drop everything and smother me with love. I just wanted to curl up into a ball and disappear. I didn't need company for that, but I was glad I wasn't alone.

For now, I just wanted time to stop so I could use it all up to recover. If I could, I'd spark a joint and blaze my way high up into the sky, so I could walk amongst the clouds and never come down.

On that day, my Mom and I held the most candid conversation we ever had. I gave her bits and pieces of the full story, and she finally gave me advice that would stick with me forever.

The Rules to Navigating a Broken Heart:
STEP ONE—Remain Busy at All Times

I did that by throwing myself into my craft. Not only did I work on perfecting my sculpture every single day after school, but I found new inspiration in oil paintings with my free time.

No longer did I use bright colors like yellows, pastels, or gold, but I felt drawn to colors that matched the tempo of my heart. Deep velvety reds, the darkest hues of blue, and a black so deeply shaded, it painted holes right through the canvas.

STEP TWO—Focus on Your Future

With all the extra work I'd created by trying to keep myself busy, I finally had the courage to actually click apply to Ivory Middleton. Suddenly, getting a "no" from my dream school didn't scare me as much anymore. I would work for it until they had to say yes, and then I'd keep working at it just to prove everybody else wrong about me.

STEP THREE—Above All Else, Give Yourself Permission to Feel

I ignored this final step. According to Momma, it wasn't healthy to bottle up my feelings. It was okay to let myself feel hurt, and mad, and ashamed, and even love for him, but if there was any other option, I would choose it in a heartbeat.

After crying it out like a baby in my Momma's arms, it was safe to say that I had felt everything.

The days seemed to fly by and blur together. All too soon, I had only a few days to work on my sculpture before it was finally time to put it in the fire. Against Ms. Hazel's better judgment, I felt the strongest urge to make a dramatic change to my piece at the last minute.

I wanted to stand out and show my range, but at the same time, I had this nagging idea that needed to be expressed. It would haunt me forever if I didn't try. I took a deep breath and prayed before I made a move.

The sculpture sat in front of me, looking nearly perfect and pure. It was an exact replica of him, every line, crease, and indent matched him the way I remembered. It all felt too safe though, too expected of me.

With all my tools splayed out in front of me, I picked up my serrated chrome spatula and dug into my perfectly carved creation. After making the first incision, the rest felt like less of a crime to my art.

I worked and remolded and patched up mistakes until I noticed the sun begin to fall. Sweat lined my forehead and the nape of my neck from all the effort. When I was finished, I took a moment to step back and review all the changes.

If I stayed here any longer, I would find a hundred different things to add or change to make it better. This was the vision I had in my head, and I was keeping it the way it was. This was the final product.

I wasn't sure if I had made the biggest mistake of my life, or if I'd just created the piece that would get me notice beyond my wildest dreams. Either way, it was already done. I made up my mind to cook it in the kiln.

Before leaving the building, I set it in the kiln and turned on the timer. It was better to do it this way so I didn't punk out and change my mind at the last minute.

By tomorrow, I would either deal with the consequences of my actions or discover my new masterpiece. I quickly made my way home and put it all behind me. Whatever happened, I was determined to make the most of it.

The next day granted me one last chance to work at it. I asked Ms. Hazel to sit with me after school for the last bit of advice I was going to get before the show. She didn't know about the changes I'd made to the sculpture, but I was hoping she would view it the same way I did.

I got to the studio early so I could get a head start with my own assessment. I decided to paint it, to really accent the new details added to the overall piece. This was the exact opposite of the advice Ms. Hazel gave me last time. It was a lot of work for me to do only a day before the show, but I was convinced this was headed somewhere.

Since I no longer had my muse to give me a reference while I painted, I drew inspiration from memory. I thought about his even skin tone and the difference that was made under certain lights and shadows. I thought about the way he looked when he was angry; it helped me find the right colors to blend.

"What's this?" Ms. Hazel's voice suddenly filtered into the room.

She came to stand beside me with a hand placed on her hip. From the look on her face, I wasn't sure if she was surprised, or disappointed, or both.

"I made some last-minute changes," I explained.

"I can see that." Ms. Hazel's eyes never left the piece. She took in the colors I was using, going around the table to get a 360-degree view.

"What made you change it?"

"It felt too safe. I wanted to make a statement."

"Hmph." She brought a hand under her chin and leaned in.

"What do you think?"

"I think it was bold to change what you had a day before the show."

I was almost scared to ask her to elaborate.

"It's that bad?"

"Akilah," she sighed, "I chose you for a reason. It doesn't matter what I think because you're an amazing artist. There are no rules to art, it just is. We manifest our own methods of creativity in everything we do. If this is what you want to present, then you need to be able to back it up one thousand percent, knowing that you put your all into it. Can you do that?"

"Yes."

"Good."

Ms. Hazel gathered her things and headed for the door. I was confused on whether she had just given me a pep talk or a lecture.

"Hey." She caught my attention as she stood in the doorway. "It's a strong piece. Believe in it."

* * *

It was time.

It was the day of the senior art show at the Westside Cultural Arts Center, and my nerves had me bouncing with energy. After a long night of painting and preparing my sculpture, it was finally ready.

This time, I neglected to even tell my family about this opportunity. We were making progress, but I wanted nothing to break my concentration. Today was going to be stressful enough with all the other artists competing for the same scholarship.

Kayla came as my wing woman and support system for the day. She helped me bring the sculpture all the way from the art studio at CSA to the Cultural Arts Center downtown. With her help, I got set up at my station with enough time to walk around and check out the competition.

"I got your back today, whatever you need." Kayla looped her arm in mine as we strolled throughout the building.

There were so many people here from all over the county and the event hadn't even started yet. Kayla knew everything I'd been through. She stood by me like the big sister I didn't know I needed. I was glad she was here with me. I couldn't think of anybody else I'd want here more.

"Thank you."

"I mean it." She grinned. "Whatever you need. If I have to knock over a couple sculptures, or scratch up some ugly ass paintings, I'll take out all the competition."

I knew she was only joking, but she looked serious enough to make me laugh.

"Well, you can start with that one." I pointed to a pastel painting that had nothing on the canvas except paintbrush splashes and gem stones.

"What the hell is that supposed to be?"

Kayla broke stride and walked over to the viewing station. She pulled a bobby-pin out of her hair and made it seem like she needed a closer look. I ran to catch up with her before she could do any actual damage.

"I was just kidding, Kayla!" I took her by the hand and steered her away from the piece. "I can take out the competition on my own."

"Now that's what I like to hear! I'm proud of you, AJ."

"Thank you." I smiled. I was proud of myself too. I'd come a long way from the girl who was scared to even look at her dream school for too long. Now, I was ready to take on all of Atlanta with my art.

"Let's go find Ms. Hazel. She wants to meet with all her students before the show."

We walked back up to the front where more people flooded in. Students from different schools congregated around their teachers. It was time for everybody to get their final pep talks in because the show would officially start in less than ten minutes.

"Alright, huddle up!" Ms. Hazel fanned around herself as we all formed a circle around her. "This is it, the big day! I want you all to know how proud I am of you, since the first mistake you made by taking my class. I was hard on you and I know I made most of you want to quit, but I pushed you because I knew your potential. I knew how great you all were.

"Today, I don't want you to think about the competition. I don't even want you to think about the scholarship money. You should focus on making new connections. Even if you don't get the outcome you want, there is plenty of potential just walking around the building.

"Talk about your dreams, network with alumni from the colleges you want to go to, put yourself out there. Each and every one of you should come out of this with your foot in somebody's door. If not, then I chose the wrong students to be here. Be bold, be brave, and most importantly, never apologize for your passions. Good luck!"

At that, we broke apart and did just as Ms. Hazel said. I set my eyes on every person in a business suit or a dress that went past her knees. Even Kayla helped a little, talking up people in the crowd and bringing them over to my station while I talked about my piece. I made it a point to mention Ivory Middleton any chance I could, hoping I'd run into somebody with connections there.

Critics walked around in disguise, viewing everybody's work. They wouldn't reveal themselves until it came time to judge, but it wasn't hard to figure out who was whom. The critics were mainly the ones who stared the hardest. They took notes and asked the most detailed questions.

I hardly paid attention to the people coming in and out of the building, but I happened to look up just as *he* walked through the door. My whole world came to pause around me. It felt like forever ago since I last saw him.

If it were at all possible, he looked even better than the last time I paid him any attention. He couldn't see me yet, but I noticed him immediately out of the crowd of people surrounding us.

Kayla was at my side in an instant. "Do you want me to take care of that?"

"No, it's okay. This is a public event. Anybody can come." I turned my attention back to the viewers. "Any more questions?"

There weren't any more questions, and I was thankful. When the people left, I took a minute to go get some water and calm my nerves. I prayed he didn't see me.

Today was not the day for whatever he had up his sleeve, yet already he was throwing me off my game. I was doing well, talking and mingling amongst the crowd. I was putting myself out there, making connections, and sticking my feet in all kinds of doors. Then he had to show up and rearrange every one of my brain cells.

"Akilah?" Ms. Hazel found me by the drinks, pretending to be interested in every flavor of sparkling water set out on the table. "Why are you hiding? There are people taking in your work. You should be over there talking yourself up."

"I got thirsty," I lied.

"Okay, well hurry up. Do you see that man right there?" She pointed to a short balding man in a tweed suit and thick glasses.

I nodded.

"That's Hyram Wiseman. He's a critic and editor of the *New York Times*. I've been talking his head off about you. You should go introduce yourself."

I gulped. If the pressure wasn't already on from the competition and my ex walking into the room, I felt like it would strangle me with the presence of such a powerful man. Still, I finished the cup of water in my hands and walked back over to my station.

I noticed Trisha first out of the group of people around my sculpture. Her pixie cut was styled differently, laid flat with finger waves all around her head. She wore black lipstick, and a royal blue pant suit. She smiled big with a wave, like it wasn't a surprise for her to be there.

"Here she is," Ms. Hazel announced, pushing her way through everybody to get to Hyram Wiseman. My audience was growing. I needed to say something, anything.

"Hello, Ms. Johnson." He extended his hand to me. "Hyram Wiseman."

"I know who you are." I gave him a firm handshake so he knew I meant business. "It's so nice to meet you."

"It's nice to finally put a face to the name Hazel's told me so much about."

"Hope it didn't disappoint."

Was I flirting with him? It was a knee-jerk reaction to that type of statement. I was so nervous, I just said the first thing that came to mind.

Thankfully, Hyram seemed to have a sense of humor, as well as everybody else that crowded around my station. They all shared a laugh which brought me at ease a little.

"Tell me about this piece. I'm very impressed by the hyper-realism and attention to detail. What was the inspiration behind it?"

This was the moment. I looked down and drew up my speech from memory. It was what I used all day to describe the meaning behind it to the viewers that came up to my station.

"Ahh, I see," Hyram interrupted before I could even begin.

I looked up to find him staring behind me in awe and surprise. Not surprisingly, everybody else followed his line of vision and I did too. It was him. Jevon stood there, tall, silent, and handsome. Just like the statue before me. A work of art in his own right. While everybody else stared at him, his eyes were set on me.

"Jevon Williams, this season's champion—well, last season most recently. Soon to be this season again, I hope?" Hyram lit up.

"Yes, sir." Jevon shook his hand, instantly turning on the charm. "You're a fan of MMA?"

"Not really. My wife's into it more than me, but I could appreciate the art. She'll be mad that she missed seeing you. I have to be honest though, I wouldn't have pegged you as an art connoisseur."

"Me either." Jevon turned his attention back to me. "But I could appreciate the art."

I ignored how that made my heart flip. A flurry of butterflies crept into my belly as Jevon brought himself closer to the station.

He was now standing right next to me in front of the crowd that continued to form around us.

"Well, now I'm really interested," Hyram cut in. Jevon had me locked in his gaze, just as tongue tied as before. "Tell us more, Akilah."

"Right. Um." I cleared my throat. "Jevon was—is my muse for my art. This piece is titled *Fighter*. As you can see, this wasn't the original design I had in mind. This version of Jevon is battered, beaten, and bruised all over. He's been through a lot, but he's still standing and ready to take on what's next."

Having Jevon so close to me made it hard to focus. I could feel him watching me, absorbing my every word. I couldn't even turn his way. I didn't want to know what he was thinking.

"I wanted to make a statement with this piece," I continued. "A lot of us are fighters in our own way and we don't even realize it. Some of us go through life looking exactly like this on the inside. Others wear their scars with pride. Either way, you find a way to pick yourself up, dust yourself off, and stand ready to take on what's next, like a true fighter. Like Jevon."

I added the last part a little lower than the rest, but the intent was still there. It was eerily quiet when I finished. Nobody said anything at first, but I zeroed in on Hyram's reaction. Only his opinion mattered to me.

He pulled out a monocle and placed it over his left eye to scan the perimeter of the sculpture. It was old-fashioned, yet it made him look like so much of an expert that people moved out of his way so he could get a better view.

"That's a powerful message, Akilah," Hyram finally commented. "The detail on this is phenomenal. You can almost feel his pain. I'm assuming she learned this technique from you, Hazel?" He turned to Ms. Hazel, who watched him just as closely as I did.

"Where else was she going to learn?"

A few people laughed at that, including Hyram as he tucked the monocle back into his pocket and took a few steps back.

"I have few more pieces to observe, but it was such a pleasure, Akilah. Very impressive. Good luck!" Hyram shook my hand a final time before facing Jevon. "Good luck to you too, Jevon Williams."

"Thanks."

I hadn't realized I was holding my breath until Hyram walked away. An enormous weight had instantly lifted off my shoulders. I didn't care about anything else.

I was satisfied with the fact that I could impress someone like him. The other viewers slowly dispersed, leaving only Kayla, Trisha, Jevon, and me at my station. The four of us stared at each other awkwardly for a while. Kayla was the first to speak up.

"I'm just going to say it." She shrugged. "If you don't win, then this whole thing's rigged. He was eating out of the palm of your hand, AJ."

"He's not the one judging, Kayla. It's not over yet."

"It might as well be," Trish cut in. "You did great, Akilah!"

Trisha pulled me in for what I thought was a hug, but she was really trying to give me a message. I wasn't sure if anybody else noticed, but when she hugged me she whispered, "Just give him a chance, please." Then, loud enough for everybody else to hear, she said, "It's good to see you."

"It's good to see you too."

"Kayla, can you show me where the restroom is? I feel like I've walked around the building three times, and I still can't find it."

Trisha was very slick. She looped her arm through Kayla's and steered her away, leaving just Jevon and me there at the station. With everybody gone, I had nowhere to hide and no excuse not to talk to him. He started to say something, but I was quick to beat him to the punch.

"Walk with me?" I asked.

He nodded, following my lead as I took us strolling throughout the build to view the other artwork. We walked side by side, both of us with our hands tucked deep inside our pockets.

This was new for us. I couldn't remember a time where we were this close yet so far away from each other. I had the sudden urge to touch him, but I resisted by burying my hands deeper into the skirt of my white dress. Jevon seemed to have the same idea because his hands were balled up in his pant pockets too.

"I'm glad you came," I said to break the silence between us.

"You are?"

"I should really be thanking you." I smiled. "If not for you, Hyram probably wouldn't have been as impressed with me. I think he was more interested in you than me, anyway."

"I didn't mean to steal your shine."

"You didn't. It made sense for you to be there."

Silence fell over us again as we made a circle around the building, walking past the same pieces we had already seen.

"Did you mean all that stuff you said back there about being a fighter, like me?" Jevon asked.

At some point, we had stopped walking. We got lost in an empty part of the building where not many people mingled around. Most of the action was at the front end, so it felt like it was just us there.

"Honestly? I winged most of that. I was so nervous that I forgot half of my speech as soon as Hyram shook my hand." I admitted. "But you're not just my muse because you look good, Jevon. I admire you; I always have. If that didn't reflect in my work, then how could I call myself an artist?"

Jevon's gaze went from my eyes to my lips, like he was drawn to them. I felt a flutter of those emotions I tried to bury drift up to my consciousness. They flapped around my belly with the strength of a small bird.

Jevon bit down on his lip while he took in all of me. It was like he was seeing me, really seeing me, for the very first time.

"Akilah," his voice was husky and full of purpose, "there's something I should've said to you the other day."

"Jevon, don't," I didn't even want him to finish that statement. "Not today. I don't want to argue. It's bad enough that—"

"I'm not here to argue," he interrupted.

Jevon took his hands out of his pockets and brought himself closer to me. With his eyes never leaving mine, he reached for my hands. They slipped out of my pockets easily and intertwined with his like muscle memory. His hands were warm and strong. He gave me tingles with his proximity.

He smelled so good it almost made me forget what I even resisted for. Jevon crooked a finger under my chin, bringing me to attention. It was a lost cause. He had total control, and he knew it.

"Jevon," I whispered, trying and failing to put a stop to this. He was going to kiss me, and I was going to let him.

"There you are!" We broke apart instantly. I jumped a whole foot away as Kayla and Trisha came into view. "We looked everywhere for you," Kayla complained.

I tried to play it cool, but I couldn't even attempt to pull myself together. Jevon was annoyed by the interruption, but he was doing a way better job at playing it cool than I was.

"Kayla," Trisha played dumb, "do you know where the drinks are? I'm kind of thirsty."

"Trish," Jevon shook his head, "it's okay. We should get going."

"Are you sure?" She looked between us, a million different questions on her face.

"Yeah, let's go."

They walked back up to the front, talking quietly amongst themselves. I could only stare.

Rule #4 to navigating a broken heart: Don't forget, you're only human.

"Perfect timing, right?" Kayla asked when she was sure they were gone. "You okay?"

"Yeah."

...Perfect timing.

CHAPTER FORTY-THREE

Jevon

"Kayla's smarter than I gave her credit for. She caught on quick," Trisha explained as we walked toward the car, "but I held her off for as long as I could."

"It's okay, Trish."

"What happened? Did you tell her?"

"No."

Trisha deadpanned. "If I didn't know you, Jevon, I would swear there was something seriously wrong with you. We gave you so much time. How did you miss the opportunity?"

"It just wasn't the right time."

"Well, you better find the right time because I'm running out of ideas."

"Yeah, you and me both."

Trisha made me buy her food before I took her home. She said I had to pay for her services because I couldn't hold up my end of the deal. I let her get whatever she wanted. Without her there, I wouldn't have gotten that far with Akilah to begin with.

Trish was a way better wing woman than I gave her credit for. When this was all over—if her plan really worked—I'd pay her back her big time.

I put all thoughts of Akilah behind me as I headed toward the dojo. Last week, I got the go ahead from my doctor to train again, and I'd been in and out of the dojo ever since.

I was healed enough to move forward with my regular training sessions. That meant full cardio, all heavy lifting, and best of all, I could spar with Sasha like I used to. If I could prove to her I was really improved, she promised to let me participate in the regional competition next weekend. It didn't matter that I was out of commission for most of the season. I was confident that I could pick back up where I left off.

"Glad to see you back, Jevon." Lincoln met me on the mat while I stretched. "You competing next week?"

"I don't know yet. That's up to Sasha."

"Well, do whatever you gotta do, bro, because we're going to need you. I've been struggling to hold the team up by myself all season. Look, I helped get us to Regionals, but I'm happy to give you back the reins next week. All of America is going to be watching."

I wasn't just coming back to a random competition. Regionals was a filmed competition. If I had any hope at all for Sasha to let me back in on this round, then I had to bring my A-game. There was no way she would let me embarrass the team on TV, no matter what the doctor said.

"I have to get back," Lincoln said suddenly. "Nick's going to kill me if I keep him waiting any longer. Good luck, Jevon. We're counting on you."

No pressure.

"Thanks."

I went back to my stretches while I waited for Sasha to finish up a phone call in her office. All week, we'd worked on hand-to-hand combat and, as promised, she didn't hold back or go easy on me.

It wasn't that hard to get back into my normal routine, but I definitely had to work a little harder to keep up. I knew for a fact that none of my opponents would measure up to a sparring session with Sasha. She was a master in the art of Silat. If I wanted to be the best, then I needed to train like I was going up against the best every single time.

"Ready?" Sasha asked when she finally made it onto the floor. She discarded her shoes and pulled her hair back into a ponytail.

"Yup."

I followed her lead, chucking my shoes to the side and bringing myself to first position. Sasha gave me no warning or indication that she was about to start, but I was ready when she came at me.

She swung at me wildly, but with a precision that couldn't be mistaken. I was able to block her first two swings and even dodge the third. But her foot soon came up to check my chin, making my teeth click hard together. I stumbled back a bit, tasting a little blood on the sides of my tongue.

"Anticipation, Jevon."

She didn't have to explain. I already knew. Anticipate every move, even the ones you could clearly see coming. The obvious moves were more than likely decoys for the real thing. I was expecting for Sasha to swing on me, but I made the mistake of not paying attention to her footwork. She was fast and clever, but I was strong and hungry for this.

"Let's try that again." I swallowed down the pain in my mouth. It stung, but I shook it off.

Sasha and I went at it for the next hour. This time, I was better at anticipating her moves. I was light on my feet and quick with my responses. At one point, I felt like I really had her. I had her locked up in a death grip, with her arms constricted behind her head and her legs twisted under mine.

The only way out of this type of lock-up was for her to either tap out or pass out. With Sasha, though, it was never that easy. She had somehow flipped us over and shimmied her way out of my grip. Before I knew it, she was locking me up in about the same way I did her.

With the way Sasha hemmed me up, it gave me a slim opportunity for an out. I could feel her breath at the base of my neck, close enough for me to know how tired she was from sparring with me, but far enough away for me not to know exactly where her head was.

Either way, I took the chance and dipped my head low before reeling it back to slam against hers in a headbutt. I heard the smack of bone against bone, and immediately Sasha loosened her grip on me. I rolled over and off to the side to catch my breath.

"Damnit, Jevon!" Sasha pinched the bridge of her nose, panting through the exhaustion and pain.

Her nose wasn't bleeding, and it didn't look broken, but I knew how bad a hit like that could hurt.

"You okay?" I asked.

Sasha tipped her head back. "Yes, I'm fine. We're done for today."

At the sight of his injured wife, Nick rushed over to check the damage.

"It's not broken, honey." He chuckled. "But he got you good."

"I know," she grumbled.

I grinned. "So, does this mean I can compete next weekend?"

* * *

Regionals.

It was a breath of fresh air. Even with all the pressure on me between Pops, my team, the deal with Shane, and the cameras that were bound to catch everything, I was feeling good.

Being forced to sit out for most of the season had given me a lot to prove and way more to fight for than before. I wasn't nervous about it, not yet anyway. Pops and I were on conditional speaking terms for the time being. If it had nothing to do with fighting, or plans for the future, then there wasn't much for us to say.

He knew how I felt about the way he'd treated Akilah, and I knew why he'd done it in the first place. Yet like always, he just assumed I would get over it and focus on what was important.

Today, I was willing to play the part with Pops while he gave me a pep talk on the way to the arena. Traffic, which was already bad, was made worse by all the people headed downtown. This gave my Dad something to boast about while we waited to move up in line.

"I know it's only Regionals son, but look at the crowd you're already bringing in." He pointed at the long row of cars we sat behind.

"All of this has more to do with Shane than me, Pops."

Shane Tithers, along with many other up-and-coming fighters like myself, would all be there. I wasn't dumb enough to believe that all these people were here for me alone, but what Pops said had some truth to it.

"Shane is here to see you, and all these people are going to know why very soon. I'm proud of you, Jevon."

"Thanks, Dad."

If his pride weren't so contingent on how well I did in the ring, I might've believed him. Conversation between us died down to a minimum as we slowly made our way through the throng of traffic.

I took the time to block out all the noise and concentrate on the competition. Teams from all over the state were coming to prove their worth for the major leagues. I wasn't really worried about a specific team or person I would be up against.

After Jao Shang, I couldn't imagine anybody else getting to me, but in the world of MMA, surprises tended to come out of nowhere.

There was always going to be somebody just as hungry as I was for a title, so I'd keep my guard up.

My phone suddenly lit up in my pocket, and I was quick to check it. Normally, I would've turned my phone off to avoid any and all distractions before a fight, but ever since the day I showed up to Akilah's show, we texted each other from time to time.

It started off as a "Thanks for showing up," to "What was the homework assignment?" and even "How was your day?" The texts were random and not as frequent as they used to be. We were both more busy these days. Even so, it was progress.

"Jevon." Pops gestured to my phone. "What are you doing? We're almost there."

"Uh, nothing. Just checking the time."

"Oh, well put your game face on, son. Work starts now."

As soon as he said it, the bright flashes of a few cameras suddenly blinded my vision. I looked up to see that we were finally pulling into the arena. Camera men and photographers lined the VIP entrance as fighters made their way in.

Blinking away at the spots that dotted my vision, I prayed my Dad would drive a little faster. I didn't want to stay in one place long enough to take pictures or answer questions shouted at me through the window.

"Your first round of interviews start in about thirty minutes. I need you to think about the questions we went over and how you're going to answer them."

"Round of interviews?" I asked. "You mean, more than just one?"

This was the part of my life that I'd probably never get used to.

"Yes. You have preliminary interviews before the fight, and then after you win, you'll be interviewed with Shane."

Pops explained it like it was his last time going over something I should've already known.

"Right, got it."

We got parked and headed inside the building. Most of my team were already getting set up in one of the rooms at the back. I could hear other coaches, trainers, and managers shouting out different commands and words of encouragement to their teams as we moved through the hall.

The amped up energy from everybody bounced off the walls. All the voices that echoed from the growing crowd out in the stadium and the antsy fighters behind the scenes became just a loud buzz of noise. I took it all in. I was home.

"Go get changed," Pops instructed. "I'll come and get you when you're up."

I nodded.

I found the cubby with my name on it and the suit hanging on the rack for me to change into. Interviews were always touch-and-go for me. They either went really well or just all-out bad. There was no in-between.

I tried to avoid taking interviews as much as I could. The media often had a way of twisting your words to fit whatever story looked the best on the screen. Again, today wasn't about any of that. I'd do the interviews and tell the truth like I always did. Whatever story they wanted to publish wouldn't make much of a difference in the end.

"Ready?" Nick asked. "Your Dad's getting things prepped for you now."

I was never ready for this part of it, but I fixed my tie and followed him out to the table that was set up for interviewing. Already, the lights, cameras, and the press crowded around the table.

They all fought for the attention of Chris Erickson, who was in the middle of his interview when we got there. He grinned like he had already won, telling them everything they wanted to hear.

When it was my turn, I took a seat in the middle of the table next to my Dad. The microphones that lined the edge of the table were adjusted to fit my height, and with all eyes on me, I took in the crowd of interviewers that waited for me to notice them.

"Jevon! Jevon Williams! Jevon!" they called to me.

I pointed to the closest person. He looked the most eager and shouted my name the loudest.

"Glad to see that you've fully recovered from your recent injury, Jevon. Are you worried about how that might affect you in ring?"

"Affect me how?"

"Well, you *have* been out for most of the season. There'll be lots of players aiming to take your position tonight. Have you thought about that?"

I shrugged. "Everybody's fighting for something. I don't spend my time worrying about what that is. That's not what I'm here for."

I pointed to someone else, a woman who got lost in the crowd. She didn't seem as eager to get my attention.

"Jevon Williams, you have become quite the household name." She grinned cunningly. "Since the finals last season, you're considered one of the most infamous fighters in the league."

"What's your question?" Pops leaned over the mic to intervene. I could tell he didn't like where she was headed.

"Right." Her smilc faded. "We have word that Jao Shang will be in attendance tonight. His older brother, Bo Shang, will be taking his place while he recovers. Your fans want to know if you share the same rivalry with Bo Shang as you do with his brother. It will make tonight very interesting."

There it was. The thing that made me "interesting" to the public. Every fighter had some kind of beef. It was how most of us made names for ourselves.

To be honest, I didn't know Jao Shang had any siblings, but with him out of the picture, it made sense for his brother to target me.

"Just answer the question, son. We don't have a lot of time. It's almost over," Pops whispered away from the mic.

"I've never heard of Bo Shang, but if he's anything like his brother, then I'll be ready for him tonight."

The woman wrote my answer in her notepad and asked no other questions. After that, the rest of the interview went in about the same direction. They asked me more questions about Bo Shang and my plans for the future, but I kept it short and straight to the point. The more time I spent answering questions, the less time I would have to warm up before the fighting began.

When it was over, Pops walked me back to my team. They huddled in the middle of the room, chanting our dojo name loud enough to make the floor rumble. Not every team would make it through Regionals, so we made it a point to celebrate every step of the way.

I pulled on the neck of my tie to loosen it just as I was pulled into the huddle. We got louder, eventually gaining the attention of one of the security guards who came to check in on us. He warned us to keep it down, but nobody listened. It wasn't like he could kick us out anyway. It was Regionals! We were hyped. Who could blame us?

I quickly got changed into my uniform. The announcer had just started addressing the crowd in the stadium. This meant the competition was about to start.

My team headed out, still riled up from our group huddle. I could hear them shouting through the halls. In no time, I was dressed and able to catch up to my team at the stadium.

We were seated at the very front, ahead of all the other teams. It had been a while since I was at any major competition, but I could've sworn the crowds got bigger every year. There were a few familiar faces in the crowd. I noticed a couple fans I had grown used to seeing as they showed up early enough to get the good seats.

They held signs with messages like "It's my birthday, please hug me!" or " Your #1 Fan!" It felt good seeing all the people who'd consistently supported me throughout the years. Even the unfamiliar faces all held an excitement that was hard to ignore.

"Let's welcome the first two contenders on stage!" the announcer bellowed in the overhead speakers. The lights suddenly dimmed and the crowd quieted down to a rush of whispers.

He singled out two fighters from the teams huddled around the ring. Both guys were clearly in two different weight classes. The smallest one didn't seem to mind the size of his opponent. He had to be either really cocky, or damn good. Either way, I was surrounded by six of the best teams in the entire state of Georgia, so I was guessing he was just that good.

While they fought, I took the opportunity to gaze around the stadium. It was packed to capacity. Even with the lights dimmed as low as they were, I could just make out the heads all the way at the top of the stands.

The various camera men posted behind them shined lights that lit the center of the ring up like a stage for the world to see. Watching the other competitors go at it made me antsy in my seat. My leg jumped as I waited for my name to be called.

One by one, the announcer picked from a pre-selected list of competitors. I didn't have to guess who I would go up against. The reporter from my interview had already given it away. Jao Shang was somewhere in the crowd, watching and waiting for my round just as anxiously as I was, but it was his brother I would contend with.

Out of all the fighters I had ever gone up against, Jao Shang was the only person with the ability to intimidate me. Now with the news that Bo was looking to pick up where Jao had left off, it made me wonder how big the stakes really were in this fight.

I had no intention of letting either Bo or Jao Shang get into my head, but I'd be crazy not to question it all. Bo Shang had never even crossed my radar before. He'd never ranked anywhere on a national scale, yet somehow he was here at Regionals, ready to take me on. It wasn't adding up.

"Jevon." I suddenly felt a tap on my shoulder, drawing my attention to my right. It was Pops. He held a barely contained grin that instantly made me sit up.

"What's going on, Pops?"

"Shane needs to speak to you."

"Right now?" I pointed to the stage. "My team is up."

"Yes, right now. I've seen the list. You won't miss your round. Just come with me."

Reluctantly, I got up and followed him out of the stadium. We went straight to the rooms at the back of the arena. Missing my first round at Regionals would instantly disqualify me from Nationals or any international competitions.

"Here he is." My father pushed the door open to a private room sectioned off from all the others.

Seated at the only table in the room was Shane Tithers himself. When he saw me, he stood to shake my hand with a smile.

"Have a seat, Jevon." Shane gestured to the empty chair across from him.

Pops took that as his cue to leave as I made myself comfortable. Shane took off his darkly tinted shades and folded them up before placing them on the table.

"I won't be able to stay after the fight, so I asked your dad to pull you away. I hope that's okay."

"It's cool."

"Great. I heard about your injury, and I'm glad you're feeling better."

"Thanks."

"I'm sure your coaches gave you all the tips you need to be successful tonight, so can I give you some life advice?"

"Sure."

"In the next few months, your life is going to change drastically. If you have something good, I suggest you hold on to it because after this tour, good things won't be so easy to come by."

"How do you know?"

He smiled. "Because I've been where you are."

I went silent.

I didn't mean to, but what he said instantly made me think of her: her smile, her face, the way she looked when she was completely in her element, the confidence she showed to the world, and the soft shyness about her that only I got to see. The thought of losing that, of truly losing her, made my stomach twist up in the most uncomfortable way.

"Everything alright?" Shane waved his hand in front of my face to get my attention.

I blinked, clearing my throat. "Uh, yeah."

"I know that look. What's her name?"

Was it that obvious?

"Akilah," I sighed.

"Hmm. Pretty name."

"Pretty girl too."

Shane grinned. "Is she here tonight?"

"No, she couldn't make it. We, um, kind of broke up."

"Oh." His brows shot up.

"Yeah."

"Well, is it fixable? Can you work on whatever happened between you?"

"I-I think so."

Shane took a minute to think to himself. Then, as if the idea suddenly came to him, he clapped and pointed to me.

"Tell you what, I'll have my driver pull up to the back, and we'll take you to see your girl before the fight."

"What?"

Did I hear that right?

"You want her back, don't you?"

"I mean, yeah, but I can't just leave. If I miss my round then—"

Shane cut me off with his hand, checking the time on his watch.

"You have about an hour until they even think about calling your name. My driver's used to getting me to places on time when I'm running late. He'll have us there and back in no time, trust me."

"No, Shane, I really can't leave. Pops would kill me."

Shane didn't seem to care about that obstacle. He leaned forward and propped his elbows on the table. In one fluid motion, he grabbed his shades, slipped them on and rose from his seat.

"You want to live Michael's life, or Jevon's?" he asked simply before turning to leave the room.

Shane's words reverberated through my skull like an echo. Every move I made, every decision, every choice in my life and career was decided by him, my dad. Akilah was the one thing, the one choice I made for me, and my father managed to take that away.

He decided that she wasn't good enough. *He* decided that she was the distraction. It was *him* who made me so cautious to let her in, and if I were honest with myself, it was my father that held me back.

You want to live Michael's life, or Jevon's?

The question echoed through my brain once again like a ticking time bomb.

"Shane, wait!" I stood up too because I had to know. "Why are you doing this?"

"I told you, I've been where you are."

He left without another word, and I was quick to follow him out. Shane dug out his phone to call his driver. I followed his lead as he rushed out the door toward the exit. What neither of us expected was my eager, almost nosy-looking Dad standing outside the door.

Nick was with him, looking just as eager as Pops was to see what we'd talked about.

"How'd it go?" Pops asked. He placed a hand on my arm to stop me in my tracks.

"Good. I just have to go take care of something real quick, and I'll be right back."

I tried again to head toward the exit, hoping he'd let it go, but his grip on my arm never loosened.

"Wait, hold up, son. Take care of what?"

"I have to go see Akilah, Pops."

"You can't leave, Jevon. It's Regionals. Have you lost your mind?"

"Yeah, I know, but I'll be back before the fight. I won't miss it."

"Damn right, you won't miss it," Pops crossed his arms, blocking our way to the exit, "because you're not going anywhere."

Pops's equal mix of shock and pure worry for my mental state of mind dared me to challenge him.

"It's fine, Michael." Shane stepped up to come between us. "I promised to have him back on time. He's in good hands."

Pops's eyes zeroed in on where Shane had lightly pat his shoulder.

"Look, all due respect, Shane, but my son's career is just getting started. I won't let you or anybody jeopardize the work we put in to get here. If you're gonna leave, then leave, but Jevon stays here."

Pop's voice rang with finality. For a moment, nobody said a word. If I didn't speak up now, I'd never get the chance again. With a deep breath, I stepped forward as a courage that I never thought I needed suddenly washed over me.

Staring my father straight in the eye, I said, "With all due respect, Pops, I *am* leaving. I have to do this because...I love her. You don't get to control who I let into my life. You manage my career, dad and I appreciate that, but you can't manage my life anymore. I'm going."

It took a moment for my Dad to get his thoughts together. His mouth opened and shut rapidly as words failed to come to him.

When he was finally able to speak, it was Nick who stepped in this time.

"Mike, I don't like this either, but I trust that he won't let us down. You should too."

I could hear Pop's teeth click together in irritation. He was out numbered, and that was something he didn't like very much. He fixed me with a steely gaze, and although I knew it was the last thing he wanted to do, he stepped aside and let us go.

"Don't make me regret this, son." He warned under his breath.

"You won't."

CHAPTER FORTY-FOUR

Akilah

I struggled to keep my eyes open as I read my history book. With midterms coming up next week, studying was the perfect excuse for me to escape my own reality.

There was too much going on that fought for my attention. Between worrying nonstop about the outcome of the senior art show, the status of my application at Ivory Middleton, and trying not to think about Jevon, I found it hard to focus.

For the third time in a row, I went over my study guide, not really understanding the words on the page. I got the dates mixed up with certain wars and laws from different centuries that all really sounded the same. If I were being honest, I could've tried harder, but my head was somewhere else entirely.

CJ watched the fight downstairs. He turned the volume up so loud it was like I was sitting there in the living room with him. I could hear everything going on from the moment the fighters hit the stage to the very moment the fights were over.

Anxiously, I secretly waited to hear his name. I wasn't checking for him, but I kept my door cracked a little so I wouldn't miss it. I promised myself I wouldn't watch him, but if he won, I wanted to be nice enough to congratulate him at school next week.

We were on good terms. Jevon and I were friendly to each other in passing, but that was all. So far, we were sort of friends, and I told myself I was okay with that. I had to be. In the end, after everything we'd been through, I'd rather be his friend than nothing at all to him.

With a big sigh, I flipped over on my bed and brought my study guide up to my face to reread everything for the fourth time. It was an endless cycle: read a few paragraphs, think about him, read a few paragraphs, think about him, and so on.

For a while, I kept up a good rhythm. The more I read and actually focused on the words written on the page, I understood more about the history of the Civil War. I quizzed myself on the dates and the laws that came from the result. It wasn't so hard when I paid attention. Reaching for a pen in the front flap of my book bag, I scribbled a few extra notes on the margins of the study guide.

There was already so much for me to remember. I tried to simplify it in my own way by drawing little reminders around certain words or phrases that stood out to me. After my fifth time going over all four pages, I felt like I had a good understanding of it all. I wasn't ready for the test, but I felt better going into it than before.

Slowly, I got up to stretch out my limbs. My bones popped and cracked from the stiffness of laying still for so long. I was on a roll and I didn't want to stop. Only when I finally moved on to a new subject did my little brother decide to disturb my peace.

"AJ!" he yelled from downstairs. "AJ! Come downstairs! Hurry!"

You'd think the house was on fire by the way he called my name. With our parents out for a date night, it was just the two of us. On any other night, CJ and I would go our separate ways.

When he wasn't on the phone, caked up with Natasha, he'd be downstairs watching the game. For me, if I weren't already with Kayla, I'd be in my room doodling or somewhere lost in space.

"Hurry up!" CJ rushed me impatiently.

"What?!" I yelled back in frustration, taking my time coming down the steps.

"Can you get the door?"

I deadpanned. All of a sudden, my brother was casually gesturing to a door that I hadn't heard anybody approach. Nobody knocked or rang the doorbell, but he seemed sure someone was there.

"You called me all the way downstairs to answer the door?"

"Mmhm."

"CJ, you're right there!" The couch wasn't that far of a walk.

"I know, but since you came all the way down here, you might as well."

I turned to go back to my room. I wasn't in the mood to play with him tonight.

"Wait, wait, okay!" CJ laughed, grabbing me by the arm when he caught up to me. "You really might want to get the door. It's for you, anyway."

"What are you talking about? Nobody's at the door, I didn't hear it—"

The chime of bells suddenly rang throughout the house, sending chills down my spine. My eyes locked with my brother's as a knowing grin stretched across his face.

"How did you know that was going to happen?" I asked.

"Look."

He pointed to the TV screen, where a bright light shined on our front porch. It was dark outside, but I watched as the camera drew closer to the front door. For a moment I doubted what I was looking at.

In what world would someone point a camera at our house to ring the doorbell? But sure enough, there it was. Our house was on TV and someone was at the door.

"What's going on, CJ?"

My heart thumped an irregular tempo, full of a nervous energy I couldn't contain. CJ shrugged, just as clueless as I was, but I knew he was up to something. None of this made any sense.

"This better not be some kind of prank, or I swear to—"

"Just answer the door, Akilah, damn!"

I gave in and went toward the door, but before I could get too far, CJ stopped me.

"Um, you wanna do something to that first?" He pointed to my hair.

On instinct, my hand reached up to my poofy, messy bun. A few curly strands had escaped the hair tie I used to loosely keep it all in place, but I didn't think it looked that bad.

All it took was one more glance at the TV screen that highlighted the accents on our front door for me to pull my hair down and fluff it out around my face. My curls pooled down to just barely graze the top of my shoulders.

In my fitted long-sleeved shirt and sweatpants, I was in no way ready to be on TV. But at the urgent sound of the doorbell ringing again, I had no time to change. After a quick glance in the hallway mirror and a thumbs up from my brother, I was presentable enough to answer the door.

I took a deep breath and slowly turned the knob. Instantly, the blaring lights from the video cameras and photographers that surrounded the door brought me to an immediate pause.

My face froze in a state of shock as my eyes adjusted to the bright lights. It took me a minute, but when my eyes finally settled, I was able to notice the tall figure standing at the door.

"Jevon?" I breathed.

"Hey." He smiled.

His eyes raked over my face, my hair, my body as if he were comparing it all exactly to the way he remembered me. I was at a loss for words, confused by his entourage of paparazzi and lights. The shiver that ran down my spine earlier had now turned into full-blown goosebumps that prickled down the length of my arms and legs.

"W-what are you doing here? I thought you..." I trailed off, unable to even finish the sentence. He was still in uniform—decked out in his black and silver Hard Knocks Dojo colors.

"I came to see you. I didn't mean to bring all this with me." He gestured around himself to the two video cameras pointed directly at our faces and the three photographers that surrounded the porch. "But it comes with the territory."

Right, this was his life. How could I ever forget? Everything had the potential to be on display for the world to see.

"Why?"

His smile fell, bringing with it a flutter of butterflies deep in my belly that left me unsteady on my feet. Jevon was so handsome, it was almost hard to hold his gaze, especially with all the cameras surrounding us.

Still, I held my ground. I wanted to know why he was here and not at his competition. I wanted to know why the atmosphere between us was suddenly so serious.

Jevon licked his lips and took me by the hand, gently pulling me out of the doorway and closer to him. Despite the dozens of clicks and flashes from the cameramen who took pictures around us, his eyes never left mine. It helped to calm the frenzied pounding in chest.

"I messed up pretty bad," he said, "and I'm here to fix that."

"Jevon—"

"No, last time you did all the talking. Now it's my turn. I talk, and you listen."

I clamped my mouth tightly shut. There was so much authority in his voice it left me with no argument.

"I should've never let you walk away from me, believing all these things that weren't true. I'll never make that mistake again." He paused, searching my face to make sure I understood his promise.

"The first lie," he continued, "was when you said that we couldn't have a future together because our lives are so different. Honestly, it doesn't matter to me where you go to school, Akilah. You could be in New York or on the South Pole for all I care, and I'd still find my way to you. Truth is, I can't picture a future without you in it. It's not one that I want."

I swallowed, doing my best to control my breathing.

"The second lie I let you believe was when you said it was best for us to end it before we got too deep." He chuckled softly to himself. "Akilah, baby, if you thought for one second that what we have wasn't deep from the very beginning, then you couldn't have been paying attention. I broke all the rules for you, and you changed everything. How could you not see that?"

I wasn't sure I could answer that, so I closed my eyes, taking it all in. At this point, my body was alit with tingles that wouldn't let up. I could feel Jevon come in closer. He cupped a hand under my chin as he waited patiently for me to open my eyes. When I finally did, I found him smiling down at me.

"And last, but most important. I couldn't let another day go by without telling you that I love you. I'm in love with you, Akilah Brielle Johnson, and I don't care if the whole world knows."

My breath hitched in my throat. There he was, basically in front of the whole world, professing his love for me. He was here, at my house when he should've been at his competition, a competition that had everything on the line for him.

He took a risk and he put me first. Jevon had bared his heart to me with bright lights and cameras all in his face. How could I not believe that what he was saying was true?

My heart suddenly felt so full. It was like he'd repaired all the broken pieces one by one. Without warning, tears welled in my eyes and spilled over just as fast as they came. I was so overcome with emotion that I didn't know to do with it.

My limbs reacted on their own, reaching up to wrap my arms around his neck. Jevon responded to me automatically, as he lifted me up off the ground. Our lips collided together simultaneously, and if not for the strong hold he had on me, I would've fallen over from the way he kissed me.

I locked my legs around his torso and pulled him in to deepen the kiss. It felt so good to be in his arms again. Regardless of the length of time we spent apart, our hands remembered each other perfectly. My lips remembered the warmth and softness of his, and I reveled in the taste of him. He was like the purest form of candy, the most decadent chocolate I'd ever tasted.

Jevon held me up effortlessly, and for a moment, all the cameras and paparazzi disappeared. I didn't care that America was watching. It didn't matter to me who was there because in that moment, nothing else existed. It was him and me and that was all that ever mattered.

Before I let myself get too carried away, I pulled away from the kiss to look him directly in the eyes. My tears had yet to stop, but I didn't care. I blinked them away so I could see him clearly when I said, "I love you too."